Praise for *Holding On To Nothing*

Holding On To Nothing is a resonant song of the South, all whiskey, bluegrass, Dolly Parton, tobacco fields, and women who know better but still fall for the lowdown men whom they know will disappoint them. Elizabeth Chiles Shelburne writes with extraordinary love and compassion of the lives of her flawed characters; she shines a clear, calm light on their tragedies, their joys, and their hard-won redemptions.   —Lauren Groff, *Florida* and *Fates and Furies*

With her immense empathy for her characters, Elizabeth Chiles Shelburne refuses to give the reader a simple, and stereotypical, tale of Appalachian dysfunction. Instead, we get a story of a seemingly star-crossed couple striving to create a better life in the most trying of circumstances. *Holding On To Nothing* is a gem.   —Ron Rash, *Serena* and *The Risen*

With unflinching candor imbued with love and understanding, Elizabeth Chiles Shelburne's evocative debut novel explores the meaning of family and the choices people make when the world denies them good options. A compassionate but unsentimental tale of love, loss, and hardship in modern-day Appalachia.
                         —Whitney Scharer, *The Age of Light*

Forget *Hillbilly Elegy* and read this gorgeous novel instead. *Holding On To Nothing* is an in-depth portrayal of contemporary young people caught in a life they cannot control or get out of. . . . Every detail is exactly right, from Jeptha's old mandolin and his beloved mutt, Crystal Gayle, to Lucy's job at Walmart where "the tidbits of other people's shitty lives floating past her scanner kept her from breaking down over her own." Contemporary themes of work and no work, drinking, sex, guns, music, community, and no future—along with in-depth character development and a hard-driving plot—make this a book you literally cannot put down.   —Lee Smith, *Dimestore* and *The Last Girls*

Elizabeth Chiles Shelburne's debut novel sings and burns in equal measure. *Holding On To Nothing* is a gripping story of love and place, of the small choices and large passions that determine our lives, of the gorgeous hope that tomorrow will bring something solid and sturdy, something lucky and true.
       —Bret Anthony Johnston, *Remember Me Like This* and *Corpus Christi*

Following in the literary footsteps of Silas House's debut novel *Clay's Quilt*, *Holding On To Nothing* is a tragically beautiful tale of love, loss, music, and blue-collar mountain life. Elizabeth Chiles Shelburne is a fresh contemporary Appalachian voice that I hope to hear from again and again.
                         —Amy Greene, *Bloodroot* and *Long Man*

Elizabeth Chiles Shelburne writes with a chafe and charm that makes you give a damn about these flawed characters, Lucy and Jeptha, makes you root for them when what little they have is at risk. This novel has all the makings of a true ballad—heartache and dead ends, booze and bad decisions, double-crossing relatives, a hand-me-down mandolin, and a loyal dog named Crystal Gayle. It also has a deep humming heart that knows sorrow. Like Lucy's beloved Dolly Parton, *Holding On To Nothing* is not just country, it's mountain. Shelburne is a literary force to be reckoned with. —Susan Bernhard, *Winter Loon*

In this gritty debut, Elizabeth Chiles Shelburne deftly captures the blue-collar ache and darkly comic sensibility of what it means to exist in a world of disappointment and generational trauma, where one is both cussed and cursed. It's impossible to turn away as these hardscrabble characters embark on a long shot at love despite voices real and imagined that shout in dissent. A stunning debut by a fierce new voice in southern fiction. —Kelly J. Ford, *Cottonmouths*

The shotgun wedding of ne'er-do-well Jeptha Taylor and girl-of-his-dreams Lucy Kilgore has tragic consequences in *Holding On To Nothing*, a novel whose dark humor goes down as smoothly as sweet tea in July. Elizabeth Chiles Shelburne's complex, moving portrait of Jeptha—universally dismissed as a loser in his small town in Tennessee, but who, in Shelburne's hands, is a wounded, sensitive soul who was never taught how to be the good man he longs to be— resonates long after the final chapter. Told in prose as clear and sweet as Jeptha Taylor's mandolin, *Holding On To Nothing* marks the debut of an important new author of southern fiction.
  —Lisa Borders, *The Fifty-First State* and *Cloud Cuckoo Land*

Elizabeth Chiles Shelburne writes with an unprecedented lyricism that is both highly literary and charmingly accessible. From the opening moments of this page-burner, the reader can't help but surrender to the titanic love affair that is Jeptha and Lucy. The storytelling is so masterful and enchanting that no matter what happens, you know you're safe with Shelburne at the helm.
  —Jennie Wood, *A Boy Like Me* and *Flutter*

Holding On To Nothing is a smart, wry novel filled with bourbon, bluegrass, grit, and heart. —Patricia Park, author of *Re Jane*

Holding On to Nothing is a novel of big skies and limited choices, of sweet bluegrass in a sticky hometown bar, of tobacco and guns, danger and desire. Shelburne shoots straight, never allows us to turn our heads. And even non-praying folk will pray for the desperate mismatch of Lucy and Jeptha and their lonely, shivering hearts. Shelburne has done the small-town novel a wondrous turn.
  —Michelle Hoover, *The Quickening*

HOLDING ON TO NOTHING

HOLDING ON

— TO —

NOTHING

a novel

ELIZABETH CHILES SHELBURNE

BLAIR

Blair is an imprint of Carolina Wren Press.

*The mission of Blair/Carolina Wren Press is to seek out, nurture,
and promote literary work by new and underrepresented writers.*

This book was supported by the Durham Arts Council's Annual Arts Fund and the N.C. Arts
Council, a division of the Department of Natural & Cultural Resources.

Library of Congress Cataloging-in-Publication Data
Names: Shelburne, Elizabeth Chiles, author.
Title: Holding on to nothing / by Elizabeth Chiles Shelburne.
Description: Durham : Blair / Carolina Wren Press, 2019.
Identifiers: LCCN 2019020643 (print) | LCCN 2019021951 (ebook) |
ISBN 9781949467208 (eBook) | ISBN 9781949467086 (hardback)
Subjects: LCSH: Working class families—Tennessee—Fiction. |
Country life—Tennessee—Fiction. | Domestic fiction.
Classification: LCC PS3619.H452265 (ebook) |
LCC PS3619.H452265 H65 2019 (print) | DDC 813/.6—dc23
LC record available at https://lccn.loc.gov/2019020643

To Tennessee:
my heart, my home, forever

We're holding on with nothing left to hold on to
I'm so tired of holding on to nothing
the years have shown no kindness for the hard times we've been through
We've squeezed the life from every dream and still go right on bluffing
with really nothing left to hold on to

— "Holding On To Nothing," performed by
Dolly Parton and Porter Wagoner

I know there's California, Oklahoma
And all of the places I ain't ever been to but
Down in the valley with
The whiskey rivers
These are the places you will find me hidin'
These are the places I will always go
These are the places I will always go

— "Down in the Valley," performed by
The Head and the Heart

HOLDING ON TO NOTHING

—PART ONE—

—1—

JEPTHA TAYLOR HAD BEEN in love with Lucy Kilgore since he was sixteen and her smile was the reason why. She had a smile that made people feel safe. Jeptha, particularly. He wasn't sure why exactly—he just knew a warm, contented feeling stole over him that struck him as exactly the kind of silent bliss a newborn baby feels when his mama feeds him. But when Jeptha pulled his Camaro, dark and shiny as a pond at midnight, into the parking lot behind Judy's Bar on a hot Friday night in June, he had no idea that Lucy's smile would be for him tonight, that it would spark through him and spread to her like a hay blaze—fiery, fast, and destructive.

No, as far as Jeptha was concerned, tonight was only about bluegrass and ass, if he could get it. It was his first time at Judy's Bar, and he felt a bit disloyal for being there. The bar had been open for four months and—being run by a Yankee—had been in disfavor for all those months with the local drinkers. Except for the real drunks, neighbors all, whose loyalty extended only to Jack, Jim, and whatever bar gave them the best shot at driving home shit-faced without getting caught. For those who could afford to be principled in their place of vice, the bar of choice was Avery's Place, owned by a hometown boy named Avery who had spent ten years fighting the Pentecostals and the Baptists, both Freewill and Southern, for the right to open a bar in what previously had been a dry county. That a Yankee swooped in five years after Avery's long fight finally ended and made use of the same provisions he had fought so hard to establish was enough for Jeptha, his friends, and the rest of the town to stay well clear of Judy's Bar. Until, that is, four boys, so far unnamed in the paper even though everyone in town knew who they were, got high behind Avery's Place one night in early July, lit a small fire in a patch of grass already dried out in the summer's drought, and ran like hell when it whooshed into a patch of wiring that snaked up the outer wall of the bar. The fire caught hold in the electrical system and sparked its way from wire to wire, finally nesting in a box of receipts that Avery kept under a couple of bottles of 151-proof Everclear, reserved for the worst of the worst drunks. Within minutes, there was only a wall of flame where once there had been a bar, and Avery's customers ran, taking their principles with them.

Jeptha, not being a subscriber to the *Review*, the town paper, or really much of a reader generally, heard about the fire two days later from his friend Cody. Jeptha and Cody were bandmates in a Boy Named Sue, a bluegrass group that played Friday nights at Avery's—Cody sang and played banjo, with Jeptha on mandolin. After a respectful period of silence, in which they thought of the drunken nights—both good and bad—they had enjoyed at Avery's, Cody explained that Judy had called him two days after the fire ("Typical Yankee. Didn't even wait for the damn ashes to stop smoking.") and offered the band a job playing Friday nights at her place. Cody was principled, yes, but a fool? No. He'd accepted and gone on to call his bandmates. Jeptha was happy to keep the gig, and all too happy to forget any moral stand he'd once had. He'd agreed to be there on Friday.

And so, Jeptha pulled his mandolin off the passenger seat of his car and made for the front door. He was showered for the first time in two drunken days, and most of the stink had worn off. He wondered if the girl who'd been in his bed last night—Brandy? Brandy Anne? She'd been bendy for sure, that one—would be in the bar and up for another go. Bluegrass and sex wouldn't be such a bad Friday. He wondered if he'd need to remember her actual name to get her back to his place.

Occupied as his mind was, he hadn't absorbed the fact of the full parking lot, so when he opened the door—happy to smell the right scent of beer, sweat, and leather that came flooding out—he was shocked to see the place packed to the rafters. He wasn't sure he'd ever played in front of so many people. A trickle of fear gnawed at his belly. He elbowed his way through the crowd. He gave a quick nod and half smile to the girl from last night. She laughed and looked down at the table, but not before Jeptha saw a blush creep up her cheeks. He smiled to himself, pretty damn sure she'd be up for it again, assuming he could finesse the fact that she was sitting with a girl he'd slept with a few months back and never called again. He gripped his mandolin case and worked his way into line, feeling content. It had the makings of a good night.

Jeptha finally caught the eye of the bartender and owner, Judy. She was in her sixties and, rumor was, had moved down to Tennessee to run this bar with a local man she'd met up in Boston. Jeptha was hard pressed to imagine why someone would move to Boston in the first place, and then, having flown the coop, decide to come back and with a Yankee in tow, no less. Still, here they were. Jeptha couldn't say that Judy appeared happy about it. Her gray hair, which looked to have never seen the inside of a beauty salon, was pulled into a loose bun from which haphazard chunks escaped, and her t-shirt, wet in spots from the ice she dumped into glasses without so much as an attempt at aim, strained over a set of sagging, ponderous boobs.

She widened her eyes at Jeptha. "Yeah?" she said.

"Hi. How're you?"

"What do you want?"

"Um, I'll have a Bud Light, ma'am." Jeptha shut his mouth. She was clearly a Yankee with no time for formalities.

"A Bud Light and what?"

"Just the beer, ma'am."

"Don't call me ma'am."

"Okay, ma—" Jeptha cut himself off when her lips pursed and her eyes narrowed. "Just a beer, please."

"You guys are too damn polite for your own good." She slid the bottle across the bar and nodded at the stage. "You with the band?"

"Yes, ma—" Jeptha stopped. "Yes."

"If you guys need anything tonight, grab Lucy. She's helping out with the tables."

Jeptha turned to see the Lucy she was pointing at with her chin, and the trickle of fear in his belly grew to a flood. There she was—the wavy blond hair tickling her waist where her shirt rode up from bending over to take people's orders; the pert little nose, turned up at the end in a way that was more cute than beautiful; and her cut-off skirt hugging curves he never got to see in church, back when he used to go. Most of all, there was her smile. Every time he saw it, he fell a little bit more in love.

Jeptha knew Lucy's smile didn't mean anything when it was turned to him—birth had given her a nice one and she was polite enough to use it often, but Jeptha had never been able to help the feeling he got the few times she flashed it his way. Even though her smile made others feel safe, she rarely looked as if she felt that way. She instead sported a hunted look, as wary as a deer stopping to nose through a leaf pile for acorns in the fall, the kind of deer that looked so nervous, so ready to bolt, that Jeptha could never bring himself to even sight his rifle on it. Every time, a few seconds after warmth flowed through him at the sight of her smile, he'd see that wariness on her face and realize that he may as well have been standing in the woods without a gun, for all the chance he had of getting her. Especially now. He'd heard from his sister that Lucy was leaving town, moving to Knoxville to work and go to school. At least he wouldn't have to see her anymore, though his stomach bottomed out at the thought.

Jeptha grabbed his beer off the counter for a much-needed sip of courage. Despite the pulsing needs of the crowd, he could feel Judy's eyes still on him. Her lips flickered. It looked like her last real smile had occurred sometime in the 1970s, and yet here were her lips, the edges moving up subtly toward her eyes. Jeptha mumbled thanks and walked toward the stage, uncomfortably aware of being watched. He kept his head down, trying to avoid making eye contact with Lucy. If he looked at her, the fear he was feeling would travel out to his hands and make them as useful as an arthritic bird dog.

"Y'all ready?" Cody asked, as Jeptha stepped up on the stage and wedged his beer between two amps.

Cody nodded once and then tapped his foot—*one and a two and a here we go*—and launched into a riff on his banjo, which Jeptha and the fiddler and the drummer raced to catch up with. His fingers were stiff and stumbling. His stage fright, which usually decreased as he played, grew into an untamable creature, fed by the fear of playing poorly in front of Lucy. He played like he was eight years old, holding the mandolin for the first time—his fingers glancing off the strings, missing his intros and staring into the crowd at Lucy during what was supposed to be a solo. It was the kind of pitiful performance that makes a pick-up band think they ought to start practicing. The crowd had quieted with the first bars of the song but gradually ratcheted up until the conversations nearly drowned out the band completely. Jeptha was grateful, hoping the noise would keep Lucy from hearing how bad they were.

During the fourth song, he watched, mesmerized, as Lucy's hips snaked this way and that through the crowd toward the band. She had a small tray in her hands, on which rested five shot glasses, full of what looked tantalizingly like whiskey. She waited at the left side of the stage a few feet from Jeptha until the song ended.

"Hey," she said after they wound the song to a half-hearted close. "It's Jeptha, right? Deanna's brother?"

"Unfortunately."

"You said it, not me," she said, her eyebrow raised. "Judy told me to bring these over. Said y'all couldn't sound any worse drunk than you did sober."

Jeptha winced. "I was hoping y'all couldn't hear that," he said, passing out shots to Cody and the other guys. He nodded at the tray. "Who's that one for?"

"Me, I think."

"You get to drink on the job?"

"You are." She wrinkled her nose at him and straightened her shoulders, clearly annoyed. Jeptha felt like a fool. "Besides, Judy said I needed to loosen up, get some better tips."

"You look to be doing all right to me."

"If you count slaps on the ass as tips, then yeah, I'm rich as hell. Cheers," she said and tipped the shot down her throat. In his hurry to keep up with her, a few drops of whiskey went down the wrong pipe, and he coughed so hard tears welled in the corners of his eyes.

Lucy cocked her head at him, a teasing smile on her lips. Jeptha's insides fizzed with a longing so fierce he felt it in his fingertips. "I'll tell Judy to make the next one a lemon drop," she said.

"Hey, that ain't nice," he said to her, but in his head he was thinking, *Do it again. Please, God, do it again.*

All trace of teasing dropped off Lucy's face, and she nodded seriously. "You'll be great. I heard you play at church back when."

"You did?"

"Yep. Besides, if you get nervous, imagine all these people naked. Not me, though. I want no part of that, thank you."

It was the longest conversation Jeptha had ever had with Lucy. She walked away as Jeptha tried and failed to keep his mind off the much-nourished fantasy of her naked. Finally, he shook his head and tore his gaze away. He nodded thanks to Judy, who mouthed, "For what?" followed by the tiniest, coolest of smiles. He relaxed under the influence of the whiskey and the image of a naked Delnor Gilliam tapping his foot against the floor, his gray, straggly beard bouncing off his belly in time to the music. He nodded at Cody, ready to play again.

The next forty-five minutes belonged to Jeptha in a way that no other moment in his life had. He was on fire, ready to take on the devil at any minute. His band was the first to notice. They kept punting solos his way on three different songs that had never had solos before. The crowd quieted to listen, roaring to cheer him on when his solos ended. But Jeptha only had eyes for his mandolin and for Lucy. He stumbled only once in his playing, when he looked up from a complex part and didn't spot her anywhere in the crowd. His hands momentarily ceased all movement until he saw the bathroom door open and Lucy stood in the hall watching him play for a minute. The light glowed off her hair and the sheen of sweat on her nose. He picked right up playing again, joy coursing through him and out his fingertips.

When their set ended, Jeptha bounded off the stage, mandolin in hand, pushing through the crowd until he stood in front of Lucy, his body bouncing with the energy of a set well-played.

"You were amazing!" she said, her smile huge, well past polite. Jeptha could tell she meant it. He had to grip his mandolin with both hands to keep from crushing her to him, sweaty t-shirt and all.

"You don't have to say that."

"I'm not saying it because I have to; I'm saying it because it's true," she said, her fingers toying with a wisp of hair that hung over her shoulder.

Jeptha had joined the band because Cody had promised him they'd rarely practice and there might be groupies. No practice and the possibility of sex? Jeptha was in. But he had never expected the girl in thrall to be the one he'd been in love with since he was sixteen.

No one had ever looked at him like Lucy did then—like she was a kid spying the newest Christmas toy for the first time. He flashed to his mother's face, searching for one memory where she looked at him like he was something special. None surfaced. Rather, her face was lined with the disappointments of having married a man who couldn't stop being mean long enough to direct a little bit of his paycheck toward the upbringing of his kids rather than to alcohol and drugs and gas for the many affairs he conducted across the county. His mother had never had the time or the inclination to shower admiration on her children. If Jeptha or his siblings had demonstrated any talents, they were more likely to be squashed as a dangerous rebellion against the Taylor norm. For generations, his family had worked as hard as they could at doing as little as possible outside of making moonshine, stealing cars, and collecting as much social security as they could con the government into giving them. Jeptha's grandfather had been arrested more times than anyone could count, and his father only slightly less. If there was a break-in, or a bar fight, or a drunken accident on the road, everyone in town expected a Taylor to be involved. So far, no Taylor had killed a person, but it wasn't for lack of trying. His father had been so drunk the day he had tried to kill Jeptha's grandfather that all six shots he'd fired had missed the old man, who stood stock still, as if getting shot at happened every day. When his dad had thrown the gun away in disgust, the old man shook his head and walked back into the house to finish his drink.

Jeptha's mom had married in and tried for the first few years to make the future something other than an unedited rewrite of the past. However, by the time Jeptha was born, her spirit had been worn to a nub and her skin to an ever-present mottled green sheen in trying to fight against her husband, and she had come to learn that putting her head down and getting through each day was best for everyone. It was no way to be happy, but it was a sure way to survive. The only thing she wouldn't concede was church—there was no sin so great that church on Sunday couldn't atone for it.

Even though the church ladies like Mrs. Slocum were nice to him, Jeptha had long understood it was only because it was their Christian duty to do so. He'd been ten when he snuck out of the sanctuary one Sunday and down into the fellowship hall where the church ladies were preparing the after-service snack. There, hidden under a card table covered in a floral paper tablecloth eating a stolen donut, he had heard Mrs. Gilliam whisper to Mrs. Slocum, "Them Taylors now, they is as direct a rebuttal of that evolution nonsense as anything Pastor Terrance says. He is mean as a snake like his dad and his dad before him and, bless her heart, she's dumb as a bag of rocks. Them kids don't seem no better. Ain't a one of them evolving."

Mrs. Slocum had hushed her quickly, but not before Jeptha's cheeks flared with the heat of shame. He was suddenly aware that other families weren't like his. He understood the looks and whispered conversations when his dad walked into a store; recognized that near-weekly visits from the sheriff weren't the norm for other families; and saw with sudden and painful clarity why the kids laughed even harder than usual when he stumbled over a word in reading.

Everything changed in that moment. No matter what he did, he'd always be a Taylor. He'd become a man then, huddled under that card table. He sometimes wished it had made him a different kind of one. But if he was going to be a Taylor no matter what he did, he'd quickly decided he might as well enjoy the reputation. He'd stopped trying in school, dropped out as soon as he could, and got his own visits from the sheriff. He'd gone to church with his mom until he was seventeen, but when she died of lung cancer that summer, he'd looked around during the funeral service and realized that no one much cared if he came to church anymore, nor did they much want him there. It was much easier to hate the sin and love the sinner when he wasn't standing among you every week. For the last five years, he'd worked only when he had to, drunk as much as he could afford, and took advantage of the loose morals of any number of girls named Chastity and Honor. He reckoned he had been as happy as any Taylor could expect to be. But now, drinking in the look on Lucy's face that made him remember his name was Jeptha, not just Taylor, his sweaty fingers cradling the neck of his mandolin in the way his hand wanted to be holding the back of her neck, he understood for the first time in his life the value of giving a damn.

"Jeptha?" Lucy said, touching his arm lightly.

"Oh, God. Sorry. I . . . I guess I spaced out for a second." He blushed, embarrassed to think how he must have looked.

"It's all right. Judy wanted me to ask if y'all want another round?"

"She buying again?"

Lucy nodded. "On the house."

"I'd be a damn fool to say no to that."

"I'll tell her you're not a fool then," Lucy said, and walked toward the bar.

"Lucy! Hey, Lucy," Jeptha yelled until she turned to him. "Only if you have one too."

She weaved her way back to him and stood on her tiptoes, her lips lingering by his ear. "I'll tell you one thing I'm *not*, Jeptha Taylor, and that's a fool," she whispered.

She walked to the bar, not looking back once. Jeptha stood stock still, his face on fire with the recent nearness of her touch. A second, a minute, a day later—Jeptha wasn't sure—Delnor Gilliam tapped him on the elbow. "Hey, ain't you gonna get up there and play with them boys no more?"

THERE'D BEEN SEVERAL more shots after that second one. At the end of the last set, when he saw Lucy walk out the back door, looking at him before staggering against the doorframe, he knew this was his last chance before she left his life for good. He followed her out and kissed her before either of them had a chance to say anything. To his surprise, she kissed him back. What started as a drunken whim quickly grew too heated for the wall of a bar. They stumble-kissed their way to his car, where he clawed open the door and followed her into the back seat. By the time he got there, he was too drunk and too excited to listen to the quiet voice in his head wondering if drunken sex with Lucy Kilgore was a good idea.

After a few minutes of awkward tangling in which his boots caught in the straps of his rifle's case, he sat firmly in one seat and slid Lucy onto his lap, pulling her shirt off as she undid the five tiny buttons on his fly with one strong pull and shimmied his pants down. Her mouth tasted like hot whiskey and fried food, and all he wanted to do was kiss her forever. And get her skirt hiked up. He had never done anything in this back seat that felt remotely as good as this did. Jeptha's mind flashed to the fire at Avery's place and the way it had leapt from wire to wire and finally exploded into flame. He gripped the headrest of the seat in front of him and yelled into Lucy's hair. As he caught his breath, he bowed his head against her chest, suddenly aware of the sweat and the silence and the fact that the small, perfect breasts moving up and down in front of him belonged to Lucy Kilgore.

"Wow," he whispered.

"Did you . . ." Her voice trailed off as she pulled back and glanced down to where her denim skirt lapped against his belly.

"Yeah."

"Oh." Lucy widened her legs, their sweat-slick skin unsticking with a smack, and heaved herself over to the other seat. She groped around underneath Jeptha's feet for her shirt.

Jeptha's heart, still thumping with joy, came to a sudden, deflated halt. But he forged on. As he hitched his pants up onto his hips and elbowed his way back into his shirt, he took a deep breath and asked, "Do you want to go get something to eat? Maybe Waffle House?"

"I'm at work, remember? I gotta get back in there and clean up."

"Oh, right."

Lucy suddenly bolted toward the door, her hand scrabbling desperately for the handle. She wrenched it open and dry-heaved. Jeptha stared. Finally, he reached out his hand and rubbed her back in a way that he suspected was more awkward than comforting.

"Are you okay?" he asked.

"No. I shouldn't have had so much to drink. I feel like shit," she said, pulling her head back into the car and closing her eyes.

"I'm sorry," he said. He wasn't, though, not really. He didn't want her throwing up, of course, but if drinking had got her in his car, it seemed worth it to him.

"I should go. Judy'll be wondering what happened to me. My last day's not for a few more weeks."

"I heard you're moving," he said.

She nodded as she extended her leg into the air to pull on her red cowboy boot. He watched as her tanned calf slipped into the shaft with a sudden pop as her heel slid into place. He wanted to run his hand up her leg, feel that smooth skin against his fingertips, all the way up to the fringe of her skirt. He shook his head and shifted in his seat.

"Can I see you? You know, sometime?" he asked. All the drunken confidence of fifteen minutes ago had fizzled, leaving his voice breaking like he was in fourth grade.

"I work here. You play here. You'll see me."

"I meant for, like, a date."

"Jeptha, I've got to go. I can't talk about this now. I'll see you later, okay?"

"I can drive you around front," Jeptha offered. He knew it was ridiculous as soon as it was out of his mouth, but he couldn't help it. He wanted as much time with her as he could get.

"It's fine. I can go in this door. Might be better if you went around the front though."

She got out of the car and leaned down to the window. "Bye, Jeptha."

She didn't look back at him as she walked away this time, but unlike an hour before, when her whisper still shivered within him, Jeptha sensed no promise in her refusal to turn around. The sight of her shuffling back toward the bar—her body bathed in a sickly orange glow from the parking lot lights, her hair a mess of tangles in the back from where he'd run his hands through it, and her denim skirt hanging hunker-jawed off her hips—produced in Jeptha only a deep sense of sadness.

If someone had told him that he would have sex with Lucy Kilgore and feel worse after the fact than before, he'd have called that man a liar. And yet, here he was, having been closer to her than ever before and somehow, he felt farther away from getting her than at any point in his life.

"**D**AMN. DAMN. DAMN," LUCY said, punctuating the words with elbow-jarring smacks of her palm against the rim of the porcelain tub on which she sat. She stared at the tidy collection of plastic wands arrayed on the sink's edge and watched as, one after another, the line indicating the pregnancy test had worked grew a faint twin, both lines pink and parallel in their certainty that her life, never so great to start with, was now officially ruined.

Until the fourth test turned pink, she hoped the positives were the result of Clear Blues gone clear wrong. As wrong as the decision—if one could call it that—she had made three weeks ago to have sex with Jeptha Taylor. Whiskey had obliterated every objection she ordinarily would have had, scouring out the institutional memory everyone in town was born with where it concerned the Taylors. She'd forgotten all about the rumors of the girls he'd slept with; how he'd dropped out of school; how he had no parents (not that she could hold that against him, not having any herself) and spent his days drunk and wild. She even, for a moment, forgot that it had been his dad whom everyone first suspected when her parents had been killed by a drunk driver when she was only thirteen. Even after the trucker—so drunk he would maintain for years afterward that it "wasn't me, officer, it was my pig"—came forward, no one quite believed that Jimmy Taylor wasn't the real culprit. But that night, drunk on whiskey and full of an addled sort of awe at how good Jeptha's mandolin playing was, every single one of those reasons had escaped her mind, like chickens flying the coop.

She had spent the next three weeks alternately berating herself and praying, hoping contrition and begging would be enough to spare her the consequences of not only sleeping with Jeptha Taylor, but doing it without a condom. Staring at the tests in front of her, she knew with certainty that

God, that old Peeping Tom, figured any girl who had sex in the back seat of a car deserved to get pregnant—even He could see that the sex back there wasn't that great.

She had known Jeptha to say hello to for much of her life. She'd even had a moment or two when she caught his eye and felt something for him— it wasn't interest, so much as appreciation for his good looks and the hungry way his eyes devoured her. But she had never found herself moved to such wanton behavior until that whiskey-fueled night when she had seen something new in him as he played up on the stage, something haunted and passionate and just plain hot. And, up to a point, the night had been exactly the kind of fun that Lucy never allowed herself to indulge in. Kissing behind the bar, fumbling their way to his car, climbing into the back seat—there had been a certain reckless abandon in that. She remembered a joyful, drunken anticipation, a feeling so novel Lucy had a hard time recognizing it. She gave herself over to it, swept away by the insanity of the moment. It was, she remembered thinking, how people she knew described the feeling of heroin.

But all the pleasure had been in the recklessness of it. As soon as the sex was over, the wild joy of the moment evaporated as quickly as rain off the summer sidewalk. A creeping sense of dismay stole over her as she tried to catch her breath. In the orange glow of the parking lot lights, staring down at the deep V of their shared bodies, she remembered it was Jeptha Taylor, emphasis on the Taylor, whose stubble heaved against her chest, whose un-condomed penis was shriveling inside her.

NOW, WEEKS LATER, she was disgusted with herself all over again, particularly since she could tell, if not before the sex, then definitely afterward, that their short encounter was the culmination of some dream of Jeptha's, some hope he had nursed for years. She knew it would never work between them, a feeling only reinforced by the heart-breaking pity she'd felt for him as his voice broke when he asked her on a date. She'd understood then that she had not only done something mind-blowingly stupid, she had done it with a guy who—despite all evidence to the contrary—turned out to think it might actually mean something.

Tears sprung up in Lucy's eyes as she stared at the tests. She shook her head so violently that they blurred into nothing. It turned out the act had meant something to Lucy too. It meant her plan—of getting out, of leaving this town, of doing something more with her life, even if it was moving an hour away to slowly but surely work her way toward a degree, one class at a time—was now, if not impossible, much, much harder. Since she'd lost her parents, she'd been plugging away at their dream for her, anticipating nothing but checking off the boxes they'd set up as defenses against their only daughter living the life they'd hoped to escape themselves: graduate high school, move out of this small town, go to college. Some days, she wanted those things too. And certainly the whole town wanted them for her. When her mom and dad died, she'd become a ward of the town, in a sense. She had been chosen as the one who would leave, a vessel for whatever dreams of escape that flitted through their own minds from time to time, and then were dismissed as hopeless without ever really being considered. But not so for Lucy. They watched out for her, made sure she had what she needed to succeed in school, raised money for her when she needed it. Even in those moments when Lucy thought of giving up and accepting that she'd live here all her life, someone was there, pushing her on. But none of those Good Samaritans considered how devastatingly hard it would be to accomplish even the most basic of those dreams once Lucy lost her parents. She was already two years behind their schedule in trying to move to Knoxville.

Late at night, when Lucy was alone and brave enough to admit it, what she imagined finding in Knoxville was not herself, or an education, or what she wanted to do with her life. It was finding a family. She had a vision of going to class and meeting a nice guy, whom she'd date until they eventually decided they were good enough for each other to get married and have kids. The education part of it was an afterthought—merely the means to a happy end. Going to Knoxville meant finding a family and becoming whole again.

Trying to live that dream had kept her centered. She kept moving forward, working hard, and caring about something so that she wouldn't become another careless slut boozing it up because she had nothing better. The dream of Knoxville, of the family she'd find there, was the thing that kept her going, the reason why the church ladies could say, without resorting to their Christian duty, that she had done "real well, considering." She stayed on the path her parents and the town had made for her, like a tractor running the same grooves year after year.

But now, looking down at the pink lines in front of her, she felt a deep pit in her stomach as she imagined the looks on the faces of those who had helped her. The utter disappointment and devastation when she told them she'd gotten drunk and destroyed their dreams. Even worse, though, was the dissolution of her own dream. A crushing sense of dismay overtook her as she watched her dream of a family—solid, stable, settled—disappear. She thought of the boxes packed in a corner of the living room, the ones neatly labeled with their contents and marked Knoxville on the top. Boxes that would need to be unpacked and probably never packed again. Her future would be here now—in this small town, her name forever etched beside Jeptha's, even if they never spoke again.

The thing that scared her most about that looming fact was not the loss of the future she'd planned, her disappointment or her anger at herself for being so stupid. Those were feelings she knew and could understand. What scared her most was that slippery, joyful fear. Pregnant by Jeptha Taylor was bad. Undeniably bad. But there, muddled in with the fear and horror of carrying the town drunk's kid, was a flicker of delight. It welled up, like oil suddenly seeping out of a long-abandoned well. This baby would be her family. Nothing pieced together, nothing cobbled. Her blood, her genes, her body would make this baby. And no matter what happened, it would be her family. It wasn't what her parents, the town, or she had ever dreamed of, but Lucy suddenly knew it didn't matter, none of that did. Some part of her wanted this.

"Hey-lo!" a voice called out from the hall, and then again from outside the bathroom door. Lucy moved to hide the tests, but before she could, the door swung open, catching the edge of one of the sticks and sending them all tumbling to the black and white tile, where the pink lines seemed to glow.

LouEllen Moss filled the doorway, her red cotton shorts and matching red shirt accented by a pair of bright purple Keds, one toe of which was nudging one of the pregnancy tests. The outfit made her look like a large, bright red apple, as if the Fruit of the Loom guys had recruited a woman to their ranks. Most women would have avoided the look once they got past a size 14, but LouEllen was not most women.

Lucy had a fleeting moment of hope that LouEllen wouldn't notice the tests. But when she moved her foot forward an inch, the plastic capsule she stepped on cracked. LouEllen looked down and inhaled sharply.

"Oh, Lucy. No."

She had been living with LouEllen, her mom's best friend, since her parents had died, and she'd never managed to keep something from her. There was no such thing as a secret from LouEllen. It was inevitable that she'd learn the truth.

"Oh, Lucy. Please tell me those belong to a friend of yours. Please tell me you are holding them for her for some reason that doesn't even have to make sense. Please say you aren't pregnant."

"I'd like to," she said, unable to meet LouEllen's eyes. "Not sure those lines are gonna let me."

"Well, shit," LouEllen said, her accent slipping into that of the holler she'd been raised in—one that Lucy knew she had spent a lot of time getting away from. She lowered herself onto the rim of the tub beside Lucy. They stared down at the tests together.

"Whose is it?" LouEllen finally asked.

"An idiot's," Lucy said, shaking her head.

"Well, that narrows it down in a town absolutely peopled with 'em."

"I don't want to say."

"Is he really that bad? I mean, it ain't like it was a Taylor."

Lucy wanted to hold onto this moment, where no one but her knew it was Jeptha's kid she was carrying. But it didn't matter. LouEllen would find out eventually. Everyone would.

"Jeptha's not so bad," she finally whispered.

"Oh, Lucy. You didn't."

Lucy risked a look at LouEllen's face. Her nostrils flared into perfect round circles, and her lipsticked lips were pursed into tiny railroad tracks of anger. Lucy had slowly been losing the memory of her mother's face, but seeing LouEllen's expression, she suddenly remembered. Her mom would have hated this with a fury so hot it would have kept her warm on the coldest day.

"Why now? You had one foot out the door. You were about to leave. About to do the thing you always wanted."

"The thing they always wanted," Lucy said, between sobs.

"You wanted it too," LouEllen said. "Otherwise, what the hell was the point of all of this?"

"All what?"

"The trying, the working, the encouraging you to get up and get out, to be something."

"I don't know. I don't know what the point of any of this was," Lucy said.

LouEllen rubbed her hand over her eyebrows three times until they stood up wild and then pinched her nose between her thumb and middle finger. It was what LouEllen always did when she was angry, frustrated, and didn't know what to do.

"Jesus, Lucy. Jeptha Taylor? He's the one you had to do this with?"

Lucy stared at the floor, silent. She had been asking herself the same question for three weeks.

"I'm sorry. I shouldn't have said that. You had your reasons," LouEllen said, her hand slowly coming to rest on Lucy's back.

"I was drunk."

"Well, it ain't the best reason in the world, but I guess it'll have to do."

Lucy laughed softly and looked up at LouEllen. "What am I gonna do?"

"I imagine cry for a while."

"After that?"

"Are you . . ." LouEllen stopped.

"What?" Lucy couldn't read the look on her face. "Am I what?"

"Going to Knoxville?" LouEllen said, her eyebrow raised.

Lucy scoffed. "How can I move there with a new baby?"

"Not to move there, Lucy. To . . ." LouEllen said, nodding at Lucy's belly.

"Oh!" Lucy finally understood. She shook her head no. She couldn't imagine getting rid of the baby. Even if she hadn't accepted that some part of her wanted this baby, it went against everything she had been raised with, everything she'd been taught. She knew a girl in high school who had done that, or was said to have done it, and no one ever let her forget it. Even the guy who had gotten her pregnant had stood in the hallway during lunch the week after she returned, loudly calling her a whore and a baby killer, though Lucy saw a glimmer of relief in his eyes to have avoided a kid at sixteen. The poor girl left school in tears every day for a week and then finally never came back. The general consensus was that it was better to be a slut and pay the price than be a slut and get off Scot-free, even if it might ruin your life. Lucy hated the way everyone had treated that girl and didn't think it was right. Even so, it just wasn't a choice Lucy could make. Besides, Lucy couldn't imagine taking that step, having to live with the knowledge that she had destroyed her only possible family. She hadn't wanted a baby, but now that it was here, she couldn't stomach the thought of getting rid of it.

"No. It's all the family I've got. I can't."

"Well, I had to ask. I don't really believe you'd go to hell for it, but God, I'd hate to have to die to find out."

Lucy stared at the pink lines pulsing on the floor, her mind blank except for the words "damn" and "baby."

"What am I going to do?" Lucy asked again. She desperately wanted some answer that didn't involve giving up everything her parents had dreamed for her, everything she'd worked toward the last seven years. She tried to imagine life in Knoxville with a baby. She'd be in a brand-new place, all on her own. She'd have to find a restaurant job that was only during the day. A daycare for the baby. Everyone bitched about how expensive having a baby was. It had to be even more so in Knoxville. And what about school? That was the whole reason for being in Knoxville, to take classes at UT. But, how could she work all day and go to class at night if she had another person to take care of?

She'd finally have some family but be all alone.

"You need to call the doctor," LouEllen said. "We'll get you some vitamins and deal with the rest." She patted Lucy's leg briskly and stood up. "We got that back room sitting empty. Be perfect for a baby."

"Wait, what?" Lucy asked.

"We can do this together," LouEllen said.

The pink lines glared at her as Lucy held her head in her hands, trying to think about what to do. She remembered her dad reading her the story of the Three Little Pigs and how even at five, she'd been horrified by the stupidity of the first two pigs. But here she was at age twenty, a vision for her life all constructed, and it turned out she was one of the stupid pigs, the one who built her home of sticks or straw. It was now crumbling down around her. Part of her wanted to piece it back together, try to shore it up.

But then, she looked up at the walls around her, at LouEllen's comforting bulk smiling down at her—offering Lucy her home again, even with a baby in tow. Maybe this was the house built of bricks, the one that could withstand. It had been in the past. Lucy opened her mouth to speak.

"You know me, I've always wanted a baby," LouEllen said.

Lucy shut her mouth. Some long-dormant maternal hackles rose up at the notion of this baby belonging to anyone but her. Lucy would always be grateful to LouEllen, for taking her in, raising her, loving her even—but Lucy was always painfully aware, even if LouEllen never quite seemed to be, that she was not her mother. They had settled into a relationship that worked for them, even as Lucy bristled at LouEllen's occasional smothering attempts to be her mother. And now her not-mother seemed to think this might be her not-baby. But Lucy would need someone's help. And who else would offer it but LouEllen?

"You okay?" LouEllen asked.

"I guess," Lucy said. "As okay as I can be."

"All right then. Aren't you supposed to be at work around now?" LouEllen asked, holding out her hands and hauling Lucy up off the tub.

"Yeah. I'm thinking about calling in sick," Lucy said. She wasn't sure she could face the scene of the crime so soon after learning the penalty.

LouEllen shook her head at Lucy and then pulled her in for a hug. Tears welled up again.

"It's gonna be all right," LouEllen said. "We'll make it. But there's gonna be plenty of days that you'll need some time off down the road, so you better not get off on the wrong foot just yet."

With that, she pushed Lucy toward the door.

LUCY HAD WALKED into Judy's bar dozens upon dozens of times since she started working there six months before, but she had never felt so conflicted upon seeing the place. It was both the scene of her worst mistake and the source of this flickering sense of joy; she didn't trust either emotion. And even the joy didn't cover up the fact that she had slept with Jeptha Taylor and gotten pregnant for her trouble. She had loved working at Judy's from the start—and loved it even more once they finally had more than ten customers following the fire at Avery's. But today, as she pulled into the lot, all she could see were the weeds sprouting up from the hundreds of cracks in the asphalt, the beer bottles tumbled down from the dumpster out back, and the dirty concrete wall, lined with wiring and more weeds, where she and Jeptha had first kissed. *Damn whiskey*, she thought to herself.

Lucy knew Judy had meant well when she started handing out whiskey like so much water. Judy wasn't from here, though, and she didn't know any better when it came to encouraging someone to see more in a Taylor. Hell, Lucy thought, saying Jeptha was "a Taylor" didn't mean anything to Judy. And even if it had, Jeptha seemed to have uncovered a soft spot in Judy that Lucy still only saw glimpses of and doubted for weeks after. Maybe it said something for Jeptha that Judy liked him.

Judy nodded at her as Lucy walked through the door. "How's the packing going?" she asked.

"What packing?"

"For your move? Aren't you moving in two weeks?"

Lucy thought of the boxes packed in the living room and of the ads she'd printed out at the library from the apartment listings online. Her favorite was dog-eared and circled: "1 BR Avail 7/1, no students. HW, EIK, $WD." It had taken her days to discern the lingo of the ads and a week more to get up the courage to call. She was supposed to send her deposit to the landlord in tomorrow's mail. She had enough money saved up to live without working for a couple months, but her plan was to hit the ground as soon as she moved in—she wanted to get there before the college students arrived and took all the good jobs. If she got there a couple months before classes started, she figured she would have enough saved to sign up for one class this semester. Turns out, she should have been buying diapers instead.

"It may not be happening now," Lucy said.

"What do you mean—may not be?" Judy asked.

"Just not sure I can do it."

"Really?"

"Don't get so excited." Lucy's stomach dropped as she took in Judy's near-smile, her eyes twinkling. She held onto the bar stool to keep herself from collapsing into a teary heap.

"You don't want to go anymore?"

Lucy scoffed. "I don't know what I want. And I'm pretty sure it doesn't matter anymore either."

"So, I don't need to hire a replacement?"

"Not yet, anyway."

"I could hug you," Judy said. "I won't, but I could. I hate hiring. Thirty-four drunks, fifteen heroin addicts, and three meth heads show up seeking easy access to a cash register and wondering why you won't give them a job."

"Well, lucky you," Lucy said, gripping the back of the chair to keep from yelling at Judy. "What do you want me to do for tonight?"

Judy recoiled from Lucy's sharp tone and peered at her. "You okay?"

"I'm fine."

"Want to talk about it?"

"Do I look like I want to talk about it?" Lucy asked, her voice softening.

"Good. I was worried you might say yes," Judy said, sweeping the bar towel over the bar and up on her shoulder. "In that case, do the usual. But bring up some extra cases of Bud. It's Friday."

"Dammit," Lucy said. She stared up at the ceiling as tears threatened to fall again. "It's Friday."

"That a problem? It's usually your best night for tips."

Lucy shook her head and headed for the back stairs. Friday meant Jeptha's weekly gig. As she broke down the boxes in the basement, dragged two cases of Bud upstairs, and swept under the tables, she thought about what she would say to Jeptha. The week after they'd had sex, she'd been off on Friday and had never been so happy to miss out on a tip-heavy night. She had kept him at arm's length the week after that, even though she could see the wounded look on his face as she sidestepped him when he asked to see her again. He must not have had her phone number, or she figured he'd be calling. But she couldn't avoid him tonight. She'd barely had enough time to get her own head around what the pink lines tossed in the bathroom trash meant for her, much less for him. She couldn't imagine sharing the news with him tonight. Or maybe ever. Maybe, she thought, she could pretend this was someone else's baby, some mysterious person whom she planned to never name. Or she could claim immaculate conception. It had worked at least once. Maybe it was time for another try.

Lucy unlocked the door for Delnor, who treated the bar as his living room every night come four o'clock. She poked her head out the door to check for Jeptha's car. The parking lot was clear. She returned to the bar, serving up a shot of the cheapest bourbon to Delnor and fending off his ever-present requests for a free beer. Every time the door opened, her stomach jumped until she could assure herself it wasn't Jeptha. Gradually, the place filled to the point that she lost track of newcomers.

Delnor was nursing his fourth shot when Lucy felt a tap on her shoulder. Her armpits prickled with sweat and her stomach soured when she turned and saw Jeptha. He wore a tentative half-smile as his blue eyes searched hers. He was looking, she was sure, for some sign of warmth. All Lucy could think was *How did I let this happen? How could I have been so stupid?*

"Hey," she said, finally. "How are you?"

"I'm good. Been thinking about you."

"Yeah?" The sick feeling in her stomach got worse, and she could swear her heart had never beat this fast.

"I was hoping you'd listen to us play tonight."

"I don't have much choice, do I?" she said.

His face fell. Lucy's stomach felt even worse for having hurt him. "I'll listen, Jeptha. Right now, I've got to get beers for these guys and food for that table. I'll see you later."

He nodded at her and walked, shoulders stooped, to the stage. Now she was sick to her stomach, sweaty, and guilty to boot. She ducked behind the bar to unload glasses from the washer. She not only needed to take care of this baby, apparently, but Jeptha's feelings too.

"Dammit. Dammit. Dammit. Stupid. Stupid," she grumbled with each glass, her anger mounting. Suddenly, she felt fingers grip her arms, hard enough to leave a mark.

"Lucy. Stop. You're going to break those."

Lucy looked from the glasses, which were stacked twelve high and swaying with each beat of the drum, to Judy. She hadn't realized how hard she was slamming them.

"I'm sorry."

"Why don't you go grab some more Jack from downstairs?" Judy asked. As she headed downstairs, she heard Judy gingerly unstacking the glasses.

Lucy grabbed two large handles of Jack. She'd been tossing back shots of the stuff three week ago, but now all she wanted was to hurl the bottles against the wall. Instead, she stomped back up the stairs and placed them on the counter with a ringing clunk.

"I've seen people look at liquor in a lot of ways, but I don't know that I've ever seen anyone look at a bottle of whiskey with such anger before," Judy said.

"Now, that surprises me," Lucy said. "It makes people do such damn stupid things."

"I'm guessing you won't be having a shot of whiskey with the band tonight?"

Out of Lucy's mouth emerged a single rueful laugh, followed by a tear. And then another one fell. She turned to face the liquor bottles along the wall, mortified to be crying at work in front of Judy. Judy moved closer to Lucy, and a moment later, Lucy felt the lightest pressure on her back, as if Judy's hand were a sun-warmed leaf that had floated softly onto Lucy's shoulder. Judy cleared her throat.

"Is he really that bad?" Judy asked.

"Who?"

She nodded up at the stage. "That mandolin player."

"Yes," Lucy stopped. "No. I don't know. Maybe I'm the bad one," Lucy said, wiping her eyes with the towel Judy had handed her.

"He doesn't ever take his eyes off you."

Lucy was silent.

"From that first night in here, a few weeks back. If you're in the room, he's watching you like a Sox fan seeing Fenway for the first time."

Lucy wasn't sure what Fenway was, but she knew the look Judy was describing. She had been trying to ignore it, hoping that if she pretended not to see it, no one else would either. Her father had looked at her that way—his face lit with so much wonder and love. Then, it had made her feel like she could do anything, be anyone. Now, seeing that look on Jeptha's face made her want to hide.

"I know," Lucy sighed. "But you aren't from here. You don't know him. Besides, there's more to it than that."

"I may not know much about him or about the people down here generally, but I know that's not a look you come across every day. I'd think twice before I squandered it."

"Squandered it?"

"I'm just saying, maybe you should give the guy a chance."

Lucy gathered the three beers for Table 6 by their necks and made her way out from behind the bar. "Maybe," she said.

A FEW HOURS later, the band ended their set, and Lucy watched as Jeptha carefully put away his mandolin and stepped off the stage. Three of the trashiest girls in the bar leapt to their feet, their nearly identical miniskirts and hacked off t-shirts bearing a little less skin than a gaggle of strippers. Lucy couldn't help but laugh when they flashed Jeptha candy-bright smiles and tossed their hair, their frosted tips all the same white blonde of lightning. He'd left with at least one of these girls before—and despite it being clear to even the most casual observer that all he planned to do was sleep with them, they kept coming back for more. She expected he'd stop and talk with them, maybe give one the nod, like she had noticed him doing whenever she had seen him out at bars in the past. She'd even seen him do it at church once—the girl had left her parents sitting in the pew and snuck out with him, coming back in after the final hymn with her hair all mussed up and her dress wrinkled. Lucy stopped laughing when she saw that he ignored them all and was heading straight for her like a cow to fresh hay. The looks they gave her were not warm ones.

"Hey, Lucy," he said, his voice cracking. Lucy smiled for a moment; there was something sweet about the fact that she made him as nervous as a twelve-year-old boy.

"Y'all sounded good tonight," she said. She pulled at a loose string on the bar towel, wishing she had a counter to clean. She'd wiped it down three times already.

"Thanks. We wasn't as good as that night."

"Well, that night was special," she said. Jeptha's face brightened like a small child seeing snow for the first time. "I mean, we were all drunk," Lucy hurried to say. "Everything sounds better when you're drunk."

"Oh, right. Yeah. I guess that's true," Jeptha said, his fingers fidgeting with his belt buckle.

"No. That didn't come out right. I don't mean y'all sounded bad, just everything sounds better when there's alcohol. Everything seems like a good idea at the time, right?"

"I suppose," he said, shrugging and not meeting her eye. "Guess I'll see you later."

"Jeptha, wait. I didn't mean . . ." Lucy stopped, not sure what she wanted to say. She looked up at him. His dark blond hair was shorn, and his blue eyes were bright with expectation. He was wearing the same gray t-shirt and jeans he'd worn that night. He looked good in them. She remembered then the feel of him under her, the planed edges of his body moving against hers. She shook her head against the vision and forced her breath to slow. It was Jeptha Taylor, for God's sake. Judy's words came back to her. Given the fact that his kid was currently dividing cell by cell inside her, maybe she should give him a chance. He was, she realized with a small shudder, sort of family now.

"Do you have plans tomorrow? I was thinking of going to Carter's Fold, if maybe you wanted to come," Lucy said.

"With you?" Jeptha said, his voice cracking again as he broke out in a grin that he couldn't contain. His face was so hopeful that Lucy couldn't help but smile.

"Yes, with me."

"I do," he said, nodding his head so hard Lucy was sure he'd give himself a headache.

"Pick me up at six? Here's the address," she said, and wrote "512 Maple" on a bar napkin.

He stared at the napkin like it was a treasure map. Lucy had a sudden vision of Jeptha as a child, back to a moment when he'd never had a drink, slept with a girl, or gone drunkenly careening around town. She was touched to think that that Jeptha was still in there.

"I'll be there. I can't wait," he said.

Once Lucy saw the door close behind Jeptha, she turned to look at Judy, who had been pretending to clean up while listening to the whole exchange from the other end of the bar. "There, you happy?" Lucy said.

"What do I care? I just said maybe think about giving him a shot, but what's that you guys say? 'I don't have a dog in this fight.'"

Lucy grabbed the empty beer bottles off the table closest to her and wiped it down. "God, I wish I didn't either."

— 3 —

JEPTHA WOKE EARLY ON Saturday morning. He cautiously opened his eyes, expecting the pounding headache, alcohol-dried throat, and ache of regret in his belly that he'd been waking with for the last three Saturdays, and most other days since he was fifteen besides. But his head was blissfully clear, and his stomach still danced with sheer astonishment over Lucy asking him to Carter's Fold. The fingers that usually shook with tremors instead pulsed with the bluegrass from last night's set. Wearing nothing but a pair of bright orange UT boxers, he lay on the wrinkled sheets and smiled up at the cratered surface of the ceiling tiles. He grabbed his mandolin off the bedside table and picked out a few notes from the song in his head. He was surprised to find after a minute or two that he was playing and humming along to "Twinkle, Twinkle Little Star," the very first song he learned to play.

He had been eight the first time he picked up a mandolin. Once a week, his Meemaw had taken him over to her friend Miss Irene's house, a one-story structure whose living room sloped from one end to the other so much that Jeptha always stuck a ball in his pocket to play with on the incline. No matter how much fluffy white peanut butter candy she gave him, he never got over his fear of her powdery smell, which barely covered a whiff of decay. One visit, fidgety and full of sugar, he had wandered around the house, hoping Meemaw might decide it was time to leave if he got too close to Miss Irene's collection of tiny blue glass animals.

Next to the animal collection, a small, pear-shaped wooden instrument, a kind of shrunken guitar, leaned against one corner. He heard Meemaw's voice drop into the half-whisper she used when she had some story she didn't want Jeptha to hear about his dad, whose marriage to Jeptha's mom Meemaw was always calling "ill-advised." Miss Irene nodded in that understanding way Jeptha had noticed women had when they were talking smack about men. He reached his hand out toward the instrument. Neither woman looked over. Unsure how to grapple with it, he picked it up by the strings. His thumb and forefinger slipped off the metal wire, and he had to grab the wooden back with his other hand to keep from dropping it. His pinky finger hit the strings and bounced off, the sound rolling off Miss Irene's living room walls the way the ball had sped down the floor. He hurriedly put it down and backed away.

"Do you know what that is?" Miss Irene asked, peering at him over her glasses.

Jeptha was too afraid to speak.

"That's a mandolin. You ever heard one?"

He shook his head.

"Lord, Betty, why ain't you ever brought him over to Carter's Fold? Boy needs some music in his life. He's old enough." Turning back to Jeptha, she said, "Well, bring it here, Jeptha. I'll show you. That's right, grab it by the neck, not the strings."

She took the instrument from his hands and held it up against herself. She strummed the strings until its soft, tinny sounds filled the room. Jeptha's hands involuntarily reached out to touch it. Miss Irene smiled. He picked at the top string and heard a note ring out.

"You know 'Shady Grove'?" Miss Irene asked.

"Yeah."

Even as a kid, Jeptha had recognized something magical in the high, forsaken sound her fingers made against the pear-shaped instrument's double strings. It made him feel lonely and understood all at the same time. As soon as she played the last note, he thrust his hands back out, desperate to hold it again.

Since that day, a mandolin was never far away from his hands. Jeptha used to sneak over to Miss Irene's most afternoons to play, with Meemaw's help. In addition to songs like "Twinkle, Twinkle Little Star" and "Shady Grove," Miss Irene taught him the mandolin's notes and quirks. She showed him the beauty of the sound and how to draw it out so that the notes seemed to go straight to his heart. With her hands guiding his, he fell in love for the first time.

But, ten months later, Meemaw died. He saw Miss Irene at the funeral and walked the five miles to her house later that week. There, with tears in her eyes, she gave him her father's mandolin. It was the most beautiful thing Jeptha had ever seen—it had a mother-of-pearl fern on the peg head and a swirl of wood at the bottom. It was far too nice for an eight-year-old, but because Miss Irene trusted him with it, he had kept it safe, even if he never went over to her house for lessons again. He wanted to, often, but he missed Meemaw too much to go to a place he'd only been with her.

This was the mandolin he kept beside him on the bed, the one he played with his band, and the one he played on the porch most nights, picking away while the sun set. Now, lying in bed, Jeptha was happy to hear the notes ring out, as true to the sound as they had been the day the mandolin was made. He moved deftly from the lullaby to "Shady Grove," softly singing the words to himself.

> *Peaches in the summertime,*
> *Apples in the fall,*
> *If I can't have the girl I love,*
> *I don't want none at all.*

> *Some come here to fiddle and dance,*
> *Some come here to tarry.*
> *Some come here to fiddle and dance,*
> *I come here to marry.*

Until last night, for the three weeks since he'd had sex with Lucy in his back seat, he'd been drinking steadily. Every day that he didn't see her, and even more on the days when he did and she brushed him off, he'd realized he had made a mistake taking her back to his car. His heart drained away faster than his beers, and he knew it was over before it had begun. He tried to tell himself that he was right back where he'd been before that night—lusting after her with her paying him no mind. But having been close to her, his neck still tickling occasionally from her whisper, his body aching to feel her weight on him again, it was no use. He'd called up one of his old girlfriends—a Chastity who had never been chaste—but the night had been a failure. It wasn't sex he wanted, it was Lucy. Alcohol was the only thing that dulled the pain, and poorly at that. It'd gotten so bad there for a few weeks that Jeptha had toyed with calling up the friend of his who always had something on him, whether Oxy or heroin. But he resisted, grabbed another beer, and fiddled around on his mandolin a little more. He couldn't forget the time his and Cody's friend Dustin had died of a heroin overdose in the Porta Potty at his construction job, where Jeptha— who'd been stranded at the top of a lift for an hour when his friend took a break—found him, hunched over and blue. The sight had scared Jeptha straight from even thinking about touching the shit, right into the well-known and loving arms of his mandolin and booze.

But finally last night, the words tumbling out of her mouth were the ones he'd been wanting to hear for more than half his life. Happy as he was, he couldn't shake the feeling that he'd started the whole thing out wrong, with a level of seediness that was so far from what he wanted with her. Tonight would be what he'd envisioned; tonight would be their fresh start.

He lay the mandolin down in its case and scratched his belly, trying to get up the energy to get out of bed, pee, and make some coffee. He was mid-grunt and halfway up when his brother Bobby's bear-paw knock sounded at the door.

"Jeptha! You up? I been waiting on your ass for near on twenty minutes. Let's go."

"Damn, Bobby, you don't need to yell," Jeptha shouted as he shuffled to the door. "I got ears. And I'm up." He pulled the door open. Bobby narrowed his eyes and grimaced at Jeptha's boxers before looking away. "What? A man can't sleep without a shirt on?"

"Frankly, Jeptha, I don't give a damn what you sleep in, as long as you are up and ready to top some damn tobacco in about three minutes."

"Alright, alright. I'm coming."

Bobby turned without saying anything. He pulled on his gloves as he clomped down Jeptha's stairs, the trailer swaying slightly with each step.

Jeptha threw on a pair of dirty jeans and a t-shirt. He dumped a quarter of a mug of instant coffee into a cup and filled it with lukewarm water from the sink. He had completely forgotten they had tobacco to top today. The farm never failed to ruin his day.

When Jeptha's parents had died—his dad in a spectacularly fiery drunken car crash that luckily only killed him and his mom six months later from a found-too-late cancer that leeched whatever spirit she had left from her body as if she were a tire with a pinhole—they left the farm to their three kids equally. Jeptha's trailer, which sagged a bit on the right side where he hadn't jacked it up quite right, sat a couple hundred feet away from his sister Deanna's house, which had been his parents' house when they were alive. Deanna had inherited the house by virtue of being the only one of them who had kids. It had been that rare case when having kids before you were ready turned out to be a financial boon, and Deanna wasn't going to waste it. At the point of a triangle, Bobby's trailer butted up against the trees at the back of the property. The farm was situated on the slope of a small hill, with the valley and its road running from left to right in front of them. Each house had a view of the road, Jeptha's dad's car up on blocks, a fence, and the field of tobacco. Plus a view straight into each other's homes. Deanna could see Jeptha drinking beer on his porch, while Jeptha listened to Bobby yell at the game on TV.

They had a twenty-two-acre tobacco allotment, all the profits split evenly between them. Deanna did none of the back-breaking work—none of the plowing, planting, topping, or sticking. She dealt with the money, the insurance, and the Farm Bureau. Even though he had no head for figures and couldn't have done it himself, Jeptha was sure she was getting off easy.

He had come to hate growing tobacco, or least growing tobacco with his siblings. He hated seeing the stalks loom up in the summer, hated how aware he was of how much work went into every cigarette he smoked. In every leaf looming up over the long, hot summer, all he could see was the misery of being forever yoked to his family. He dreamed of buying a plot of land for himself and growing whatever he wanted on it. Even if he failed, it'd be his failure. But Jeptha had no cash, no extra reserves of money set aside for something like that. Instead, he settled for telling Bobby there had to be a better way to make money off the land. Bobby kept asking what he had in mind. Jeptha had no idea, but he was sure that no man was meant to work so hard for so little.

Bobby had insisted they plant tobacco, like their dad and his dad before them. But it didn't take a genius to see that hefting three hundred pounds around the tobacco field was no easy job. As a result, every awful task— every knee bend, root check, or crawl through a row in ninety-two-degree heat to look at the underside of the biggest leaves—fell to Jeptha. At the end of every day, he emerged filthy from his fingernails to his ankles and smelling of fresh tobacco, a scent that made him both crave and despise the thought of a cigarette. They did as much of the work themselves as they could, but still, between fertilizing, topping off the flowers, and paying a couple of Mexicans to come out and help stick it into four-foot bunches that hung to dry in the barn, profit wasn't something Jeptha was terribly well-acquainted with.

Suppressing a gag at the taste of the coffee, Jeptha closed the door behind him and started into the field. His long legs caught up with Bobby's waddle in a few steps. Together, they waded into the tobacco, six feet high and already lacing the air with the leathery, spicy scent that would intensify when it was hung and dried in a month. Theirs was quiet, long, hot work—checking for fungus, topping the flowers to force the tobacco to put its energy into the leaves, and keeping an eye for tobacco worms that would mean spending money they didn't have for spray.

"Damn, man. Ever time I look over there, you got a smile on your face. You just get some or something?" Bobby asked from the row next to Jeptha.

"Get some? Did you see anybody in my trailer just now?"

"Then how come you're so happy?"

Jeptha hid his face behind one particularly tall plant. "Just enjoying life," he lied. "Ain't you ever felt that way?"

"Not when I'm sweating my way through a field of untopped tobacco, I ain't."

"I ain't saying I'm happy about this," Jeptha said, gesturing at the long rows in front of them. "But I got something good happening tonight."

Bobby stopped and eyed Jeptha. "Oh yeah. Like what?"

"Heading up to Carter's."

"Me and Kayla was thinking of heading up. You don't see me smiling like a dumbass kid at Christmas."

"I'm taking someone with me."

"Like I said, I'm taking Kayla."

"Y'all been doing that forever. This is someone new."

"Who?" Bobby asked, his eyes narrowed and lips curled.

Jeptha didn't want to say Lucy's name, didn't want to ruin what seemed so precarious. But Bobby squeezed his way through two plants and into Jeptha's row. He stood in front of Jeptha waiting for his answer.

"Lucy Kilgore," Jeptha said quietly.

"That's hilarious. Who are you really taking?"

"I'm taking Lucy Kilgore," Jeptha said, his voice raised.

"Damn, man. She's a little out of your league, ain't she?" he asked.

"She said yes. So I guess I'll let her decide," Jeptha said defensively, fidgeting with the plant beside him.

Bobby rustled back through the row. "Well, good luck. Don't do nothing too stupid."

Jeptha looked down to see he had shredded the tip of the leaf in his hand. He dropped his hands. "Thanks, man. That's real helpful."

They were quiet for a few minutes as they worked their way to the end of the row, going faster as they neared the end.

"She don't think I'm stupid," Jeptha said as he got to the last plant.

"What's that?" Bobby asked as he straightened up and wiped his forehead.

"I said, she don't think I'm stupid."

Bobby wiped his brow again and looked back toward the other end of the field. "Well, she don't know you real well yet, does she?"

Jeptha tried like hell to ignore Bobby's words. He tried to focus on the work and on the thought of Lucy's face when she'd asked him to the Fold. But the words followed him through the rows of tobacco and into his trailer a few hours later. He stood in front of the fridge, staring sightlessly into the depths, wanting to rebuke Bobby, but lacking any ammunition to do so. When he thought of Lucy's face that first night—as he held his mandolin and played the best set of his life—he could almost believe he was something better, someone worth her time. But Bobby's words pricked at him, made him want to dive headfirst into the case of beer in front of him and never come out.

He knew he wasn't much, wasn't ever going to cure cancer or be famous for something or, hell, even be known as a hard worker. He wasn't much better than his father had been. But, prior to the night with Lucy, he had forgotten that he ever wanted to be.

When he thought at all about the kind of man he was, which was rare as a summer blizzard, he figured he was no better or worse than any other man, especially the ones from his family. He worked as much as he needed in order to survive and drank more than maybe he should, but there wasn't anyone else counting on him. He couldn't see that it mattered much, despite what Rick Mullins said when he pulled him over early in the summer, trying to pin another drunk driving charge on him. But now, with Bobby's words needling him, he worried that his brother was right. He thought of how Lucy had dodged him when he first asked for a date, how she'd wanted nothing to do with him when he tried to talk to her last night, and, mostly, how her face had fallen immediately after they'd had sex. She'd probably asked him out last night out of pity. Jeptha could not stand pity. He'd rather she hated him than pitied him. She probably thought as little of him as his brother did.

He shivered as the fridge's cool air wafted over his skin. He wrestled an Old Milwaukee out of the cardboard case on the top shelf, where it sat beside a jar of pickles and a block of cheese fuzzed with green mold, and gulped the beer down in two breaths. His stomach and mind calmed as the beer reacquainted itself with his body. He immediately stooped to grab another one and drank this one slowly, savoring the sea of calm that swept over him. This was more like it. More like himself. Maybe he should say fuck it about tonight, drink himself stupid with Cody, and pretend none of this shit with Lucy had ever happened. The sex had been great, he thought as his body stirred, but everything after had unsettled him, made him think all kinds of thoughts he didn't have any use for.

He got in the shower, needing to scrub the tarry, spicy scent of tobacco off his body. The beer had dulled the drumbeat of Bobby's words to a barely noticeable hum. He reached out to the soap shelf and found it empty. With the water still running, he hunted around under his sink, dripping water all over the floor. All he could find was a bottle of bright green no-scent soap left over from last year's deer season. The stuff didn't lather for shit, but at least he wouldn't smell like a tobacco field. Before he went back into the shower, he finished off the third beer he'd left on the sink for just this purpose. The words quieted again. He soaped himself down— his legs and trunk and shoulders a stark white against the warm brown of his forearms and hands. It was only July but, like every man in the county, his farmer's tan was in full effect.

With the towel wrapped around his waist, he checked his phone. He still had an hour and five minutes before he was supposed to be at Lucy's. An hour and five minutes to decide whether he even wanted to go. He stood in the foot of space between his bed and dresser, reveling in the unusual smell of fresh laundry. He'd finally gone to the Laundromat for the first time in a month yesterday when everything had been worn many more times than twice. He looked out at the tobacco in front of him and Bobby's words in his head got louder for a minute, but he took a sip of his beer and pushed them away. He picked out a blue plaid shirt with shell snap buttons, the last present his mama had ever given him, remembering how she had told him it would bring out his eyes. He didn't know if he should even go through with it tonight, but a man had to get dressed regardless. At least this way he was ready. He snatched his clean jeans off the floor and slipped on his well-worn brown boots. The toes were scuffed nearly to his socks, but they were still wearable. He ran a hand through his buzz cut, not sure it made any difference at all, and then, as happy with his looks as he ever was, he walked into the kitchen.

Jeptha heard his dog, Crystal Gayle, nosing around on the porch. He grabbed his mandolin and what was left of the case of beer and joined her. As he sat on the graying fabric of the red lawn chair, Crystal Gayle nuzzled her head under his hand. He lay the mandolin down on the porch far away from her paws and rubbed her down from muzzle to tail. She quivered with joy. Crystal Gayle had a lab's build, tall and lean down the back, but verging on stocky up front. Like her namesake, she had a long lustrous coat of hair, chestnut-colored in the dog's case. She would have been gorgeous but for two lower teeth that stuck out like an upside down vampire and a Mohawk of thick, spiky hair down the middle of her back, exactly the color and texture of the German Shepherd two doors down. That local valley stud had knocked up her mom, Loretta, because Jeptha, Bobby, and Deanna had been too broke and lazy to get her fixed. Loretta had produced a legendary litter of eleven of the mangiest mutts anyone had ever seen. Crystal Gayle was the runt, the ugliest of the bunch. But, a day after the pups were born, she had taken eight toddling steps over to Jeptha's outstretched hand, climbed aboard, and fallen asleep on his chest as he stroked the Mohawk on her back with his finger. They had tried to sell the puppies, but the poor things were too ugly for anyone to buy. They gave away as many as they could, five in all.

Jeptha had told no one about the night Bobby had appeared at his door with a squirmy burlap sack in one hand and a huge rock in the other, saying, "I'm heading to the creek. You coming?" Jeptha had shook his head no and shut the door in his brother's face. He had gone back to the couch, where a three-week-old Crystal Gayle lay curled on the pillow that used to be his, and petted her until she fell into a deep sleep.

Three years later, he was still glad he'd hidden her from Bobby that night. He spent more time talking to her than anyone. He leaned down and hugged her to his chest. "You're a good girl, aren't you, Crystal?"

She wagged her tail and licked his cheek.

"Supposed to go on a date tonight, with a really nice girl. You'd like her, probably more than you like me," he said, scratching behind her ears. "Bobby thinks I ain't good enough for her. I can't decide if it's even worth trying. You think I oughta go?"

She woofed twice, then turned in a circle three times and lay down so that her head rested on the edge of the porch, her body curved around in front of Jeptha, placed so he could stroke her with his foot while he played.

"Was that a yes?" he asked.

Crystal Gayle looked over her shoulder at him and arched her back closer to his foot. He rubbed her with his foot, and she lay her head back down, contented. "You're the only one on this farm thinks I'm worth a damn," he said to her. "And that's only 'cause I rub your back."

He grabbed his mandolin then and picked out the opening notes of "East Tennessee Blues." He'd been trying to get the tempo down for weeks, but between the beers and the heat, his fingers wouldn't move fast enough. He soon gave up trying. He rested the mandolin on his lap and looked up at the sky, his eyes heavy under the influence of the five beers he'd had.

IT WASN'T UNTIL he heard a truck crunching up the gravel driveway that he realized he'd fallen asleep. Jeptha jerked his head up as his friend Cody lumbered out of the dark blue Ford F-150, pulling a black Harley Davidson t-shirt down to cover his belly, a job the shirt had long since sized out of.

"What are you doing here?" Jeptha asked.

"Brought you a present," Cody said, hefting up a case of beer.

"Aw man, you shouldn't have," Jeptha said. He thought about going in to check the time, but the light looked the same as it had when he fell asleep. He was sure it had only been a minute. Besides, the drunker he got, the less he thought he was going to go at all. Maybe he'd call up that Bendy Brandy girl—she didn't seem to care much what kind of man he was.

The porch swayed from side to side as Cody mounted the steps. His friend's black hair curled long in the back while the front stopped above his eyebrows. Jeptha had never had much use for the mullet, but it had been Cody's cut since he was seventeen. The man was loyal to it. There was something about it that brought out his small, upturned nose and his pink cheeks, where baby fat had solidified into adult fat. Jeptha would never have said as much to his friend, but sometimes when Cody spoke, Jeptha saw the talking pig from that kids' movie they'd once showed in school, about a pig and a spider. Like Jeptha, Cody sported the same farmer's tan on his arms, but unlike Jeptha, Cody wasn't embarrassed by it. He cut off the sleeves of his t-shirts himself, and his shoulders shone white and blubbery.

"You look awfully dressed up for sitting on the porch with me," Cody said.

"This ain't for you."

"Well, I wondered. Thought maybe you'd gone gay on me all of the sudden."

"Look at you. Ain't no way I'd go gay for you."

Cody smiled and handed him a beer before collapsing into the other lawn chair on the porch. Jeptha winced as he did, sure it was going to break underneath him one of these days.

"Marla loves me," Cody said. "That's why I don't got to get dressed up anymore. What's your story?"

"I'm supposed to be taking Lucy Kilgore to Carter's tonight."

"Sure you are," Cody said, looking away from Jeptha over to the tobacco. "Looks good out there."

"You and Bobby," Jeptha said, shaking his head.

"Me and Bobby what?"

"Y'all don't believe me when I say I'm taking Lucy."

"'Cause it ain't believable. Who're you taking?"

"Lucy."

Cody turned back to Jeptha and narrowed his eyes at him. "Wait, serious? Shit. That's awesome. You've been stuck on her forever."

"No, I ain't."

"Please. We've all thought about her. She's a beautiful girl. A little skinny for my tastes, but I could handle it. But you? You think about her nearly every damn day," Cody said. They both paused to take a sip of beer. Jeptha slapped a mosquito off his leg. "I wonder why she said yes," Cody said.

Bobby's words and now Cody's pulsed in his head. He downed his beer and crushed the can hard under his foot. Crystal Gayle glared at him.

"I don't know why," Jeptha said. "Especially since I'm coming to find out none of y'all think I'm worth a damn." He grabbed another beer.

"Man, don't take it like that. It's just—Lucy Kilgore. She ain't on our level—not like Marla or Deanna. She's smart. Different. Better than us, I don't mind saying."

"Oh yeah? Not so much better; she ended up in my back seat three weeks ago." Jeptha wanted to take the words back as soon as they left his mouth.

"You did not have sex with Lucy Kilgore," Cody said.

Jeptha wondered if he could say nothing and hope Cody would forget. One look at his friend's astonished face told him no.

"I did. But don't say nothing," Jeptha pleaded.

"Holy shit," Cody said.

They were quiet then, listening to the cicadas start their nightly drone and watching Crystal Gayle stir when the first faltering movements of the lightning bugs appeared. She growled low in her throat and lunged when one sparked near her head, then ran down the steps, nipping at the air.

Cody finally spoke. "So why'd you say you're supposed to be taking her? You thinking of bailing?"

"Probably."

"Why would you do a fool thing like that?"

"Don't know if it's worth it. What would she want with a man like me?"

"You was just yelling at me for saying that exact thing," Cody said, half out of his chair.

"Just 'cause something's true don't mean I want my friend saying it about me."

"Fair enough."

Jeptha reached down and grabbed another beer. He was drunk and getting drunker. Cody watched him as he drank down half.

"The way I see it is, you got two options," Cody finally said. "Sit here, get drunk, and be the man we all know you to be. Or get up from your goddamn chair and see if you can't prove us all wrong." He held out another beer to Jeptha.

Jeptha looked at it for twenty long seconds and finally stood up. "Aw hell, man."

Cody smiled. "What time you supposed to be there anyway?"

"Six."

"Man, it was after six when I pulled up."

"Dammit," Jeptha yelled. He jerked his door open, grabbed his keys off the counter, and jumped over the steps to his car.

IT WASN'T UNTIL Jeptha arrived in Lucy's neighborhood of small shotgun houses tufted by weeds on long, narrow lots that he realized he had forgotten the small napkin on which she had written her address. He knew it was Maple Avenue, but he had no idea of the number. He peered up the long straight ribbon of road that ended at the highway. There must have been a hundred houses between him and 11W. He scrounged in his pockets one more time, hoping that he would find the slip of paper, but there was nothing but a penny and a well-tumbled piece of lint.

"Dammit!" He banged his forehead against the steering wheel, hoping by some chance he could knock out the stupid and the drunk. He briefly considered heading home, back to his porch where Cody probably still sat working on that case of beer. But he was here, and in that long moment on the porch weighing Cody's words, he knew he wanted to be here. He regretted every drink he'd had past that first one and wished he could go back and punch himself in the face for being so stupid all afternoon. He'd been lucky as hell to get a date with Lucy, and now he'd have to work his ass off to make up for being both drunk and late for it.

Jeptha parked at the bottom of the street. Skipping any houses with Big Wheels or kids' toys in the yard, he began knocking on doors.

After twenty minutes and a set of mighty sore knuckles, he knocked on 510 Maple Ave. An old lady answered the door in a multicolored floral housedress, her short, graying hair already set in curlers for bed. She clutched the doorframe with all the strength left in her frail, liver-spotted hands.

"Yes?" she said.

"I'm looking for Lucy Kilgore. Does she live here?"

"Why, no. She lives next door. Right there," the lady said and pointed to a mint-green house with a tiny sliver of concrete front porch. The swing was slowly moving back and forth, as if someone had gotten up from it a minute before.

"Thank you!" Jeptha shouted over his shoulder as he ran across the yard. According to the clock in the lady's living room, he was forty-five minutes late picking up Lucy.

He wrenched open the screen door and knocked on the wood behind, recoiling as the sound echoed off the houses nearby. After a minute, he heard the sound of footsteps. He started apologizing before the door even opened.

"Lucy, I'm so sorry! I was late leaving and then I got all the way here and realized I forgot your address. I been knocking on every door on the street trying to find you—"

Jeptha stopped when he realized he wasn't talking to Lucy, but to a woman he'd seen around town all his life. Her white hair poufed in a halo around her head, and she wore a matching set of red cotton shorts and t-shirt, topped with a massive purple necklace. The bright colors, though, were at odds with the look on her face. She stared at him with her eyebrows arched and her mouth puckered to the side.

He stuck out his hand to shake hers. "Sorry, ma'am. I'm Jeptha—"

"Taylor. I know. I knew your father. You are his . . ." She stopped and surveyed Jeptha. He could tell she was taking in everything from his scuffed boots, bleary eyes, and beery smell. "Spitting image," she finished.

Jeptha dropped his hand. "Oh. I, uh, was coming to see if Lucy was here."

"Young man, I'm LouEllen. I'm not Lucy's mama, but I'm going to talk to you like I am," LouEllen said, moving toward the porch swing and gesturing for him to sit down on it with her. "Now, showing up an hour late is not the way I would have played this one."

"I know," Jeptha said, easing into place beside her. He hung his head. "I can explain."

"Can you now?" LouEllen eyed him with an intensity that made his stomach roil. He scooted as far away as he could on that little swing, keenly aware of the sour mash smell of beer coming off him.

"If I could just see her . . ."

"She's not here."

"She's not?" Jeptha said, his voice cracking.

"You made a big mistake tonight."

"I know." Tears sprang to his eyes, and he looked down at the porch. The glass in LouEllen's hand clinked with ice cubes and two fondled lime wedges as she sat beside him. The piney scent of gin wafted up from her glass. He thought helplessly of all the time he'd wasted today, wondering if he should even show up. This was the only place he wanted to be, and he'd ruined it.

"But I'm a nice woman, and I believe in second or third—or whatever this is—chances. So I'm going to tell you that she waited for forty minutes and then drove herself to the Fold. Said she was already dressed, might as well go."

Jeptha stood up. "How long ago did she leave?"

"Probably ten minutes. But she's angry, so more like fifteen with how fast she's driving."

"I'm sorry, ma'am."

"It's not me you need to apologize to. Save that for Lucy."

Jeptha nodded his thanks at her and hustled toward the stairs. He turned at the top step and said, "Do you think it's worth trying?"

"It's always worth trying, Jeptha," she said, giving him another thorough once-over. "Frankly, you don't look like you've done a lot of trying in your life. And I doubt you'll succeed. But it's always better to have tried than not."

"Thank you, ma'am."

LouEllen nodded and, taking a large sip of her drink, gave herself a big push with her feet. Jeptha could feel her eyes on him all the way back to his car.

WHEN JEPTHA BLEW through the doors of Carter's Fold in ten fewer minutes than it had ever taken him before, he was sweaty and out of breath. He stopped at the bottom of the amphitheater, suddenly aware of how big the Fold was. Cut into the side of a hill, row upon row of wooden benches were slapped together and hay bales stretched out the last few rows. A tin roof covered the seats, but the sides and back were open to the breeze, or as much breeze as could sneak past all the people sitting on the edge of the cinderblock retaining wall and camped on the grass trying to peek in. On summer nights when a really good band played, every seat would be claimed by 7:00 p.m.

Jeptha had never needed to find a jilted date in the midst of all these people before. He needed a systematic approach, like hoeing a row. He'd work up one side and down the other. He stood at the bottom, his eyes scanning each row as if he was reading a page. He lost his place ten times before he finished the left section and started on the center column of seats. It felt like a hundred rows, but finally about three-quarters of the way up, his eyes passed a girl who looked like Lucy. When his eyes came back to her, he saw it was Lucy. She was staring at him.

He smiled and waved. Nothing. She was still looking at him but didn't lift her hand. He waved again. She held his gaze for a moment more and then looked pointedly away from him.

Jeptha took the stairs two at a time, coming to a hard stop just before knocking over a toddler who had wandered off his seat in order to get a good look at an abandoned piece of popcorn on the steps. He stepped around the little guy, touching his light brown curls for luck, and bounded up to where Lucy sat. He must have said, "Excuse me," to twenty people before he got to her. Then he had to beg those same people to pretty please scoot down the bench enough so that he could squeeze in beside her.

"Lucy, I'm sorry."

Her face was diamond hard—her usually plump cheeks sharply planed and her nose pinched and severe. Finally she said, "You're more than an hour late."

"I walked out the door without the piece of paper you gave me. I knocked on fifty-two doors before I got to yours."

"You smell like a bar."

"I had some beers with Cody after work. But I ain't drunk." He was, but he knew better than to tell the truth.

"I don't care."

"Lucy, I'm sorry. I was sitting on my porch with my dog—she's got this weird thing where she likes when I pet her with my foot. I didn't realize how much time had gone by. And then I forgot the damn paper. I'm an idiot. I'm sorry . . ."

"Your foot?" she asked, looking at him for the first time since he'd sat beside her.

"What?"

"You pet your dog with your foot?"

"She likes it. I swear."

"She sounds dumb as you. Y'all deserve each other."

Jeptha winced. She was saying the things he'd been hearing in his head all day, exactly what he'd said to Cody. Still, he couldn't disagree—he was an idiot. But Crystal Gayle wasn't.

"She's way smarter. I'm the idiot," he said.

Lucy shook her head at him. "I thought maybe everyone was wrong about you. Guess they weren't. Please leave."

"Aw, don't be like that," he said. "I'm sorry."

"If you don't move, I will," Lucy said. She excused herself down the row, and Jeptha hurried to follow after.

Everyone in the row must have been able to feel Lucy's anger flaring off her. They practically jumped out of their seats to let her by. For Jeptha, though, every pair of knees was an obstacle course. They glared at him and one old lady even shook her head as he stepped over her feet. Jeptha saw Lucy sit on the edge of a bench five rows down.

He started down the steps, but that same curly-headed toddler whom Jeptha had tripped over before stepped out of his row right in front of Jeptha's feet. Jeptha bowed his body back, just managing to keep his heels on the stairs, but bumped the little kid with his knees. Jeptha could only watch as the kid teetered back and forth and then, in slow motion, finally tottered over onto the step below and then the one below that before he caught himself on his cheek. He burst out with a scream so loud the band stopped playing for a second. It seemed the entire audience was now glaring at Jeptha, none more so than Lucy. The look of disappointment and anger on her face reminded him of nothing so much as the look on his first-grade teacher's face on the first day of school when, at Bobby's prodding over that long summer, he had answered "penis" instead of "here" at roll call. Jeptha reached down to try to pick the boy up, but his mom got there first, her eyes narrowed with revulsion and a too-late protective instinct. Jeptha looked up at the ceiling and mouthed a silent "Damn."

When he looked back down, Lucy was another ten rows in front of him. "Lucy, wait," he yelled to her.

"Sorry," he said to the boy's mom before he rushed down the stairs.

When he finally caught up with her at the entrance of the Fold, he began to beg. "Please, Lucy," he said, touching her arm. "Stay. I'll make it up to you."

"There's nothing to make up. There is nothing between us. Do you hear me? NOTHING," she said, her voice laced with acid. She jerked her arm away and walked to the doors.

"But that night . . ."

"Was nothing. I was drunk. It didn't mean a thing."

"It did to me. I know I messed up. Lemme make it right."

"How could you make it right, Jeptha, when you don't even know how wrong it is?" she yelled. She banged open the door and strode onto the field full of parked cars.

"At least let me walk you to your car," he begged, having to run to catch up to her.

"Leave me alone."

In the dusk, Jeptha could see her nostrils flaring. Her deep brown eyes were like a well gone bad. "I got to make sure you get home okay."

"I've been getting home just fine every day of my life up to now, without you. And I'll continue to every day going forward. Also without you."

She stopped at a beat-up black Honda Civic and dug her keys out of her pocket.

"Give me another chance," he said quietly.

"What for? What's the point? It's not like anything is ever going to come of this."

"It ain't like that, Lucy," he said, watching in despair as she got in her car. She looked up at him for a moment, and he brightened, hoping maybe she was softening.

"I should never have gotten in that car," she said. "I know better than to do something like that with a Taylor."

"With a Taylor? You think I ain't good enough for you?" Jeptha yelled, finally losing his control on his temper. Here it was—Bobby, Cody, and now Lucy. None of them thought he was good enough for her, for anything or anyone, really. None of it mattered. He'd apologized a dozen times, and she didn't care. He could apologize a hundred more, and it wouldn't make a whit of difference. Hell, he could have showed up at her house an hour early, and she probably still wouldn't care. He was a Taylor, no matter what. He banged his fists on the top of her car and then took a step back.

Lucy shrugged in agreement and drove away too fast. Angry as he was, he still found himself throwing up a prayer for her to get home safe and then berated himself for it. She didn't care about him. Everyone was right. Lucy was too good for him—she always had been. She'd always been the one smart enough to leave this town, and there was no way she would stay around for a man like him. That night had been a fluke. It would never matter what he did or how well he played. Nothing would ever make Lucy Kilgore want to be with him. He listened for a moment to the bluegrass filling the night air, the sound of the mandolin and the banjo competing with the rise and fall of the cicadas' drone and the insistent rhythm of the tree frogs. The music struck him as a dirge for what might have been.

He got in his car and slammed the door. Fiddling though the stations, he found a screaming Metallica song and turned it all the way up, wanting to obliterate the bluegrass sounds he associated with Lucy. He tried to stop thinking of her. He focused his attention on the ten or so beers he expected remained in the case beside Cody, who was no doubt passed out on the couch—beers that Jeptha planned to drink in a slow and orderly fashion until he was too drunk to remember why he'd ever thought his life might change.

—4—

"**D**ID HE FIND YOU?" LouEllen asked as soon as Lucy pushed the door open. Lucy threw her keys and purse down on the table. She flopped on the couch, then stood right back up, her fingers shaking.

"I guess so," LouEllen said, taking Lucy in. "You look pissed as a hornet with a crushed nest."

"More," Lucy said. She paced back and forth, her belly a sloshing pool of rage. She stopped in front of LouEllen. "He was drunk. Drunk! Did you know that?"

"He'd been drinking."

"That asshole showed up an hour late. And drunk. For a date. Who does that?" she said. She thought of his voice breaking in his car, after they'd had sex. She had felt sorry for the man, but not anymore. "I'll tell you who. Jeptha Taylor. What on earth was I thinking?" Lucy paced again. Every time she stopped moving, her anger overwhelmed her.

"What happened?" LouEllen asked. Lucy could hear the pity starting to tinge her tone. The fire in her grew.

"What do you mean, what happened? He showed up, said 'I'm sorry' a hundred times, and I drove away. I don't need to listen to the apologies of a man who can't even be bothered to show up on time for a date with the woman who is carrying his child."

"But he doesn't know that, does he?"

"Does it matter? All he's been wanting since that godforsaken night we had sex was for me to go on a date with him. 'Can I see you again? Wanna go to Waffle House? How about a drink? Blah, blah, blah.' Then I finally give him a chance, feel sorry for the asshole, and he does this. I'm like a glutton for punishment. I sleep with him, I get pregnant. I give him a chance, I get stood up." Lucy pushed her hair back behind her ears with both hands and stared at the ceiling.

"I mean, what the hell is wrong with me? Could I be any dumber?" she asked. She shook her head as tears started to fall. "I must want to ruin my life, right? That's what this is."

"You made a mistake," LouEllen said, reaching out for her hand. Lucy pulled it away. She didn't want comfort, didn't deserve it.

"Hell of a mistake." Lucy bit her lip, trying to keep the tears from falling. Tears weren't going to make this go away. They weren't going to fix anything. She looked around wildly, her gaze landing on the boxes stacked in the corner. Her boxes, still packed, ready for a life she hadn't even been sure she wanted, now forever out of reach.

"We all make mistakes. It happens. But if you're going to keep this one," LouEllen said, nodding at Lucy's belly, "then you need to at least go to the doctor. Get some vitamins. Take care of yourself. Ain't no fair punishing that baby in the hopes it'll go away."

"I'm not doing that," Lucy said, slamming pillows into place and folding and refolding the blankets on the couch.

"Really?" LouEllen asked. "Have you been to the doctor? Gotten your prenatal vitamins? Decided what hospital you'll deliver at? Asked for more shifts at Walmart and Judy's to try to save up some money? Done anything that might signal that you understand that you are now pregnant, and going to, in seven short months, bring a baby into this world, who will be yours and yours alone?"

Lucy hugged the blanket tight to her chest. The tears that fell now weren't angry ones. "No," she said, with a sigh. "I haven't."

"Don't you think you should?" LouEllen asked, gently.

"I . . . I just . . ." Lucy didn't know what to say. She wasn't ready to face it yet. To admit the finality of what she'd done.

"You need to let go of this pipe dream of yours—that Jeptha will be a totally different kind of person and y'all can settle down in a sweet little family and raise your baby and live happily ever—"

Lucy tried to interrupt.

"Don't try to deny it," LouEllen said, ignoring her objection. "I know you, I know what you're hoping. Hell, every woman ever pregnant like this hopes that. But, I'll tell you right now, it ain't gonna happen. Not with that one. Not with Jeptha."

Lucy thought back to earlier in the night, before Jeptha was late. She had sat on the porch swing waiting for him, hugging her belly. She pushed herself hard, smiling into the wind as it blew her hair back and forth around her face. She'd felt oddly whole sitting there, like one of her missing pieces had been found and put into place. Now, the swing hung forlorn and abandoned, and all Lucy could see was Jeptha's bleary, drunken face apologizing to her. LouEllen was right, even if Lucy didn't want to admit it. She'd been constructing a fantasy.

She finally made eye contact with LouEllen. "There's no chance, huh?"

LouEllen took a step closer and put her hand on Lucy's arm. "I don't see how."

"You're probably right," Lucy said with a sigh. "Goodnight, LouEllen. I'm going to bed."

LUCY DIDN'T WANT to know that Pearline Hammond, the Bear Creek Free Will Baptist minister's wife, was using contraceptive film, in clear violation of that church's beliefs, but there it was, skillfully hidden under two packs of size-three diapers piled on the ever-moving conveyor belt of checkout lane seventeen, of the thirty-seven available at the Walmart where Lucy now worked five days a week, in addition to her night shifts at Judy's.

"How are you doing?" she asked, smiling at Pearline as she picked up the diapers and the film and swept them past the scanner and into a bag before anyone could see.

"And how are y'all?" Lucy said to Pearline's kids. The three boys were fighting over what flavor gum was in a green package, while the oldest girl held the baby, whose diaper sagged ominously beneath her sister's forearm. The baby stared at Lucy, snot caked around her nose, and chewed her finger.

"We're good, Lucy. Thanks for asking. You?" Pearline said, her body relaxing visibly as the film disappeared into the bag.

"Doing fine, thanks."

"Heard you were moving to Knoxville on us soon."

"Not sure that's going to be happening now," Lucy said. She allowed herself a little growl under her breath, pissed she'd mentioned it to anyone.

"Everything all right?" Pearline asked. She sighed, a hank of hair escaped from her messy bun floating up in the air, and turned to the boys.

"Y'all, stop. It don't matter what kind of gum it is, you ain't getting any."
She turned back to Lucy and cut her eyes toward her kids. "Sorry."

"Don't worry about it. Everything's fine. Just wanted to save a little
more money." She knew it was only a matter of time before she'd have to
stop telling this lie, but for now, she didn't want to say the truth out loud.

"Don't we all? Well, good luck. Always thought you've done real well for
yourself. You'll get there one day."

Lucy nodded, suddenly unable to speak. If Pearline only knew how far
away her parents' dream was now. Her mom would have been polite, sweet
to Pearline even, and then sworn up and down afterward that she would
give anything to keep Lucy from that fate. Now here Lucy was, handing
over Pearline's bags and smiling weakly at her future. Pearline gave her a
look that seemed almost encouraging, her harried face relaxing from the
worry lines that were a permanent fixture. "You'll be all right," the look
said. Lucy almost believed it until she took in the view outside of Pearline's
face: the boys trying to shove a pack of gum down the shorts of the youngest as he cried, aware it was wrong but unable to stand up to his older
brothers; the older daughter smiling naughtily at a teenaged boy two lanes
over; and the baby staring at Lucy, expressionless, disengaged, caked in
dirt, and never wearing pants. How on earth could Pearline peddle a future
where things would be all right?

"Um, miss?"

Lucy turned toward the voice. She looked down and realized the conveyor belt was stacked four items high, and a lady, unknown to Lucy, was
staring at her with narrowed eyes and pursed lips. Pearline and her family
were already heading through the door.

"I'm sorry. How are you today?"

The lady nodded and continued loading more groceries onto the belt.

As Lucy swept the unsmiling lady's fiber supplements and Tucks pads
past the scanner, she tried to ignore the items on the aisle and zone out like
she usually did during her shifts. She didn't really want to know the secrets
she could learn by paying attention to a person's purchases. Since she had
gotten pregnant, though, she couldn't ignore the tidbits of lives floating
past her scanner. Dwelling on the evidence of other people's shitty lives
kept her from breaking down over her own. And so, she noted that Pearline
was using those films without her husband's knowledge; that Sheila Parker

paid with food stamps; and that Rick Mullins, the police officer, had eaten nothing but Hungry Man dinners since his wife left him. On some deeper level, it made her sad to see their secrets swing past her scanner, the consumer goods telling a story that none of these people would dream of whispering to their best friends. But if she stopped focusing on their lives, all she had inside her was a raging ball of fury: at herself, for getting pregnant; at her parents, for dying; and at Jeptha, especially, for being too drunk and stupid to show up for one date.

It had been a month since she'd left Jeptha in a spin of dirt and grass from the Fold's parking lot. Every day she thought she would stop being so mad, but every morning, she woke up as furious with him and disappointed in herself as before. He'd tried to call a couple times, but she'd hung up on him. She ignored him the two times he knocked on her door. When he came in the next Friday night, nearly a week later, to play his set, he'd looked at her, his face buoyant with hope, but when she'd turned away, stony-faced, he hadn't even bothered to come up to her. LouEllen was right—it was ridiculous for Lucy to have hoped he could be something more.

Lucy was relieved to see that it was almost five-thirty. For the next three hours, people would rush in to grab that one ingredient they'd forgotten for dinner or run through the doors, pulling a child by the arm, to buy supplies for some school project that the kid had forgotten to mention was due *tomorrow*. This part of her shift always flew by—she'd be ringing things up so fast the beep would barely register before the next item went through. Lucy would barely have time to look at the clock, much less think about her own life, until nine o'clock, when, as if by magic, the entire town quieted down.

When the rush finally ended, Lucy got the nod from her boss Teresa and gratefully took her break. This was a job she had dreamed of quitting, but the night after Jeptha stood her up, she had swallowed her pride and asked for more shifts at both Walmart and Judy's, accepting that providing for this baby was up to her, and her alone. She headed toward the break room but turned away sharply when she heard tired laughs coming from inside. Rhonda, Ashley, and Kelsey were already in there. Without seeing them, she knew they'd all be in the break room gabbing away over a large bag of Doritos. Listening to them go on about disrespectful kids and drunk, cheating husbands, Lucy felt like she was trapped in some God-awful country song that had no end. It couldn't end, really, since their lives were always going to be this way. Lucy didn't need to look at their weary, lined faces and sagging, overweight bodies to know her own body's future, and she didn't need to hear their stories to know what her own would soon be. The certainty of it made her desperate. Tonight, she'd rather be alone.

She rarely entered the music section because she was too broke to indulge in buying anything. She looked wistfully at the rows of CDs, their shiny cellophane packages tantalizing her. She knew she should walk away. But then, Lucy saw the end cap of the aisle. It was a retrospective of Dolly Parton, with every one of her CDs laid out in neat rows, already loaded in the CD player, ready to be listened to. She flicked through the row. After ten albums of bright colors, a black-and-white photo caught her eye. On the album cover, Dolly's blond hair cascaded down from an almost insurmountable height above her head, her arm hooked over the back of a wooden chair. Apparently, this was the subtler side of Dolly.

But no black-and-white photo could tame Dolly Parton. Lucy had the feeling that if she turned away, Dolly would jump out of her chair, suddenly dressed in one of those little pink suit numbers, buttoned up tight under her boobs—what Lucy had heard Dolly call her "big 'uns" in an interview—and start making jokes and letting loose with that laugh as high-pitched as a panther's scream. She didn't much care which side of Dolly the picture showed—she loved them all. As did everyone in town. She was a hometown girl, even if she'd grown up seventy-five miles to the west. Dolly Parton was mountain, not just country, and she sang about it to people all over the world who might not otherwise give a damn.

Lucy picked up the headset attached to the display. She knew that settling the headphones on her head—feeling that slight pull on her ear drums as the cups of the headphones sucked air in and hearing that tinny echo before the song began—was tantamount to buying the album. But she couldn't help herself.

With a slight hush beforehand, as if the CD itself were drawing breath, Dolly's voice burst out clear and high. Lucy held her breath, listening to Dolly open the title song, "Little Sparrow," without a single instrument. Tears welled in Lucy's eyes as she put her hands over the headphones, pushing the sound deeper. Her throat began to clench. She loved Dolly's

voice, the way it seemed to go somewhere deep inside her and find whatever pain she was feeling and bring it out, give it life. The mournful notes
of a bow dragging against the strings of a fiddle sounded through Lucy's
ears, and Dolly's voice came on again. She warned Lucy to beware of men,
that they would break her heart, or worse.

They will crush you like a sparrow,
Leaving you to never mend.

"I'm crying in a Walmart," Lucy whispered to herself. She hastily
slipped off the headphones and wiped the tear away. She wished this song
had been playing that night on the porch as she sat on the swing, waiting
for a man who would never show, nauseated and exhausted from being
pregnant and feeling some small piece of hope she didn't even know she
had leak out of her.

She looked around the store, terrified someone might have seen her.
Crying in the country aisle was the last thing she needed. Lucy picked up
the CD and placed it in her basket. If that song could make her cry in a
public place, she better get that CD home and listen to the rest of it there.

Walking aimlessly until her break ended, she found herself in front of
the baby section. Realizing where she was, she slowed and finally stopped
in front of it. Some part of her wanted to handle all the newborn clothes,
hung on the smallest hangers Lucy had ever seen, closest to the aisle where
women couldn't help but touch them, a rush of hormones prompting them
when necessity did not. She could see a turquoise outfit, hemmed in yellow, with a lion no bigger than a hummingbird whispering a roar into the
world. Lucy ached imagining her baby wearing this onesie, imagining the
life they would lead, just the two of them. Theirs wouldn't be a family like
she so desperately wanted, but it was what she could give. She felt an odd
rush of love, she guessed it was, for the nameless, faceless being inside her,
who was slowly starting to become not something that had happened to
her, but something she wanted. Her little boy would wear this with pride.
Or her little girl would get her first taste of fierce in it.

Lucy reached out to finger the sleeve. It was the softest thing she'd ever
touched. She could swear she caught a whiff of baby powder. Lucy moved
to grab the hanger.

"Doing some shopping, huh, Lucy?" Deanna Taylor, Jeptha's sister,
suddenly smirked from her elbow. Lucy's face burned, and she dropped

her arm. She stared at Deanna as her mouth uttered "ums," surprised to find that some part of her brain was still occupied with being jealous of Deanna's whole look: her hair was white blond, bleached to within an inch of its life, and feathered at the ends. She wore a red tank top that hugged her boobs, miraculously still pert after two kids, and junior's-department-small denim cut-offs.

Lucy still remembered the first time she had ever talked with Deanna. It was a Sunday, a few months after her parents died, and the preacher droned on and on about a passage that had been her dad's favorite. She felt hot, trapped there in the pew, hemmed in by all these well-meaning Christians and the memories of her parents. LouEllen's gentle pats on her knee felt like bone-jarring thumps. Lucy suddenly stood up and rushed out of the pew. She knew tears were coming, could feel them starting to fall down her cheeks before she made it all the way out of the church hall. She crouched down in the gravel and let go, the grief of the last few months catching her like a fist to the stomach. She wanted to howl with rage but knew the congregation would hear her if she did, so she stifled her screams and gave in to the tears behind them. After ten minutes, her tears began to ebb. Good thing too, because just then, she heard the crunch of gravel coming around the side, and the hurried whispers of two girls. She hastily wiped her face with the hem of her dress and stood up.

"Oh," Deanna Taylor said when she rounded the corner and saw Lucy. She had a cigarette already between her fingers. "What are you doing here?"

Lucy hoped like hell she didn't look like she had been bawling her eyes out for the last ten minutes. Deanna was three years ahead of her in school, but her reputation loomed large enough for even someone as young as Lucy to be aware.

"Couldn't stay in there anymore," Lucy mumbled. Her fingers twisted the hem of her dress. She now wished she'd sat in her pew and cried.

"Tell me about it. This is Marla," Deanna said, gesturing to the plump girl beside her, whom Lucy recognized from school only as the girl who was always beside Deanna. Marla nodded, looking too scared to say anything, like she wasn't sure if Deanna was going to be nice or punch Lucy just for fun.

Deanna peered closely at Lucy. "You're that girl whose mom and dad died, right?"

Lucy nodded.

"They thought my dad did it. He didn't, you know," Deanna said, her chest thrust forward.

"I know," Lucy whispered.

After a tense minute of silence, Deanna finally slumped against the wall. "You want a cigarette?"

Lucy wasn't sure if this was a trick. She had never smoked but was too scared to say no.

The first breath in was like the devil himself had taken up residence in her lungs, burning and scratching with fury. She hacked the smoke out and felt like a fool when Deanna laughed, then Marla.

"First time?" Deanna asked.

Lucy was coughing too much to answer.

"You get used to it."

Swelling out from the church behind them they heard the sounds of the doxology, signaling the end of the service.

"Shit. We better go," Deanna said to Marla. Looking at Lucy, she said, "You should come over sometime."

"Okay," Lucy said. She didn't want to go over to Deanna Taylor's house. But she knew better than to say no.

Their friendship hadn't lasted long. Lucy snuck out of LouEllen's a couple times and watched TV uncomfortably with Marla and Deanna, knowing she was failing every test Deanna put her way. Like Marla, she was mute most of the time, in sheer astonishment at the meanness Deanna could summon in the most casual conversation.

When Deanna had dropped her—marked with only the mildest gossip about her being a stuck-up bitch—back into the freshman lake two weeks later, Lucy felt like a fish on catch-and-release day, bloody but gratefully alive.

And now, years later in the Walmart baby aisle, her mouth still gaped uselessly open and shut as she struggled to come up with some convincing reason why she was misty-eyed and fondling baby gear.

"For a friend. Um, a friend who's pregnant," Lucy said. Was that enough? She watched as Deanna's eyes grew interested.

"Cassidy?" Deanna asked.

"No."

"Leigh Anne?"

"Uh, no."

"Tonya?" Deanna hated not being on the inside of gossip, and the idea that Lucy knew something she didn't clearly bothered her. Lucy didn't know what else to say. She didn't even know who Cassidy or Leigh Anne were. Was that Tonya girl from high school even pregnant? And if she was, why the hell would Lucy be buying a gift for her? She hadn't talked to her in high school, much less now.

"Yeah," Lucy nodded. "Tonya."

"Uh-huh," Deanna nodded. She sized up the outfit. "I mean, that's real cute. If you like lions. Which, like, almost no one does."

"Well, I'm just looking."

"Anyway. You still working at Judy's?"

"Yes," Lucy said. "Four nights a week."

"Heard my brother's playing there."

"Friday nights."

"Y'all must be real hard up for music," Deanna said, yawning. She waved bright red talons in the direction of her mouth.

"I guess." Mad as she was at Jeptha, Lucy still felt bad lying. Jeptha was good. But she didn't feel bad enough to want to do anything that might provoke Deanna. She needed Deanna to forget she'd seen Lucy and forget about the baby outfit. Otherwise, Jeptha and the rest of town were liable to find out she was pregnant before the sun set tomorrow.

Deanna yawned again. "God, I'm bored. I'm gonna go check out make-up. You wanna come?"

Lucy pointed to her badge. "I'm working."

"God, you work here too? That sucks."

With that, Deanna walked away, her hair bouncing off her shoulders with the uniformity only half a bottle of AquaNet could achieve. When she was out of sight, Lucy exhaled the breath she'd been holding. With one quick look to make sure Deanna was well and truly gone, she threw the turquoise lion outfit into her cart and fled back to lane seventeen, feeling her breathing calm as she swept her own items past the scanner and tucked them under the cash register.

She was onto her second customer when Teresa came over, her face creased with annoyance.

"What are you doing here, Lucy?" she asked.

"Working. I just finished my break," Lucy said, confused.

"You're supposed to be over in guns tonight. It's Saturday."

"Shoot, I forgot. I'm sorry," Lucy said. She nodded to the customer in line. "Let me finish here and I'll go over."

"Go on. I got it," Teresa said, waving Lucy out of the way.

It hadn't been the case under the old manager, but under Teresa, it was policy, if unspoken, that pretty girls sell guns. Every year, two or three of the young, prettier cashiers would get trained up on guns enough to talk with the men who wandered over. The sales records backed it up. Lucy had grown up shooting cans for target practice and using 22s on squirrels. She'd even gone through the hassle of getting her hunter safety certificate as a kid so she could go deer hunting with her dad. But, when she killed her first deer and her first words were "I'm sorry," she had stopped hunting, fairly sure she'd never develop the stomach for it. So she knew enough to designate between a shotgun, a 22, or a 30.06 rifle. But the store also stocked real guns, semi-automatics that Lucy knew nothing about until she took the one-day training course. She wouldn't say she was one of the boys, but her knowledge didn't even really matter. Most of these guys, especially the Saturday night ones, knew everything about the guns they were admiring. She was really there to give them something they'd want to protect. Once the baby belly was showing, she knew she'd get staffed there even more. She figured if pretty girls sell guns, then pretty pregnant girls must sell big guns.

As she slid behind the counter, she looked up and cursed. Big Jim, Deanna's husband, was on his way over for his weekly date with a gun he'd probably never be able to buy. The Taylors were determined to follow her tonight. Lucy punched in her code and slid the key to the gun counters out. She had the door open by the time Big Jim strolled up.

"This one again?" she asked.

He nodded, his eyes full of reverence for the grained silver body and matte metal finish on the semi-automatic. The gun looked almost puny in Big Jim's arms. His name was honestly given: he was six-four, if an inch, and must have weighed close to three hundred pounds. He worked at the ammunition plant fifteen minutes down the road and spoke just enough to have risen up to manager over there. Lucy wouldn't have called him gentle, but he was a quiet man. She could never figure how he or anyone put up with Deanna.

"This the week?" she asked. He had been coming to check out the gun nearly every Saturday night since it'd come in. Even Lucy had to acknowledge it was beautiful. But it cost over a thousand dollars, an amount that took Lucy's breath away every time she saw the tag.

"Maybe," Big Jim said. He only had eyes for the gun. He turned it this way and that, then hoisted it to his shoulder and peered through the scope, tracking one of the dozen or so captive sparrows flitting between the warehouse's metal struts. He brought it down with a sigh and laid it on the counter, his fingers caressing the grain of the butt like it was a woman he'd finally and inexplicably gotten to lay down in his bed.

"It's a beauty," Lucy said. She would love to close this sale, get Big Jim to buy this gun so he'd stop coming to the counter every week. She wanted as few interactions with the whole Taylor family as it was possible to achieve in this small town.

Big Jim tore his eyes away from the gun and looked up at Lucy. "Hear you're working with Jeptha over at Judy's."

"I mean, I wouldn't say working with. He plays there."

"Plays there," Big Jim huffed. "That sounds about like him. Getting paid to play."

Lucy nodded, not sure what to say.

"Least it gets him off the farm. Be easier on all us if he weren't involved at all," he said.

"Doesn't he do most of the tobacco?" Lucy asked, curious despite herself.

Big Jim laughed, rough and low. "That what he said?"

"I don't really talk to him, to be honest."

"Wise choice. He does some. But mostly he's drunk. Gets out in the field at ten thirty, works for an hour, then passes out for the afternoon. Kills Deanna we have to split anything with him."

"Does Deanna work the field too?"

Big Jim really laughed now. "You're funny. My wife would as soon ride an elephant as work in the fields. She does the books, insurance, and whatnot."

"Oh," Lucy said. She'd never heard Big Jim string so many words together.

"Does more than Jeptha, though. That's for sure. That kid ain't worth shit."

"That's what people say," Lucy said, thinking of LouEllen's take on Jeptha from a few weeks back.

"People ain't wrong."

If this is what having family was, Lucy thought, maybe she and the baby were better off on their own. Or with LouEllen.

Big Jim slowly took his fingers away from the gun and shook his head. "Not today, I reckon. One day."

Lucy picked up the gun by the base of the barrel and loaded it into the counter behind her.

"Anything else?" she said as she locked it. She heard the rhythmic plop of flip-flops coming up behind him and looked up to see Deanna.

"You work guns too?" Deanna said, gnashing a piece of gum like a cow with cud.

"On Saturdays," Lucy muttered. Her stomach had done a sudden violent turn, and it wasn't the return of Deanna that had done it. She felt green and hot all over and had to clench her jaw to keep her dinner down.

"Excuse me," Lucy mumbled. "I don't feel good." She ran out from behind the counter, her hand clamped over her mouth.

"Mm-hmm," Deanna said. "I bet you don't."

Lucy glanced back at Deanna long enough to see the malicious glint in her eye. She knew.

— 5 —

I T WAS A RARE thing indeed when Deanna deigned to enter the tobacco fields, but when Jeptha wiped his forehead, there she was, picking her way down the hill to where he and Bobby were working. She usually kept herself as far as possible from the land, as if the whole farm, their childhood, and the house she lived in hadn't come up as a result of the dirt she so studiously avoided. His sister was as prissy as she was mean. She was tiptoeing through the grass like it would infect her. He had no great love for working the fields, but he was damn sure it wasn't going to kill him.

He saw someone beside her and peered through the thick long leaves of the tobacco stalks to see if her kids had come with her. Jim Ed and Cassie Ann were his blood, but Jeptha had never had an affection, much less an affinity, for them. Jeptha thought all six-year-olds liked playing outside. But not his sister's kids. Except for school, they almost never left the house during the day. They liked it that way—eating crap and watching TV. They would come by every once in a while when he was playing his mandolin on his porch but soon start sneaking glances back at their house, scratching at their arms and kicking their feet at the grass like meth heads in need of a fix. Without bothering to say goodbye, they'd start walking away, breaking into a run when they got close to their house in order to win their never-ending battle over the remote. He guessed you could call it running—it was as fast as they knew how to move, but God, it was embarrassing to watch them do it.

But it wasn't the kids coming down with Deanna. It was Marla, Cody's wife. Her mousy brown hair and short, plump figure stood in sharp contrast to Deanna's thin, blond, and brittle look, and, as usual, she seemed to be shaking her head in slavish agreement with whatever Deanna was saying. If Marla had ever had an independent thought outside of Deanna, Jeptha wasn't aware of it. He was fairly sure Cody wasn't either. Cody never said it out loud, but Jeptha knew he hated the way Marla slobbered all over Deanna, like she was the queen and Marla a lowly servant. Jeptha winced watching them walk down the hill toward him. He was reminded suddenly of how they had once been friends with Lucy, and how that friendship had been the cause of the second most embarrassing moment of his life when it came to Lucy Kilgore.

His belly still roiled with shame when he thought of the day six years ago when he had walked into his parents' house and seen Deanna lying on the floor with two girls. Deanna had introduced him as "My shithead brother, Jeptha" with a lazy wave of her hand. Lucy said hey with a half-hearted smile on her face and went back to the TV.

At seventeen, Jeptha thought love songs were for losers and poems were shit, so he felt alone and abandoned there on the edge of the living room, swept away suddenly by a strange emotion he didn't know much about. He wanted Lucy; that was true. He could feel the strain of his penis against his jeans. But there was more than that. He was breathless, lost. He wanted to stare at her, the way her red flip-flop dangled off her right foot as she swung it slowly back and forth, how the tattered cut-off edge of her jean shorts moved slightly with each swing, and how her summer-lit blond hair fell in unbrushed tangles down her back nearly to her belt loops. At that moment, with that "hey," Jeptha understood the need for an outside resource on love.

He went into his room and turned on the stereo. He had a pretty nice voice—even if he did say so himself—and once he found the song he was looking for, he turned the volume up and sang along. It was one of his favorite songs—he thought it was a summer anthem about drinking beer and driving a truck in the summer, but as he listened to the words today, he realized it was about a girl. He sang out loud and danced around the room in his cowboy hat, wishing that his singing was the kind that could make a girl—Lucy—fall in love with him. He imagined that he was living the song: him and Lucy in a truck, his arm around her, driving around on a hot summer day looking for a place to stop and mess around once the sun went down.

He sang the last line at the top of his lungs, ending with a long, drawn-out "chillin' it."

Then he heard Deanna's laugh followed by the titters of the two other girls. The girl he was singing about was laughing at him.

·

He opened the door, furious and breathing heavy.

"What . . . were . . . you . . . doing?" Deanna asked, every word broken up with laughter. "That was hilarious."

Marla was laughing too but sneaking glances at Deanna to make sure she didn't laugh for a second longer or louder than Deanna. Even then, she was like a dog that's been abused and keeps coming back for more. Lucy stared at Jeptha with a small, private smile on her face. He blushed even harder when he looked at her.

"Jesus, Deanna, what the hell do you want?" he yelled at his sister. "Why don't you shut up and go back to watching your stupid show?"

"Why? This one's funnier than that one," she said, her seventeen-year-old mouth honed for sass and quick comebacks. She'd stop at nothing to make others feel small. It seemed like everyone—from their parents, to Jeptha, to other students at school and even the teachers—knew that words in the hands of a girl as evil as Deanna could hurt no matter how old you were.

"Deanna, shut the hell up," he said, slamming the door in her face.

He sat down on the bed, near tears, and pulled the cowboy hat off his head. He'd bought it at the saddle and feed store for way more than he could afford. He thought he'd seen a hot country star in its lines on his head. Now though, he saw the terry cloth brim was soaked and graying with grime, the supposedly leather edges were fraying, and the entire structure was caving in on itself. Lucy must have thought he was ridiculous. That little smile wasn't an interested one, but a mocking one. She had been laughing silently at him, which was so much worse than Marla's loud hysterics. Lucy got no credit from Deanna for silent mocking. She'd found the whole thing funny. He had no shot with her.

That one encounter, six years before, had convinced Jeptha that Lucy was the girl for him and that there was no chance he would ever get her. He wanted to, God knew, but he wasn't sure what he, Jeptha Taylor, could bring to the table that would convince her. He had no idea what had changed in her that night at the bar—maybe it was the alcohol—but something had. And then he'd gone and messed it up so much that he wished to God he had never even met her.

Deanna's wave from the edge of the field caught his eye. He took his time picking his way through the plants and avoided eye contact with

Deanna when he arrived in front of them, knowing she'd take it as a sign of disrespect, and wanting her to.

"How're you, Marla?" he asked.

"All right. Cody said y'all had a good set the other night," she said.

"I doubt that," Deanna snorted. Jeptha reacted the same way he always did whenever his sister said something awful, which was pretty much every time she opened her mouth: wish like hell he had a beer to down so he could throw the bottle at her head.

"Gonna make any profit this year?" Deanna asked, looking around at the field, her mouth pinched tight and her nose wrinkled.

"Hope so," Jeptha said. He pointed down to the end of the field, where the plants were standing tall and lushly green. There were a couple of days in the middle of the season, where, when he stood in the middle of them, he could imagine he was in a rainforest. "We planted more down there, but who knows how much we'll end up making."

"Not enough, I'm sure," Deanna said.

Jeptha shrugged his shoulders. "I can't say."

Deanna looked out over the field, her eyes narrowed. Jeptha smiled as he watched a ladybug fly into her hair. She brushed at it and screwed up her mouth when her hand touched it. Deanna raked it out of her hair with such hatred that it was shredded by the time it landed on the ground. "Ugh," she said, shuddering with disgust. "Can't the damn things see?"

"Did you get it? Want me to check?" Marla asked.

"Marla, I think I can handle getting a bug out of my own hair."

Marla looked down, pink spreading from her cheeks up into her hairline and down her part. Jeptha spoke to save her from any further embarrassment.

"Is there something y'all needed? I'm guessing you didn't come down to jaw about tobacco prices," Jeptha said.

"Well, we were just talking about some real interesting news, but if you're busy . . ." Deanna trailed off.

"What?" Jeptha asked. He wasn't interested, but he might as well take the break she was offering.

"You want to tell him, Marla?"

Marla looked up then, her face shining with excitement. Gossip was to Marla what the tobacco in the field was to cigarettes. Cody was always complaining about it: like every man Jeptha knew, Cody hated gossip, but his wife was addicted. She spent $25 a week on the shitty magazines full of celebrities trying to pretend they were "just like us," even as the pictures showed no life Jeptha had ever seen. Marla worked as a hairdresser at Snips 'n' Bangs. Jeptha thought it was a job like any other, but as it turned out, Marla didn't much care about hair; she wanted whatever job was at the pinnacle of gossip.

"Well, you know the Cartwrights?" Marla began, her face animated and her hands waving. "Their youngest boy, Travis, he got kicked out of school. For sleeping with a teach—"

"Not that news, Marla," Deanna interrupted. "Jeptha doesn't give a shit about the Cartwrights. No one does."

"Right. But, wait . . . Oh, the thing you told me? About who you saw at Walmart?" Marla asked. She looked confused for a moment and then she whipped toward Jeptha, her eyes widening with sudden understanding about something.

"Never mind," Deanna said. She looked at Jeptha. "Lucy Kilgore's pregnant."

The color drained from his face. Deanna, Marla, the sun, the tobacco—all seemed to disappear as he tunneled into that word, *pregnant*. The back seat of his car, the dented headrest came to him, her mouth on his, his pants sliding down. He'd never thought of protection.

"Caught her buying baby clothes. She was going on about buying it for a friend but wouldn't say who. Finally, I asked if it was for Tonya, and Lucy said yes. Total lie—Tonya's not even pregnant."

"Baby clothes? That don't mean she's pregnant," Jeptha said.

"Then she ran off puking a few minutes later. Jim saw it too. Said I looked like that with our kids."

Jeptha wiped sweat that had nothing to do with the sun off the back of his neck. Did Deanna know about him and Lucy? He didn't think so, but she played a long game, so it was hard to tell. He knew Bobby wouldn't have said anything about them going to the Fold—his brother barely spoke if it didn't concern the farm. From the look on Marla's face, though, he was pretty sure she knew he'd slept with Lucy, but it didn't seem like she'd told Deanna. He'd have never thought she had that much restraint. He smiled weakly at her.

"God, I hope it's true," Deanna said with a smile on her face. "I hope she's stuck here—she's always going on about leaving, like she's so much better. I hope it was someone awful—"

Deanna stopped and stared at Jeptha for a minute, then shook her head. "Too bad it wasn't you, Jeptha. You'd have been happy to be the stud horse on that one, God knows. And imagine if she was stuck here. With you? Man, I would love to see that."

Deanna's words barely touched Jeptha. He put his hands in his back pockets and looked up at the sun, too shocked to take much of anything in, even his sister's insults.

"Jeptha?" Deanna said, prodding his shoulder with a long pink fingernail.

"Yeah?" he said.

"Thought you'd be more upset, is all. Sad you missed your chance. Not that you had one, come to think of it."

Jeptha nodded. Disappointment flashed across Deanna's face. He imagined she wanted a bigger reaction from him—but being called a loser by his sister was everyday fare. The possibility of Lucy Kilgore carrying his baby was not. He had to see her. He had to know if it was true.

"Good to see you, Marla. Tell Cody I'm gonna come by later, maybe borrow his truck."

"I will," she said. Deanna stared at both of them, a look of pruned outrage on her face that neither of them had responded the way she'd expected them to. She huffed, rolled her eyes, and walked up the hill.

JEPTHA WORKED LONG enough to see Marla drive off and Deanna close her door behind her, then he walked with long, fast strides to his trailer where his phone was charging. It had died two days before, and he had only this morning gotten around to plugging it in. But now, he couldn't get it on fast enough. When the screen finally came on, it flashed 0 MESSAGES. He wavered for a moment, his tobacco-stained thumb hovering over the 4 of Lucy's phone number, a number he'd had to beg off of Judy. Wouldn't she have called him if the baby was his? Or maybe she'd wanted to tell him that night at the Fold, but he'd fucked it up entirely. He thought of her in her car, looking wounded and beaten. Despite how loudly she'd been yelling at him, she didn't even look that angry, just tired. He hit the digits of her number on his phone before he could lose his nerve and waited, clearing his throat for the five rings it took for someone to pick up. He almost hung up when he heard a drawn-out "Helllllooo?" that could only be LouEllen's. He willed his thumb away from the end button.

"Is Lucy home, please?" he said.

"May I ask who's calling?"

Jeptha swallowed, preparing himself for her to hang up. "Ma'am, it's Jeptha Taylor."

"Now, Jeptha. Do you really think this is a good idea?"

"I just want to talk to her."

"Well, honey, she tried that. If you recall, you messed it up pretty good." He'd thought maybe LouEllen might be on his side, after she told him where Lucy had gone that night, but it didn't seem much like it. Still, no amount of LouEllen could keep him from finding out if Lucy was having his baby.

"I want to ask her one question."

"Jeptha, there's no question you could ask that she wants to answer."

"Please, ma'am. Just let me talk to her."

"Jeptha, I've been real polite. I even told you where she went that night. But, she's said her piece and you need to respect it. If you can't listen to what I'm saying, I'm going to give Rick Mullins a call. I believe you know him? I don't think you want the police involved, now do you?"

"No, ma'am," Jeptha sighed.

"All right, then. Now you have a real nice day. Bye-bye."

———

JEPTHA STARED AT the phone for ten minutes, not sure what to do. He had to see Lucy. He had to try one more time. He would have to risk the wrath of Lucy and LouEllen and the possibility of a run-in with Officer Mullins. It wouldn't be his first.

He hopped in the shower and mulled his options. Flowers seemed flimsy. Chocolates weren't enough. Besides, maybe pregnant women couldn't eat chocolate? He dried off as he walked into his bedroom, then let his towel puddle on the floor under him. He opened his drawers, but they were empty. Jeptha turned to his bed, pulled some clothes off the footboard, and brought them to his nose. He stopped, staring at the bed in front of him.

A crib. That's what he'd bring to Lucy. He threw on his clothes, grabbed his keys, and hightailed it to Cody's, where he borrowed the truck off his very confused friend, and screeched into the parking lot at Walmart a half hour later. After checking to make sure Lucy wasn't working any of the registers, Jeptha spent ten minutes searching for the baby section and another hour figuring out what to buy. The number of choices was overwhelming. Light wood, dark wood, white. Curved ends, flat ends, sleigh ends. The baby beds were nicer than anything he'd ever slept in. And more expensive too, he thought, as he looked at the price tag. The one he liked the best was the display one—a simple white one. He dragged over a girl working two aisles away and pointed to it.

"Do y'all have this one?" he asked. "I didn't see it boxed up over there."

She shook her head. "It's all out. You can maybe have this one, though."

"The display one?"

"It's pretty new," she said. "It ain't been up but a few weeks. These things is a pain in the ass to box back up once they's put together."

"I'll take it," he said. He walked an aisle over and grabbed a box of diapers. He threw it into the crib. He picked it up by the sides and walked awkwardly toward the checkout, stopping only once to grab a big fuzzy teddy bear on the end of the toy aisle and chuck it into the crib.

After paying, Jeptha hoisted the whole thing up over his head and carried it out to Cody's truck. He set it down in the bed of the truck and stood back. There was something disturbing about a fully assembled baby bed standing up in the bed of a truck. Besides, the way his luck went, no matter how many tie-downs he put on it, it'd probably bounce right out and get smashed to pieces on the highway. So Jeptha dug around in Cody's truck until he found a set of Allen wrenches and took the crib apart right there in the parking lot. He laid the sides flat in the bed and tied them down with some webbing he found in Cody's back seat.

Now, driving up Lucy's street in the dark, he wondered if he'd gotten the right thing. Maybe she would have liked that wood crib rather than the white one. Maybe he should have gotten a box of size one diapers, which apparently diapered babies seven to fourteen pounds, rather than newborn, which diapered babies five to ten pounds. He remembered Big Jim and Deanna bragging about their babies' weights, like it was important for some reason, but he'd be damned if he could remember the numbers.

He parked in front of Lucy's house. The teddy bear sat next to him on the bench seat, strapped in by a seat belt so it wouldn't fall over onto the muddy floor. He and the bear looked out the window toward her house. They saw her pass by the window, her shape too blurred by the curtains for Jeptha to make out if she had a belly. He hoped like hell that LouEllen was out; this was going to be hard enough with Lucy.

He stopped with his hand on the door handle. It suddenly occurred to him that he could drive off and never acknowledge the responsibility that might be his. It didn't seem like she had any plans to tell him. He had an out. He didn't have to get out of the truck. He could take the crib and the diapers back and pretend that no one had ever told him he might be a father. No one would know, least of all Lucy. He watched as she passed by the window again. Her silhouette was clear this time. Jeptha could see the slightest round in her belly, the smallest indication that his kid was making itself known inside the body of a girl he had loved since he was sixteen. He remembered that curly-haired toddler from that awful night at the Fold and how silky his hair had felt against Jeptha's palm, how much trust the little boy had put in him—a complete stranger—not to hurt him. Of course, that trust had been misplaced, but Jeptha's knocking him off the stair and onto his head had been an accident. When it was his kid, he'd be more careful. He wouldn't squander that blind trust this time.

Jeptha unbuckled the seat belt from around the bear and, hugging it to him, opened the door. He walked lightly up the sidewalk, with the bear and the diapers under his arm, and set them by the door. Then he went back to the truck for the crib, which now lay in a heap three feet from where he'd originally loaded it into the truck. He hoped it wasn't too scratched. Staring at the disassembled crib in the back, he worried he wouldn't be able to get it all back together again. He fingered the screws and washers in his pocket and tried to calm himself.

Finally, he got all the parts up on the porch. His mouth was dry and his hands were sweating. He should have something in his arms. He wiped his palms on his jeans and picked up the bear. Then he picked up the diapers. Two things would be good—he'd hold the bear and the diapers. This would work. She would have to forgive him.

Jeptha leaned down and rang the doorbell.

— 6 —

"**O**H SHIT. YOU KNOW," Lucy said, after a full minute of silent, open-mouthed shock. Her brain would not process the sight of Jeptha in her doorway, a massive teddy bear and a box of diapers clutched in his arms.

The smile on Jeptha's face faltered. "Uh, hi," he said, hoisting the bear and the diapers a little higher, as if for her to see better.

"Hi." Lucy squinted in astonishment at the sight in front of her. How did he know? And why was he here?

"Can I, uh, come in?" Jeptha asked.

She was so suddenly, violently sick to her stomach that it took her a minute to hear the question. Then she shook herself out of her stupor and nodded. "You'd better, I guess, before my neighbors see you."

"I came to bring you this stuff," he said. He shrugged and looked down at his feet. "To apologize."

"Well, you better get to it. I'll take that bear." Lucy hugged the bear to her belly and eyed Jeptha as he stacked four sides of a white crib against the wall. It was pretty, she thought, nicer than the ones she'd been looking at.

"How'd you even find out? I haven't told anyone but LouEllen," she said.

"Deanna. She guessed you was pregnant," Jeptha said. "Based on your reaction, I guess she was right."

"Your sister ruins everything," Lucy said, feeling her stomach rise all over again as she thought of Deanna's knowing smirk the night before.

"That's always been my experience," Jeptha said. He wasn't looking at her, but at a piece of carpet that had come loose years before. He nudged it with his toe. "She didn't guess nothing about it being mine though."

He paused and cleared his throat, looking up at Lucy. "Is it?"

A wave of anger swept over her. "Yes. You ass. It's yours." She suddenly felt like a woman, more than being pregnant or turning twenty-one had ever made her feel. It was the pure, unmitigated fury provoked by a man's stupidity that had done it. "I'm not some slut."

"I never thought that. Never," Jeptha said, violently shaking his head. His eyes turned white blue in their seriousness. "That night in my car . . . It was the best . . . Um, I mean I've never regretted it for a second."

He loved her; Lucy knew it for sure in that moment. Everything she had been dying to escape in the last few months was, for Jeptha, a dream come true.

"So, do you know how to put this thing together?" she said, putting a hand on the crib parts stacked against the wall.

"Well, I took it apart, so I think I can put it together," Jeptha said. Lucy smiled a little as she noticed him nervously fiddling with something in his pocket. He pulled out a handful of screws and washers and laid them on the floor in a pile. Then he grabbed the crib sides and laid them on the floor too, like a tiny hurricane had collapsed the four walls. "Is this one okay?" he asked. "It's the display one. The girl sold it to me for cheaper, but it ain't been used or nothing."

"I honestly have no clue, Jeptha. It's a crib. That seems good." She stopped herself when she saw the hurt look on his face. "It's pretty, I mean."

"Ain't you looked at any cribs?"

"Not really. I've mostly been trying to pretend none of this is happening."

"How come?"

"I think I hoped it might go away if I didn't think about it too much," Lucy said, slowly.

"You aren't . . . you aren't going to Knoxville, are you?"

Lucy sighed. Every once in a while, she caught herself imagining what her life would be like if she was okay with going to Knoxville for an abortion. She'd be on her way to leaving this town instead of taking extra shifts, trying not to throw up in front of Deanna, and being worried about everyone knowing her business. She wouldn't be spending twenty minutes before bed every night examining every crackle and pop in her stomach to see if the baby was moving yet. She wouldn't be experiencing bone-chilling waves of fear about how she would care for a baby when she'd never so much as kept a fish alive.

"No," she said, shaking her head. "I can't do that." She watched as his body grew slack with relief. It surprised her. She would have expected him to be thrilled with the notion. She kneeled on the ground beside him.

"What can I do?" she asked, nodding at the crib.

Jeptha's sleeve brushed her bare arm as he reached over her. A shiver worked its way down her spine. Was it possible that after all this she still had a flicker of excitement over him? She could hardly get in more trouble than she was already in. That horse had definitely left the barn.

"So these long pieces go on the sides and these are the ends," Jeptha said. "It was pretty easy to take apart. Can't be much tougher to put it together."

Lucy watched as Jeptha counted and sorted the screws and two different kinds of washers. He slid two washers over the bottom of each screw before laying them down on the floor, four to each end of the crib. He nodded at the tall piece toward the couch.

"You want to hold that other end up and I'll screw this side in?" he asked.

Lucy knee-walked over to the other end and held it up straight. Jeptha's long tanned fingers quickly slotted the necessary screws into the wood without even having to check the directions. It was like watching him play mandolin, as if his fingers knew what to do, without him having to think about it. Her father had always pored over directions, asking questions, calling the number, and still assembling things wrong, all while her mother stood, arms crossed, sighing pointedly. Once her parents were gone, it was just Lucy and LouEllen, struggling to figure out directions worded in such a way that she was sure actual Chinese would have been easier. No one had ever done something like this for her, and with such ease.

Is this how he would be as a father? Would he be the kind of dad who could make anything, fix any problem as long as he had his pocketknife, a hammer, and some duct tape? Lucy could imagine the steady joy in that, the satisfaction of seeing something come together. Was a man like that really so bad? Lucy knew what everyone said—he was a Taylor, he was a drunk, he was lazy, he couldn't hold a job. Hell, he hadn't even been able to be on time—or sober—for their date. But watching him work, she wondered if maybe there were worse fates than a man like the one in front of her. Maybe this was the real Jeptha, this quiet, sweet man, not the drunk, late, shambling one from a few weeks before. She remembered then the earnest singing she'd heard from his room years before during Lucy's brief try-out as Deanna's friend. He'd actually sounded good—Lucy hadn't been able to force herself to laugh along with Deanna and Marla because goose bumps had risen up when he got to the chorus. He'd been sweaty and flushed when he came to the door, as if he were putting on a true performance in there. She wanted to tell him it was good but was too afraid of Deanna, so she smiled at him and hoped it was enough. Long after Deanna had dropped her, Jeptha's voice had floated through her head for weeks, its gravelly depth catching her unaware.

"Can I?" Jeptha said, holding up a screw near her face. She started, brought out of her memory by the man Jeptha had become. He was kneeling on the ground right by her, one hand above hers on the corner of the crib. He had a clean, leathery smell that Lucy remembered from his back seat. She wanted to lean into his neck and fill her nose with it.

"Sorry, what?" Lucy said, pulling her face back and looking down so he couldn't see her blush.

"Can I just get in there and put this one in?"

"Of course," she said, and scooted out of the way. "So, Deanna told you about me throwing up?"

"Yeah," he said.

"Bet she loved that."

Jeptha laughed. "Nothing my sister likes more than people embarrassing themselves."

"She doesn't know it was you?"

"No. I think Marla may have figured it out, but she ain't told Deanna."

"Really? I didn't know she was capable of that."

"Me either, honestly."

"How'd Marla figure it out?" Lucy asked.

Jeptha looked embarrassed, his face bright red. "I told Cody. That night I messed everything up."

"Jeptha, I'm sorry about what I said that night. I shouldn't have."

"I deserved it. I was late. Drunk too. I shouldn't have been," he said. He looked her in the eye. "I'm sorry. I really am."

"Thanks," Lucy said, hurriedly looking down at the floor.

"Can you hand me that little Allen wrench?"

Lucy handed him the Allen wrench at her side, his fingers brushing the palm of her hand as he picked it up. She pulled her hand back.

"Can I ask you . . . Why were you late?" Lucy asked.

"It ain't worth saying."

"I'm asking. I want to know."

"I wasn't gonna come, actually. Seemed like everybody I mentioned it to thought it was a waste of time, thought there was no chance you'd give me a shot. Bobby didn't even believe me when I said I was going on a date with you."

"But I'd asked you," Lucy said. She knew she ought to be angry that he was going to stand her up, but she was sad for Jeptha. He actually went through life believing he was as bad as everyone said. Maybe he was, but it didn't seem like it in this moment.

He shrugged. "Yeah. But you'd avoided me a lot too. Besides, I ain't a fool. I know I don't bring a lot to the table."

"You brought this crib," Lucy said. She wasn't sure what more to say.

Jeptha moved to the other corner of the crib, inserting the last two screws into the slots. After a few minutes of silence, he nodded at the boxes in the corner marked Knoxville. "You still planning on going?"

Lucy looked over at them and sighed. She shifted positions from her spot on the floor, stretching her legs out and pulling the waistband of her jeans down so it would stop cutting into her belly. She hadn't been able to bring herself to unpack the boxes, as if she might, by some stroke of divine intervention, still be able to leave town and rent that apartment. She knew it was never going to happen now, but she still avoided that corner of the house.

"How can I? I'm going to need LouEllen to help. We're going to turn that back room into a baby's room."

She turned away when Jeptha stared at her, not wanting him to see the tears in her eyes.

"I'm sorry," he said.

"It's not your fault," she said. Then she looked down at his crotch and laughed. "Well, not on purpose."

"Definitely not on purpose," he said, smiling.

"Thank you, by the way, for this stuff. This was nice of you."

Jeptha nodded, but didn't say anything more, just went around the crib, tightening each screw in turn until it was steady on all sides. He straightened up and offered Lucy his hand. She scrambled up and stood beside him, looking at the crib. He leaned over the side and touched the coils at the bottom of the crib, the metal clanging slightly as he bounced his hand against it. She heard him curse so quietly that she couldn't even hear the word he used. She heard the anger behind it, though, and saw his shoulders deflate, his whole torso sinking in on itself in a way that made her think, *Aw, there is the Taylor in you.*

He looked up but couldn't meet her eye. "Should have known I'd fuck this up somehow," he said. "I didn't get a mattress."

"Well, we don't have a baby yet either, so I'm not too worried."

"I can't believe I forgot that. I'm sorry."

They stood side by side. Lucy put her hand out and touched the crib's shiny white finish—she didn't know much about these things, but it seemed like a beautiful crib, a place a baby would be happy to sleep for the first few years of its life. Jeptha thumbed the crib as well. She had to hand it to him; showing up at her door with a crib and a teddy bear and diapers was about the only thing he could have done to make her forgive him. Standing there with him and looking at the crib their baby would sleep in, everything felt real. She was going to have a baby. An honest-to-God baby. Hers. And Jeptha's. Lucy reached out her hand and rested it lightly on his.

"Thank you again," she said. "It's beautiful."

Jeptha looked at her, for so long and so quietly that a flush swam up from her belly. His eyes were doe-soft, and a smile flickered on his lips. He opened his mouth to say something, but LouEllen came swanning through the front door, her gargantuan bag swinging in before her hips made their entrance.

"Jeptha. You're here," she said. Lucy saw her mouth tighten for a moment before she smiled at him. "And you brought a crib. Lucy told you the good news?"

"Something like that. Yes, ma'am."

"Well, there you go. It looks . . . real nice," she said. "Have y'all tried to get it through the doorway of that back room?"

Lucy and Jeptha looked at each other. Lucy hadn't considered that. And the look on Jeptha's face said he hadn't either.

"Maybe it'll fit. They usually don't, but maybe this one will," LouEllen said.

"I hope so," Jeptha said. Lucy noticed his fingers fiddling with the frayed edges of his pockets.

"If not, we'll take it down and put it back up. Jeptha did it in five minutes," Lucy said.

"Did you now?" LouEllen said. She appraised Jeptha. He fiddled more.

Lucy couldn't stand seeing him suffer under LouEllen's gaze. "Jeptha was on his way out. Weren't you?"

"What? Oh. Yeah, I was. I am." All was quiet while he leaned down and pocketed the Allen wrench and one extra washer. "Should I try to get it through the door now though?"

"It'll be fine, Jeptha. Don't worry about it. If it won't fit, we'll leave it right here until you can come back and help us girls out," LouEllen said, her hand gesturing to the door.

Jeptha took the hint. "Okay. Just let me know, Lucy, when you want me to come help. Tomorrow, next day, anytime."

"I will," Lucy said. "And Jeptha?" He turned so quickly she worried he'd hurt himself. "I appreciate it. Really." She faced him, and then kept her back to LouEllen until Jeptha closed the door and she heard his truck drive away.

"Well, wasn't that just precious of him?" LouEllen said from behind Lucy. Lucy's belly tightened when she saw LouEllen's hands casually touching the crib. "It's pretty. Couple dings, but nothing a little white-out won't cover."

Lucy leaned on the crib edge opposite from LouEllen and averted her eyes from the dings she now saw around the edges, tiny flecks of missing paint that she might never have noticed if LouEllen hadn't pointed them out. "I think it's perfect," she said.

"It was nice of him—I'll say that. I thought you weren't sure you were going to tell him?"

"I didn't. He figured it out."

"And didn't run screaming? That *is* nice of him."

"I think maybe he isn't as bad as his family is."

"Maybe not."

"I'm serious," Lucy said, angry at the tone in LouEllen's voice. She would always be grateful to LouEllen for taking her in, but sometimes, she wanted to tell her to get the hell out of her life.

"I am too, Lucy. It's just—you're young. I believed people could change when I was young too. But I've seen a lot of Taylors over the years. And I ain't never seen one of them that wasn't drunk or mean or tomcatting, or all three. Believe me, I want that not to be the case for you. For that baby. But history doesn't bode well for him."

Lucy thought of the times she'd seen Jeptha roll out of church early, off to get up to God knew what trouble; or the times she'd seen him in high school strolling through the halls, the smell of booze lingering in the air behind him; or that time he'd come into the Laundromat where she was doing her clothes, his eyes bleary red and his clothes smelling like a skunk. Lucy only figured out later that he was high as a kite.

"I'm not sure about him either," she said to LouEllen. "I wish I was. It'd be good to have someone to count on in the middle of this."

"Well, what am I? Chopped liver?"

Lucy looked at LouEllen—her red-lipped smile lighting up her face, her white hair tipped to the side, and her teal-blue outfit blaring against the white walls. She laughed. "No, you are certainly not chopped liver."

"Well, alright then. You aren't alone in this. You don't need to depend on Jeptha. You got me."

"That's good to know," Lucy said, giving LouEllen a hug, even as her skin pulled a little at the words. She knew she should purely be grateful that LouEllen had been willing to take her in and wanted to be involved now that Lucy was bringing a baby into the house. But she worried. LouEllen had once told her that the worst mistake she'd ever made with her life was not having kids. But if Lucy was going to do this, she knew herself enough to know that she wanted to be elbows deep in bottles and baby poop. She wanted to make the mistakes millions of others already had made rather than have someone tell her constantly how to do it better or differently. She wanted a family, her own family, one that made all the mistakes families make when they are exhausted, broke, or unsure. She wasn't sure that could happen with LouEllen standing beside her, marshaling the world into order.

She looked at the crib she and Jeptha had assembled and then back to the doorway it needed to fit through. LouEllen was right, of course: there was no way it would fit. But then she thought of Jeptha's long fingers slotting their baby's crib together, like he was playing an instrument he'd been handling all his life. He would have to come back—undertake the whole crib exercise all over again. At the thought of that prospect, Lucy felt a flutter in her stomach that had nothing to do with the baby.

J EPTHA EASED HIMSELF INTO a seat at Judy's. "The usual?" she asked, her hand already halfway into the cooler before she finished asking the question.

There was no one else in the bar so early on a Friday, just a half empty beer at Delnor's usual place, marking his spot while he went to the bathroom. Like old, unmarried, crotchety Delnor, Jeptha didn't have anywhere else to go. The tobacco didn't need tending until tomorrow; Cody was at the plant; and Jeptha was, as always, in between construction projects. He had no one to get into trouble with. Besides, after he took that crib by Lucy's two weeks ago, trouble hadn't seemed as appealing as it usually did. Even drinking, his oldest and best friend, had lost some of its appeal. It'd been two days since he'd had a beer at all and two weeks since he'd been drunk. Lucy and the baby were taking up all the space in his head that alcohol usually did. He saw her a week ago at his regular gig—they'd talked after the set while she cleaned up, but when he'd said, "Well, I better get out of your way," hoping she'd ask him to stay, she'd merely said, "All right," and patted his arm good night. He'd called and talked with her a time or two, wanting to see her, but she was working every night he'd asked her about. He'd gone by her house twice too, to see if she needed him to move that crib, but she wasn't home—LouEllen had answered the door. Her words had been as nice as could be, but her raised eyebrows and knowing smile had made Jeptha so nervous he could barely mutter Lucy's name. He trembled thinking about it. He was sure LouEllen hadn't mentioned his visits to Lucy. But the idea that, at any given time, Lucy was a few minutes away from him, his kid growing inside of her and he couldn't see her, set him on edge. He put his hand on his leg to stop the jittering that was his constant companion these days.

"Jeptha? Hey. You in there?" Judy asked, her arm deep in the bottom reaches of the beer cooler. She pulled out a Budweiser and set it in front of Jeptha.

"Oh, sorry. I'll just have a Coke."

"A Coke? You?" Judy said, her hands hovering over the beer, about to pop the top on it.

"Yeah."

"Well, all right then," she said. She wiped her hands on her t-shirt and grabbed a pint glass off the shelf, dragging it through the ice and filling it from the fountain dispenser. She set it in front of Jeptha and narrowed her eyes at him. "You getting on the wagon?"

"Haven't felt much like drinking," Jeptha said.

"New leaf?"

"Guess," he said, not sure what name to give this new feeling.

"Well, as long as you can play tonight, it's all the same to me. Just don't tell everyone I said that. I'd be out of a bar if all my regulars started drinking Coke."

"Won't say a word," he said. He turned away from her watchful stare, gazing toward the stairs and hoping he'd see Lucy coming up them to restock the beer cooler. He'd come in early in the hopes of getting to talk with her. His leg jittered again as he looked.

"She isn't here," Judy said.

"Who?"

"Jeptha, please. Delnor's in the bathroom, and even he knows you're looking for Lucy," Judy said, crossing her arms over her body.

"Oh," Jeptha said, looking down at the bar, knowing his cheeks were as red as his t-shirt.

"What's going on with you two anyway?"

"Hell if I know." Jeptha sighed.

"Can I ask you—is she all right? She's been sort of off recently—pretty distracted and keeps using the bathroom like an old guy with a prostate problem," Judy said. "I've been wanting to ask, but it's not strictly my business."

"Um, well, I, she's . . . she's okay. Ain't been feeling great, I think, but it'll pass." Jeptha tried to keep a smile off his face when he thought of Lucy being pregnant, but he failed.

Judy leaned in close and stared at him until his underarms stunk with fear. "Jeptha Taylor. Is she pregnant?"

"I . . . I . . . it ain't mine to say. Well, I mean, it is mine, but—damn. Forget I said anything."

Judy slapped the bar with her hand and very nearly smiled. "I suspected as much, but I'd have never guessed you were the reason why. I was pretty sure she hated you."

"I think she did. Still might. I don't know." He wiped a blade of condensation off his glass with his thumb, remembering the smooth white paint of the crib and the slight touch of Lucy's hand on his when she had thanked him.

"What happened?"

"Nothing." He felt weird talking to Lucy's boss about it but also like he wanted to open his mouth and tell Judy everything.

"Yeah, I know a lot of women getting pregnant from nothing. I hear that's the chief way it's done, in fact." She rolled her eyes at him. "So, what's the story?"

Jeptha didn't know how to put all that had happened into words. He knew other people could probably do it—Cody, say. That man could out-talk a woman. But Jeptha didn't know, and never had, how to put the words together, how to parse out his feelings and arrange them into sentences. He knew he was happy when he thought of Lucy's hand on his but miserable when he thought about not having seen her for two weeks. He didn't know how to tell Judy any of that. Not for the first time, he wished he'd been gifted with the skill of making his mouth say what his heart felt.

"It's . . . it's a long story."

Judy rested her hands on the bar and scanned the empty room. She crossed her arms back over her tremendous chest and stood up tall, staring down at Jeptha. "Yeah, I could see how you'd be real worried about telling it, given how busy I am."

"Delnor may want a drink?" he protested weakly.

"You're worse than either of my husbands at talking," Judy said, shaking her head with disappointment. "Besides, it's four o'clock. If history is any guide, Delnor will be in there for a good twenty minutes yet."

"I . . . I don't know what to say."

"Do you love her?"

"Damn, Judy." The jitter in his leg kicked into high gear, and he looked around for the tenth time to make sure no one was listening. The bar was as empty as it had been two minutes before.

"Well, do you?"

"I . . . um, I . . ." Jeptha stopped, not trusting what might come out of his mouth. He settled for a nod.

"Now, was that so hard?" Judy asked. "Actually, to look at you, it was. Never mind."

Jeptha was silent, relieved to have admitted he loved Lucy and weak with the desperate knowledge that it didn't matter. He could bring a thousand cribs, all the diapers in the world, and love her forever. He was still Jeptha Taylor, and no woman in her right mind, especially one like Lucy, would give him a shot.

"What are you going to do? You love her. She's pregnant. What's next?"

"Nothing," Jeptha said. He put his head in his hands, his legs still jackhammering away at the floor.

"What is that noise?" Judy asked, peering over the edge of the bar. "God, is that you? You are nervous as all get-out, aren't you? Why don't you ask her to marry you and get it over with?"

"Marry her?" Jeptha croaked. "I can barely get up the nerve to ask her on another date."

"Well, you better find it and quick."

"Ain't no use," he said. He'd thought about it, a dozen times or more since she'd told him she was pregnant, vaguely imagined her saying yes to his proposal. But when he tried to think of specifics, he got panicky. He imagined bringing her back to his shitty trailer after the wedding, trying to find space for a crib among the rusted red couch, pizza boxes and beer cans on the floor. All the things about his life that had never bothered him before were making him sweat now, imagining them through Lucy's eyes. She'd run screaming. He'd be left alone. And Jeptha was smart enough to know that having her and losing her would be way worse than never having had her in his life.

"You are pitiful, Jeptha, just pitiful."

"Like I don't already know it," he said.

"I mean seriously," Judy said. Jeptha looked up at the note of anger in her voice. "Another man might see this pregnancy as the answer to his prayers. She's way more likely to say yes now than she ever was."

"Not if it's me doing the asking," Jeptha said. He sipped his Coke, wishing it was a beer.

"How come?" Judy asked.

"I'm a Taylor," he said, waiting for the expression on her face to change to one of disappointed disgust. When it didn't, he shook his head. "Don't you know? We're the worst of the white-trash—we drink too much, shoot each other, cheat. You may not give a shit, but Lucy does."

"Maybe. But carrying a man's baby has a way of changing a woman's mind about things. Besides, you don't seem so bad to me. And even if you are, you can change."

Jeptha scoffed. "Yeah, right. How can I change?"

"Get a job, be there for her. Stop blaming who you are on your name. You've already stopped drinking. Seems to me your biggest problem is being a coward."

"A coward? The hell?" Jeptha stood, nearly knocking his stool over.

"You are too chicken to ask Lucy to marry you, no matter the answer. Even if she says no, isn't asking the right thing to do? I mean, even where I come from—the Godless North as you all keep calling it—that is generally the way these things work. Aren't you guys real big on all that honor stuff down here?"

Honor. There wasn't anything more in the world Jeptha wanted to do, but there was no honor in asking a question when he already knew the answer was no. Jeptha got angry sitting there, across from Judy's crossed arms, her looking down at him like his grandma used to do, looking at him like he was family and she knew anything about anything. She moved down here for a man, one she wasn't even married to, and she wanted to lecture him on honor? Jeptha didn't want to hear it.

"Ain't you heard, Judy? I ain't got no honor," Jeptha said. "And I'll take that beer now."

"Aw, fuck that, Jeptha. Be better than that." Judy threw him a sharp look and walked away.

JEPTHA SAT THERE as the bar began to fill up, trying to ignore the dirty looks Judy cast his way while casting more than a few of his own at her. He talked to Delnor for a few minutes and nursed the half-foam beer Judy had grudgingly set in front of him thirty minutes after he'd asked for it. He just wanted to see Lucy. He knew seeing her wouldn't make him feel any better—probably worse if his past experiences held true—but he didn't care. He turned around in his seat every four minutes to see if she had snuck in behind him, but there was no Lucy, just a couple of people sitting at tables, eating jalapeño poppers and waiting for the show to start.

"This thing's warm as a homeless man's bottle of piss," Judy said, picking up his half-drunk beer and shuddering. "You want another one?"

Jeptha shook his head. "Just a Coke."

Judy set down his drink and leaned her elbows on the bar in front of him. "Here's the thing, Jeptha. You only get one shot at something like this—believe me. How you're feeling right now? It doesn't come around every day."

"How do you know?"

"I was young once," Judy said. "A hundred years ago."

Jeptha laughed.

"I'm serious. You don't get a dozen shots on goal when it comes to this. I've been a bartender all my life and I've seen people in every stage of love there is. But you—you're miserable in love. That's the worst kind. The kind that can only be treated by doing something about it. Whether she says yes or no, you've got to ask. It's the only way you'll stop that leg." Jeptha stilled it with a massive force of will. "You've got to try."

Jeptha was quiet, his gut twisted as he thought of Lucy. He nodded at Judy. "Maybe."

———

THE MINUTES UNTIL the rest of the band arrived dragged by. Jeptha lifted his head off his arms every few minutes to peek around for Lucy and then collapsed back into a heap. He knew he should get up, figured he should at least try to look semi-respectable and not like a drunken bump on a log passed out at his place of work, but he didn't know when his head had ever felt so heavy, his limbs so bone-tired. He was even more miserable now than he had been when he walked in. He stared at the beers, wishing that a drink would help but knowing there was no cure for this ache in a bottle. Ask Lucy Kilgore to marry him? Lord knew he wanted to, but it'd be a cold day in hell before he'd ever man up and do that, and an even colder one before she'd say yes.

He jerked as he felt a touch on his shoulder and looked up so quick he gave himself whiplash. It was Cody, shaking his head as he stared down at him.

"Drunk before we even start our set?" Cody asked. "That's a new low."

"I ain't drunk. Just had a half a beer," Jeptha said.

"Sure? You look like shit."

"That's just my face."

"What's in that glass?"

"A Coke."

"Serious? Shit, man. You all right?"

"Just tired, that's all. Tired of being me."

"Aw, Marla feels that way about me every day. You don't see me drinking Coke 'cause of it. Come on, let's go play," Cody said. He pulled Jeptha's arm until his feet had to hit the floor to keep him from falling like a Slinky to the ground.

Jeptha took one last look around and shuffled to the stage. He hitched up his pants and clicked the locks on his mandolin case. Even seeing his mandolin didn't give him the usual lift. He tuned it half-heartedly, staring idly about as he did. He missed Cody's nod to start playing and had to hustle in twenty seconds late on the first song. No matter how hard he tried, he could not keep up. It was like all the music had left him, the rhythm gone. Three songs in, the band stopped playing under cover of needing to retune, but it was really so Cody could step over to Jeptha. He barely heard what Cody was saying—he stared at the ground, wishing he could stop this farce and go home now.

Then he saw something behind Cody's broad back. A hint of movement, female, carrying a tray of drinks. He put his arms on Cody's shoulders and moved him bodily to the side. There was Lucy, staring at him with concern in her eyes. She had never been more beautiful—her hair piled up on her head, a few soft curls escaping down her neck and her face, slightly plumper than it had been a few months before all this began and lit from within as if by a fire. A crackle ran through him. He thought again of the fire at Avery's and how Delnor described it as leaping from one bottle to the next until the entire bar was lit up like Christmas in July. She smiled at him, and that crackle burst into open flame.

"You all right?" she asked.

He nodded, not trusting his voice. He barely noticed as Cody edged out of the way.

"Judy had me bring these up," she said, handing him drinks for his band-mates. "Said this one is yours." She sniffed it. "What is this? Coke? Now I *am* worried."

Jeptha swallowed hard against the lump in his throat. He tried to speak, but a froggy croak was all that came out. He swallowed again. "I'm okay. How are you?"

"Feeling better."

"You was sick?"

"Pregnant. Apparently it makes people throw up."

"I'm sorry." Jeptha wasn't sure what else to say.

Lucy shrugged. "Price I have to pay, I guess. Besides, I'm feeling better. I'm more than two months, so maybe the worst is over."

"That's good."

"Y'all want anything for later?"

"Probably the same."

"Another Coke? You aren't drinking?"

"Ain't been as appealing as usual. Besides, you can't drink."

Lucy cocked her head and narrowed her eyes at him, surprised. The half-smile on her face made Jeptha want to grab her in a hug that would remove all the worries she was toting around. Instead, he asked, "Can I play you something?"

Lucy thought for a moment and brightened. "Shady Grove? I remember you used to sing that at church."

"Shady Grove, then." He moved to stand up and go back to the band, but she put her hand on his arm.

"Thank you, Jeptha," she said, and kissed him on the cheek.

"You're welcome," he whispered as she walked away, his nose full of the scent of her, all bar soap, sun, sweat, and an earthiness he couldn't name. Jeptha stayed there, crouched down and swaying slightly, until Cody tapped him on the shoulder.

"I think you promised her a song. Want to sing it for her before the sun comes up?"

AT THE END of the night, Jeptha made his way over to Lucy. She was behind the counter, wiping off the abuses of a night's worth of beer, liquor, and mixers. More curls had tumbled down the back of her neck, and her cheeks were flushed from hustling around the bar all night.

"Do you need a ride?" he asked.

"I got my car. Thanks, though. Looks like Cody might want one," she said, nodding behind Jeptha. He turned to see his friend staring at them, an empty glass in his hand, miming drinking it. Cody smiled so big his eyes closed and waved when he saw them looking at him—the man was six sheets to the wind.

"You sure?"

"I gotta close up and get home. I'm worn out."

"Another time?"

"Yeah," she said, moving down to wipe the rest of the counter. "I'll see you later."

Jeptha began to make his way to Cody. Ten feet away, he caught Judy's eye. She had her arms crossed again, looking at him like a bouncer about to kick him out for bad behavior. He closed his eyes for a minute, took a deep breath, and walked back to Lucy. He paused in front of her, wanting to make sure the words came out right.

"Do you want to do something tomorrow? We could maybe try the Fold again?" He spat the words in such a rush that he saw her have to work through them to make out what he'd said.

"You sure you want to go back down that road?" she asked.

"I'll be there. Early even."

"Jeptha . . ."

"I'll sit there all night to make sure."

Lucy eyed him, silently.

He pulled his keys out. "All right, I'm going. I'll be at your house when you get home. All night. All day. 'Til six."

"You better not. LouEllen's liable to call Rick Mullins on you. They were high school sweethearts, and she says he still loves her." Lucy smiled.

"Might be worth it," Jeptha said.

"Being shot or in jail is no way to prove yourself," Lucy said. "All right. Six o'clock tomorrow. My house."

"I'll be there."

"You better."

— 8 —

L UCY WOKE UP CONFUSED. Chirping birds had woken her instead of the nausea that usually had her sprinting for the toilet. She waited for her stomach to roil and her toes to twitch and writhe in a fight against the queasiness. When five minutes passed with nothing, she cautiously stretched. Still nothing. The only thing she felt was hungry. It was the most glorious morning she had had since finding out she was pregnant.

All right, baby. We may get along yet, she thought.

Thinking of the baby made her think of Jeptha. Watching him sing "Shady Grove" last night had made her shiver—he sang it with a burning intensity, his soul pure and shining up there on stage. She thought of the way his voice cracked when he talked to her, like he was a fourteen-year-old boy asking a girl out for the first time. He looked at her sometimes like she was the sun to his earth, her presence responsible for all the basic biology of existence. It both exhilarated and terrified her. She recalled his hands putting the crib together, the focused and deliberate way he threaded each tiny washer onto the screws. She thought of his long, thin fingers methodically turning each screw with the Allen wrench, tightening them until they wouldn't go anymore, then backing each one off a quarter turn. She remembered the way he had held the two sides together before the screws went in, one hand palming the gap and his knee holding them up. She flushed there in bed, thinking of his fingers spread wide around her waist as she straddled him in his car.

But then she remembered him that night at the Fold—drunk, late, and knocking over that little boy as he tried to chase her down the stairs. Her stomach turned with embarrassment at having kissed him on the cheek last night. Why had she done that? She knew how he felt about her. Then she'd gone and said yes to another date. She wanted things to return to how they'd been when he had fucked up their date. That Jeptha was easy to deal with, more black and white. She could just hate him and get on with it. This Jeptha—the one bringing cribs and diapers, and singing her songs, and promising to show up early for dates—he was much more complicated.

Lucy emerged from her room to the smell of eggs and toast, and for the first time in weeks, the smell didn't send her running to the bathroom. She forgot about Jeptha, hunger dominating her brain.

"God, that smells amazing," she said to LouEllen as she walked into the kitchen.

"You're up!" LouEllen said, turning around from the stove.

"Did you put my name in the pot?" Lucy said, peeking at the mound of scrambled eggs studded with half-melted chunks of cheese in the skillet.

"I hope so—I can't eat all this," LouEllen said. "Sit down. Get some coffee."

Lucy sipped a cup of coffee and then, when it went down easily, took larger sips. She was exhausted with relief at being free of unrelenting nausea—even if it came back later today, she wouldn't mind. It was a treat to have an hour without it now.

"You look like you're feeling better," LouEllen said, setting a plate in front of her.

"I do," Lucy said between bites. "I hope it lasts."

"You're ten weeks and two days, right?"

She stopped chewing, surprised by LouEllen's precision. Lucy had to do the math every time.

"I'd say you're almost in the clear. The first tri is the worst, and you're about out of that now."

Lucy stared at her. "How do you know that?"

"I've been doing some reading," LouEllen said, her cheeks flushing slightly. "Don't you have your ultrasound soon?"

"A few more weeks yet—August fifteenth."

"I've been wanting to ask, can I come?" LouEllen asked haltingly.

Lucy had pictured herself in the room—and there was even a daydream she'd had a time or two of Jeptha being there. She'd never imagined Lou-Ellen. But maybe it wouldn't be so bad—in case something was wrong. Plus, LouEllen had been beside her at so many points in her life. This was a small thing. Why should she deny the woman who had taken her in—cared for her as if she were her own—something she so clearly wanted?

"Sure," Lucy said, forcing a brightness into her voice.

"Your mama would have wanted to see it, I bet," LouEllen said.

"You think?" Lucy asked.

Seven years later, her memories of them had faded to specific moments—a special look from her dad, like she was the most amazing thing he'd ever seen, and fights about nothing that she'd had with her mom on her way to and from school that she could now see were fought from love. Death had made them seem more perfect in Lucy's head—she knew there had been plenty of fights, mostly over money and some over her. Her dad had worked hard as a manager at the chemical plant in Kingsport, but it was a far cry from the glamour of living in town that her mom had craved. She'd once told Lucy of the vision she'd had for her life—marrying a doctor, living in Kingsport or maybe even Knoxville, buying and decorating a house in one of those neighborhoods where everything was a beige-brick variation upon a two-story, large-foyer theme. Instead, she'd found herself settled down with Lucy's dad, who had gone to college—unlike most people her mom knew, herself included—but was happy to work hard as a middle manager and come home to his family. His ambitions had never been enough for Alice, Lucy's mom. It was Alice who had dreamed of Lucy leaving this town, of getting out and doing something else. It had always been her mother's dream, unrealized and now forever so. Lucy wasn't so sure that her mom would have wanted to be at the ultrasound. She thought that the woman she had known might have seen it as a black-and-white proof of Lucy's failure to live up to either of their dreams.

"I do," LouEllen said. "I know she wanted you to get out of here, move to Knoxville, or hell, even Kingsport. But she'd have been excited by a baby. A little sad for you, maybe, but excited to have a grandkid."

"As excited as you are?" Lucy asked. She had spied a book about being a good grandparent on LouEllen's nightstand.

"Well, she was never one to get as excited as I get about things, probably for the better."

Lucy smiled at LouEllen and reached for another piece of toast.

"Speaking of, do you have any ideas what you want to do with that back room for the baby?" LouEllen asked.

"God, I don't know. I have a crib. What else do I need?"

"A changing pad, a diaper bin, more diapers, wipes, a comfy chair, a rug, some paint, books, bottles . . ."

"Stop, please," Lucy said, burying her head in her arms. "I'm already overwhelmed with everything. I don't need to figure all that out today."

"I can help, if you want."

"No, I can do it. I just don't want to deal with it now."

"What if I just get a few things?"

Lucy nodded, happy to be able to scratch a few items off her list. She guessed this was what a mom did—helped out with things you were too overwhelmed to take on yourself. She'd scrolled through a few websites at night before bed, enough to know that she didn't want anything to do with those pale yellow or pale green "gender neutral" themes she saw floating around. She wanted something bright and cheerful—maybe a happy bright yellow or a calm turquoise. Nothing that featured pastel, soft-faced animals gallivanting around the room like members of a demented animal kingdom. She liked the lion on the onesie she'd bought, roaring proudly into the world. She wanted something that would let this baby know the future was bright, not prescribed—something that said this baby's origins were better than the back seat in which he'd been conceived.

It was a lot to ask of a baby room.

"Okay then! So, what's on your agenda for today?" LouEllen asked.

"I'm at Walmart today. And tonight . . ." Lucy trailed off. She hadn't meant to say anything about Jeptha.

"Ooh, something fun?"

"Just the Fold."

"Want company?"

"I . . . I have some," Lucy said, still not looking LouEllen in the eye.

"You are going with Jeptha, aren't you?" LouEllen said. Her voice was considerably less warm than it had been a minute before.

"He asked. Last night."

"And you said yes."

"It's just the Fold."

LouEllen stared at Lucy. Her lips were pursed and her face furrowed in anger. After a minute, Lucy saw the lines relax, replaced by a look of renewed purpose.

"Did I ever tell you I dated his dad for a little bit?" LouEllen said.

"Jeptha's dad?"

"Yeah, for a month or two. My parents were horrified—the grandfather had been involved in every break-in this side of Hawkins County. But I was sure he was different. Sure I could make him more than any of his family had been. And I did—right up until he showed up drunk for the first dinner with my family and crashed his car through our mailbox."

"You never told me that," Lucy said. "But I don't think I am going to make Jeptha better. I'm not asking that."

"Sure you are. Every woman in every relationship is asking for that. Don't fool yourself."

"We aren't in a relationship. And you weren't pregnant with his kid," Lucy said, getting up to pour more coffee in her cup.

"You keep saying that like you're alone—like you don't have a place to live and a person to help."

"It's not that, LouEllen. It's just . . ." Lucy stopped. How could she explain to the woman who was the closest thing she had to family that she didn't feel like she had any family? "I've spent the last seven years wanting to have a family—and I know I have you. And God, I am grateful for that. But how can I deny my kid the same thing I've been wanting for so long? How can I keep him away from his father? All because Jeptha was late for a date and *might* be like the rest of his family? It doesn't seem fair."

"There ain't a lot of fair going around the world, as far as I can tell," LouEllen said. But she reached out and patted Lucy's hand. "I don't want you to feel like he has to be it."

"He's not. It's the Fold, LouEllen. I'm not falling in love. I'm not getting married. I'm not leaving you," Lucy said, finishing her cup and setting it down in the sink. "Except I am, because I have to go to work." She kissed the top of LouEllen's feathery white head, which smelled of powder and dandruff shampoo. "Thank you for the eggs. I'll see you later today."

A FEW HOURS later, Lucy was in such a groove that she had scanned four bags of cheese puffs before she looked up to say hello to the customer on the other side. She half-expected to see an Oompa-Loompa, but it was Delnor Gilliam, his face turned up in an oddly warm smile that she'd never seen before. His teeth were black and jack-o-lanterned, but his clothes were pressed, and his beard was clean. He was a committed alcoholic, but mostly a functional one.

"Well, Delnor Gilliam. Am I at Judy's right now?" Lucy asked.

Glancing around him, he said seriously, "Don't look much like it. And, it ain't got a lick of booze. That was my first clue."

"You're smarter than you look, aren't you?" Lucy said, laughing.

"Don't tell nobody."

"Not a soul."

He unloaded two more bags of cheese puffs, three two-liters of Sunkist, and a cantaloupe.

"Got kind of an orange theme going, huh?" Lucy asked, waving her hand at the items on the belt.

"What? Oh," he said, looking down at the cantaloupe. "Well, they say as fruit is good for you."

Lucy laughed so hard her shoulders shook but stifled it quickly and turned it into a nod when she saw that Delnor was serious. "That's true. They do say that."

"Hey, what's this I hear about you and LouEllen? Y'all is going to have a baby?"

"Me and LouEllen? No. I mean, I am. But not LouEllen."

Delnor looked confused. "Huh. 'Cause she's going around telling everyone who will listen that you and she are going to raise that baby. At first, I was confused. Like, was it part of one of them lesbian kind of couples? But then I said, 'Delnor, now. Lucy's half her age. That can't be right.' But then I thought, it must be like how we got my brother—Aunt Betsy come over crying one night when I was a kid and supposed to be asleep. This was before she up and left, you know. Anyway, she was talking about she was too young to be having a kid. My mama said she'd take care of it, and next thing you know, I wake up and we've got a new brother. I figured maybe that's what LouEllen is doing for you."

"What? No! This is my baby. No one is taking it and saying it's hers," Lucy said, her arms wrapped protectively around her middle.

Delnor held his hands up. "I didn't mean to start no trouble. I probably misunderstood is all."

Lucy could feel her nostrils flaring and could see the fear in Delnor's eyes. How dare LouEllen talk about this baby like it was hers? Was this why she'd been doing all that reading, all that studying up on babies? Lucy very much doubted that LouEllen had any expectation that Lucy would up and leave her baby, but it was clear that LouEllen expected to play a primary role in this baby's life. She was walking around town making Delnor and who knows who else think she was about to be a lesbian mom, for God's sake. Lucy closed her eyes and tried to breathe.

"Don't get bothered about it now, Lucy," Delnor said. "I'm sure I just heard it wrong."

Lucy opened her eyes and smiled weakly at Delnor. The poor man. He'd stumbled straight into a snake pit. One that Lucy was about to have to walk into herself.

"It's okay, Delnor. That'll be $14.20," Lucy said, and waited patiently while he counted out a ten, four crumpled ones, and two dimes. The ones had probably been in Lucy's hands at some point, or in her wallet even. At Judy's Delnor didn't tip much, but he always left one hand-smoothed dollar under his glass at the end of every night.

As he handed the money over, he looked up at her shyly and said, "Sorry about that. I'm glad to hear it. I was right sad to think you might not raise that baby."

"Thanks, Delnor. I appreciate that," Lucy said.

Grabbing his bags, he nodded goodbye at her. Lucy reached up and flicked her light off. Teresa could shove it. She needed a break.

9

JEPTHA HAD FALLEN ASLEEP with his hand cupped against the whisker-roughened spot where Lucy had kissed him the night before, wanting to hold on to the warmth of the moment. Clear of the booze that he usually steeped in, he'd dreamed of nothing but Lucy all night. When he awoke, the sun was topping the trees on the mountains across the valley. It had been weeks since he'd woken this early and this sober—in fact, he realized, it had been the last time he was supposed to take Lucy out to the Fold. Shaking his head of the memory, he pulled on a sweatshirt, grabbed his mandolin, and went out to the porch, Crystal Gayle padding along behind him. Fog clung to the valley bottoms where the sun hadn't hit yet. But higher up, the early morning sun, bright and clarifying, was starting to touch the world. Even the tobacco looked pretty in the morning—the leaves glowed caterpillar green.

As he picked out the notes to "Shady Grove," he thought of Lucy's smile when he'd played it the night before. It was a little thing, playing a song for someone, but it made her smile. Jeptha would be happy to make her smile every day for the rest of his life. If he felt like that and didn't ask her to marry him, maybe Judy was right. Maybe he was a coward. But he didn't want to be. Not anymore.

He set the mandolin down on the floor and stood up. Within a second, Crystal Gayle was up from her nap, her tail wagging as she leaned her weight against his legs.

"I'm going to do it, girl," he said to her. "I'm going to ask her to marry me."

Her tail stopped wagging.

"You worried?" Jeptha asked, petting her from ear to tail the way she liked. "Worried she'll replace you? Never gonna happen."

Crystal Gayle woofed and flopped back down.

Jeptha smiled. He rubbed his chin, trying to think of what he had saved up. He had the $200 Cody had given him last night from their gigs, but he was pretty sure he'd spent everything else he had. No self-respecting man, particularly one with as hard a row to hoe as he had in getting Lucy to marry him, could hope to persuade a girl to say yes with a $200 ring. The tobacco payment would be coming soon—he hoped he'd get a couple thousand, like last year, but who knew. It would get him through to the new year, but it wouldn't help him much with getting Lucy a ring tonight. He groaned, knowing what he'd have to do. At the sound, Crystal Gayle looked up at him, worry in her eyes.

"I'm alright, girl. Just got to go do something I really don't want to do," he said. Jeptha went back in, pulled on his work jeans and a t-shirt already stained brown from last weekend's work, and set out to find Bobby.

He combed the fields for five minutes, looking up and down each row, grumbling as he saw how much work they had to do. The plants were over his head, their tops green with accumulated chlorophyll that they'd need to be cured of in the barn, the bottoms already turning a crinkly, tawny brown. He'd be dog-tired by the end of the day. Still, he smiled when he saw he'd beat Bobby out to the fields for the day. He couldn't think of the last time that had happened. Jeptha plopped down on an overturned cinderblock on the edge of the tobacco to wait for Bobby to come plodding down the hill.

A few minutes later, Jeptha saw a flash of blue on the next farm over. He shaded his eyes and peered through the morning haze at Bobby crossing the barbwire fence back onto their property from the next farm over. Jeptha inhaled sharply as he saw Bobby straddle it, the barbs dangerously close to his balls. Bobby had always been too lazy to crawl under a fence. He'd rather risk castrating himself than have to get all the way down on the ground and then all the way back up. Jeptha's brother had inherited their mother's family build—short and stocky—while Jeptha's long legs and rangy figure were all from the Taylor side. Jeptha could clear that fence with barely a thought, but since it wasn't their farm, he'd never needed to. What on earth was Bobby doing over there?

Bobby tramped over to Jeptha's trailer, banged on the door so loud the trailer jarred a little, and then stomped back down the stairs, a look of fury on his face. Jeptha laughed to himself as he watched Bobby's angry little trot down to the fields.

"Hey there, slowpoke," Jeptha said when Bobby got close.

"What the hell?" Bobby said, his eyes narrowed at Jeptha. "You're here? I been up there banging down your door."

"I'm here."

"Is this some kind of joke? Are you still drunk from last night? Did you sleep out here?"

Jeptha stood up lazily and stretched his arms overhead. "Thanks for the faith, brother. Nope, not drunk—went to sleep stone-cold sober in my own bed last night and woke up ready to work. You got a problem with that?"

"Will wonders never cease? I'll take it," Bobby said, a smile on his face.

"Hey—what was you doing over on Old Man Keller's land?" Jeptha asked. The smile fell from Bobby's face.

"I wasn't," he said, his eyes looking up to the sky.

"Bobby, you've been a shitty liar all your life. Even if I hadn't of watched you climb over that fence, I wouldn't of believed you."

Bobby took his tobacco-stained cap off his head and stared at the ground, his hands twisting the brim until it was nearly a circle.

"He letting you use it or something?" Jeptha asked.

"He . . . um. Well, truth is, I bought it," Bobby said.

"You what? When?" Jeptha asked. He hadn't heard hide nor hair of it being for sale or of Bobby buying it. They'd talked for years about how much better it would be if they could work a larger plot, buy up Keller's quota, and really make a go of it. And now, here Bobby went and did it without him. Jeptha stood up, hot with rage that his brother had cut him out of the deal.

"Last fall," Bobby said. "He was sickly and looking to offload it."

"Why didn't you talk to me? I'd have gone in on it," Jeptha said.

"With what? You got some cash hidden away somewheres?"

Jeptha's cheeks burned, even more so because he knew he'd have to swallow his pride in a few minutes and beg Bobby for money. He felt that occasional ache of wishing he was another kind of man, the kind who could get a job, keep it, and stash money away. He'd thought it when he found out Lucy was pregnant, and again right now.

"I might have been able to find it if you'd let me know there was the possibility of doing something with it. Where'd you get the money?" Jeptha asked. He knew Bobby worked hard, but somehow the numbers didn't add up. How'd he saved that much? They did the same thing, both of them out here farming the same land. Somehow Jeptha had hardly anything to show for it—not even enough to buy a ring for Lucy—but Bobby had enough money laid back to buy more land.

"In case you ain't noticed, Jeptha, I work. I save. I don't spend my money as soon as it comes in. Unlike some of us, I'm not sitting at Judy's every day of my damn life." It was a righteous-sounding speech, and even in his anger, he knew Bobby had a point, but he couldn't ignore the fact that Bobby hadn't yet looked him in the eye.

Jeptha had no reply. He was so angry and confused he didn't trust himself to speak. He picked up his knife, a bundle of sticks, and the spear, and turned into the fields. He nodded to Juan and Santiago, the two Mexican migrants they hired every year at the cheapest price they could possibly pay, who were standing at the edge of the field, waiting for Bobby to give them instructions. Most farms the size of theirs would have hired a bunch of guys, but they hired as little help as they could and tried to keep as much of the profits as possible. *What had been the point of that if he had nothing to show for it at the end of the day?* Jeptha found himself wondering as he walked all the way to the other end of the field to put as much distance as possible between himself and his brother.

Once he reached the end of the row, he angrily stuck the stick deep into the ground, not even feeling bad that he was pretending the ground was Bobby's heart. He jammed the sharp metal point on top of the stick. Leaning down, he aimed one expert hack at the very bottom of the stalk closest to him. It split in two with a satisfying thwack, and he hefted up the plant with his free hand, ramming the bottom of the thick, fibrous stalk through the point and onto the wooden stick below. He bent down to get the next stalk and did it all over again.

Before he even realized it, he was through three rows and he'd left the worst of his anger somewhere about halfway down the second. Bobby's purchasing the land still galled him, there was no doubt about that, but he couldn't deny that Bobby was right; he didn't have any cash to put up for it. No bank or person in their right mind would have lent him the money. Maybe Cody. But it wasn't like he had extra cash rolling around with two kids of his own. Besides, Jeptha was the first to admit he wasn't a great investment.

Jeptha grabbed another bundle of sticks and headed back the way he'd come. He worked steadily for the next four hours, the repetitive work and the hot air calming him in a way that nothing but his mandolin usually did. He paused only to sip water out of a gallon milk jug and check his phone to make sure Lucy hadn't called to cancel. Looking out, he felt no small sense of accomplishment as he slowly decimated his part of the field until he was finally able to see out to the cars traveling on the road in front of the farm.

"You ready to call it?" Bobby called out from two rows over, startling Jeptha with the first words in four hours.

"You sure? It's only—" Jeptha pulled out his phone from his back pocket. "Twelve."

"Yeah. We're in good shape. I'm all right doing more tomorrow if you are. Especially if you are able to work like you was today."

Jeptha nodded. "I will be." It was the first compliment he could ever remember his brother paying him.

"All right then. Be the first year ever I won't be bitching about splitting the money with you."

Jeptha took a deep breath, once again choosing to ignore his brother. "Hey, speaking of money . . ."

"This ain't about that land again, is it? I should of maybe told you, but I knew it wouldn't matter."

Jeptha's belly tightened with renewed anger. He swallowed it down, along with his pride. "No, I don't want to talk about that. I was wanting to know, could I get an advance on this year's split? Even five hundred dollars would help."

"Why?"

Jeptha wiped sweat off his forehead and stared over the highway, up to the sun-hazed hills that formed the valley they sat in. He didn't want to say anything to anyone, particularly his family, until he knew Lucy's answer.

"You up to something, Jeptha?" Bobby asked. "Shit. I should have known there was a reason you was up early, so ready to work. What are you into?"

"Nothing."

"Is it that pot idea you talked about that one time? Am I gonna find a bunch of plants hidden over in that side of the field?" Bobby said, nodding at the rest of the uncut crop.

"No, man. It's nothing like that. It's nothing bad," Jeptha said, blushing as he thought of the ring he wanted to get Lucy.

"You're going to ask Lucy to marry you, aren't you? Son of a bitch." His brother laughed so hard the fat around his eyes crinkled up until there was no space for him to see. Everyone knew she was pregnant by now; word had got out it was his. There was no use denying what he was about to do. Jeptha nodded.

"Oh, man. That is amazing," Bobby said, still chuckling.

"I know," Jeptha said. The smile that momentarily lit his face fell away when he realized Bobby didn't mean it kindly. "She's pregnant. And I . . . well, she's pregnant."

Bobby was shaking his head. "She ain't never gonna say yes."

"She might. A baby has a way of changing a woman's mind," Jeptha said, parroting Judy's words from the night before.

"That'd have to be a hell of a pregnancy," Bobby said. "Way I hear it, she was lighting you up at the Fold couple weeks back. Didn't seem like she liked you much."

"I made it right."

"You got her pregnant. How you ever gonna make that right?"

"I'm gonna be there for her. Don't that count?" Jeptha felt his face flush, knowing his brother would never respect him. He'd done everything that needed to be done for the crop this year, barring those few drunken weeks after sleeping with Lucy, but Bobby would never think better of him. To his brother and sister, he'd always be a lazier version of his dad.

"Not if she didn't never want you or that baby to start with."

"Dammit, Bobby," Jeptha yelled. "I ain't done nothing to you today. I worked my ass off and asked you to borrow some money that's by rights already mine. You aiming to give it to me or what?"

"Oh, I'm gonna give it to you. I'd give you extra if you'd let me be there when you ask her. I'd kill to see you fall flat on your face."

"She might say yes."

"You keep telling yourself that," Bobby said, laughing. As he walked away up the hill, he said over his shoulder, "Come on up to the trailer after you get a shower. Better make sure you read the fine print on that return policy at the jewelry store. That's my only advice."

THE GLASS OF the jewelry counter creaked ominously as Cody shifted his weight onto his elbows. "I got to say, I could not fucking believe it when Marla told me about Lucy being pregnant," Cody said, his breath steaming up the glass.

The Zale's sales lady in front of him stiffened at Cody's language. "That one," Jeptha said, and pointed at a small round diamond in a gold band. Jeptha was starting to wonder if he'd made a mistake in bringing his best friend with him on this mission.

"I mean, we ain't had a chance to talk about it, but wasn't you surprised?" Cody went on.

"You could say that," Jeptha answered, holding the ring up to the light. "Think she'd like this one?"

"It's all right," Cody said, shrugging his shoulders. "I mean, I can't say I was surprised when Marla got pregnant. That was like the natural order of things. Not that I would have minded a few more years of freedom. It *was* the prom, after all. But Lucy? With you? Now that one set me on my heels a bit."

"You and everybody else, apparently," Jeptha said. Giving the ring back to the woman, he pointed at another one, the stone slightly wider at the top and set a little closer to the ring. "I'm beginning to wonder why I'm friends with someone who thinks I'm such a piece of shit."

"Don't be like that, Jeptha. I mean, it's surprising is all. Lucy Kilgore. Pregnant. With your kid. That is not the natural order of things, I'll say that much."

Jeptha liked the sparkle of the one he was holding, liked the way the stone nestled close to the finger, not sticking up high and asking to get caught on every single thing. He could see this on Lucy, see her wearing this around, even at the bar. It wasn't anything huge—even Marla's was bigger—but it was what he could afford, sort of, and Jeptha reckoned that anything else ought to go to the baby.

He nodded yes at the woman as he handed her back the ring and turned to Cody. "So, should I not be doing this? Bobby says there is no way she is going to say yes. Am I an idiot for asking her?"

Cody scratched his belly through his t-shirt, thinking on it. His head was turned to the left slightly, as if the thought required some real work on his part. Finally, he clapped his hand on Jeptha's shoulder. "Hell, man.

You've done got further than anybody thought you would. Might as well go all the way."

———————

JEPTHA DROVE LIKE a maniac home from the store, Cody snoozing in the seat beside him, his knees up around his shoulders in the Camaro's deep bucket seats. At a stoplight on 11W, Jeptha double-checked that the ring box was still in his shirt pocket and then pulled out his phone and saw it was already getting on five o'clock. He wanted Lucy to know he was there, ready for their date, not about to mess this one up. He wanted everything to be perfect so that she had no reason to say no—other than the fact it was him doing the asking.

He looked over at Cody, a small snore flaring his perfectly round nostrils with each breath. It was like watching a sow sleep. Jeptha sighed. He hated to do it, but he didn't have a choice. When the light turned, he pushed the gas and drove a few miles on down the road.

Finally, right before the turnoff for Lucy's house and a mile or two from the turn-off for Cody's road, he nudged his friend. "Hey, man. Wake up."

"Hmm? What? Huh? Oh, shit. Did I fall asleep?"

"Yeah."

"Why we stopped on the side of the road?"

"You gotta get out."

"Here?"

"I need to go pick up Lucy. I can't drop you off."

"Are you fucking kidding me, man? I go with you to pick out a ring for your pregnant not-girlfriend, and you kick me out of the car on the side of the highway?"

"I don't got a choice."

"I'm not getting out."

"Well, you ain't coming with me, and I ain't driving you home."

"Aw, man, come on."

"Call Marla. She'll get you."

"She's shopping with her mama and the kids all afternoon. They ain't gonna be home 'til seven."

"Well, they say as walking is good for you," Jeptha said, eyeing the strip of fat escaping from the bottom of Cody's shirt.

Cody tugged his shirt down. "I hate walking."

"Cody. When have I ever asked for anything?"

"You borrowed my truck two weeks ago. And two weeks before that. And my ladder and jack a few months before that, which you still ain't returned."

Jeptha rested his head on the steering wheel. "Something big?"

Cody was silent, his arms crossed over his belly. He sighed. "This is that important to you?"

"Cody, I'm set to ask Lucy to marry me. Tonight."

Cody growled and rolled his eyes. "Fine. I'll walk. You better hope she says yes, though, because I don't plan on forgiving you for a while."

Jeptha nodded. He would agree to anything if it would get Cody out of his car so he could make that left turn toward Lucy's house. He could feel his whole body aching in her direction.

"I mean it, not for a long while. If you need a shoulder to cry on, or someone to drink with, you better hit up ol' Delnor at Judy's. I ain't it. And you can't borrow my truck no more neither."

"I owe you. Big."

"And don't think I am gonna talk to you tomorrow. I don't care whether she says yes or no. You are on your own."

"I get it. I'm sorry, man. But I got to do this," Jeptha said. He paused for a minute, staring at Cody, waiting for him to move toward the door. Finally, he reached across his friend's belly and opened the handle for him. "Like I said, I owe you."

Cody stared at the open door and back at his friend, his mouth set in a thin line, shaking his head back and forth slowly like this was the most disappointing thing he'd ever witnessed in his whole life.

"You gotta go," Jeptha said.

Cody heaved himself out of the car, shuffling his pants up and his shirt down once he was standing. He put his hands on the roof of the car and leaned down so Jeptha could see him.

"You're cold, man. Ice cold," he said. He stared at Jeptha for a minute, then smiled and hit the top of the car. "Aw, hell. Go on. Good luck, ass-hole." He slammed the door.

Jeptha drove off, his car tires thudding over the grass and gravel on one side, leaving Cody in a cloud of dust. In his rearview mirror, he saw Cody scratch his belly and hitch his pants up one more time. As Jeptha drove over the hill, Cody kicked the ground and started walking home. As his friend disappeared from view, Jeptha's stomach tightened, fear filling his body at the prospect of what he was about to do. For about ten seconds, he considered turning the car around, heading to Judy's and getting shit-ass drunk. But the moment passed. He bit his lip, touched the ring box in his pocket, and turned onto Maple Avenue.

10

LUCY THOUGHT WORKING THE rest of her shift would lessen some of her anger at LouEllen. She hoped her body would be so tired that she'd be too worn out to hash it out with her tonight. But, no, she was still spitting mad as she stomped through the parking lot, slammed her door behind her, and pushed the gas pedal to the floor. How dare LouEllen assume this baby was hers—or at least part hers? How dare she go around telling people in town that *they* were having a baby? Far as Lucy could tell, no one else but her was throwing up forty times a day, gaining ten pounds, or generally feeling like shit. Lucy had wanted LouEllen to help, to be a part of her life, but she envisioned that help as a kindly grandparent willing and able to babysit. Not some kind of co-parent who, knowing LouEllen, would make all the decisions before even telling Lucy.

Lucy slammed the wheel to the left just before her street. She came to a quick stop in front of the house and stared up at it. Angry as she was, it was a bad idea to run in there primed to fight. She and LouEllen got along as well as they did because they didn't fight. For the first few years, Lucy had been so lost without her parents that she'd leaned on LouEllen exclusively. She was the best-behaved teenager anyone had ever seen. Not because she cared about her behavior, but because she was so sad and so confused and so angry about their deaths that she couldn't muster the energy to misbehave. Then, once the clouds had lifted, it was easier to go along with LouEllen. Lucy had mostly been happy with the arrangement. She disagreed when she really meant it, but for the most part, her life with LouEllen had an easy, workable, livable rhythm. If it was one that was mostly driven by LouEllen, Lucy didn't mind. Or hadn't minded. Until now.

She took three deep breaths in the car, remembering how her mom used to make her do that when she was little and needed help calming herself down. If she could get to her room and rest for a little while before she had to get ready for this stupid date, she'd feel better. She could get up in the morning and have an adult conversation about the baby and what role she wanted LouEllen to play. There was no need for a fight—just a calm, rational conversation between two adults. Decision made, Lucy thought of a nap, and her pace quickened up the walk to the house, like a cow smelling the hay in the barn. She was so close to her bed, so close to being able to avoid the drama of a fight. Six feet from her door, her shoulders drooped in relief. Then LouEllen stepped out of the kitchen. Lucy's stomach grew hot at the sight of her.

"You're home!" she said to Lucy.

"I'm wiped. I've got to lay down for a few minutes," Lucy said, trying and failing to keep the anger out of her voice.

"I know, I know. But let me show you one thing first," LouEllen said, grabbing Lucy by the elbow and pulling her down the hall. "I know I said I was just going to pick up a few things, but I got started, and everything was so cute. And I'd already done the paint, so I said, 'Let me finish this for her so she doesn't have to think about it.'"

"Done the paint? Finish what?" Lucy said. She had no idea what Lou-Ellen was talking about.

"Ta-da!" LouEllen said, as she flung open the door to the back room.

The crib was in there, alongside a changing table with a yellow changing pad stocked full of diapers and wipes, a bookshelf full of board books, a comfy nursing chair, several tiny outfits and sleepers folded neatly in baskets on the shelves of the changing table, and what looked like more than a dozen stuffed animals. The room was perfect: it had everything a baby would need, like something out of a magazine.

Lucy hated it.

"What do you think?" LouEllen asked.

Lucy burst into sobs. It was everything she didn't want in terms of style: pale yellow; wallpaper trim in those pastel safari animals that looked like no lion or giraffe she'd ever seen; a rug that had matching animals running around its border. But far worse than the style choices was the fact that she had wanted to do this herself—pick a wall paint, put together the bookshelves, swearing as she did so, and pick out pillows for the chair, laughing when things didn't quite match, all while entertaining smudged-edged visions of her and the baby using these things. She was so tired, so worn out, and so angry as she thought of all the hovering LouEllen would do, all the love in which she would smother Lucy and her baby. Lucy knew it was ungrateful: complaining about too much love, about a perfect baby's room, what was wrong with her? But love done LouEllen's way could be torture. Lucy had been fine being waterboarded by love when it was just her. But now she had someone else to worry about, and she'd be damned if she'd let LouEllen take it all away from her.

"You love it," LouEllen said. "I knew you would. I wanted to do this one thing for you, so you didn't have to worry. But you better stop crying, or I'll start. And we know I can't stop." She patted Lucy on the shoulder.

"Don't," Lucy said, jerking away. "Don't touch me."

"What?" LouEllen asked.

"Just stop. Stop all of it. Stop this room, stop acting like this is your baby, stop telling me what to do," Lucy said. She tried to keep her voice even, tried to remember that she had wanted to do this in a nice, calm way, but she was losing the battle.

"What on earth are you talking about?" LouEllen said. Her voice lost some of its liquid sweetness and took on a harder edge.

"This! All this!" Lucy said, waving her arms around the room.

"The room? You don't like it?"

"This has nothing to do with the goddamn room. Which, incidentally, I hate." A sense of power flooded over Lucy when she saw how LouEllen's face sunk at that. "It has to do with the fact that none of this is yours." She pointed at her stomach. "This isn't your baby. It isn't your life. It's mine. And it's messed up all to hell right now, but I'm not gonna let you take it away from me."

"I'm not trying to take it away from you. I'm trying to help."

"You took this away from me," Lucy said, waving her arms around the room again. "All this. This was the one fun thing I had in front of me. The throwing up, the getting bigger, the stress, the figuring out how I'm going to raise this kid on my own. . . . None of that is fun."

"Why do you keep saying on your own? From the first moment this happened, you've been walking around like you are by yourself. Like you suddenly found yourself pregnant in the middle of Timbuktu. But here you are, still here, still living in this house with ME, the lady who has been taking care of you for six years now."

"You know what? You did take care of me when I was a kid. That's true. But now, I take care of myself. I live here, but I have a job, and I take care of my stuff. I'd pay rent if you'd let me, but you won't cash the checks. And all that's fine. But you are acting like this baby is going to be yours, or at least part yours. Like you are going to be a second mom to it."

"I'm not behaving like I'm going to be a second mom," LouEllen said, rolling her eyes.

"Oh, really? Then why did Delnor have to stop and think for a minute about whether you and I were a couple?"

"A couple? From Delnor? If that wasn't so utterly ridiculous, I'd commend him for being so damn progressive."

"You were so insistent about how this was *our* baby that he thought that meant you were going to raise the baby, take it from me, and maybe I'd see y'all sometimes. Like it'd be your kid, not mine."

"Lucy, it's Delnor Gilliam. He's a drunk. Are you seriously picking a fight with me 'cause of something he said?"

"It's not just that, LouEllen. I know you. I know you get excited. You go overboard. You smother people. And it's mostly smothering them in love, but that's my job with this baby. And I don't know if you can hold yourself back."

"Do you honestly think that a baby can get too much love?" LouEllen said, shaking her head at Lucy, her eyes wet with the start of tears.

"Too much love, no. But I can definitely get too much of you—too much attention, too much making decisions that I should be making, too much doing things for me when I want to do them for myself," Lucy said.

"You can't do it all by yourself. You can't raise this kid all on your own."

"Who says I can't?"

"You will need help. And what are you going to do? Ask Jeptha?"

"Leave him out of this."

"Why? He's the whole damn reason you are in this mess."

"I don't know why you hate him so much," Lucy said.

"I don't know why you *don't*," LouEllen shot back. "He got you pregnant. He's a drunk. A lowlife who is never going to be anything, and yet, you keep giving him chances."

"He's this baby's father."

"You'd be better off thinking of him as a sperm donor."

"Jesus Christ, LouEllen!" Lucy said, slamming a teddy bear to the ground. "What is wrong with you?"

"Calm down, Lucy."

"This is what I'm talking about. You telling me what to do. Do you honestly think that I'm going to exclude Jeptha from this baby's life because of his past? The answer is no. Do you honestly think that you telling me different will change my mind? Yes, you do. You will think that about everything. The color of paint in this room. The kind of car seat. The baby's doctor. What formula I buy. What friends he should have. What sports he should play. And on and on and on and on. I'm already sick of it, and I don't even have a baby yet."

Lucy, her chest heaving, stared at LouEllen, who held her gaze. The older woman's face was impossible to read. It was one of the only times that Lucy hadn't been able to tell exactly what she was thinking before she opened her mouth.

"I had no idea you hated me this much," LouEllen said.

"Dammit, LouEllen. I don't hate you. I just don't want you as a partner in this baby's life."

Lucy watched as a dust mote floated down to the floor, illuminated in a shaft of light sneaking in through the side of the blackout shades LouEllen had installed. Lucy waited for LouEllen to speak. Instead, just her nostrils flared.

Finally, LouEllen flung open the door of the closet. Hauling out a large cardboard box, she began slamming stuffed animals into it.

"Don't want a partner, huh? Don't want me? Well, you know what? I'm not so sure I want you. In fact, I think I'll pack up all this baby stuff for you, get it all nice and assembled so you can take it with you, wherever the hell it is you think you are going to go. I don't want to hold you back. Or make you do anything you don't want to do. And believe me, I'd love not to be woken up six times a night by a screaming baby. If I'd have wanted that all these years, I would have had one myself."

LouEllen flew around the room, throwing animals, diapers, and clothes into the box with an uncanny accuracy. Lucy bit back tears, hoping that keeping them inside would keep the sheer and utter panic from overtaking her.

"Oh, but wait," LouEllen said, stopping suddenly, a tub of Desitin in one hand and a stuffed alligator in the other. She stared hard at Lucy. "I remember why I didn't have a baby now. I got *you* in the middle of the night, in the middle of your life. A kid I had to raise, from a friend I often couldn't stand. A kid too old to be parented and too young to be on her own. But lucky me! It seems like you are the perfect age to be on your own now! I don't need to worry about you, I guess."

"Are you kicking me out?" Lucy asked, her voice barely above a whisper. This fight had spiraled out of control. And yet, looking at LouEllen packing up her stuff, she felt a sense of utter fear combined with sweet relief.

"I . . ." LouEllen stopped. Her arm, poised to throw yet another stuffed animal into the box at maximum speed, relaxed until she was hugging the bear to her chest. "I—"

The front bell rang.

LouEllen looked at Lucy, a question in her eyes. But almost instantly Lucy saw her eyes narrow, followed by her lips clamping down into a tight grimace and her nostrils flaring. It could only be Jeptha at the door.

"It's Jeptha, isn't it?" LouEllen asked.

"I'm guessing. He's early."

"Of course he is," LouEllen said. "The one time in his whole damn life. I'll get the door. You go get changed."

Lucy had forgotten she was still in her work clothes. She hated to leave Jeptha to the mercy of an angry LouEllen, but more deeply, she wanted to get him and herself out of that house before either she or LouEllen jumped off a cliff too high for them to come back from.

Lucy strained to listen to the conversation as she brushed her hair and threw on whatever clothes still fit. LouEllen's voice took on that syrupy sweet drawl she used when she was being fake. Poor Jeptha's voice was so soft that Lucy could barely hear him. But as she put her hair up into a ponytail, she heard them walk down the hall. She heard LouEllen throw open the door with a flourish. She heard Jeptha breathe in sharply.

"Hey," she said to Jeptha as she came up behind him.

"Hey," he said, turning to her. His eyes were wide, his face drawn and ashen.

Lucy looked over at the room. The box of animals was gone, the space somehow miraculously returned to its pastel glory. She looked up at LouEllen, who stared back with a wide smile and a self-satisfied gleam in her eye.

11

JEPTHA HAD NEVER BEEN so glad to leave a house than at that moment. LouEllen smirked once more in his direction as he held the front door open for Lucy. The door closed an inch behind him with more force than was strictly necessary. He broke out in a cold sweat all over again. He helped Lucy into the car and hoped she wouldn't notice.

"She's sort of scary, ain't she?" Jeptha asked, as he drove up the hill.

Lucy laughed the heartiest laugh Jeptha had ever heard from her, the kind that makes a person ugly unless you love them. He laughed too, until both of them were going so hard that they were nearly crying. They kept on for ten whole minutes, until finally only random giggles emerged. Lucy wiped her eyes and giggled once more.

"Oh, God," she said. "I don't know why that was so funny, but it was."

"Glad you thought so. I was terrified. I'm still sweating."

Lucy glanced at him and giggled again. "I know. She can be sort of scary. I'm sorry—we were fighting earlier. She means well, but she can't help herself sometimes. I think she's worried about me. We've been a unit, just her and me, for a long time."

"How long have you lived with her?" Jeptha asked.

"Seven years. Since . . ."

"Since . . . your parents."

"Yeah."

"I'm sorry about that. About them, I mean."

"Thanks."

"I remember that. When I was a kid. Seeing you at church after."

"It wasn't a good time."

"You always seemed okay to me. Like you'd be okay no matter what."

"I've gotten good at putting on a face."

"They found the guy who did it, right?" What he most remembered about that time was the sheriff showing up at his house in the middle of the night, rousing his dad out of bed, and wanting to talk to him about where he'd been thirty minutes earlier. He'd been home, which his mom said too, but her word meant nothing to a cop who knew well the kind of lies an abused woman will tell. The only thing that convinced the sheriff was his dad's car, broken down once again. Only when both the sheriff and his deputy couldn't start it did they believe his dad had had nothing to do with the crash. He wanted to make sure Lucy knew it wasn't his dad that had done it.

"They did. An hour later, they pulled over a guy rocketing down 11W. His truck was all scratched up on the side, same color paint as my parents' car. He was so drunk that when they asked him if he'd been involved in an accident earlier, he said, 'It wasn't me, Officer. It was my pig.'"

"That's a sorry man that'd say it was a pig."

"Who knows? Maybe it was. They found a pot-bellied pig in the front seat. Rick Mullins told me a few years later that he could have sworn the pig was drunk too, the way it smelled, but he'd be damned if he knew how you tested a pig for sobriety."

"No, I can't imagine how you'd pull that off," Jeptha said, shaking his head.

"Anyway, LouEllen took me in after that. I've been there ever since."

"She family?"

"No. Not blood anyway. She was my mom's best friend from childhood."

"Was your mom like that?"

Lucy's eyebrows went way up. He'd always loved how expressive her face was, and he saw now it was because of her eyebrows. They were like delicate worms, arching and dancing and wiggling off the line of her forehead. "Like LouEllen? Oh God, no. LouEllen is a power unto herself. She's big, and warm, and full-throttled. My mom was quiet. Reserved. Cold, even."

"Cold as a mom?"

"Sometimes," she said. Jeptha waited to see if she'd say more. "I remember my mom used to hang up the phone sometimes with LouEllen and say, 'She's like a steamroller coming at you.'"

"She about run over me tonight."

"Just about," Lucy said, grinning at him. "She's a lot. But she's got a good heart. And everything she does is so full of love and worry. My mom loved me, I know that. But it was never like LouEllen's love. But now I don't know what to do."

"What do you mean?"

"You saw that baby's room, and she wants to come to the doctor's appointments. It's like she thinks this is her baby. And I need her, don't get me wrong. But I want to do all that stuff, you know?"

Jeptha nodded. He hadn't even known that was an option, coming to doctor's appointments, but he felt a pang of desire to be there himself.

"Besides, I think she is partly doing all this because she's worried I'm going to make a mistake."

"What kind of mistake—oh," Jeptha said. He heard Cody's and Bobby's disbelief echoing in his ears and felt the ring box scratch through his shirt. "It's me, right? I'm the mistake?"

She nodded, her eyes on the floor.

"Do you think that too?"

She looked him in the eyes. "I'm sitting here, aren't I?"

"True."

Jeptha stared straight ahead, his jaw clenched. Here he was getting ready to ask her to marry him, and she still regarded him as a mistake she'd made one drunken night. He couldn't even blame her. He'd knocked her up and fucked up the first date. It wasn't like he was starting from such a great place.

He wished he had the words to convince her that he was worth the risk, that she could hold on to him. But he didn't. Besides, he wasn't sure it was even true. He knew that when he was with her, he wanted to be worth it. But could he be a man she could count on? He'd never been before.

His throat tightened up as he looked at the mountains around him. The sun was setting off to his left, lighting up the fawn-colored hay and the barns, especially the unpainted ones, with a rose-gold hue, as if God himself had painted the scene. Jeptha had driven up here in exactly this light before, when he brought his mother up to watch him play at Carter's the first (and only) time. His dad scoffed at the whole thing when Jeptha asked his mom if she'd come, but his mom, for once in her life, shushed him and said she'd love to go. Said she was sorry Meemaw wasn't here to see it. The day of the show, Jeptha had found a new shirt laid out in his bed—the sky-blue plaid that matched his eyes with mother-of-pearl buttons. It was his one good shirt, the one he was wearing tonight for his date with Lucy, and had worn on their first failed date. He looked down at the buttons, thinking of his mother picking it out for him all those years ago. She'd been so proud of him, smiling the whole time she watched him play. He'd been playing backup, nothing special, but she'd acted like he had hung the moon. He knew that his mother loved him, in her way, but he'd never felt like he was anything special in her eyes until that moment.

After the show, she'd wisped her way over to him, the cancer they didn't yet know about already stealing away all the solid parts of her. She'd hugged him tight around his middle, her tiny arms strong for their size. He couldn't remember the last time she'd hugged him. She leaned back and put her hands on his face.

"God gave you a gift, Jeptha. Now, He mixed it up with all kinds of sin too, but He put that gift in there. Don't you forget it, neither. It's something special."

It was a moment that Jeptha would never forget. Looking over at Lucy, he saw how the light played off her nose and lit her face with the same warm glow as the rest of the valley. His love came jumbled up with all kinds of sin, and only he could say which was going to win out. It was up to him. In that moment, he knew what he wanted: to be something special for her, to be the kind of man she and the baby needed.

Jeptha stopped the car on the side of the road. They were a few hundred feet away from the parking lot for the Fold, but he didn't think he could make it any longer.

"Would you mind if we parked a little closer?" Lucy asked. He didn't say anything, just came around to her side of the car and helped her out. He guided her over the biggest ankle-twisters and down to the fence. His heart was beating so loud he was surprised cars weren't stopping to wonder at the sound.

"What are we doing here, Jeptha?" Lucy asked.

He bit his lip. He could barely speak, he was so full of love for her and determination to be the man his mom had seen that night.

"Jeptha?"

He took a deep breath and dove in.

"I know this ain't the way it's supposed to go," he said, fishing the ring box out of his pocket and holding it out to her. He ignored her gasp. "And I, um, I know who I am. I know you and LouEllen and Cody and Bobby and well, everybody else in this town, think I'm the kind of mistake a girl should run away from as fast as she can. And I can't give you nothing like what LouEllen did with that baby room. Hell, my trailer don't have but one bedroom, so I can't even give you a baby room. But I do love you. And have for half my life. And I want to be the man that you and that baby need. That's got to count for something. And I was hoping that you might, well, learn to love me too. Or at least be willing to be my wife."

The sound of the cicadas swelled suddenly around them in the cool night air, so loud they left a faint vibration in Jeptha's chest, exactly in rhythm with his heart. Say yes. Say yes. Say yes. He could hear his hopes in their tempo. Then, with one last full-throated drone, they stopped. A hushed quiet descended as Jeptha waited. The silence went on and on and on.

"No," Lucy said.

Jeptha's heart broke. His throat parched.

12

"**N**OT YET," WAS WHAT Lucy had meant to say on that night three months ago when Jeptha asked her to marry him. But no had come out first. Her heart felt like it would fly up and out of her chest, like one of those sparrows from Walmart blindingly in search of the sun. Jeptha's lips were a tight, bloodless line, his eyes drooped down like he'd had a stroke, and his tan skin was gray. There had never been a sadder man in all of human history. Staring at his face, she was shocked to realize that the answer wasn't a flat no, even if that's what had come out of her mouth. In the silence that followed that one devastating word, a whispery flutter bumped within her belly like she was a fish bowl and the occupant inside had flitted a tiny fin against the side of her. It was the first nudge of the baby inside her, her first physical sense that the thing that had started all this trouble might actually be worth it.

"Not yet," she'd told Jeptha then, grabbing his hand and pulling him up. "My answer isn't no. It's just not yes. Not yet, anyway. Everything is different. The baby. Me. You are different than I expected. I don't know yet."

And she'd kept on not knowing, even as they'd spent more and more time together. She'd called him the next day, to talk, and hung up the phone smiling after twenty minutes. He'd brought her to dinner at Cody and Marla's a few nights later, and she'd spent the whole night laughing. Cody and Jeptha together were like a comedy show—she just had to lean back and let the act wash over her. Since then, they'd done something every couple days. LouEllen never let her forget how much she hated it, but with every kick of the baby, Lucy's resolve strengthened. This was Jeptha's son, she reminded herself. Why shouldn't she know him? Why shouldn't she give them a chance to be a family of some sort?

LOUELLEN POKED HER head in through Lucy's half-open door early on Thanksgiving Day.

"What are you doing?" she asked.

"Getting ready. Deanna asked if I'd come over and help out some before everyone got there."

"Got where?"

"The Taylors' place," Lucy said. "For Thanksgiving."

"I thought you were joking about that. I was about to get the turkey going."

"Haha," Lucy said, thinking LouEllen was the one who was joking. But when she looked up, she saw LouEllen's face was deadly serious.

"I told you, LouEllen. We're doing Thanksgiving with Jeptha's family."

"We?"

"Me and Jeptha. And you. You're invited. I told you that."

"You're really going there? What about me? We've done Thanksgiving together every year of your life."

"And we can this year too. I thought you were coming. I need the support. Lord knows, Deanna hasn't gotten any nicer 'cause I've gotten bigger," Lucy said, trying for a joke to lighten the mood. Besides, Lucy really did want somebody else there with her, someone besides Marla, who had turned out to be a sweet and funny woman, prone to painfully accurate under-her-breath imitations, mostly of her husband. But if Deanna was around, she turned into something else entirely—that same scared, cowed girl that Lucy remembered from when they were kids.

"No. I don't think I will. And I don't think you should either," LouEllen said.

"I'm sure you don't, LouEllen, but I am going. And I wish you'd come with me."

"That's the way of it then, huh?"

"The way of what?" Lucy asked.

"The way this is all gonna go between us going forward," LouEllen said, pulling herself upright and taking a deep breath in. Her nostrils flared with purpose.

"If you mean me making my own decisions—yeah, that's the way of it," Lucy said, facing LouEllen head on. "That doesn't have to be a bad thing, you know."

"I wouldn't care about you making your own decisions if you'd make the right ones."

Lucy laughed, even though nothing was funny. "The right ones according to you, though. No one else's opinion really counts."

"I am right on this one, Lucy. He is going to break you. Your heart, your spirit, something. You don't take a chance on a Taylor. Like it says in Jeremiah, a leopard can't change its spots."

Lucy shook her head in amazement at LouEllen. If it wasn't her life, it would have been funny. LouEllen was as much leopard as Jeptha. She was quick to judge, a rash decision-maker, and could hold a grudge for a lifetime. There would be no changing her mind. Lucy went to the kitchen and picked up her purse and the pecan pie she'd made last night.

"I'm going, LouEllen. I wish you'd come with me. I'll miss you."

"Doesn't seem much like it. Your parents would be so disappointed right now."

Lucy turned back to look at LouEllen, tears flooding her eyes. It was as if one foundation was crumbling beneath her while another one was being built beside it. Standing there, with the baby depending on her, she wasn't a hundred percent sure which was the most stable, but she'd be damned if she'd go down with the one that was falling apart.

"Well, good thing they aren't here then," Lucy said, and slammed the front door behind her.

———

"LOUELLEN COULDN'T MAKE it?" Jeptha asked, looking behind Lucy, as if LouEllen, either in spirit or in bulk, could ever have hidden behind someone.

"No," Lucy said, staring down at the wood floor of the porch. "Said she wasn't feeling good."

"You mean she hates me and doesn't want to look at my face? That kind of not feeling good?"

"That's the one," Lucy said, laughing.

"Hope it's not contagious," Jeptha said, opening up the door.

"Believe me, if it was, I'd have caught it by now."

"Well, come on in. Deanna's already yelling at anybody in ear shot, so you may as well come get yours."

Lucy made a face at Jeptha. "Do I have to?"

"She knows you're here now. It'll be worse if you wait. Besides, I think she mostly needs some help. If you don't mind."

"Why aren't you helping?"

"I ain't getting stuck in the kitchen," Jeptha said. Lucy cocked her eyebrow up at him. He rushed on, "Not that there's anything wrong with the kitchen, or a man can't be in there. Just I, Jeptha Taylor, ain't no good in there."

Lucy rolled her eyes and thrust the pie toward him. "Carry this, will you? I'll go help."

Jeptha smiled and kissed her on the cheek.

DEANNA BEHAVED ALMOST like a human being the entire day. Even Marla seemed surprised. Lucy felt sorry for her—she looked like a dog who got beat every day who couldn't understand why today's beating hadn't arrived. She cowered every time Deanna opened her mouth, but gradually relaxed as each sentence passed without any comments on her.

When Lucy got up to clear the table, Jeptha quickly stood to help.

"What are you doing?" Deanna asked Jeptha, poison in her voice.

"Helping."

"Well, that's a first."

Lucy walked to the kitchen, but not before she saw Jeptha narrow his eyes at his sister and whisper, "Shut up."

"Sorry," Jeptha said when he came in behind her.

"For what? It's been fun."

"Deanna."

"She's been pretty good so far. For her," Lucy said as she scraped off the plates.

"For her," Jeptha agreed, taking the plates she handed him and stacking them in the sink.

"Poor Marla. She looks like a beat dog."

"She's probably feeling pretty good about today actually," Jeptha said, as he stacked the last plate on top. "Deanna won't make it through the whole day, though. She always loses it at some point."

Lucy grabbed the pie she'd made. "Think it's time to bring these out?"

she asked Jeptha, nodding at the pie that Marla had brought. "Maybe some sugar will keep Deanna sweet?"

"It ain't never worked before, but sure, let's give it a shot," he said and followed her back into the dining room with the other pie.

"Well, Lucy, I don't know what you did to my brother to get him to be so sweet today, but it sure is nice," Deanna said.

"Stop it, Deanna," Jeptha whispered.

"Jeptha, given the size of that belly, I'm pretty sure you've already made your impression on Lucy."

No one spoke for a moment.

"Actually, Jeptha's always been pretty sweet to me," Lucy said. "Must be 'cause I've been pretty nice to him."

"Nice is one way of putting it," Deanna said, her eyes narrowed.

Lucy shook her head, feeling her heart rate pick up a bit. "Deanna, if you're trying to make a point about how me and Jeptha had *sex* and that's how I got *pregnant*, I think you can come right out and say it. I think even Bobby over there is acquainted with the concept. And I know you are."

Everyone at the table busted out laughing, even Deanna's husband. Lucy put the pie down on the table and sat down. She'd promised herself she would keep her mouth shut today, but here she was, mouthing off to Deanna, giving her the kind of ammunition she loved.

"So, Lucy, how *are* you and Jeptha going to pay for this baby?" Deanna said, primly putting the tiniest bite of pecan pie in her mouth before making a face and putting her fork down.

Lucy looked over at Jeptha, whose face was bright red.

"Same way everyone does, I guess. With jobs."

"Surely, you can't keep on working two jobs. And who on earth is going to take care of that baby while you're at work? I've seen Jeptha with kids, and I can't say I'd recommend him as a babysitter."

"Deanna, stop," Jeptha said. "We'll figure it out."

"How? It's not like y'all are living together. Or even married. Oh, sorry, that's a soft spot, isn't it? I forgot you turned my brother down."

"I . . . I . . ." Lucy stopped. She didn't know what to say. These were the very same questions she'd been asking herself. She didn't want to have this conversation with Deanna, though. Lucy looked up at Deanna then and saw that her eyes were narrowed and she had a smug, mean smile on her face. She felt sorry for Jeptha, having such a bitch for a sister.

"I don't know, Deanna. You offering to watch him?"

"Lord, no," Deanna said, her face curdled with disgust. "Babies is the worst."

Everyone was silent for a moment, listening to Deanna's kids fight over the TV with Marla's kids.

"I'm just saying, it's not like Jeptha can support you. He barely makes anything . . ."

"I make as much as Bobby," Jeptha protested.

Bobby, who had taken a sip of water, started coughing. Jeptha stared at him.

"Right, Bobby?" he asked.

Bobby kept coughing until finally he was able to take a deep breath. His face was bright red. "Yeah, that's it."

"But Bobby don't got nothing to do with his money. No baby. And Kayla don't seem to be aiming for marriage, does she, Bobby?"

"Hell if I know. 'Sides, we aren't talking about me and Kayla," he said.

"True," Deanna said. "Well, I'm sure you will figure it out somehow, Lucy."

"You mean, me *and* Jeptha will figure it out. It's not just me," Lucy said. Jeptha took her hand then, and Lucy had never been gladder for it.

"Sure. You keep telling yourself that," Deanna said, laughing as she walked her still-full plate into the kitchen.

"I'm sorry," Jeptha leaned over and whispered to her. "Ignore her."

"I know. I will," Lucy said, trying to ignore Deanna and the pit in her stomach.

"Well, now that Deanna's come at everybody like a hurricane, how about some football?" Cody said, standing up and rubbing his belly. "Lucy, that pecan pie was delicious. I think I'll take another piece with me for the game."

He picked up the pie tin and eyed the remaining half. "Aw hell, I think I'll just take the whole thing actually. Y'all coming? Bring a fork."

———

IN THE PAST, Lucy would have spent the next day with LouEllen talking through the whole exchange with Deanna. But not now. There wasn't an ounce of Christmas spirit in LouEllen after that Thanksgiving. She communicated with Lucy primarily through glares, and the next time Jeptha came to pick Lucy up, LouEllen had ignored him entirely. Lucy told him to stay in his car in the future and she'd come out when she was ready. Lucy knew it was the right call when Jeptha didn't even try to argue the point.

Lucy didn't know what to say to LouEllen. It was like they had just moved in together all over again, except instead of nerves, this time it was sheer anger that kept them from speaking. On the few occasions when Lucy had wandered into the living room to watch TV with her, LouEllen had waited until Lucy had gotten all settled in and then pointedly walked out of the room.

"Fine," Lucy called out each time and changed the channel. They were both behaving like two-year-olds, but Lucy didn't care. She was never going to change LouEllen's mind, and LouEllen's angry silence wasn't going to change hers.

Two weeks before Christmas, Lucy finally dragged out the Christmas decorations, including the fake pine tree. She'd always hated that tree. It was so mechanical and antiseptic to put a tree together rather than put one up like she had with her mom and dad. But LouEllen was dead set against a real tree, and not even a grieving thirteen-year-old who wanted some piece of her old traditions had swayed her. Lucy had stopped asking.

"What are you doing?" LouEllen asked as she watched Lucy drag out the box.

"Getting out the Christmas stuff."

"Why? You aren't ever here to see it."

"LouEllen," Lucy said, staring at her. "We do it every year. Don't you want to put this up with me? I thought we could spend some time together."

"I'm sure Jeptha will come on over any minute to ruin it."

"He's not coming."

"Well, I don't care. I don't want any of it this year."

Lucy straightened up from where she was sorting through the fake garland and red plastic balls. "Are you serious?"

"As a heart attack. I'm not doing Christmas this year. Not in my house. Not with you."

Lucy dragged the box back to the closet without a word. Her chest was rigid with fury. Lucy knew it was bad between her and LouEllen, but she hadn't realized it was this bad. She sat on her bed and stared at her wall in mute anger for five minutes until her hand hurt. Looking down, she realized she was squeezing a snow globe she'd pulled out of the box. She shook it gently and held it up to watch the snow fall softly against the faces of Mary and Joseph staring down at baby Jesus. Lucy was fairly sure there hadn't been snow at the birth of Jesus, but she had never cared—it was the stocking present LouEllen had given her the first year she moved in. Tears filled Lucy's eyes as she sat on the bed, like they had seven years ago when LouEllen had given it to her.

"They are a family," LouEllen had said gently. "Trouble after trouble, but they found a home wherever they could and made a family. I thought it was a good reminder of your mom and dad, but also what we can be, if you'll let me."

Lucy gave the snow globe another half-hearted shake. Some family. She'd thought she and LouEllen would be okay, that they could weather any storm, but she wasn't sure about this one. Some part of her didn't even want to try.

Her phone pinged in her back pocket. She set the snow globe down on the bedside table and dug it out to see Jeptha's name.

"Free? Wanna get a tree for the trailer?"

Lucy could see LouEllen sitting stock-still on the couch, her mouth set in a hard line.

"Yes," she wrote back. "Please yes."

"THAT ONE," LUCY said, pointing to the tree, as tall as herself and perfectly shaped. But when they turned it around, there was a ragged lump sticking out from the back like the tree trimmer had walked away from his job and forgotten to come back. Lucy didn't care. Misshapen or not, this was their tree. Jeptha lugged it to the car and up to the trailer on his back, where it left a sticky trail of resin on his jacket that would likely remain for months afterward. He set it down with a grunt into the stand that Lucy had already filled with water. When she tried to drag her belly onto the ground to put more water in, Jeptha had laughed, taken the pitcher from her, and hauled her back up onto her feet.

"You look like a beached whale," he said. "A beautiful beached whale, but one that definitely ain't supposed to be down that far. Why don't you get the lights out? I'll finish that."

She waddled over to the boxes of lights, the baby's weight swaying her body from side to side. Her feet and hips had naturally turned out in the last month, making room, she guessed, for how much more was to come. She collapsed onto the couch with a sigh of exhaustion.

"We can finish tomorrow," he said. "If you're tired."

She shook her head. "No. I want to see it with the lights on tonight."

"Yes, ma'am," he said, with a salute that made her laugh. "Hand me that first string and I'll get going."

He plugged the string in. Warm, soft light filled the room.

"Do you mind if I turn out the big lights?" she asked.

"Nope. Makes it easier."

The trailer looked more beautiful than it ever had. Lucy turned on a Dolly Parton Christmas album she'd been listening to nonstop, like every Christmas, and sat back on the couch. She watched Jeptha in the semi-darkness, as he stretched up to the top of the tree. He curled the first end around the top, nestling some pieces deep into the branches and some out closer to the edge. Every few turns, he'd step back from the tree, examine the lights, and fine-tune the arrangement. With each string she handed him, the tree grew brighter and more beautiful. After a bit, she pulled out the boxes of red and gold balls they'd bought earlier that day, five dollars for a dozen, and attached the wire hangers. She hung them on the parts of the tree he'd finished putting lights on, smiling at him as they crossed paths. When every branch held as much as it possibly could, she stood back to admire it all. Jeptha joined her.

"Never had a tree in here before," he said. "How's it look?"

"Beautiful," Lucy said as her eyes filled with tears. "Why'd you do this?"

"Do what? The tree? Just thought it'd be nice. And I remember you saying you don't never get a real one anymore. Thought we could do that, maybe start a new tradition. For us. For the baby."

"Like a family," Lucy said, under her breath.

"Exactly. Like a family."

Lucy smiled at Jeptha and then went back to staring at the tree. She thought of the Mary and Joseph figures in the snow globe. No matter where they were or how little they had, they were a family, bound together against the world. She wanted that, even if this wasn't the way she'd imagined she'd get it. She looked over at Jeptha. His eyes were lit up by the lights of the tree, and he had a look on his face she had never seen before, a smile of contentment.

"I will, you know," she said into the silence.

"Will what?"

"Marry you."

Jeptha spun around to look at her. "You will?"

She nodded, then broke into a smile. "I will."

Jeptha pulled her into a hug, a hunk of Christmas lights still in his hand. Her heart beat faster, and her nose twitched with sudden desire as Jeptha hugged her tighter and tighter until, finally, one of the little lights he was holding deep against her back broke with a tiny ping of shattered glass.

"Are you okay?" Jeptha asked, pulling her away from the shards of glass on the floor. "I'm sorry. I got so excited."

"Me too," she said, and kissed him. For a minute, she could tell he thought this was their usual kiss, sweet but staid. But staid wasn't what Lucy wanted in that moment.

"Oh," he said, stepping back a hair. "You want to . . ."

"Yes," she said, glad the lights were low enough to hide her red cheeks.

"It's okay? For the baby?"

"Yes," she said, reaching her arms up around his neck. "It's definitely okay."

She pushed him gently toward the couch as he pulled her shirt over her head, his roughened hands stroking her breasts, two sizes bigger now than they used to be. Lucy shivered. Jeptha smiled and did it again. Lucy peeled the elastic panel of her maternity jeans down over her belly and slid them down her legs.

"You are beautiful," Jeptha said, tracing a line with his finger from her collarbone down to her thigh.

"You must be blind," she whispered in his ear.

"Best view a blind man ever had."

"Why am I the only naked one here?" she asked. She unbuttoned his pants as he pulled his shirt off. Lucy drew in a sharp breath, enjoying the sight of him. She kissed him again, feeling her naked belly jutting between them but not caring. He sat down on the couch, pulling her down to him, her legs straddling him. Lucy was reminded of the only other time they'd had sex—like this, but in his car, both too drunk to remember what they were doing. This time, sober—and now committed—was another story entirely.

After, as they lay tangled up in each other on the couch, the soft, warm glow of the Christmas lights washed over her belly. They watched as the baby moved from side to side, Jeptha's hand on her belly feeling the kicks.

"Are you happy?" Jeptha asked her.

"I think so," Lucy said, not exactly sure what name to give the feeling that was warming her up inside. "I think that's what this is."

———

THE NEXT MORNING, when Lucy came home, still in her clothes from last night, it was to a house as quiet and tense as the valley before a thunderstorm burst through. The air looked almost yellow around LouEllen, who sat staring out the kitchen window, a cup of coffee cooling in front of her, her lips pressed together so tight they almost disappeared.

"You stayed over," she said.

"I did."

LouEllen toyed with the handle of her cup. "Y'all talk about getting married again?"

"We did." Lucy prayed to God quickly that LouEllen would stop right there, not ask the logical next question. When she'd said yes last night, she hadn't thought about how she'd tell LouEllen this morning.

LouEllen nodded slowly, her face pale. "You said yes this time, didn't you?"

Before a thunderstorm breaks over the mountains, there is a moment when the world is silent. Birds, insects, people. Every living creature knows what is coming and freezes in anticipation of the violence. LouEllen looked up at Lucy. They stared at each other for a good thirty seconds, neither of them wanting to hear the answer that was going to bring down the heavens.

"I did."

LouEllen's face split apart like a ripe peach. But just as quick, or so it seemed to Lucy, her expression was gone, cleared away in favor of hard granite.

"You can leave."

"What?"

"You can leave now. No, let me rephrase. I want you to leave."

A hole gaped in Lucy's stomach, pain she hadn't felt since her parents died. She'd somehow thought she was special, that LouEllen would never cut her out of her life. But here it was. Lucy had been right. You can't trust anybody. Nobody has your back, nobody but blood, and probably not even them. LouEllen had been saying for so long that she was family, but as soon as Lucy decided to go another way, to make a decision contrary to LouEllen's wishes, that family was gone.

Lucy's throat burned. Some piece of her wanted to argue with LouEllen and beg to stay until she married Jeptha. But the other part of her knew it was pointless. Besides, there was something comforting, after so many months of indecision and not knowing what she was doing with herself and her life, in being committed. If there had been any hesitation in her step this morning after saying yes to Jeptha, it was gone now. She was sewn into her decision. She swallowed down the lump in her throat.

"Now?" Lucy asked. "I don't have work."

"Seems as good a time as any," LouEllen said, without meeting her eye.

Lucy bent down to grab a few trash bags from under the sink. In her room, she tossed all of her clothes into the bags without folding or sorting them, knowing she'd regret it later but too angry to care. Then she grabbed all of the knick-knacks of her life—pictures of her with her parents; a ticket to Dollywood, where she'd ridden her first and only roller coaster ride before throwing up on her dad; a few books she'd saved from high school; her diploma; and the three stuffed animals she'd saved from her childhood. She had a vision of passing them on to the baby, but looking down at the small unicorn, its horn dirty from years of being chewed on, a ragged raccoon puppet, and a used-to-be-pink elephant tossed upon the debris of her life, they seemed like a terribly sad inheritance to pass on. And yet, so very appropriate, especially for a girl who could pack her whole life in twenty minutes. She left the snow globe she'd unearthed yesterday on her bedside table.

Lucy paused in the hallway, staring at the baby's room. There was nothing she wanted to take from there. It was all LouEllen's—except for the crib, which she'd have to come back for. She took three steps down the hall and stopped. The lion onesie. That was hers. That was something she could pass down to her child, something good.

"Be like this," she would say. "Be like this fierce little lion. Roar like this at the world."

Lucy grabbed it from the drawer in the room that would have been her baby's. It was as beautiful as ever, but even less about Lucy than it had been the day LouEllen revealed it. Lucy took a deep breath and put her hand on her belly.

"We're gonna be all right," she said to the baby.

She shut the bedroom door behind her, picked up her trash bags, and walked out of the house.

———

LUCY AND JEPTHA married on a stark, gray Sunday in January. The trees were stripped bare, the sky was flinty with clouds, and a mean wind cut through the valleys. No bridal magazine would have picked it for a wedding, Lucy thought as she stared at the sky through the window at the back of her church's sanctuary. She shivered as she watched the branches rub against each other like spindly, decrepit old aunts leaned up against each other for support. She heard a quiet buzz from inside the church and moved to look through the doors into the hall. Lucy counted ten people in the pews: Deanna, Big Jim, Cody, Marla, Bobby and his girlfriend, Kayla, Judy, and, off to the side of Judy, Delnor Gilliam. Lucy couldn't believe he'd shown up, but then, about everyone he knew in the world was inside the church at the moment. She smiled as she imagined him telling her, in all seriousness, "I didn't have nowheres else to be." She saw the minister come out then and take his place up front. Jeptha followed behind. He was twisting the knot on the tie he'd borrowed from Cody like it hurt him and stopped only when he realized that everyone in the pews was staring at him. He smiled weakly at the small crowd there, his eyes wide. Then he looked to the back doors.

Lucy's breath went wild, and her eyes widened with the same fear she saw on Jeptha's face. She ducked so Jeptha couldn't see her. She needed air. She burst through the doors of the church so hard they slammed behind her and ran to her car. Leaning her arms on the trunk, her breath only grew shallower as tears flooded her eyes. She felt so alone. She hadn't spoken to LouEllen since the day she kicked her out, but she missed her now with a physical intensity. She wanted one of her hugs. Lucy heard a car slow down on the highway and looked up, every cell in her body hoping it was LouEllen. But the car drove on slowly, the man and woman inside staring at her until they drove over the hill. Lucy realized what a sight she must be, wearing the long white dress she'd bought for this, her belly grazing the trunk of the car, tears streaming down her face.

She closed her eyes for a moment, feeling the cold wind blow right through her dress. She breathed in deeply and blew out through her mouth, remembering the tricks that had helped her stop crying in the middle of class after her parents died. She'd gotten through that. She could get through this.

She thought of the night with the Christmas lights, remembering how full of certainty she had been. This was the right choice. She would walk back into the church, marry Jeptha, and give her baby a father. They would build a life and a family together. She didn't need LouEllen to do that. This was her family now.

The baby kicked then, his foot digging deep against the side of her belly, so hard she could see a little ridge in her dress. "Shh," she said to him, rubbing the hard spot. "It's okay. We will be okay, you and me." After a minute, the baby shifted inside her, and his foot pulled away from her side to parts unknown. Following his lead, she walked back into the church to get married.

— 13 —

JEPTHA WASN'T SURE THERE had been a happier day in his life than his wedding. He spent much of it pinching himself, sure there was no way it could be true. But Lucy had walked down the aisle, her white dress falling gently over her belly. She wore an expression he had never seen: her lips curved up in a small smile that trembled on and off, her eyebrows pinched together slightly. Like a doe with a new fawn, she looked both older and younger, tougher and more vulnerable than ever. Jeptha felt a sudden hunger for her. Not sexual, just all-consuming. He had to stop himself from rushing down the aisle and hustling her into his car. Instead, he gripped his wrist with the other hand and squeezed until it hurt while smiling so big his cheeks hurt for two days after.

Lucy held out her hand. His palm was sweating like he'd just washed it, so he wiped it on his dress pants before he took hers. A few people in the congregation laughed, but he didn't care. He held on tight. He saw Lucy glance behind her for one brief minute, and his heart stopped. But then she squeezed his hand tighter and nodded at the preacher to start. The man said things, Jeptha knew, because they were married at the end, but all Jeptha heard was a drone like Charlie Brown's teacher. He couldn't stop smiling at Lucy, stunned that he'd somehow found himself here in front of her. She was the most beautiful girl he'd ever seen, and she was marrying him. The preacher had to ask him twice if he wanted to marry Lucy. "Yes," he finally said, never taking his eyes off her. "I mean, I do." It was a testament to how shocked he was to be in this moment that he hadn't even blushed when Deanna had whispered loudly, "About right, him not listening at his own wedding."

He paid attention when the preacher asked Lucy the question, though. He was terrified she'd say no. He watched her as she looked at the preacher, listening to his words, nodding along. He saw her swallow hard before she answered. She looked at Jeptha and then out into the crowd. Afterward, everyone in town joked with him about how she was thinking of pulling a runner, but Jeptha knew it was LouEllen she was searching for. She turned back to Jeptha and gave him a smile before she said, "I do."

Of course, LouEllen never showed. Not to the ceremony. Or the reception, such as it was. Just punch and cookies in the basement with a few baby gifts sprinkled in. Jeptha hated her for hurting Lucy that way. But as the weeks stretched on and he had Lucy all to himself, he loved her a little for leaving him as the only family Lucy had.

THERE WAS A simple joy in being sober and living the kind of life with Lucy that he imagined everyone else did. He was so caught up in it that he didn't even miss drinking that much. Trying to be a better man for her and the baby seemed like the least he could do. The easiest way for him to be a better man was to stop drinking.

Instead, he woke up with Lucy at 6:00 a.m. and made coffee—half regular and half decaf—and got out the cereal stuff while Lucy showered. They ate together, talking about their days and the baby before Lucy left for work. While she was gone at work, Jeptha spent his days cleaning out the trailer to make room for all the baby stuff Lucy insisted they needed. They both knew that the pitiful corner of the living room they'd assigned to the baby was a sad cousin to the room that LouEllen had all done up in her house. But Lucy never said anything, so neither did Jeptha. There was no way he could get his trailer looking as nice as that, but he was determined to try. Remembering that Lucy had once said she wanted a bright turquoise room, Jeptha set to making it happen for her.

Standing in the paint aisle at Walmart, he called her. She was only about three hundred feet away from him, manning her checkout lane, but he wanted the paint to be a surprise.

"What's your favorite color blue again?" he asked.

"Jeptha, I'm working. Teresa's gonna kill me if she sees me on the phone."

"I know! But just quick, when you say turquoise, do you mean like that pale robin's egg color or bright turquoise like the sky in summer before sunset?"

"The sky in summer before sunset. Bright."

"Thank you kindly!" Jeptha said and hung up. He hauled two cans of flat paint up to the mixing station and, handing the paint chip he'd picked to the kid manning it, told him, "This one, bright as you can make it."

He grabbed a brush, some tape, and a roller, determined to do this right. He checked out at the aisle farthest from Lucy and ran out the door before she could see him. Back at the trailer, he taped around the windows and the floor and moved all the baby stuff they'd shoved into a corner into the bedroom. He slapped up one coat. While he waited for it to dry, he assembled the crib he'd picked up at LouEllen's house a week back, where he'd wilted under her hard gaze the whole time he took it apart and hauled it out. When the first coat was only a little tacky, he did the second, grateful that today was a long day for Lucy. This was Jeptha's first home improvement project on his own home, and it was taking longer than he'd thought it would. Finally done, he sat on the couch and surveyed the room, thinking how good it looked and how nice a beer would taste.

Fingers fluttering, he pushed all the furniture back where it belonged and brought the crib over. He set it in the corner between the armchair and the couch. They'd have to lean over the arms of both pieces of furniture to get the baby out, but it was the only spot for it. He found the bag of baby stuff that Lucy had bought and put a bright yellow cover on the changing pad. He laid it down on the kitchen table beside a basket she'd assembled full of diapers and wipes and such a vast variety of ointments that Jeptha wasn't sure if they were having a baby or prepping for surgery. It seemed unsanitary to have poopy diapers on top of the table where they ate, but it was the only flat surface, and they'd both agreed it would have to do. Then Jeptha assembled the swing Lucy had bought. It was a no-go. The damn thing took up six feet of real estate, a fact that Jeptha didn't realize until after he'd pinched his finger three times setting it up. They'd have to settle for the bouncy seat that Lucy had mentioned. It would fit under the kitchen table.

Exhausted, Jeptha finally sat on the couch. The idea of a beer flickered briefly in his mind, but he pushed it away and turned on the TV, watching *The Day After Tomorrow* for the eight hundredth time until he nodded off.

"Jeptha," he heard from beside him on the couch. "Jeptha."

He opened his eyes. Lucy was staring at the room, smiling.

"You like it?" he asked.

"It's perfect."

"You're not just saying that?"

"No," she said, holding his hand. "It's perfect. I got to pick everything out and you did the hard part."

He laughed. "Well, I've got to take that swing down. You can help with that."

"Yeah, that ain't trailer-sized," she said, looking over to where it took up their whole kitchen floor. "I about killed myself getting past it. I'll take it back tomorrow. Get that bouncy chair."

"I measured. It'll fit under the table."

Lucy squeezed his hand and leaned back against him. "I love this movie," she said, tucking her legs up under her and spreading the blanket over them both. He put his arm around her and held her to him, thinking he'd be okay if he could spend the rest of his life right there.

BUT AS THE days passed, costs added up, Lucy's exhaustion grew, and Jeptha got more and more stressed. Never more than when he thought about how little money they had and how much more they would need once the baby actually arrived. The tobacco was all in and sold, so there was nothing to do but wait for the check from Bobby, who'd been dropping hints about it not being as much as he'd hoped. Jeptha couldn't figure that—they'd grown more and lost none of it this year. But Bobby kept insisting costs were up and prices were low, quoting Jeptha this number and that number. Jeptha had never had a head for figures and eventually stopped asking, accepting that he'd get what he'd get and there wasn't much to do about it.

He'd called around to see if anyone was doing any construction work that he could get on, but the projects were all shut down for the winter. He had gotten a couple days of work helping Dick Slocum frame out an addition for him and Ethel's grandkids to stay in when they came to visit, but the last day of work had been tacking up heavy plastic sheeting to keep the winter out for the next few months. They wouldn't start up again until after the baby was due. Jeptha grew desperate—he'd never minded being out of work and having just enough to get by, but now the look on Lucy's lined, exhausted face and the oncoming train of baby expenses made him bow to pressures he'd heard about but never understood.

He spent three days eyeing his dad's old suit in his closet, hating the man and everything that had touched his abusive, drunk, cheating body, but finally one cold morning, he manned up and got dressed. When he came out of the bedroom, awkwardly adjusting the shirt collar where it scratched against his neck, all the weariness on Lucy's face lifted. The old Lucy—the light, happy child he first remembered from church when he was a boy himself—surfaced.

"You're going to an interview?" she said, her voice full of as much hope as he'd ever heard.

"Gonna try," he replied, and kissed her hair, loving the soft, purply scent of her shampoo. He walked out the door that day, feeling like a Taylor who might make something of himself. Then he came back in to grab the job ads he'd forgotten.

The look on Lucy's face sustained him through the drive to town and down through the ammunition plant's gates. Parking his car, he began to imagine commuting down here every day, getting a paycheck, being the kind of steady man that Lucy could depend on. He walked through the doors to the receptionist, paper in hand.

"I come about the job y'all got, ma'am," he said.

She was all done up and looked him up and down like he was her equal. The suit, he thought.

"Wonderful. Which one?"

"Um, the open one?" he said, unaware there was more than one.

"Okay, please go down this hall and to the second door on the left. They are interviewing candidates. Oh, and fill this out," she said, handing him an application form.

Jeptha looked down at it. It was double-sided, covered on both sides with boxes asking about work experience. He made his way slowly to the room, reading it as he went. It was nice of them to give him a pen, but he wasn't sure what he'd need it for. He could fill out his name, of course, and he was fairly sure he remembered his social, but the work boxes were a mystery to him. Tobacco grower, he guessed he could put down, but for dates? He'd been doing it all his life—could he put that? And construction, well, it was odd jobs here and there. How did he put each of those into dates?

By the time the HR lady stuck her head through the door and called his name, Jeptha had sweated through his undershirt and his button-down and was working his way through the already rank fabric of his father's uncleaned suit. He thought he'd been nervous at his wedding, but that was nothing.

He shook the woman's hand, not catching her name because he was too caught up in her perfect hair and red lacquered nails, cut short and professional, and sat at the chair across the desk from her.

"Now . . ." she said, looking down at the paper, "Jeptha. You have worked construction."

"Yes, ma'am."

She was silent. Jeptha was silent.

"What kind?" she finally asked.

"All kinds, really, ma'am. Framing, painting, roofing. You name it, I've done it."

"With a company? I don't see one listed."

"No, ma'am. On my own, as they needed me. Nothing full time," Jeptha said. That didn't seem to be the right answer, given the pursed lips and throat-clearing that followed.

"And your farm?"

"The sin crop."

"Excuse me?"

"Tobacco, ma'am. Sorry, that's just what we call it. On account of them saying it ain't good for you." Jeptha wiped his soaking palms on the suit pants, horrified to see visible sweat marks. He pressed his hands against them so the woman wouldn't see.

"I see," she said. "But no plant experience."

"No, ma'am. But I can handle equipment. All kinds. Been doing it all my life."

She sighed and removed her glasses. "Well, thank you, Mr. . . ." She glanced back down at the paper. "Taylor. Oh. From Allen County?"

"Yes," Jeptha said, slowly. That couldn't be good.

"Well, thank you for coming in," the woman said, stacking up her papers.

"That's it?" Jeptha asked, confused. Wasn't she going to tell him what the job was about, show him the plant floor?

"We'll be in touch," she said, standing up and motioning to the door.

He understood then. She was saying no but didn't want to dirty her pretty red nails with the actual word. He couldn't help himself. "So I ain't getting this job," he said.

"We'll be in touch," she said again.

A simple "no" would have been easier, he thought as he trudged back out the door. At least that word meant something. "We'll be in touch" was useless, a meaningless statement that would never be true. Jeptha was sure the devil would be shoveling snow in hell before he ever heard this woman's voice breathing down his phone line.

He flopped into his car. His fingers twitched—they were alive and nervous in a way that Jeptha recognized and hated. He ached for a drink, for the numbness that flowed through him, suddenly remembering the joys of alcohol. Then he saw a shirt of Lucy's, abandoned there on the passenger seat. He lifted it to his face—the grapey, earthy smell of her filled his nose. He picked up the paper, found the next job he'd circled, and pointed the car down the road.

———————

JEPTHA SPENT THE next two weeks trying for jobs. He left every morning, buoyed by the look on Lucy's face, and returned every night as beaten down as he'd ever been. He heard "no," or some version of it, more times than any man ever should. Against all odds, Lucy kept a sense of hope. Jeptha couldn't bear to be the one to bring spit-moistened fingers to that flame. Any hope he had had was worn down to nearly nothing by the end of the two weeks, and he was right back where he knew he belonged. There was no suit-wearing job at the end of the rainbow for him. Never would be. But Lucy still believed, so Jeptha forced himself on.

At breakfast one Thursday, Jeptha emerged in the suit, and there was no change in Lucy's face. Maybe she was just tired, he told himself, worn out from not sleeping at night.

"Good morning," he said.

She flashed him a tired smile and then looked back down at her cereal. "You all right?"

"Couldn't sleep last night," she said. "It's a long day today and tomorrow."

"I know you got Walmart and Judy's today, but what's tomorrow?"

Jeptha saw her take a deep breath, her nostrils flaring. He closed his eyes, trying to think what he'd said to piss her off.

"You don't remember," she said flatly.

"Remember what?" He was panicking. He had no idea what she was talking about. Her due date, he thought wildly. No, that was March 4th. They were still weeks away.

"Childbirth class. It's at six tomorrow night," she said, glaring at him.

He looked at her blankly. Then a vague memory came trickling into his head—her telling him to make sure he put a certain date in his calendar, at which point he'd thought, but hadn't said, *What calendar?* Looking at her face, he guessed he should have found one and put this date on it.

"Of course you don't know what I'm talking about," she said, sighing in a way that sounded more disappointed than angry. Jeptha recognized it because he'd heard it all his life, from everyone who had ever asked anything of him. She sounded like his mother, like his teachers, like she had the night he'd shown up so late at the Fold.

"If you can't remember childbirth class, I don't know why I've been hoping you might be able to get a job. What on earth was I thinking?" she asked, putting her head in her hands.

He wished she was angry still, wished that he was trying to counter that as opposed to this deflated, resigned Lucy.

"I've been trying," he said, his voice rising slightly. "Ain't nobody hiring right now." He knew that was a lie. They were hiring. They just weren't hiring him.

"Uh-huh," Lucy said. She clearly knew the truth too.

"What do you want me to do?" he asked.

Lucy shook her head, and he could see her eyes were glossing over with tears. "I don't know, Jeptha. Sometimes I just wish . . ."

He stared at her, feeling his nose prickle. For the first time, Jeptha didn't want to know everything in his wife's head, sure she was still regretting the night last summer that had gotten them to this place. His shoulders slumped forward, the last tiny smidgen of hope he'd been nursing slipping out of him as easily as a bar of wet soap off the bathtub's edge. She was right. They'd both been fooling themselves, playing house and hoping they could construct a real life out of foolish dreams, with no nod to the reality that surrounded them.

"You know what, sometimes I do too," Jeptha said. "But I can't. So why don't you text me that class info, and I'll be there tomorrow." Then he walked out the door.

———————

HOURS LATER, THREE rejections under his belt, he found himself parked in a chair on Cody's front porch as the weak winter sun set. "What are you doing here?" Cody asked as he came out on his porch with a sweating beer in his hand that Jeptha's eyes went straight to.

"Just drivin' around. Wound up here."

"It was weird enough seeing you in a suit on your wedding day. Why the hell are you wearing one today?" Cody asked, motioning Jeptha up on the porch with a lazy wave of his hand. He sat in one of the wicker rocking chairs and took a deep pull on his beer. Jeptha took a seat in the rocker beside him, where Marla usually sat.

"Job hunting."

"Worst kind of hunting there is," Cody said. "How'd it go?"

Jeptha poked his finger between the collar of his shirt and his roughened skin and pulled. On his wedding day, the suit had given him a sense of promise. Today, it scratched him all over and seemed to echo the word "no" with every step. His father's alcohol-infused sweat seemed to linger in its fibers.

"Ain't no one gonna give me a job. I wouldn't," Jeptha said. Today was nothing like his wedding day.

"Aw, shit, man. It ain't that bad, is it?"

"Tried over at the plant where you are, couldn't get past that red-taloned HR lady."

"Stephanie? She's the worst. Ain't got no idea what happens there once the carpet ends."

"Well, she was damn clear she didn't want me on any surface over there, carpeted or no."

"What about Wal—"

"Nope. Can't even get on there."

"Oh."

"Yeah."

"Well, that ain't been a problem before now."

"Before now, I didn't have a wife and a little boy on the way."

"What's Lucy say?"

"Not much. Just sighs."

"She working?"

"The bar three nights and Walmart forty hours. Looking for some cleaning jobs too."

"Ain't she about to have that baby any day?"

"Yep."

"Damn, man. You need a beer," Cody said, and heaved himself out of the chair. Jeptha didn't stop him.

"Here," Cody said, thrusting a can toward Jeptha. The cold, heavy beer felt right in his hand. He stared at it, the circle of the pop top the perfect size for his finger. He slipped his fingernail under it and flicked it up the smallest amount he could without opening it, over and over, listening to the tinny little rings it made. His mind was immersed in imagining the soul-pleasing sound of giving in—pop, thwack, fizz—and then tasting that first sip. His mouth watered and he bit his lip.

"So what are you going to do?" Cody asked.

"About what?" Jeptha said, still staring at the unopened can.

"Work."

"I ain't got a clue."

"You gonna drink that beer or stare at it?" Cody asked.

Jeptha took a deep breath and put it back on the table. "Nah. It's been five months. Don't wanna go back down that road."

Cody stared at him, a look of surprise on his face. After a minute, he said, "Why don't you come by the plant tomorrow with me? Shift starts at eight. I can introduce you to Tom, see if maybe they's a spot for you. He can hire people without having to go through Stephanie."

"Yeah?" Jeptha asked, his voice two octaves higher than it had been. "Man, that would be awesome. You sure?"

Cody glanced quickly at the unopened beer again and nodded. "Yeah. Come on."

Marla stuck her head out the screen door. "I'm putting on dinner. Jeptha, you staying?"

"Nah, I'm good. I got to get home." He smiled at Cody. "I got a job interview tomorrow."

"Damn right," Cody said.

"Good for you. Good luck," Marla said. "Say hey to Lucy for me." She looked at Cody's beer, and then up at her husband, one eyebrow raised. Then she went back into the house.

"Wish you *was* drinking. Now this one's gonna go to waste too," Cody said, putting the beer down on the table beside Jeptha's.

"Marla got you on a beer diet?"

"Something like that. Don't like me drinking too much. And not in front of the kids."

"Ouch."

"She got the idea from watching you, asshole. Said you was like a new man. Got her thinking she wanted one too."

"Sorry about that."

"Aw, don't be. I kind of like it, actually. Plus, I done lost ten pounds. And Marla likes that," Cody said, with a quick wink. He stepped into the house, and the screen door swung shut behind him.

Jeptha's eyes were on that half-empty beer, his fingers twitching beside his leg, desperate to grab the can and chug it down in one sip. What was half a beer? Nothing. He didn't need to open the other one, just keep Cody's from going to waste. It wasn't like it was falling off the wagon to have half of a beer. He took three steps toward the can, his hand already reaching out.

"Eight o'clock, Jeptha. I'll see you there, right?" Cody said from behind the screen, his eyes narrowed.

Jeptha jumped backward and shook his head. "Yeah, eight," he said and ran off the porch to his car.

IT WAS QUIET in the trailer that night. Jeptha and Lucy tiptoed around each other, polite but neither quite ready to make amends. Jeptha wanted to tell her about the interview but didn't want to jinx it. Besides, no matter what he did or what he looked at, all he saw was that beer can, drops of condensation dripping down its side. In bed, when Lucy scooted her butt toward him and he put his hand on her hip, he felt a cool, metal can in his grasp. When she rolled over to kiss him, apparently ready to apologize, if not in words, he tasted sparkling, hoppy beer instead of his wife. When she climbed on top of him, her long hair hanging down over her now-huge boobs, he had to force his eyes open because whenever he closed them, he saw not her body, but a can of beer, foam frothing out the top. After, he grabbed onto her waist and held her tightly until he fell asleep, afraid of what might happen if he let go.

—14—

WHEN JEPTHA LEFT THAT morning, dressed once again in his suit, Lucy was sure he wouldn't remember the childbirth class. He'd left as determined as she'd seen him in weeks, even whistling "Shady Grove" as he walked down the steps. The sex, she thought. She'd been willing to forgive him enough to have angry, pity sex with him, but not enough to remind him about the class before he left. It was as obvious as those rainbow-hued tests of the emergency broadcast system that used to come on TV. This was a test and one she dearly wanted him to pass. If he didn't, it wouldn't just be LouEllen's voice that echoed through her head, saying "I told you so." Jeptha was trying, she knew that, squaring his shoulders a little more every day to deal with the rejection he faced after every interview. If she hadn't been pregnant, she wouldn't have put so much hope on him. But then, she thought with a rueful laugh, if she hadn't been pregnant, she wouldn't have been here with him at all.

There had been good moments these last few months. He was sober, for one thing, which was a minor miracle. He'd put together all the stuff for the baby, never complaining when he pinched his fingers assembling a swing that he must have known would never fit in their trailer. He had stood with her in the baby aisle at Walmart, offering whatever opinions he had on diaper cream and nursing pillows, and hadn't even seemed annoyed by the process of it. He had worked hard to try to get a steady job. She would never have thought it would be the case, but there was a core of sweetness in Jeptha, especially when it came to her. Every instance of it surprised her. There were moments—at their wedding, when he had stared at her, open-mouthed with awe when she walked down the aisle; when she saw the bright blue living room he'd painted for her; when he brought her Krispy Kreme hot nows as a surprise—when she found herself liking him, maybe even loving him. In those moments, she was sure that not only could they could do this, but that they *were* doing it—they were a family. They could raise a kid, not perfectly, but with some amount of love that would be enough.

She'd held onto this notion so tightly that she'd allowed herself to hope when Jeptha came out in his dad's suit. He looked handsome, like he had at their wedding, and capable, even driven. But after a night of almost no sleep and with the baby due in a few weeks, Lucy had woken up without blinders on. He was never going to get one of these jobs he was going out for. She was an idiot for ever hoping.

Crystal Gayle's face appeared below Lucy's head on the table. Lucy smiled. The dog harrumphed deep in her throat, like she had been shouldering forever the frustration Lucy was feeling. She wagged her tail and nudged her nose under Lucy's leg.

"You think he'll ever change?" Lucy said to her, rubbing the Mohawk that sprung up between the dog's ears. Crystal Gayle woofed softly, a sound of hope. Poor thing, she'd been sticking it out on a hope and a prayer for much longer than Lucy had. She was a smart dog, though—Lucy hoped maybe she knew something that humans couldn't see.

"All right, girl. I'm gonna head to work. He said he'd see me at class, so let's hope so, huh?"

WHEN LUCY WALKED into the community room of the hospital that night, she was alone. Six happy couples, each with their own pillow, sat in a circle, all cuddled up with each other. She nearly fled in tears. But the instructor spotted her then and waved her over. She was an older woman, her graying brown hair cut in an unattractive bob, with a teddy bear embroidered on the roll of her turtleneck and breath that smelled of onions and uncleaned dentures. When Lucy came closer, the instructor adopted an expression like a sad gummy bear, her eyebrows smooshed together and the corners of her mouth pulled in and down, as if she were smiling and frowning at the same time. Lucy wanted to punch her in her pity-laden mouth.

"Forgot your pillow? On your own?" she said, her voice quiet and mousy, probably intended to be kind. Lucy fell into a pile beside her and sat in a static of anger, her hands clenched together so tightly her knuckles were white.

"My name is Phyllis, and we are here for childbirth class, to learn about childbirth and how you and your partner—" She stopped and looked over at Lucy. "Excuse me, how *you* can navigate your way through what is a beautiful, natural process that will bring your baby into this world."

Lucy stared at the floor to avoid the wall of pity that surrounded her. She squeezed her hands tighter.

"Can I help you?" Lucy heard Phyllis ask.

Lucy looked up, and there in the doorway was Jeptha, a pizza-stained pillow from the couch clutched under his arm. Lucy sighed audibly as tears of joy came to her eyes.

"He passed," she said under her breath as Jeptha strode across the room and sat beside her as the other dads had done.

"Oh! Welcome! Our last dad is here!" Phyllis said. She clapped her hands and beamed with joy—relieved, Lucy was sure, that she wouldn't have to spend her whole night having to change her lecture to accommodate the sad, single mother she thought Lucy was.

"Hi," Lucy whispered to Jeptha. "You came."

"Sorry I was late. I was at work."

"Work?"

"At the plant. Cody got me on. Full time."

Lucy leaned over and hugged Jeptha, not caring at all that the other couples were staring and Phyllis was bungling her lecture about the naturalness of childbirth. She kissed him on the cheek. "I'm so happy. And proud of you," she said.

Jeptha squeezed her hand. "Me too," he said. He nodded at Phyllis. "We supposed to be listening here?"

Lucy was so happy she barely heard any of the words Phyllis said for the rest of the night. First labor is a lot longer than you think. Try to breathe. Put your hand in this ice water and see how long you can stand it. She and Jeptha kept laughing at all the wrong moments until it was clear they were Phyllis's least favorite couple in class. Lucy didn't care. It was worth it.

––––––––––––

TWO WEEKS LATER, Lucy was uncomfortably aware of Judy's eyes on her lumbering, waddling form as she came through the door for her shift.

"How are you feeling?" Judy asked.

Lucy yawned. "That," she said, as she tucked her stuff under the counter. She tied her apron around her waist, grabbed a rag, and lifted up Delnor's beer to wipe under it. "Hey, Delnor," she said.

"There she is," he replied, his voice sleepy. "How's that baby doing?"

"Causing as much trouble as you, Delnor," she said, smiling at him.

"So raging against the machine."

"Pretty much. He's in there, kicking and swimming around, getting cooked. Making my belly hurt."

"Aren't you getting pretty close?" Judy asked.

"Five weeks or so," Lucy said. In the beginning, she'd been so excited when people asked when she was due. She had no idea how much she would come to hate that question.

"How's Jeptha? I don't see him in here anymore except for when he plays," Judy said.

"He's good. He got on at the plant a couple weeks ago, full time. He's liking it. Gets to work with Cody," Lucy said, cautiously. Lucy hadn't mentioned Jeptha's job to anyone, not wanting to jinx it, but now that he was a few weeks in, she felt more comfortable.

"What I've noticed is he don't hardly drink no more," Delnor said.

"I know," Lucy said. "He gave it up."

"Why'd he do a damn fool thing like that?"

"Don't know, Delnor," Lucy said with a laugh.

"Probably love. It'll make a man do crazy things," Delnor said.

"Will wonders never cease," Judy said, rolling her eyes at Lucy. "Delnor Gilliam, a romantic."

"Ain't nothing wrong with that. I got a heart in here somewheres," he said, pawing at the front of his shirt.

"Probably hard to find under all that alcohol," Judy said.

"Speaking of which . . ." Delnor trailed off pitifully, holding up his empty glass with a pleading expression on his face.

"Oh, fine. Just this once," Judy said and put a new beer in front of him.

"I might fall in love with you if you keep doing that," Delnor said to Judy.

"Keep talking and I'll take it back."

Hearing that, Delnor wrapped his beer in both hands, took a huge sip, and promptly spilled some down his chin and into his lap. Judy shook her head and threw a towel at him.

"So, Lucy. How're you feeling about work? You thinking about scaling back a bit?" Judy asked.

"I don't know. Can't go down at Walmart or I lose my insurance. And Jeptha just got on, and I don't have much longer to work before I'm gonna go out anyway."

"You know I don't tell people what to do . . ."

Delnor stared up at Judy and grumbled. She flicked her narrowed eyes at him and his beer. He stopped. "Unless they need it. And I'm not going to tell you. But Jeptha's full-time now. You're full-time now. You may want to think about resting a little."

"I'm fine," Lucy said, feeling anything but.

"Lucy. You had to lay down in the basement the other day because you were having such bad contractions. That floor is disgusting."

"I just needed a few minutes. I was fine."

"What does Jeptha say?"

"You think I need to obey my husband?"

"Don't insult me like that. I'm asking because he sees you at night when you aren't here putting on your best face."

Lucy sighed and leaned back against the counter. "He says I should tone it down a little. Says now he's got a job, I don't need to have two."

"I think you may want to listen to him."

"I just worry, Judy," Lucy said. She dropped her voice to a whisper. "This sober business is new to him. So is the steady work. If he lost it . . ."

"You could come right back here and work again."

"You'd keep my job for me?"

"You think I want to hire someone else permanently? You're my best worker. But Brandy Anne, or whatever her name is, says she's between chairs at the salons and could use a couple months of work."

Lucy closed her eyes and let herself imagine not having to come to work at Judy's three nights a week after her eight-hour shifts. She loved the job, but she was flat exhausted. She could go home, finish getting the baby stuff together, clean the house, read the baby books. Or sleep, she thought with a groan. Her belly tightened up then, and she rubbed hard against it with her hands, her face tense with pain. Whoever said Braxton-

Hicks contractions didn't hurt had never had any. When it subsided, she opened her eyes.

"Are you really serious?" Lucy asked.

"Brandy Anne is coming in twenty minutes. Thought you could train her and then take off."

"Thank you, Judy," Lucy said, relief flooding her voice. "I can't tell you how much I appreciate it."

AFTER A WEEK of working only one job, Lucy felt like a new person. Instead of collapsing onto the couch during her break, she walked the aisles trying to think if there were any last-minute baby items they needed. They had used Jeptha's first check to stock up on diapers, formula, and clothes. Everything had a place, even if that place was tucked into a basket under the couch. Everything looked ready. But, with just a few weeks left to go, Lucy was a ball of nesting nerves. Her doctor had told her to relax and rest as much as she could, but she couldn't stop walking the aisles, sure she'd forgotten something.

During her 2:30 break on Tuesday, Lucy saw a flash of purple ahead. She turned the corner into the gardening section, and there was LouEllen, camped out on the patio furniture. Used to be, before they'd stopped talking, LouEllen could be found three days a week using the swing and chairs set up in the gardening section as her own front porch, chatting with whomever she happened to run into that day. Lucy hadn't seen LouEllen in months, since she asked her to leave the house. She'd heard her voice a couple times an aisle or two over but had turned the other way so she didn't have to talk to her. Lucy's stomach knotted, both fearful of what LouEllen might say and missing her so much it hurt. But Lucy remembered that she and Jeptha were ready. He had a job. She had only one job. The house was ready. LouEllen had been sure they would fail, but she was wrong.

"Hi, LouEllen," Lucy said.

"Lucy!" LouEllen yelled so loudly people turned around. She stood up, waving Lucy over. "Come here. Let me look at you!" She looked Lucy up and down, her eyes lighting up when she got to her huge belly. Her hands reached out, but she stopped short of touching Lucy. "Can I?" she asked.

"If you want."

"You look great. And—oh! It kicked."

"Yeah, he does that."

"He? Wait, what am I doing? Sit down, sit down," LouEllen said, gesturing to the chair beside her.

As they settled in, Lucy said, "You know, LouEllen, I don't think they set this up for you to use."

"If they don't want me to sit in them, they shouldn't put them up. If they have a problem, they can talk to me about it."

Lucy laughed at the thought of Teresa, who could be such a pain as a boss, taking on LouEllen. Teresa was fierce with her employees, but Lucy knew she didn't stand a chance against LouEllen. Lucy allowed herself to relax against the green-and-white-striped cushion, thrilled to put her feet up for a minute.

"So . . . it's a little boy? Do you have a name picked out yet?"

"Jeptha and I haven't decided." Lucy noticed LouEllen's hands clench at the sound of Jeptha's name.

"How is Jeptha?" LouEllen asked.

"He's good. We're good. He got on at the plant full-time. And I quit Judy's and am only working full-time here now." Lucy heard the note of smugness in her voice, and she didn't care. It gave Lucy no small amount of pleasure to prove LouEllen wrong.

"You quit Judy's?"

"Yeah, last week. Judy brought it up. And Jeptha and I had been talking about it. Seemed silly to be working two jobs when Jeptha had one."

"But what if something happens?" LouEllen asked. It was a question, but her tone sure made it sound like a certainty.

"Nothing's gonna happen. Besides me having this baby. We're good. You don't have to worry. We're a family. We'll take care of each other."

There was no trace of a smile left on LouEllen's face. "I hope so, Lucy. I'm glad for you. I hope it stays that way."

"Do you want me to let you know when the baby comes?"

LouEllen's face softened into a smile. She took Lucy's hand and squeezed it. "I'm counting on it," she said. "Good luck, Lucy. You know I love you."

"I love you, too, LouEllen," Lucy said, her eyes filling with tears.

"Okay, then. Well, now. We can't be crying in Walmart. You know that's one of my rules. You probably need to get on back to work anyway."

"I do," Lucy said, lumbering out of the chair. "But I'll see you soon."

"Oh, hey," LouEllen said. "I keep meaning to ask—are Jeptha and them buying that land across the road from y'all?"

"I haven't heard a thing about it, if so. Why?"

"Just things I'm hearing. It's a good piece of property. Be smart if they did."

Lucy thought to herself that that was a sure sign the Taylors weren't involved but shoved the thought away. Things were good now, she reminded herself. "It would be, but it ain't us. We hardly got anything out of last year's tobacco crop."

"Serious? I heard it was a good year."

Lucy shrugged. She knew what Jeptha had told her, what the check on their kitchen counter had said before she'd deposited it. Two thousand dollars had gone quick. But it didn't matter now. Jeptha had a steady job.

"Guess not for us," she said. "I'll see you, LouEllen."

When Lucy looked back before she turned the corner, she saw that LouEllen's face was creased with concern and lit with joy, like a mother's might have been.

— 15 —

JEPTHA SAT IN FRONT of the trailer after his shift ended, picking at his mandolin and waiting for Lucy to get home. He'd been on at the plant for three weeks and, for the first time ever, life seemed good. He liked his work all right and had found there was something steady and boring, but in a good way, about getting up to go to work every morning. He guessed it was how normal people felt every day, but since he'd never been sober enough to be a part of the working world in any kind of routine way, it was a new and surprisingly pleasant feeling for him. He went to work, did his job making sure the shells were lined up before another machine inserted the shot, and came home to his wife, who was generally a much happier person now that she wasn't working sixty-five hours a week, especially since she was literally due any day now.

Jeptha put his mandolin down and watched three deer cautiously nose their way out of the tree line on the next farm over. It was dusk, the time when they preferred to reveal themselves in search of food. It was growing cold in the shadows where he sat, but Jeptha could still see the sun lighting up the eastern part of the valley. Every part of him—his hands, his lips, his stomach, his mind—craved a beer, but it had been five months, the longest he'd ever gone, and he pushed the thought away. Lucy liked him sober and working, and he loved Lucy. So, sober and working he'd be, even if it was a struggle every single minute.

Jeptha looked around for Crystal Gayle. This was usually the time of day when his dog nudged her head under his arm and rested her muzzle on his lap. He didn't see her anywhere. She'd taken to hanging out at the bottom of the driveway now that Lucy was so close to her due date, grumpy with concern for her, and he guessed Crystal Gayle was down there.

Just then, brakes squealed on the road. Jeptha heard that high, lonely whelp that dogs make only in the face of a moving car grill. His heart fell into his stomach as he took off running, praying it was some other dog but knowing it was her, knowing she'd bolted out into the street, thinking she saw Lucy's car. He might have forgiven the driver, knowing how hard it is to see at that time of day, but whoever it was peeled off in a screech of tires and stinky rubber and was over the next hill by the time Jeptha got down to her. Skinny as he was, and with a haircut so short it suggested a fit military past he didn't actually have, he was out of breath when he got there. He skidded to a stop beside Crystal Gayle's heaving, misshapen body, panting along with her as blood seeped from her nose into a shiny red puddle that slowly soaked into the variegated roadway.

Jeptha knelt down in front of her, knowing from the way her eyes tracked his that it was hopeless. He stroked her head, starting right above her green eyes and going back past her still-alert ears to the top of her neck, trying to soothe her in her moment of bewilderment.

"Hey girl . . . it's okay, girl," he said. "You're going to be okay."

Jeptha eased one hand under her belly and the other under her chest, nearly crying as he listened to the whimpers Crystal Gayle made with each movement. He kept talking to her, trying to keep her calm as he struggled up to his knees, her broken body in his arms, and then stood, his left leg faltering under her weight. She cried out then but didn't make another sound beyond labored panting as Jeptha walked up the driveway, aware of every piece of gravel crunching underneath his feet. He laid her down as gently as he could on a soft piece of earth up by his trailer that was carpeted in grass turned soft by last week's rain. It broke Jeptha's heart to watch Crystal Gayle try to nose her injuries. Bested by pain, she gave up and laid her head back down on the ground, her submissive and beseeching eyes turned up to him.

"I'll be right back," he told her.

Jeptha walked over to Deanna's house. Crystal Gayle had really been his dog, but he figured he ought to tell his brother and sister and see what they wanted to do. Deanna's kids had all loved her too, and he figured they'd want to say goodbye. When Deanna came to the door, Jeptha simply said, "Crystal Gayle's hurt. Bad," and walked off the porch to Bobby's house. When he got down the hill, with Bobby in tow behind him struggling into a wife-beater, he saw Deanna standing over Crystal Gayle, her face marked only by an absence of emotion.

"What happened?" she asked.

"Got hit by a car just now," Jeptha said.

"She wasn't never the smartest dog," Bobby said.

"It wasn't her fault," Jeptha said, his voice rising with anger. "She didn't ask to get hit. Some asshole just couldn't see shit and ran her over. Didn't even have the decency to stop."

"Well, what are we supposed to do?" Deanna asked. "I mean, is she gonna die or what?"

"How the hell do I know, Deanna?" Jeptha said, although he did.

"Guess we could take her to the vet," Bobby said.

"I ain't paying five hundred dollars for some vet to tell me this dog's gonna die," Deanna said. "She ain't gonna make it. Y'all are better off putting her out in the woods and letting her go peacefully." With that, Deanna walked away.

"Don't your kids want to see her?" Jeptha yelled at her back.

She didn't even bother turning around. "Nah. I asked 'em, but they said they's watching something."

Jeptha shook his head, frustrated with himself for imagining that those kids might be better than their mama. They were mean as snakes, just like her. She had never cared enough about anyone to get involved if it required the tiniest bit of inconvenience to herself. It was a wonder she had ever managed to keep her children alive, come to think of it, given how little regard she had for any life outside of her own. And yet, Jeptha could see them through the window, silhouetted against the light of the television, their faces so fat with McDonalds that their eyes were nearly squeezed shut.

"Well, what do you want to do?" Bobby said. "I'll take her over to the vet in the morning, if you want. Let them put her down."

"No. I'll take care of it."

"You sure?"

"No. But I'll do it."

Jeptha watched as Bobby walked back to his trailer, slowly shedding himself of his shirt as he went, so that by the time he mounted the stairs, his corpulent upper body was fully revealed, his shirt crumpled in his hand. The screen door slammed shut behind him, and Jeptha saw the blue light of the TV flicker for a moment as Bobby crossed in front of it before settling himself in his chair.

Alone in the night, Jeptha listened to the cicadas drone around him, their song a low, quiet dirge. He knelt down by Crystal Gayle, petting her from her nose down to her tail, shushing her quietly and trying to convince her it was going to be okay. She played along, her body relaxing as his hand swept over her in a rough rhythm, but she seemed to know this game was as much for him as it was for her. She'd known as soon as the car hit her.

Although he had never found himself in this situation before, Jeptha knew the truth of the matter: a real man shoots his own dogs. A real man doesn't, like Bobby suggested, pay some over-educated, clean-shaven guy, probably a Yankee moved down here for the weather and the hospitality, five hundred dollars to send his dog off into that good night with some namby-pamby concoction of drugs shot through a delicately placed IV. Looking into Crystal Gayle's eyes, he could see that she knew the truth as well—hidden deep in her wolf-like genes, she knew that the world was violent and that death, properly delivered, ought to be violent too. Jeptha thought that dogs, maybe even those pink-bow-wearing lap dogs, felt cheated of the last measure of their long-suppressed feral natures by a drug-induced death. Jeptha would take death at the end of a barrel any day over floating away in a hospital, delirious and confused.

"Okay, girl," Jeptha said, putting his hands on his knees and pushing himself up. "It's all going to be okay. You're not going to be hurting anymore."

Jeptha shuffled over to his trailer, stumbling over one of his wife's sneakers lying in the grass. Lucy had given it to Crystal Gayle in frustration—she thought if the dog had one that was specifically hers, she would stop taking all her others. To Jeptha's surprise, it had worked. Much as Jeptha knew that Lucy would want to say good-bye, he could not countenance the idea of his dog suffering through the next two hours in excruciating pain while Lucy finished up her shift. Crystal Gayle's eyes were already beginning to slip backward in time with the shakes that were racking her body, and her long shaggy coat, the reason for her name, was matted with blood. While Jeptha had been wasting time talking with his siblings, she had begun to hack up a bloody foam, her gums gone pale. It was only a matter of time, Jeptha knew, and he would not wait for Lucy to do what needed to be done.

Jeptha emerged from his trailer with his pistol in one hand and, in the other, the only dog toy besides Lucy's shoe that Crystal Gayle had ever had. The squirrel's stuffing puffed out from a hole in the side where she had ripped out the squeaker before she'd had it an hour. He laid the toy and the shoe down beside her nose, and she smelled them briefly before resuming her eye contact with Jeptha. He scratched behind her ears, rubbed down the full length of her body, and stood up.

"Alright, girl. It's gonna be okay now," he whispered as he loaded a bullet into the pistol's chamber. "You're gonna be alright now, girl. Yes, you are. I love you, Crystal Gayle. Always will."

He kept talking nonsense as he crouched down close to her, the pistol mere inches from the spot where her mouth and her ear nearly met. He took aim, although it was hardly required at such close range. Still, he was determined to do this right, determined to avoid causing his dog any more pain than she already felt.

"Goodbye, girl," he said. Tears crept down his face as he took a deep breath. Then he exhaled and squeezed the trigger.

FORTY-FIVE MINUTES LATER, Jeptha had buried Crystal Gayle, along with her squirrel toy and her shoe, in her favorite spot by the trailer where she could see the whole valley pass before her. He washed his hands, changed his clothes, cleaned his gun, put it away, and made his way to the Minute Market by the highway.

"Hey, Jeptha," Bill said from behind the counter. "Ain't seen you in months."

"Yeah." Jeptha made his way to the back. He had no more tears. Just a hard-headed desire to be as drunk as possible, as quickly as possible. A row of coolers lined the wall. He pulled open the door in the middle where the beer was stocked in between Styrofoam containers of night crawlers. It was awfully optimistic to stock bait year-round, but he guessed there must be some guys who fished every day regardless of their chances of actually getting anything. The upturned dirt in the containers made him think of the grave he'd left behind, the dirt still caked under his fingernails no matter how much he'd scrubbed. Worms like these would soon be tunneling their way into Crystal Gayle. He straightened his shoulders against the tears that were trying to come back and grabbed two cases of Old Milwaukee.

"How's Lucy doing?" Bill asked. The cans clunked against the linoleum countertop.

"She's all right." Jeptha withdrew the rubber-banded stack of cards and cash from his back pocket and withdrew a twenty.

"Due any day, ain't she?"

"Couple days more," Jeptha said.

"You sure about this?" Bill said, nodding at the beer.

"You want to shut the hell up and sell me this beer, or do I need to go somewheres else?" Jeptha asked. It wasn't any of Bill's business what he did. Bill had no idea what Jeptha had just done, how hard it had been. He deserved as many drinks as he could possibly put down.

He pushed the twenty at Bill, who paused for a moment but finally took it with a sigh.

"Tell Lucy I said 'Good luck.'"

"I will." Jeptha clenched the cases under his arm and walked out. He threw himself and the beer into the front seat and ripped open one end of a case. Three beers spilled to the floor. Jeptha swore, knowing he'd forget and spray them all over himself at some point. Still, three beers seemed as good a place to start as any. He grabbed a can from the inside of the pack and popped the top.

The first beer went down so easy, he was halfway through the second before he even realized the first was gone. Jeptha surveyed his body, pleasantly awed by the buzz that went from his fingertips to his toes. He reclined his seat slightly, enjoying the comfort of his bucket seats. He drank another. He wished he had his mandolin. His fingers picked at invisible strings, and he sang a few bars of "Shady Grove" before grabbing another beer. He checked his phone for the time. A black screen was all he got. Dead. He never remembered to charge it. It didn't matter anyway. Crystal Gayle was gone. There was no reason to hurry back.

He grabbed another beer. "A road soda," he said to himself. It was gone before he found the song he wanted to listen to. When he found an old Alan Jackson song that had never failed to make him happy, he cranked it way up. He sang along to "Chattahoochee," feeling like he was on that hot, hot river, and laughing his ass off every time Jackson said "hoochie coochie." He was twelve again, free, and the world was hysterical. He pounded two more beers, his months-sober head going straight to hammered. He wanted his mandolin, bad. He wanted to sit on the porch with Crystal Gayle, play some music, and wait for Lucy. So he turned on his car and pointed his wheel toward home.

When he got to his driveway ten minutes later, he realized he couldn't remember the drive home from the store. There was his father's old Chevy, still sitting on the blocks the old man hefted it up on so he could spend his Saturdays ignoring his kids and working on a car that Jeptha knew would never run. Suddenly, the car was right in front of him. Jeptha stood on the brakes. His Camaro bumped the rusted body before it stopped. Jeptha hit his head on the steering wheel. All was quiet.

He rubbed at the goose egg that was already coming up on his forehead. The car looked like it was still on the blocks, but it had shifted a few inches off center, seemed like. Jeptha squinted to figure out how bad it was and gave up when he saw two and sometimes three cars in front of him. Besides, what did it matter? His dad was dead and gone, good riddance. In fact, Jeptha was tempted to back up and finish the job. That would show his dad. But he didn't want to risk denting up his own car, since it was about the only nice thing he owned. He reversed a few inches and shifted to park.

He peered up at his trailer. It was dark. Good, he thought. Lucy was probably already asleep, oblivious to Crystal Gayle's death. He'd have to tell her tomorrow, but when he was sober. He couldn't do it like this.

Jeptha saw a flash of white off to the right of the trailer. For a minute, he thought it was Crystal Gayle toting Lucy's shoe, but it was a rabbit running off into the woods. If Crystal Gayle was still alive, she'd be standing outside his door, waiting for him to get out of the car, probably giving him that disappointed look. That'd be all right, Jeptha thought. To be disappointed in someone, you had to expect better in the first place. Crystal Gayle always had.

He could almost feel her chin rubbing on his leg, feel the soft yet wiry hair between her ears, hear the soft harrumphs of her breath through her deep black nose. He wanted to remember her like this, not that broken heap she had been a few hours before. Even though he knew he'd done the right thing, he couldn't rid himself of that look in Crystal Gayle's eyes right before he pulled the trigger—having begged him to deliver her death, she seemed to rebuke him there at the last second for having come to terms with the decision so quickly, as if her last thought was dismay that she should be so easy to dismiss. Even in his drunken haze, Jeptha knew he was exaggerating, probably giving the damn dog feelings she'd never had a day in her life, but still. Her eyes haunted him.

He grabbed another beer, trying to force them from his mind.

"If you were here, girl, it'd be like old times. Just you. And me. And the mandolin," Jeptha said aloud to Crystal Gayle. He straightened up, thinking of his mandolin. That's what he needed. He'd play a dirge for Crystal Gayle, say good-bye to her the old way.

"I'ma get it," Jeptha said, talking to her, like that would bring her back. "Play us some music."

He moved his feet and tried to rise out of the seat. The ground tilted underneath him and he fell back hard, popping a rib on the steering wheel and his wrist on the gearshift.

"Aw, fuck. CG, I'm drunk," he said, and nearly fell out laughing with sheer joy at the feeling. He lay his head against the headrest and pulled his legs back into the car. "I'm gonna get us that mandolin. Just gonna finish this beer here and rest my eyes for a minute."

Jeptha could almost feel Crystal Gayle nuzzling her nose under his hand. He tried to get his fingers to move enough to pat her nose, but he wasn't sure if they were obeying his brain. He mumbled something about resting his eyes again and then surrendered to sleep and dreams where his dog sat beside him, ears alert, full of love, fully alive.

"JEPTHA? HEY, JEPTHA! Are you okay?"

Jeptha's eyes opened, and he immediately closed them against the sunshine. Where was he? Who was talking to him? He opened his eyes slightly again and saw an image of Lucy, fuzzy against the morning sun. His head echoed with her voice, the pain shooting off his skull like a bullet off a tree. He groaned.

"Good. You aren't dead then," Lucy said. "In that case, I'm going to work."

"Wait," Jeptha said, his voice barely loud enough for him to hear it. He coughed and straightened up in the seat. "Wait." He opened his eyes wide enough to see Lucy stalking toward her car as fast as her belly would allow her to go. He lurched to standing. A wave of nausea hit him so fiercely that his knees buckled, and he gripped the doorframe to keep from falling. He swallowed, thinking he'd beat it down, but no. Over the sound of his vomiting, he heard Lucy slam her door. He straightened up as much as he could and ran crookedly, still bent in half, over to her car. She started the engine and looked between the seats to back out.

"Lucy! I'm sorry. Wait."

She shook her head at him. Jeptha saw tears in her eyes before he jumped out of the way of her front bumper. "Lucy, please. I'm sorry."

The car bumped down the incline for twenty feet, and then stopped. Jeptha ran to her door. "I'm so sorry. I fell asleep in the car."

"Yeah. Fell asleep. That's what we're calling it."

Jeptha didn't know what to say. His head hurt like never before. He couldn't think. And there was something weighing on him, something he needed to tell Lucy. Crystal Gayle. He suddenly remembered. He stumbled back from her car.

Lucy shook her head, her voice quiet. "What happened, Jeptha? You were doing so good. We were good."

"Crystal Gayle . . ." he whispered, leaning his head on his arm at the top of the car. He wasn't strong enough to look Lucy in the eye.

"Yeah, where is she? I called for her last night for ten minutes and nothing," Lucy said.

"She's . . . she's gone," Jeptha mumbled into the fabric of his shirt.

"Gone?"

"She got hit by a car last night. She was dying. I had to . . ." Jeptha stopped. He gave into the sobs. "I had t-to sh-shoot her."

"Oh, Jeptha," Lucy said. The car door eased open, and he moved out of the way. She slipped her arms around him, and he leaned fully into her until they both fell against the car.

"I'm sorry," she said into his chest. "I'm so sorry."

They stayed like that for two minutes until finally Jeptha pulled away.

"I'm sorry," he said, hesitating. "For this. For me. For drinking. I didn't know what else to do." He could see now that there was nothing steady, boring, routine, or stable about falling into a case of beer and getting so drunk he passed out in his car. That was something Old Jeptha would do.

"You need to call Cody and tell him you can't come to work today. You're already late. And you can't go. Not like this."

Jeptha shook his head and looked up at the sky. Clouds flitted overhead, and a hawk flew by in search of an unsuspecting mouse. He watched the hawk for a moment more, envious of the freedom flying above his head: freedom from his blinding headache, from his dead dog, from his disappointed wife, from having proved once more the kind of fuck-up he could be. The bird flew out of sight.

He looked back down at Lucy. "I'm sorry. I don't know what happened."

"It's okay. I'm sorry about Crystal Gayle. I loved her too." She waited for a moment and then checked her phone. "I'm going to be late if I don't get going. You okay today?"

"I'll be all right. You go on," he said. Jeptha's stomach curdled as he watched Lucy pull out onto the road. He clamped his arms around it, trying to stem the involuntary lurch that he knew was coming. Then he let his hands drop to his sides—he'd lost his dog and screwed up, disappointing both himself and his wife. He deserved to be throwing up in a bush.

After, Jeptha walked heavily up the stairs to the trailer, his phone in his hand. His brain and his legs weren't communicating well, and he walked like a baby, re-creating the process with each step.

He saw his charger snaking across the kitchen counter and plugged in his phone. While he waited for it to come back to life, he grabbed a carton of orange juice out of the fridge. After a quick, guilty look out the window, he slurped directly from the cardboard, groaning with joy as the cold juice sizzled against his parched throat, sluicing through the taste of old beer and vomit that coated his tongue. He longed for the numbness of the prior night when he'd been able to forget what he'd lost.

He put the orange juice back in the refrigerator. Behind the milk, he spied a sole longneck Coors, and his body ached for it. The hair of the dog; it had been a while since he'd been forced to endure it, but now he remembered it like it was something he'd been missing. He closed the door so he wouldn't have to see the bottle. He should call Cody. He checked his phone. Still dead.

He opened the fridge again, this time for food, but there was nothing that looked good. He dug through the furthest kitchen drawer for Tylenol. He had to open the fridge again for more juice. The bottle of beer was bathed in light, the condensation on its sides illuminated like in a commercial. He shut the door. His phone pinged, back from the dead.

He had five messages, all from Lucy, her concern growing stronger and angrier with each progressive message. He deleted them all after he heard the first few words. Jeptha looked at the time. He was due at work two hours ago. He owed Cody a phone call, but, as he dialed the numbers, Jeptha prayed his friend wouldn't hear his phone on the plant floor.

"What?" Cody answered.

"Hey. It's me. Um, Jeptha."

"I got caller ID. I know who it is."

"I'm sorry I couldn't be there today, man."

"Whatever."

"I am. Really."

"Whatever. It's one day. You just can't do it again. Tom don't give many chances."

"I know," Jeptha said. "It won't happen again. It was Crystal Gayle. She got hit last night. I had to put her down."

"Oh, man. I'm sorry. She was a good dog."

"She was."

"You should have called me . . ."

"Phone was dead. And I was too busy drinking myself to death."

"Jeptha . . ."

"I know. Can't believe I did it either."

"Be careful, man."

"I will. I'll see you tomorrow."

His throat felt tight and his eyes stung. For want of anything better to do, he opened the fridge, staring at the contents like a death-row inmate at a woman. His eyes rested on the beer. He'd promised Cody and Lucy that last night was a mistake. He wanted it to be. He wanted to go back to that moment on the porch before Crystal Gayle died. He'd been content, he now realized. That's what that feeling was. He didn't want to be a drunk for his wife, for his kid. He looked down at his jeans, hay snaking up the legs and flecks of vomit splashed up around his ankles. He didn't want to be this man, not anymore. Jeptha pawed the tears off his face. He pulled his hand away and watched the fingers jitter across the air, his body aching for another drink. Just beyond his hand, the beer sweated. He didn't want to be like this, but all he could see were Crystal Gayle's eyes, haunting him. A tear dropped to his dusty shoes. He made to straighten up, to shut the refrigerator door. But his hand closed around the neck of the beer, the glass clinking against a jar of pickles as his hand shook. He sat down on the couch and opened the beer. He didn't want to be this kind of man anymore. But he didn't know how to be any other kind.

"**Y**OU GOING IN TODAY?" Lucy asked at breakfast.

This was about the extent of the conversation she and Jeptha had exchanged in the two weeks since Crystal Gayle died. Jeptha had been so sorry about getting drunk the night she died that Lucy had assumed it was a one-time thing, a mistake he could make up for. She was wrong. He'd been drunk nearly every night and for several of the days.

Jeptha nodded slowly.

"You better hurry," Lucy said. He'd already missed four days of work and been late another three. Lucy tried to quiet her rising sense of panic. She'd banked her life on sober Jeptha, and for months, she thought she'd been right to do so. He smiled weakly at her. He was still in there, the Jeptha she'd come to love. Or, at least she hoped he was.

"Please God," she prayed silently. "Let this be temporary. Let him get back on the path he was on before Crystal Gayle died."

Lucy scooted herself out from the table, groaning as she did. Even with her belly sucked in as much as she could, she still snagged a spoon on lift-off and would have taken the whole cereal bowl down with her if Jeptha hadn't reached out and grabbed it. In the mirror this morning, even her nose looked pregnant. Since she'd woken up, an emptiness had yawned in her stomach, now located near her boobs—it was Tuesday, her due date. She looked around. Everything was done. Diapers, crib, formula, bottles, clothes. It was all ready. Except one thing: Lucy knew it was crucial but could not, for the life of her, remember what it was. She almost asked Jeptha but knew he wouldn't remember. He hadn't remembered it was her due date, after all.

"I got to go," she said. "You heading out?"

Jeptha nodded again but stayed seated.

She crouched down by him. "You need to go, Jeptha. You're going to be late. We need that job."

"I'm going," Jeptha said, a note of anger in his voice.

"Okay," Lucy said, standing up so quickly she got dizzy for a second. She put her hand out on the table and closed her eyes until the spinning stopped. "I'll see you later."

As she walked out onto the porch and down the stairs, Lucy still couldn't help but look around for Crystal Gayle to come bounding up. She had loved that dog from the very minute she met her. Lucy was pretty sure the feeling had been mutual, but Crystal Gayle's love for Lucy was no match for her love for Jeptha—that was a foolhardy devotion, the kind only a mother might show. Lucy imagined that Crystal Gayle loved her because she saw Lucy as another caretaker for her beloved Jeptha. Right now, Lucy knew that Crystal Gayle would be barking at Jeptha steadily—a special bark that sounded like nothing so much as nagging—until he finally got up and out the door to work. Lucy wished that Crystal Gayle was there to do it—she doubted very much that her own nagging along those lines was going to work.

WHEN LUCY GOT to work, the store was quiet except for the sparrows nesting in the beams above. One kept flying over to a nest and chattering away to what Lucy assumed was another bird inside. He was frantic with concern. She wondered if he'd remembered his wife's due date.

Lucy threw her stuff in a locker and pulled on her blue vest. She was on checkout today, thank God, and had somehow convinced Teresa to let her drag a stool from the break room out so she could sit for at least part of her day. Lucy walked to her checkout lane, Number 37, nearly at the end of the row. If one could be said to have a favorite checkout lane in a sea of identical ones, this was it. It was at the end of the line and always busy. Busy was exactly the way she usually liked it, but today, for the first time, she winced every time she looked up and saw someone in her line.

Four hours later, Lucy finally got her break. She shut off her light, put the closed sign on the end of the conveyer belt, and ripped the vest off her shoulders, desperate for her twenty minutes. Her head rang with the beep of the purchases, and her arm periodically swept phantom products across the scanner, the muscle memory still working. She stopped to collect her thoughts outside the break room, trying to remember the last thing they needed for the baby, but failed. She gave up on sitting down for her break and went to the baby section, hoping it would jog her memory.

Finally, in the fifth aisle, Lucy remembered: a car seat. She examined the row of car seats on display, taking careful notice of an infant bucket seat in taupe that went with everything and was beautiful to no one. It had the look of the cheapest one, but she saw that it was still almost a hundred dollars. She didn't have that in her bank account and doubted Jeptha had it in his. He'd only gotten one paycheck so far and, given how much work he'd missed, it didn't seem like he'd get much in the next one. Maybe there was still some left from the tobacco money? She closed her eyes and sighed. If not, they'd have to ask Deanna or Bobby. She knew what Jeptha would make of that suggestion—his lips would pucker up and his forehead would draw forward in a sea of wrinkles. He hated being the poorest one in a poor family and would occasionally go off on a rant about how they were cheating him out of what he was owed. He hated asking them for anything. Not having to do so was one of the big benefits of having a steady job, he'd told her after a few days at the plant.

A steady job, Lucy thought. *Steady until you're too drunk to keep it*. She'd have to come back for the car seat, she decided, as she rummaged in her pocket for her ringing phone.

"Hello," she said.

"Lucy." Jeptha's voice slurred. It was only 1:00 p.m., but he sounded hammered.

"What, Jeptha?"

"They fired me. Damn assholes fired me."

Lucy was rooted to her spot in front of the car seats. All she could hear was her heartbeat pounding through her body as a wave of nausea washed over her. He'd lost his job. She wasn't sure why she was so surprised. He'd been late, drunk, or absent for most of the last two weeks. It was her fault for thinking the last five months had meant something different.

"Jeptha . . ." she said, and then stopped. There wasn't anything else to say.

"I'ma find something else. Don't worry. I know. I'ma be something steady, something good."

"I gotta go, Jeptha." Her voice was flat.

"I love you, Lucy," Jeptha said, pleadingly. "I'm sorry."

"Bye."

She hung up, hoping that maybe if she didn't move, didn't react, this wouldn't be happening. Just then, a dull cramp bloomed in Lucy's belly and snaked its way around to her back and up to the top of her rib cage. She held onto the shelf in front of her and bit her lip until it passed.

"Lucy!" a voice called out from down the aisle. It was LouEllen. Lucy gripped the shelf again to keep from running into her arms. She didn't want to tell anyone about Jeptha losing his job, least of all LouEllen. Lucy could see LouEllen's observant, beady brown eyes searching her face. She prayed that LouEllen had lost some of her skills at reading Lucy's mind.

"Are you okay?" LouEllen asked. "Looked like that hurt."

"Just those practice contractions. They aren't supposed to hurt, I guess, but they do."

"You sure it was a fake one? Are you going into labor talking to me? I *will* haul you to my minivan and drive you to the hospital if so."

Lucy laughed, knowing LouEllen wasn't joking.

"I'm fine. I've been getting a few of these. But they aren't real. This baby probably won't even come for two more weeks, with my luck."

"How do you know?" LouEllen asked.

"I don't. I'm just hoping. I'm not nearly prepared. Don't even have a car seat yet."

"Aw, you'll be fine," LouEllen said, patting her arm. "Most kids my friends had slept and traveled in a drawer half the time. They came out all right."

Lucy laughed—she could imagine LouEllen or her friends laying a baby into a blanket-stuffed drawer and strapping the whole thing in with a seat belt. But Lucy was fairly sure there was some rule now about not being able to leave the hospital without a properly installed car seat. She doubted a drawer was going to work anymore.

"That's good to know," she said. "Of course, we don't even have a drawer to spare in that trailer, but I'll figure it out, I guess."

"This one's nice," LouEllen said, pointing to the most expensive one on the shelf.

"Yep. Expensive too. I'm probably gonna get this one," Lucy said, pointing to the taupe one she hated.

"I'll help you carry it up front if you want."

"No, that's fine." Lucy looked down at the floor, her cheeks red. "I'm probably going to get it tomorrow."

"I could buy it for you. A gift?"

"No," Lucy said sharply. "No. I'll get it. Just can't today."

"Okay," LouEllen said, holding her hands up in front of her. She stared at Lucy for a minute, her eyes soft, and put her hand on Lucy's shoulder. "You'll be okay, Lucy. You always have been."

"I know," Lucy said, straightening up. "I'm just going to get the seat tomorrow."

"I've got my phone on every night, so if anything happens, if Jeptha isn't . . ." LouEllen stopped. Lucy was glad she hadn't finished that thought, knowing what she'd heard. Jeptha's spectacular fall off the wagon had not gone unnoticed or unremarked upon in town.

"Thank you," Lucy said. "I'll see you later."

Forty feet away from her lane, the same pain from before hit her, starting low and rippling up like water rings on a pond after a fish nips a bug. Lucy lurched to the side, bracing herself on a glass jewelry case. As suddenly as it hit her, it was gone. If these were practice contractions, she hated to think what the real ones were like.

"First labor is longer than you think," she remembered the childbirth instructor saying. "Try to ignore the pain as long as you can. Otherwise you're likely to end up going to the hospital early and having to go home. It'll feel like you've been laboring forever if you do that."

That was about all Lucy could remember from class. She'd been so happy to see Jeptha and so proud of him for getting a job that they'd barely paid any attention, just giggled the whole time. She saw now that that had been a mistake. *One of many*, she thought to herself.

"Ignore it," Lucy said as she straightened up and walked back to her lane. "Ignore it, ignore it, ignore it."

As she pressed in her code to log into the cash register, she remembered the numbers 4-1-1. She couldn't remember what the ones stood for, but the four, she knew, was for four minutes apart. Her contractions were nothing close to that. The last one had been twenty minutes before. She relaxed a little and flicked on the light ten feet above her head. Like shepherds navigating to Bethlehem, customers swarmed toward her. Over the next three hours, contractions hit every twenty minutes. If she could grit her teeth through the first forty seconds, the last twenty were an easy slide into pain-free territory. If she could still stand and work, she told herself, there was no way she was having a baby any time soon.

BY THE TIME Lucy got in her car, though, she'd gone from trying to ignore the pain to trying to manage it. She called Jeptha three times on the eight-minute drive home and each time it had gone straight to voicemail. As she bumped her way up the driveway at five minutes to six, she was as eager as she had ever been to see her husband. Drunk or not, she didn't care. She wanted him home. But the trailer was dark, and his car was gone.

"Please, God, let him be asleep and not gone," she said to herself, knowing it was irrational if his car wasn't in the driveway.

She opened the car door and took a step out, where she promptly had another contraction, the strongest yet. After breathing through it, she mounted the trailer's stairs, noticing beer cans scattered around Jeptha's lawn chair from what she guessed was Jeptha's pre-work drinking session, and unlocked the door.

"Jeptha?" she called out. "Jeptha?"

When she turned on the kitchen light, she saw that the trailer was empty. She had to face the truth: her husband was gone, and his phone was dead.

The contractions were coming faster. She pulled out her phone to time them. She wanted someone—anyone—there with her. She thought wistfully of LouEllen's offer and wished she'd taken her up on it in the moment. LouEllen had meant it, would come in an instant, and was exactly who she wanted there. But Lucy couldn't make the call. The East Tennessee in her wouldn't let her ask for something this big from someone who had meant everything to Lucy and rejected her, even if LouEllen had been nice to her today.

"Nope, this is all me," Lucy said out loud, hoping that speaking the words would make her believe it. She stood, swaying back and forth, and turned on the TV as another contraction hit. *Ignore it*, she thought. *Ignore it.* She started to hyperventilate over the thought of having to drive herself to the hospital like this but swallowed it down. After twenty minutes of timing the contractions, she pushed herself off the couch. They were coming three minutes apart now. It was time to leave. On her way down the hall, the next contraction hit with so much force that her knees buckled, and she banged her head against the paneling. On her hands and knees, she lowed in pain, sounding like the cattle on the next farm over on cold winter mornings. She had promised herself she wouldn't make that sound, having heard its appallingly animalistic tones on the childbirth videos. But it rose unbidden from her lungs, escaping past her clamped lips. She hung her head in defeat and tried to remember to breathe.

In the midst of the next contraction, right on top of the last one, she heard something outside. Over her own moaning, she heard footsteps. Her stomach leapt into her throat with joy as she imagined Jeptha's heavy thud bringing him into the trailer. She heaved herself to a standing position and waddled, legs spread wide and her back hunched over, down the hall. She wiped sweat off her forehead and blew air out of her lungs. Exhaustion was settling in. As she passed the bathroom, though, another contraction hit, and she felt a sudden heaviness down low. The pain was too bad to move. She pivoted toward the sink, gripping the vanity with such force that the glue that connected the fake marble top to the wood below popped loudly.

"Lucy?" a voice called out, but Lucy couldn't tell who it was over her own lowing.

"Come in," Lucy yelled, the contraction finally ending. She didn't care in that moment who walked through the door. Her dead mother, Dolly Parton, the devil himself. It didn't matter. She needed someone. Anyone.

Lucy focused on the voice as it grew closer and closer. "I know you said not to, but I got you a present. That car seat. The pretty one." Lucy smiled during a break in contractions, recognizing LouEllen's voice, but then another one hit.

"Oh, good Lord," LouEllen said when she finally got to the bathroom door, her eyes wide. "You *are* having this baby."

"Not here I'm not," Lucy whispered quickly before the next contraction peaked.

LouEllen stepped toward Lucy and stroked her hair back from her face. "Can you get in the car?"

Lucy nodded with relief. She let go of the counter and moved her right foot off the ground a few inches. But the pain swept her up again. She grasped the counter and focused her eyes on the slight variations in the vanity. "No."

"No what, honey?" LouEllen said.

"No, I cannot get in the car."

"Oh hell. I'm calling 911," LouEllen said, digging her phone out. "Is this Ethel?" Lucy heard muffled talking on the other end. Ethel Slocum was manning the phones tonight. It made her feel like someone was watching out for her.

"Hey, it's LouEllen. I'm over at the Taylors' place. Lucy's having this baby right now. There's no way we're making it to the hospital."

LouEllen was silent for a moment, listening. "Well, y'all better hurry. Like they say in the movies, I sure as hell don't know nothing about birthing no babies."

Lucy screamed out and gripped the counter again.

"You hear that, Ethel? I ain't joking. You get me those goddamn EMTs, and you get 'em here NOW," LouEllen roared and hung up.

LouEllen stroked Lucy's hair. "It's gonna be okay, Lucy. They're coming, and they'll know what to do."

Lucy barely heard her. The childbirth instructor was right: she knew when it was time to push. LouEllen, the phone, and the bathroom disappeared. Even the pain had become something different, something to tunnel into rather than retreat from. Her focus had narrowed to a tiny imperfection on the counter, a fleck on the laminate that looked like a German Shepherd at attention. Her eyes were trained on that spot as she strained, bearing down through each contraction with a groan that had gone beyond animal and into savage.

Suddenly towels appeared beneath her, and the tiny bathroom got very crowded. Blue coats pushed their way into the tiny space. The one on her right, his head totally bald, tried to coax her to lay down. "No," she whispered. He kept insisting. She tried to block him out as she pushed, but he would not stop saying, "Okay, here we go, move your leg down. Lie down."

"Dammit!" she screamed as she pushed. "I am not laying down."

She thought she would break in two then, as a massive weight pressed against her from the inside. The bald EMT cautioned her to slow down. Would the man say nothing useful? She yelled out again and pushed with all the strength she had. The pressure peaked, and with a sweet, exquisite pop, the pain stopped so suddenly she burst into tears. Hands reached between her knees. A squirm deep inside her flowed out into the space below, like the exuberant wriggle of a fish unhooked and eased back into the water. There, below her, was her baby, covered in blood and bawling. She collapsed into the EMT's waiting arms then. They deposited the baby, slippery and pink, on her chest. He smelled like iron and something earthy, and Lucy laughed when he opened his mouth and screamed in her face. Lucy held her son, in awe of the tiny human on her chest. When the EMT took him away for a moment to wrap him in a towel, Lucy recognized in the devastation of her ache for him incontrovertible proof that real love, both exhilarating and sobering, can happen in an instant.

—17—

"**A**NOTHER ONE," JEPTHA HOLLERED at the cute blonde bartender at the South Side Bar. It was the kind of dingy place on the wrong side of the tracks where people with class came only in groups and only for one drink so they could tell their friends about it after. For Jeptha, who saw in its dinginess a home, the South Side was exactly the place he knew he deserved, particularly tonight. He'd long since lost track of his drinks.

Earlier, Jeptha had shown up at work two beers in, which was why they finally fired him. Cody wouldn't even make eye contact, just shook his head sorrowful-like, when Jeptha trudged out the door. Overwhelmed by shame, he'd driven to the Tuesday-empty parking lot of a nearby church, devoured the four beers remaining in his car, and driven around aimlessly. Finally, he called Lucy. He kept wishing he didn't have to tell his wife, but he couldn't see his way clear to that. She'd find out soon enough.

The disappointment in Lucy's voice—she was due any day now (although Jeptha was too drunk to say which day)—was low and shocking. There'd been a shining moment in their marriage, a month back, when Jeptha was sober and working and they were happy. Then Crystal Gayle died, and he'd been drunk every day since. Even drunk, Crystal Gayle's eyes still haunted him. Lucy's voice joined in, playing over and over in his head. He couldn't stand either of them. The only solution was to get drunker.

"You better stop yelling at me, or I'm gonna stop bringing you drinks," the bartender said. Up close, she was older than he'd thought, but being smiled at by someone felt so good Jeptha didn't care. "You on your own?"

"Looks that way. Texted a friend earlier, but I ain't heard nothing. See?" Jeptha said, holding out his phone. "At SothSde dirkin," Jeptha had texted Cody earlier. But there was no reply. Jeptha figured Cody was pissed and likely to stay that way.

"Don't see anything. 'Cept it's six o' clock. You got off early today?"

"You could say that."

"Get fired?"

"How'd you know?"

"You aren't the first one coming in here at two o' clock in the afternoon drinking hard, full of piss and vinegar, wanting to get back at somebody."

"No one to get back at but myself," he said.

"Usually isn't . . ."

A man at the other end of the bar called out to her.

"I'll come check on you later," she said.

———————

TWO HOURS AND three drinks later, she settled back in across from him. "Your friend coming?"

"My phone died, but I don't guess so. He's the one got me that job. Probably pretty pissed at me."

"You wanna charge it?" she asked.

"Doubt it matters," Jeptha said. "But sure."

"I'll be back in a minute," she said to the other bartender and nodded her head for Jeptha to follow.

She went through a metal door into a back storage room. Napkins, salt, ketchup, and cleaning supplies nearly spilled off a set of shelves. A small desk sat in one corner, covered with papers, invoices, and empty Diet Coke bottles. "Charger's here," she said, pointing at the cord snaking out of the wall. Jeptha slipped past her. He fumbled with the charger, too drunk to make the connection even after three tries. "Here," she said, taking the phone from his hands and plugging it in.

"Thank you," he said, taking a step toward the door. But she blocked his way. She put her hand on his chest and kissed him. Jeptha pulled back.

"What are you doing?"

"I'm bored. You're cute. And had a shitty day. Figured I'd help out a little." She kissed him again, and Jeptha gave in a little. He tasted cigarettes and cinnamon gum on her lips, that old combo that had welcomed him home on a dozen other girls before he'd met Lucy, who'd always tasted like the woods smelled, earthy and sweet.

Lucy. He pushed the bartender away, harder than he meant to. "I'm married. I can't."

"I saw your ring. Doesn't bother most guys."

"Bothers me," he said, grabbing his still-dead phone. "Excuse me."

———

TEN MINUTES LATER, sitting at Waffle House, Jeptha buried his face in his hands. He was his dad all over again. Drunk, unable to keep a job, cheating on his wife.

"Double order, scattered, smothered, covered," the waitress said from above him, dropping a plate in between his arms. "You want more coffee?"

He nodded, not trusting himself to speak anymore. Used to be, he'd spend all day drunk, not working, hitting on women, and call it a damn fine day. Not anymore. How could he fix this? He had no job, no friend, a baby coming, and a wife who should hate him. His head hurt from messing it all up.

Jeptha ate a few bites of his hash browns and pushed them aside, watching the cheese congeal. He knew he should get up and surrender his booth to the eager high-school kids waiting, but he couldn't do it. Instead, he lit a cigarette and asked for more coffee.

As he sipped it, Jeptha saw a woman as hugely pregnant as Lucy lumber out of a truck and take the arm her husband offered. She waddled to the entrance where he held the door. Their faces were subtly lit with what Jeptha imagined was excitement over the child she carried. Their laughter, the way they seemed to actually enjoy being together, was like looking into a mirror that had reversed its purpose and reflected all that he and Lucy were not. This couple was the opposite image of what they had become since Crystal Gayle died. The husband was not sitting drunk in a Waffle House by himself while his wife drove home from her late-night shift at Walmart. The wife was not sitting on the couch every night watching *The Voice* or *The Bachelorette* with a face that suggested she would rather be anywhere and in any other condition than the one in which she found herself.

Jeptha watched them until the comparison became too unfavorable to bear. His marriage was in no better shape than Crystal Gayle had been when he put her down. He rubbed at his headache, caused partly by the drinks but more by his inability to decide whether a man was obligated to shoot his own marriage when it got to the same stage as a dog that needed killing. When he was drunk, he could believe that the problems in their marriage were due to exhaustion and bills and would end once the baby came. On the wrong side of drunk, like he was now, he could no longer buy his own lies. He was the problem.

Finally, he scooted out of the booth and paid, nodding at the couple as he passed. He wanted that, he knew with a deep thud in his belly; he wanted what they had. Jeptha was smart enough to wonder if it was too late for things with him and Lucy to change. But he was dumb enough to think he might as well try. And the only way to do that was to get stone cold sober again and stay that way.

———

JEPTHA DROVE HOME slowly, wanting to be as close to fully sober as possible when he begged Lucy to forgive him. He drove out into the open countryside, where farmland was broken only by the occasional gas station and churches with their well-meaning signs lit twenty-four hours a day, a fluorescent ministry for wayward souls. "If God feels far away," one read, "who moved?" He knew the answer.

When Jeptha pulled into his farm's driveway, his heartbeat quickened as he saw that every light was on in his trailer. It was 10:00 p.m. Lucy was usually asleep by now. Although her car was parked out front, he knew something was wrong. He ran as fast as he could to the trailer. They were close to, or—*Shit*, he thought, skidding to a halt at the bottom of the stairs—at her due date now. Her due date was today. He cursed himself, ran up the stairs, and jerked open the door.

There were bloody towels trailing into the kitchen and several discarded blue gloves. His heart beat faster. Small puddles of blood led from the kitchen to the bathroom. A pit opened up in his stomach.

"Lucy!" he yelled, but there was no answer.

He walked to the bathroom, fear tingling his fingers. It was empty except for a bundle of bloody towels beneath the sink.

"Holy shit," he whispered to himself. That same bucking sense of frantic fear that Crystal Gayle had shown the night she'd died flooded Jeptha. He bolted back down the hall and out the door.

From the corner of his eye, he saw something white flutter down to the porch. He bent to pick it up, and his finger caught in the peppermint stickiness at the back. He held the note toward the full moon. "At hospital," it read.

Jeptha jumped off the porch, his left ankle bending underneath him and scraping against the hard leather of his boots. He limped as quick as he could to his car. All he could think was *Please God, let her be okay*, over and over again. If there had been time to write a note, maybe things were all right. But, the blood—there was so much.

He roared down the driveway and into the street without even looking to see if a car was coming. He was five minutes down the road before he realized he didn't have his lights on. Once he got on the highway, Jeptha drove ninety miles an hour toward the soft glow that the huge chemical plant cast over Kingsport. He prayed as he drove, asking for three things: one, that he not get pulled over for speeding; two, that his wife be okay; and three, that he get there in time to see the baby be born.

In keeping with the general pattern of his life, God only granted one of Jeptha's wishes. When he finally got to the hospital—having talked Rick Mullins out of taking him to jail for going double the speed limit only because he kept insisting that Lucy was having his baby—he ran through the hallways in search of her but stopped short at the door of her room.

She was plainly okay, sitting up on the hospital bed and smiling down at their baby, who lay on her legs. She rubbed his cheek with the back of her hand and kissed his forehead. Jeptha had never before seen his wife so purely happy, so full of joy. His stomach curdled as he watched Lucy fall in love for the first time.

Jeptha knew then that he had lost her, and for good this time. In his few short moments on earth, his baby had managed to create more of a bond with Lucy than Jeptha had in all the years he'd known her. It was excruciating to watch. He would never see that face of Lucy's, the one that looked lost in love, turned to him. It was all he had ever wanted, and now that he saw what real love was, he knew it was plainly, impossibly, out of reach. He thought for a minute of walking away but instead crossed the room to Lucy's side.

"I'm sorry I wasn't here," he whispered.

"I wasn't either," Lucy said, not lifting her eyes to his.

"What do you mean?"

She looked up at him then. Jeptha fought hard to keep his face from crumpling when he saw love fall away as she stared at him, rather than the baby. "I had him in our bathroom with half the fire department."

"Are you serious?"

"It went so fast. I didn't realize that was it."

"I'm sorry. I should have been there. Today was your due date. I should have been home."

"It's okay." She stared at the baby, his hair fuzzy and his face squashed— Jeptha hoped temporarily—from being born. "I was thinking we should call him Jared. What do you think?"

"It's perfect. How is he?"

"He's perfect. Do you want to hold him?"

She scooted up toward the head of the bed, wincing with each shift of her bottom, and held him out to Jeptha.

Jeptha cradled his son awkwardly in his arms and watched him sleep. Tiny blond eyelashes wisped against his cheeks, fluttering up and down with each breath. Jeptha recognized miniature versions of his ears and Lucy's upturned nose. Jeptha held his son's head, the soft skin of the baby's scalp against his palm like nothing he'd ever felt, and wondered at how such a tiny thing could make him feel such a terrifying responsibility.

"He's so little," he said, with a smile.

"But cute," she yawned. "They're going to take him up to the nursery soon."

"I'm so sorry, Lucy. I can't believe I wasn't there."

"It's okay," she said again.

Jeptha could see that she meant it. It was truly okay with her that he had missed his own son's birth. There was no measure for the hurt he felt, for the pain he'd brought on himself. He quickly thumbed one of his tears off of Jared's forehead, hoping he had been fast enough to escape Lucy's notice. Jared's eyes opened slightly from the pressure of Jeptha's touch. He stared up, his eyes unfocused, still shiny with some sort of medical goop. Jeptha wondered if his son was disappointed to meet this grizzled, sour-smelling man who was his father. He leaned down to kiss him between the eyes, and his son's eyelids closed again in sleep.

"He *is* perfect," he whispered.

"I know," she said. Jeptha thought she had never looked more exhausted or more beautiful. It was a moment he would remember for the rest of his life.

"You ready for me to take him up to the nursery?" a nurse asked from the door. Jared's face pursed with every squeak of her footsteps on the floor. Jeptha tightened his grip. He didn't want to give his baby, his only connection to Lucy, over to a stranger.

"That would be great," Lucy said. She nodded at Jeptha, like this was no big thing. He squeezed Jared and kissed him one more time between his eyes. When he saw the pinched look on his face relax into sleep, Jeptha carefully handed the baby over to the nurse and watched her every move as she settled him in the small plastic bed and pushed him with quick steps out of the room.

"Guess I . . ." Jeptha said, stopping to clear his tear-clogged throat. "Guess I shouldn't be surprised that you had him on your own. You're about the strongest person I know."

"Well, it wasn't easy. But I didn't have much say in the matter." Lucy yawned and laid her head down on the pillows. "I've got to get some sleep. I'm sorry."

"I'll stay, wait 'til he wakes up."

"You should go on. I'm going to sleep for as long as he'll let me. You look like you could use some sleep yourself."

"You sure?" Jeptha asked, hating himself for the hope he heard creep into his voice, hope that she would want him to stay, beg him not to leave.

"It's fine. You should go on back. Come back later this morning," Lucy said, sleep already beginning to slur her voice.

"Okay," Jeptha said, his voice cracking. "I love you, Lucy," he said, kissing her on the forehead.

"Mmmm."

From the doorway, Jeptha saw that her eyes were closed, and her breathing was already moving into that steady territory of sleep. His heart, his body, his everything wanted to lay down beside her and never leave. He wiped his tears away, glad she could not see them. Finally, he whispered "Bye," knowing she wouldn't hear, and walked down the hall. The same nurse who'd taken his son gave him a sad smile from the nurse's station. Looking away from her, he saw another father stretched out in the chair beside his wife, their hands on their baby in the plastic bassinet between them. He stopped, almost returned to Lucy's room. But the image of her, staring down so contentedly at Jared, came to him. Lucy did not need him. She never had.

When he got home, he sat on his porch steps, elbows on his knees and his head in his hands. The sun was rising over the farm to the east. He waited for Crystal Gayle to rest her head on his leg but then remembered he'd never feel that comforting weight again. Two weeks ago, he'd sat in this same spot and felt an overwhelming and unfamiliar sense of contentment and happiness, like life would be okay. He should have known better. Since then, he'd killed his dog, gotten himself fired from his job, acquired a kid, and lost his wife. He'd have thought it was a country song— a bad one—if he didn't have the freshly dug grave, an empty wallet, a baby bearing his last name, and the miles of regret on his heart to prove it.

—PART TWO—

— 18 —

"MAMA! MAMA! MAMA!"

Lucy groaned and rolled over to look at the clock. Five a.m. Better than yesterday. But still not as good as the seven a.m. Jared had been doing for several months before his teeth came through. She'd thought the first three months of having a baby had been hard. But now that Jared was ten months old, it wasn't any easier. With a groan, she pushed herself up out of bed and walked down the hall, squinting her eyes against the sun.

In the kitchen, she saw Jeptha's keys on the counter. Then she saw his boot hanging off the edge of the couch and his arm trailing the ground. He *had* come home after all.

"Mama!" Jared squawked from the crib, which, by necessity, was pushed against the wall of the living room, a few feet from Jeptha's head. He didn't stir. Lucy hadn't heard him come in the night before, but given how comatose he seemed, she guessed it was late and he was drunk, as usual. Better than the car, she supposed, where she'd found him passed out too many times to count in the last ten months, but still, she'd rather he came to bed. It'd be way better to wake her up than the baby, who wasn't nearly as heavy a sleeper as his drunk father.

Lucy sighed as she studied Jeptha's face. When she watched him like this and saw Jared's face in his contours, her stomach unclenched a little. Despite her low-grade, constant anger with him, she had a softness for her husband—love, of a sort, she guessed—that she cursed herself for on a daily basis. She remembered his sober self, his desire to be better, and the steady pleasure of those months. She wished sometimes that she had given him more in return for his effort—maybe he would have stayed that way if he'd found more reward from her in it. She missed those moments on the couch, tucked beside him. There had been a safety, a rootedness there. One baby and so much alcohol later, she saw Jeptha and still wanted to save him—wanted to see that man, the one with whom she had imagined building a family, again.

"Hey there, Mister," Lucy said to Jared, whose face lit up when he saw her.

"Mama," he said. Lucy broke into a smile. She couldn't help it. She knew every parent thought their kid was the cutest, but Jared really was, with his mess of white curls and his big three-toothed grin. She loved how he had one word and used it for everything—whether he meant her, or milk, or a toy, or his lovey. He never tired of saying her name, and she never tired of hearing it. She had been incapacitated by love for him there in the bathroom when he was born, and that feeling had only grown over the last ten months. From the outside, she knew her life didn't look good—Jeptha fallen completely off the wagon, her working sixty hours a week. But Jared made it all worth it. She had never known that the kind of love she felt for him existed in the world.

"Couldn't sleep, huh?" she said, hefting him up by his armpits. "You ready for your bottle?"

Lucy set him down on the floor in the kitchen. She grabbed a bottle off the dish rack, scooped one full spoon of formula into it, and scraped out another one from the dregs of what was left. This was the last formula in the trailer. She'd forgotten to pick it up at the Walmart yesterday, so tired on her break that she had actually sat in the break room and closed her eyes for twenty minutes until Teresa had come in yelling at her for having been five minutes late that morning. She had texted Jeptha asking him to get some since he wasn't doing anything else. She looked on every counter and opened every cabinet, slamming the last few doors as she realized he hadn't done it. She'd have to run out and get more on the way to drop Jared off at Marla's. Lucy looked with fury over at Jeptha's slumbering form.

Out of the corner of her eye, Lucy saw the cord to the living room lamp within Jared's grasp. She usually kept it tucked behind the table where he couldn't reach it, but Jeptha, in his drunken attempts to turn on the lamp, must have undone all her hard work. She was moving before Jared even reached his hand up to it, but she wasn't fast enough. The whole lamp crashed to the ground, narrowly missing Jared's head and glancing off his arm. He burst into loud, angry tears. A dead man couldn't have slept through it.

"What's going on?" Jeptha asked, rubbing his eyes.

"Your son is destroying the house. And I need to shower, get him dressed, and leave in less than ten minutes, so we can go get more formula. That's the last of it in the house," Lucy said, pointing at the bottle she had given to Jared.

"Oh shit. I was supposed to get more."

"Yeah, you were," Lucy said.

Jeptha didn't answer. He rubbed the beard that had grown in over the last few months. It was no wonder Jared cried every time Jeptha picked him up—he looked like a moonshiner and smelled worse.

"Want me to take him?" Jeptha asked.

"No. It'll make it worse."

She whipped Jared up off the ground and took him into the bathroom with her. She slammed the accordion door shut behind her. But it jammed and came off the track, gaping open about eight inches. She put Jared down on the floor and handed him his bottle. She took three deep breaths while holding on to the sink, her hands exactly where they had been when she pushed Jared out of her. She shook the anger out of her hands and slowly eased the door back on its track, closing it. A minute later, she heard Jeptha trudge by, followed by the sound of the mattress collapsing under his weight. He hadn't even stopped to take off his boots.

Even though she knew it would make her late to work, she eased her head under the water, sighing as the hot water hit her scalp. She portioned out a tiny dot of her favorite shampoo, a hotel sample from a trip to Knoxville three years ago. It smelled of oranges and honey. She peeked out at Jared every few seconds, but he was happily playing with an empty Safeguard soapbox and drinking his bottle. She stuck her head back under the water, blocking out all sound and feeling nothing but the water beating down on her. Under this cascade, with the scent of orange in her nose, she could pretend that nothing existed outside of this moment. Under the water, there was no deadbeat husband, crying baby, or relentless job. There was a nice, clean apartment, where a happy, smiling Jared had his own room and a fun, reliable baby sitter. The sun streamed in through bright kitchen windows, and Lucy played with Jared in the mornings and went to class in the afternoons. Under the water, for a few minutes each day, she could imagine that was her life.

Something hard bonked against the wooden doors of the sink vanity. Lucy held her breath, but a few seconds later, Jared began to wail. Lucy counted to ten, hoping he might stop on his own, and she could go back to that vision. But then she remembered she had to get formula before going to Marla's. She pulled her head out, turned off the water, and poked her head out of the curtain.

"You're okay, Jared," she said as cheerfully as she could. He wasn't, of course, but like her, he would have to make do.

LUCY BRIGHTENED WHEN she looked up from the register and saw Ethel Slocum standing at the head of the belt. She had been about to turn her light off and pull out her cash box, but Ethel was worth staying open for.

"Hey, Ethel," she said.

"Hey, Lucy! I been walking up and down the aisles for five minutes try-ing to see if you were here."

"Well, ain't that sweet!"

"You're still open, right?"

"You're my last. About to head out to pick up Jared."

"Aw, how's he doing?"

"Getting so big. Scooting around, pulling up on everything. Says Mama like crazy."

"I'll still never forget that phone call from LouEllen." Ethel shook her head. "I was so worried about you."

"Well, it all turned out all right, thanks to you getting the EMTs out there."

Lucy bagged up Ethel's purchases. She heard the older woman inhale a few times as if she was about to say something, but every time Lucy looked up, Ethel was silent.

"Fifty-two, thirty-eight," Lucy said.

Ethel opened her mouth one more time, but then dug in her purse. She counted out the cash, giving Lucy exact change from the pocket on her wallet. When Lucy turned to drop the change in the drawer, Ethel finally spoke.

"Is Jeptha all right?"

Yep, Lucy thought. *If all right is drunk, jobless, and home sleeping.*

"I think so," Lucy said. "Why?"

"Well . . ." Ethel said, shaking her head. "No. I shouldn't say nothing."

"Shouldn't say nothing about what?"

"It's just, he was supposed to come over and help Dick out with the addition yesterday, and he never showed."

"He didn't?"

"No. We called him, but no answer. He's not sick or anything, is he?"

"I think—I think he wasn't feeling great yesterday. Real feverish," Lucy lied.

"Oh, well, that's okay. We wouldn't want him to work like that," Ethel said, nodding. "But listen, we got to get that addition done. Dick had mentioned it to another guy before Jeptha said he could get back to it. Anyway, when Jeptha didn't show, Dick called him yesterday and he came on out. So we are probably gonna keep on with him, since he's done started."

Lucy nodded, afraid to talk. She swallowed down tears and finally said, "I understand. I hope he works out. If not, call us."

"Oh, I will, honey. I will."

Lucy stared down at the floor after Ethel walked away. She hated lying, hated being forced to pretend that everything was okay when the whole town knew it wasn't. She remembered all the times she avoided the break room before Jared came, not wanting to hear the women in there bitching about working too hard and living with husbands that were too drunk. Before, she'd avoided it because she didn't want to believe that could be her. Now, she avoided it because it hit too close to home. She looked at her co-workers, though, and wondered how they did it, year in and year out. Was there really no other way?

"Miss?" an older man said on the other side of the fully loaded belt.

"Oh. Sorry," Lucy said. She wiped her eyes and rang him up.

LUCY ROARED UP the gravel of Marla's driveway after her shift ended, still furious with Jeptha for losing the only job possibility he had had in months. It was one of her three long days each week, when she worked a shift at Walmart during the day and then went to the bar at night. She had to be at Judy's in forty-five minutes, but she always came by Marla's in time for dinner so she could see Jared. She would have just long enough to feed him the dinner Marla had already made and then run out the door. She slammed her car door shut behind her. Even when he wasn't there, Jeptha could ruin a moment.

"Hey, Lucy," Marla called from the kitchen when Lucy walked in. "Jared's in his chair."

"Thanks," Lucy said and turned into the dining room. Marla's kids were spooning mac and cheese and peas into their mouths silently, their eyes on the TV in the corner. Lucy watched Jared chase a mashed pea around his plate, his fat little fingers struggling to pick it up. She walked over to him and crouched down by his side.

"Hey, bud," she said, smiling.

"Mama!" His face lit up at the sight of her. He pointed at the pea, his face suddenly serious, and said, "Mama."

"Yeah, that's a pea. Can you say pea? That one is not cooperating, is it?"

"Mama," he said, shaking his head with the dismay only an almost-one-year-old could muster.

"You want some help?"

"Mama."

Lucy dragged a chair over beside him. She mashed the peas a bit more with the back of his spoon and put a few in his mouth. He closed his eyes with pleasure, which made Lucy laugh. Jared loved to eat.

"He loves that word, don't he?" Marla asked.

"Uses it for everything," Lucy said. She looked up at Marla. "How're you?"

"Fine. The same."

"How was he today?"

"Good. He's aching to get after those big kids. He took a couple steps today holding onto the table," Marla said, hesitantly.

"He did?" Lucy asked, her heart breaking. She'd missed it, like she'd missed the first time he sat up on his own, the first time he had pulled up to standing, and the first time he'd said "Mama." Sometimes Lucy felt like Marla was more of a mother to her son than she was.

"Sorry," Marla said, quietly. "I know it's hard to miss that stuff."

"Be easier if it was fair."

"Fair?"

"If Jeptha was doing his part too. But no. He lost the only job possibility he's had since Cody got him on at the plant and he got his ass fired." Lucy looked around at the kids, who were now looking at her. "Sorry," she said to Marla.

"It's okay. Nothing they ain't heard before." Marla wiped her hands on the dish towel that she wore over her shoulder nearly every second she was in the house. "You okay?" she asked, her hand on Lucy's shoulder.

"As okay as I can be, I guess," Lucy sighed. "Nothing's gonna change. It's my fault for thinking it might."

"What are you gonna do?" Marla asked.

"What can I do? I'm gonna go to work, try to raise this baby," Lucy said, her fingers stroking the side of Jared's cheek. He turned a gummy smile to Lucy. "Speaking of which, I better get out of here."

She kissed Jared on the head, her stomach aching at the thought of walking away from him. "All right, little man. I love you. I'll see you later."

"He'll be asleep and waiting on you," Marla said.

Lucy kissed Jared one more time. He happily returned to his dinner, as if his mom walking out the door was nothing to him. Tears came to her eyes again.

"And Lucy . . ." Marla called out. "It'll be okay. Things'll get better."

She looked back at Marla and shook her head. "That's sweet of you to say, Marla. It ain't true, but it's sweet of you to say it."

Lucy walked slower than she should back to her car, breathing in the cold night air. She wanted Marla to be right, wanted to believe things would get better. But she couldn't see her way clear to believing it. She'd settle for getting a little bit more time with her son. One day a week wasn't enough. She wanted to be able to put him to bed two nights in a row, to feel that soft, warm cheek nuzzle into her neck, his warm, milky breath leaving a damp spot on her skin. Beyond that, she wanted a partner in all this. She wanted the old Jeptha back—the one who had shown up at her door with diapers and a crib, taken her to the Fold, and rubbed her feet at night. The one who didn't drink. Even out of work, that Jeptha would have been a prize compared to the one who shared her home now. He was drunk more often than not, and out more than he was home. When she did spend time with him, he stared at her, his cheeks sunken and his eyes dimmed with squashed hope. He looked at her like he was craving something—anything—from her. She wasn't the only disappointed one in their trailer at night. They were both wanting more than they got.

But Lucy didn't have anything more to give. She was purely wrung out by the soul-consuming love she had for Jared, the way it had overtaken her on first glance and continued to beat her to within an inch of her life every day. It was exhausting loving something like that; there was no more of her to go around. Jeptha could see that. She tried to hide it from him, to force her face to remain the same when she glanced from Jared to Jeptha. But there was no way to do it—the light fell away from her skin as soon as she turned away from Jared. She was just so tired. She had nothing left for her husband except for anger and frustration. And even if there was something to give, who would she give it to? The sad, grizzly guy on the couch? She barely knew who he was.

She didn't know much of anything anymore. All the certainty she'd once had was gone. The only thing she knew for sure was how much she loved Jared. Twenty-two years of living, and he was the only good thing she had to show for it.

———

WHEN LUCY WALKED through the door of the bar, Judy was wiping down the counter, lifting up Delnor's glass and paper and glasses and keys as she moved past his spot on the bar. "Damn, Delnor, you about moved in here, or what?"

"Lucy!" Delnor said, ignoring Judy and turning to the front door. "How's that baby?"

"Trouble, Delnor. Pure trouble," she said, starting to laugh. She couldn't help herself. Delnor—with his scraggly beard, habit of living at the bar, and evident drinking problem—was such an unlikely person to inquire about a baby, but he asked after Jared every time he saw her. When Jared was only a few months old, Lucy had had to bring him in for a couple hours one afternoon because Marla's kids were sick. Delnor had eased Jared out of the car seat while Lucy went down to the stock room and had him asleep in the crook of his arm before she returned. He stayed there for two hours, asleep for most of it and pulling on Delnor's beard for the rest. Both had been delighted.

"Jeptha playing tonight?" Judy asked when Lucy looked up. He'd never

come in last Friday night, and Lucy had been caught telling the truth—
that he'd been fine when she left—as Cody was spinning a web of lies about
him being sick for days. Lying to Judy was dangerous, and Cody had slunk
out of the bar after the set, eager to get away before Judy made eye contact
with him. When Lucy got home, she found Jeptha face down in the middle
of the bed, snoring. The room smelled of whiskey. Lucy had slept on the
couch that night.

"Far as I know," Lucy said, her anger flooding back in. "But I don't
know much."

Judy was silent. Her right eyebrow pointed skyward, and the right corner of her lips tucked back, rendering her whole mouth off-kilter. It was
her deeply skeptical look, the one she wore when the person in front of her
was slinging bullshit. "Y'all doing all right?"

Lucy shrugged her shoulders. Judy had been a bartender long enough to
know the signs. She had once told Lucy that the people who had had the
worst things happen in their lives rarely shared them—they stayed on the
periphery of the crowd, got along well enough with everyone, but rarely di-
vulged anything about themselves. It was the ones yelling about themselves
on the bar stools that hadn't really experienced anything terribly profound.

"Want me to say something to him?" Judy volunteered.

"Can't imagine it would make a difference," Lucy said. "Besides, who
knows if he'll even show tonight?"

"He better," Judy said, pulling a beer off the draft with a practiced hand.
"I hired a bluegrass band. I don't know much, but bluegrass seems to come
with a mandolin. If the band doesn't have one, then they're not a band. And
I'm not paying."

They needed the money, little as it was, that Jeptha brought home from
the gig. "I'll tell him," Lucy said. "He'll be here."

She dug her phone out of her back pocket as she went down the stock
room stairs. The call went straight to voicemail, of course. She'd thought
missing his son's birth might have been enough of a reminder for him to
charge his phone, but no. He was forever forgetting. She left him an acid-
tinged message that he'd get tomorrow and threw up a quick, pointless
prayer that he wasn't sitting at home drinking, totally oblivious to tonight's
show.

AN HOUR AND a half later, the band had already played half a set when Jeptha finally stumbled in. He made a beeline for her.

"Hey," he said, and tried to hug her. She pushed him away.

"What?" he asked.

The audacity of the question made her faint with rage. She took a breath and ignored it. "You are late. They already started."

"It ain't like I missed much."

"Eight songs."

"Hell, Lucy. We play sixteen. I'll get on half."

"Judy's gonna stop paying you if you don't start showing up."

"Nah, she won't."

"Yeah, she will," Lucy said. "And seems like you are rapidly running out of job options these days. The Slocums hired somebody else when you didn't show."

"Oh, shit. I forgot about that," Jeptha said. He rubbed his beard, and his eyes darted away toward the stage. "Damn. Can't believe they did that."

"You can't believe it? You didn't show up. What do you expect? It's a job—if you aren't there, the work doesn't get done. It's not like a marriage, where you can't get out no matter how often a person doesn't show up."

She strode back to the bar without a backward glance. Lucy busied herself for an hour, ignoring the band as best she could. Every time she saw Jeptha up there, trying to catch her eye and mouthing the words "I'm sorry," at her, she turned away, finding any excuse she could to clean. She wiped down tables that still had five people sitting at them, hand washed beer glasses, a first at Judy's, and took away glasses from the bar with a vigor that bordered on mania. She had Delnor hoarding his spread, one arm shielding his beer, the other his hamburger.

"Lucy!" Judy said. Her sharp tone stilled Lucy in her most recent sweep down the bar.

"What?" Lucy yelled back.

Silence followed. Lucy turned slowly to Judy and saw her boss's mouth set in a thin line, her blue eyes dangerously sparkling. "Take a break. Now."

"Fine."

Lucy ripped off her apron and threw it on the bar. Delnor cowered as she passed, picking up both his glass and his plate and holding them in his lap. She pushed the back door open with both hands and kicked it shut behind her.

"Dammit!" she screamed into the wind, finally giving in to the tears that had been hounding her all day.

A few minutes later, Lucy heard the door ease open. She tensed, thinking it was Jeptha, but breathed out when she heard mandolin notes from inside. She gave Judy a half-hearted smile.

"I'm sorry," Lucy said. "Bad day."

"You okay?" Judy asked. The tender note in Judy's voice made Lucy start crying again.

"No," she finally said. "Not really."

Judy squeezed Lucy's arm. "I'm sorry."

"What are you sorry for? It ain't your fault he turned out to be exactly what he is."

"But I . . . I told you to ask yourself if maybe there was more to him. It wasn't my business."

"It wasn't your decision, either. I made this choice."

"Still, I told you love like that didn't come around every day. And it doesn't. But love may not be enough."

"Don't worry about it, Judy. I made my bed."

"Don't mean you have to lie in it, though."

"Did you just say 'don't'? Instead of 'doesn't'?" Lucy asked, starting to laugh.

"Oh God. Did I?" Judy asked, a genuine look of horror on her face. "Been hanging out with all you rednecks too much."

Lucy's laugh petered out as she pictured her drunk husband knocking into the door on his way into the bar tonight. "Redneck is right, I guess."

"I didn't mean it like that."

"I know. But if the shoe fits . . ."

"Lucy, just because you made a choice to be with Jeptha a year ago, that doesn't mean you have to keep making it."

"What would I do?"

"What women all over the world do every day. Pack up your stuff, get your kid, and go."

"Where?"

"I happen to know you've got a nicely decorated baby room waiting for you at your old house."

"With LouEllen. Who kicked me out."

"People make mistakes. Honestly, I don't know what the right answer is. But you do. Or if you don't, you'll figure it out."

Lucy looked out at the parking lot, the site of her son's conception. The lights cast a sickly orange glow on cracks that ran through the asphalt like a dried lava field while tumbleweeds of McDonald's wrappers, cigarette butts, and smashed beer bottles heaped around the dumpster. There was no romance, no happy ending to be found here. It was little wonder that nothing after had gone well.

"You'll figure it out," Judy said. "Just because you're in this place now, doesn't mean you have to stay in it. You've got choices. You need to make them."

"I'll think about it," she said, feeling like her world was spinning and she had no safe purchase.

"All right then," Judy said, squeezing Lucy's arm one more time. "Come on back in when you're ready."

"Choices," Lucy said under breath after the door closed behind Judy. She thought of Jared's face at dinner as he'd happily shoved peas into his mouth. "We've got choices, buddy," she said, both to her son and to herself. "We've got choices."

— 19 —

JEPTHA WOKE UP IN bed for the first time in two weeks. He'd been coming home too late and too drunk to risk waking up Lucy, so he'd been passing out on the couch. Truth was, he liked falling asleep there, listening to Jared's breath whistle in and out, his little baby sighs puncturing the air every few minutes. Today, though, he stared up at the ceiling of his bedroom and waited for the pain to kick in. It always seemed to take a minute for his brain to catch up with the job the alcohol had done on his body. He looked to his right and saw Lucy sprawled beside him, asleep on her belly with her right leg up at an impossible angle, her hair in a messy halo around her face. He watched her for a moment, trying to match her sleep-swollen face with the angry one from last night. There was no malice in her puffy cheeks or half-parted lips. Still, her words played endlessly in his head, pounding along with his headache—"It ain't like a marriage, where you can't get out no matter how often the person doesn't show up."

Lucy shifted in her sleep, a sigh floating out over her lips. He leaned toward her, breathing in the air she had just exhaled, desperate to be close to her. A paralyzing tremor ran through him at the thought of losing her. It was as if a sinkhole had yawned open beneath their trailer, leaving Jeptha clinging to the sides, his hands stripping bark from the roots he clung to, hoping like hell someone would come along and save his sorry ass, but knowing he was the only one who could do so.

When Jeptha couldn't hold it any longer, he breathed out and hoisted himself up. He stumbled into the corner of the bed and out into the hall. He rubbed his hand over his face as he shuffled down the hall to the kitchen. He wondered if he should shave his beard, an outgrowth of nothing more than laziness. Then his head throbbed and the thought of a razor near it made him cringe. Just then, he stepped down hard on the edge of a plastic block. It dug deep and painfully into the meaty part of his foot.

"Ow, shit!" he yelled, jumping up and down with his foot in his hand. He banged his shoulder against the wall and finally landed in a heap on the floor. He held his breath, hoping no one had heard. The silence was deafening. Then came the storm. Jared was standing up in his crib, crying as loudly as Jeptha had ever heard him.

"Dammit, Jeptha," Lucy said as she stepped over him and made her way to their son. "It's six thirty in the morning—he was actually sleeping, for a change."

"I stepped on something," Jeptha protested. "What was I supposed to do? Why are his blocks all over the hallway anyway?"

"When did I have time to clean it up yesterday? You were here all day. Why didn't you pick 'em up?" Lucy asked.

Jeptha looked over at the blocks strewn outside the bathroom door. He wasn't sure why he hadn't picked them up. He could have. He'd been sitting on the couch twelve feet away watching TV for half the day. He'd even stepped over the damn things three times on his way to the bathroom.

"Exactly," Lucy said in response to Jeptha's silence. She held Jared in her arms. He was quiet, too quiet. Not even a year old, and Jared already knew the sound of his parents' fighting. Jeptha remembered that quiet from his own childhood. Lucy shook the bottle in her hand with about ten times more effort than it needed and handed it to Jared, who grabbed it eagerly. Jeptha hauled himself up off the floor and sat down hard on the couch, rubbing his foot.

Lucy's phone rang.

"What on earth?" she said, shifting Jared to her other side to answer it. He squirmed and started crying.

"Here," Lucy said and dropped Jared on Jeptha's lap. Jeptha quickly faced him out so he could drink his bottle and keep his eyes on his mama. Jared peered up at Jeptha, his bottle clenched in his hand. Jeptha smiled at him and then leaned down to kiss him on the cheek, but Jared closed his eyes and pulled away.

"Oh, sorry buddy. My beard's pretty scratchy, huh?"

Jeptha rubbed Jared's belly through his pajamas for a minute until he realized that something was wet. He looked down and saw that Jared's pajamas were wet with pee, which was now all over his own hand. He edged

Jared up into a sitting position and looked down at his shirt, which was moist on the front where Jared was sitting.

"Crap," Lucy said to the person on the phone. "No, I understand. You can't do nothing about that. I hope you feel better," she said. "All right, bye."

Jeptha looked at her. "Uh, Jared peed through his diaper."

She stared back at him. "Well, maybe you should change it."

"Oh. Yeah. Right."

He held Jared out from his body and took him over to the table. He laid his son down and looked around for the diapers.

"On the bench," Lucy said, pointing at a small green basket stuffed with diapers, wipes, and two of the twenty-seven ointments that seemed to have taken over their trailer as soon as they had a kid. Jeptha saw she was furiously dialing numbers and was about to ask if everything was okay when Jared suddenly rolled over on his side, spreading a night's worth of poop over the changing pad.

"Come on, Jared," Jeptha said. "Turn over. I got to get this off."

Jared laughed, turned onto his back, and waved his feet in the air, one of his heels covered in poop. Jeptha closed his eyes and took a deep breath. It was a mistake.

"Jared, I hate to tell you, but you stink," he said to his son, who laughed, delighted.

"Tink!" Jared shouted. Jeptha looked around guiltily, hoping Lucy hadn't heard. He guessed "stink" wasn't a horrible word for a kid to learn, but he was pretty sure she'd have preferred his second word be something else. Jeptha had hoped for "dada," but had to admit the baby was probably far more familiar with stink than with dada. By the look on Lucy's face, she'd heard.

Lucy sat down on the couch. She held her phone in between her legs and was staring down at the floor.

"Everything okay?" Jeptha asked.

"Marla's kids have a stomach bug so she can't take him. And I can't miss any more work or Teresa's going to fire me."

"She wouldn't do that."

Lucy looked at Jeptha with a face so hard it scared him. "You aren't real clear on the relationship between showing up for work and keeping your job, are you?"

Jeptha stared down at the ground, stung but unable to deny the truth of what she'd said. Lucy was all about the uncomfortable truths these days.

"I don't know what to do," he heard Lucy say behind him. Jeptha looked down at his son.

"Well, um . . . I could take him."

Lucy laughed like he'd told the funniest joke in the world. But when she looked up, she stopped. "Oh. You're serious."

"I mean, I'm his dad. I can keep him alive for a day." Jeptha went back to wiping his son's bottom. "Jesus Christ, what is this?" he wondered out loud, pawing at the stuck-on flakes on his son's bottom with his sixth wipe.

"Cheerios," Lucy said from behind him. He heard her sigh. "So much for having choices," she said under her breath.

Jeptha looked at her, his eyes wide and his heart beating fast. He hadn't actually expected her to say yes. Somehow he had yet to spend a whole day with Jared. With a hangover beating at his body like a July thunderstorm, today seemed like a really bad day to start. He watched Jared's face crumple as if he could tell what was about to happen.

"What do I do with him?" Jeptha asked.

"He's ten months old. Don't you think you probably should know the answer by now?"

He should know. But he didn't.

"I'll write it all for you. Are you sure you can do this?"

Jeptha bit his lip, terrified but not wanting to show it. "I think so."

Lucy found a piece of paper and a pen. After a couple of minutes of writing—during which Jeptha grew ever more scared, unaware that there was that much required in taking care of a baby—she looked up at him, her eyes narrowed.

"Jeptha." Her voice was stern and serious.

"Yeah?"

"No drinking. Not a drop. Not while you have him."

"I wouldn't. He's my son too."

"I mean it. He's my everyth—" She stopped, but they both knew what she'd been about to say. "No drinking. Use his car seat like I showed you a couple weeks ago. And keep your phone on. Everything else is written down here."

Jared cried in force as his mom walked into the bedroom and shut the door. Jeptha heard her opening drawers and pulling on clothes. She was going to change her mind, Jeptha was sure of it. He waited a minute or two, sure that Lucy would come through that door, unable to resist the sound of her baby crying. No one emerged from the door. Finally, he leaned over and picked Jared up. He set him up on his lap and bounced him on his knee. Jared cried. Jeptha put him up on his shoulder like he'd seen Lucy do. Jared cried harder.

The bedroom door opened—both Jeptha and the baby looked toward it like Christ himself had walked through. They were at the end of the hall, with Jeptha holding Jared out before Lucy was all the way through the bedroom door. Jared nearly leapt into her arms. She held him tight against her, kissed the top of his head, and then peeled his arms off her shoulders and handed him back, screaming, to Jeptha.

"You're all right, Jared. Mama's got to go."

"But he's crying," Jeptha said.

"He does that."

"How do I make it stop?"

"Give him his bottle. Or some Cheerios. Or both. Change his diaper. Play with him."

She gave Jared another kiss on his head and walked out the door. The trailer was silent, both Jared and Jeptha struck dumb at the sight of Lucy heading down the long drive.

Jared's blue eyes peered up at his dad. Jeptha raised an eyebrow at him. "What the hell are we gonna do?" he asked.

Jared cried.

"Probably the right response," Jeptha said, nodding at his son.

THE CAR SEAT had seemed much easier to install when Lucy did it. Jeptha knew a seat belt went through a loop on the bottom and the handle went the other way, but he couldn't figure out how to get Jared inside the car seat without being strangled by the belt. Jeptha's nerves frazzled as he sweated through his shirt. He wrestled with the seat and tried to ignore Jared's increasingly high-pitched cries. The poor kid had already cried for two hours as Jeptha tried method after method to make it stop. He gave him a bottle, changed his diaper, sat him on the floor and stacked blocks with him, and cuddled him. Nothing worked. His last attempt had been to make monkey noises at Jared, which had made him stop crying for about twenty seconds until he got scared and started up again. Surely, Jeptha thought, there was a limit to the tears a baby could cry. If so, they had to be near to finding it. Finally, exasperated with the crying and the car seat, Jeptha put Jared in it, did up the buckles inside as tight as he could, threw a seat belt over the entire contraption and pulled it tight.

The drive to Cody and Marla's was hellish, but Jeptha didn't know where else to go. He was hoping like hell that Marla was still there, that he could convince her to feel better. He knew she'd say no if he called to check first, so he figured his best option was to show up with Jared. She couldn't say no to helping when it was Jared's sweet face doing the asking, could she? Jeptha couldn't figure how he was going to do twelve more hours of this with the headache he had from last night. He rolled down the windows of the car, hoping some of the sound would flee the hotbox of tears. But an old lady at a stop sign stared at him, hatred on her face, like he was back there kicking the baby instead of plainly driving the car, incapable of doing anything but getting on to his destination. He rolled the window up and slunk down deep in the seats.

He sped up Cody's driveway, flying in the air as he hit a bump at the bottom of their drive. He saw Jared's car seat pop up off the cushion and resettle itself almost in the middle of the car. He took that as a pretty good indication that he had not installed it correctly. He parked the car, grabbed the car seat with Jared, who stopped crying momentarily in surprise at his father's face, and banged on Cody's door.

"Marla!" he cried, beating on the door. "Marla!"

"Damn it, man. What do you want?" Cody said, shuffling to the door, wearing a pair of threadbare tighty-whiteys, workout socks, and a head of disheveled hair.

"Oh, man. I'm sorry," Jeptha said.

"What do you want?"

Jeptha hefted up Jared's car seat, so Cody could see the baby's face. There was no sound coming out of Jared's mouth, just an O of pain in a silent scream.

"She ain't here," Cody said through the screen. He looked down at Jared. "He's pretty pissed, ain't he?"

"When's she back?"

"Not until tomorrow. She took the kids up to her mama's with her so she can rest while her mama watches them."

"How come you ain't watching them?"

"I got work at noon." Cody stared at Jared's squalling form and rubbed his face. "Hell, come on in. I can't go back to sleep now anyhow."

Jeptha followed him into the house and collapsed gratefully onto the opposite end of the couch from Cody.

"You gonna do anything with him?" Cody asked, nodding at the baby.

"Should I get him out?"

"Far as I can tell, being in there ain't working for him much."

Jeptha unbuckled Jared and pulled him out of the seat, narrowly missing clocking Jared's head on the handle. He cuddled him close to his neck like he had seen Lucy do, but Jared pulled away, his eyes screwed up tight as Jeptha's beard scratched him.

"Here," Cody said. He grabbed Jared and tucked him in tight beside him, sitting up and facing the TV. "This is what I always did with mine when they was babies."

Jared quieted instantly, his eyes focused on the television. He looked up at Cody, and Jeptha saw a smile flit across his son's face. Everyone else made it look so easy, even Cody. It seemed odd to have his son tucked beside the naked thighs of a man wearing nothing but tighty-whities on a couch, but he was quiet. For now, that was enough.

"How you doing?" Cody asked.

"All right. You?"

"I ain't the one showed up at my friend's house with a screaming baby at eight a.m."

"Eh . . . things ain't great. Lucy's pissed I still don't got a job."

Cody was silent.

"I know. I'm sorry," Jeptha said.

"It's past," he shrugged.

"I'm wanting to figure out if I can do something more with the farm," Jeptha said, haltingly.

"More? Y'all are growing as much as you can, ain't you?"

"As much tobacco as we can."

"You got another crop in mind?"

"Maybe."

"Jeptha, don't do nothing stupid," Cody said, shaking his head.

"Travis does it."

"Travis doesn't have a wife or kid. If he gets caught, it's just him."

"How's he gonna get caught?"

"Who knows? It happens, though."

Jared sniffled, his mouth turned down like a circus clown's.

"Why don't you make this guy a bottle?" Cody said.

"Another one?" Jeptha asked.

"Can't hurt."

Jeptha made the bottle and handed it over to Cody, who tipped it up for Jared to drink until his tiny hands grabbed the middle himself.

"I don't think it's a bad idea," Jeptha said, defensively.

"The bottle?" Cody asked. "No, he seems to like it . . . Oh, planting pot under the tobacco? Just don't seem that smart to me."

"What else am I gonna do?" Jeptha asked. He was genuinely interested. He had no idea what else he could do for Lucy and Jared. They'd long since spent the money he brought in from the tobacco, little as it was, and he couldn't borrow any more from Bobby. He knew planting pot was a desperate idea, but he was nothing if not a desperate man.

"Y'all ought to see if you can buy that land next to yours. Add some acres."

"Bobby done bought it."

"What? When?"

"Last year. Didn't tell me about it until harvest time. Caught him about to slice off his balls coming over the barb wire fence." Jeptha couldn't look at his friend while he spoke. It had been his dream for years to buy that land, get a bigger quota, and Bobby's doing it without him had made him madder than anything in his life. He'd been so caught up with Lucy at the time that he hadn't even realized how mad he was about it, but now, he thought about it every single day.

"Shit. Where'd he get the cash?"

"That's the part I can't figure. I mean, he works, but it ain't like he's got that much coming in. Especially since we got almost nothing for the tobacco last year."

"Well, I'm sorry, man. I know you was wanting that."

Jeptha shrugged, noticing that Jared's eyes were becoming more and more wrinkled around the edges. As he watched, they closed and then sprang open, over and over. The bottle drooped out of his mouth. Jeptha got scared—the boy clearly needed to sleep. Should he take him home now? Or could he put him down here somewhere? Before he could think through the question, Cody looked down and noticed the half-sleeping boy. He cupped one hand under his diaper, another behind his neck, and laid Jared down on the couch. Jared gripped his bottle and sucked on the nipple. After a minute or two, his hand fell to his side and Cody grabbed the bottle before it spilled on the couch. His son didn't flinch. He looked like his mother from this morning. They were both easy to love when they were asleep.

"That's what mine always did. Passed out on the couch. Think it's the TV that does it."

"I don't know what I'm going to do with him today."

"You oughta take him for a walk. Go walk your property, see if you can't come up with something legal to do with it. And ain't that farm across from y'all's coming up soon?"

"Why are you so interested in me getting more land?"

"I ain't. Just interested in not having to go to the jail every time I want to say hi to you."

"I gotta do something."

"Well, here's a thought," Cody said. "You could stop drinking."

Jeptha seethed. "You don't know a thing about it," he finally said.

"Seems like you been out every night lately. Sleeping on your couch, or your car . . ." He looked at Jeptha. "Girls talk. To Marla especially."

"I'm fine. I don't know what she's been telling Marla, but me having a couple drinks at night ain't the problem."

"Sure about that?"

Jeptha stood up. His keys clanged to the floor.

"Shh. You're gonna wake him up," Cody said.

"Don't matter. We're leaving anyway."

"Why?"

"It ain't the drinking keeping me from working. It's all these assholes in town won't give me a chance. And I sure as hell ain't gonna sit here and listen to you lecture me about it. You ain't the boss of me." Jeptha's belly squirmed with shame. Jeptha knew Cody was right, but he didn't need to hear his best friend put words to what Lucy and everyone else in town was thinking.

"I ain't lecturing. Just sayin'."

"I get enough of that at home."

Jeptha picked up Jared from his nest on the couch. He woke up, of course, and started screaming immediately. Jeptha threw him in the car seat, none too gently, and tried to steel himself against the crying. He snatched up the car seat by the handle, carried it outside, slung it in the back of the car, and strapped it in the way he had on the way over. Cody would know how to install it the right way, but Jeptha had too much pride to ask.

"You want a hand with that?" Cody asked from behind him.

Jeptha shook his head. "I know how to do it."

"Doesn't look like it."

"Dammit, Cody!"

"Hey man, I am sorry. But you are gonna kill that kid, and I can't let you do it. Move."

Cody pushed Jeptha out of the way and leaned into the car. He flipped the seat around so Jared was facing the back, pulled the seatbelt tight across his feet, and slotted the strap through the two hooks on the bottom of the seat that Jeptha couldn't for the life of him figure out a use for. He leaned onto the handle with his naked belly and pulled the belt tight. Jeptha looked away from the sight of Cody's balls slipping out the bottom of his underwear.

"All set," Cody said. "You got a pacifier for him?"

"No."

Cody closed the door. "Well, good luck with that then."

Jeptha looked away from his friend. He could apologize now, and everything would be okay. Part of him wanted to. The other part knew apologizing would be acknowledging that his friend had a point—and even though he knew it was true, he didn't want to admit it. Drinking was the only true friend he had. He couldn't lose it. Not now.

———

THE DAY DID not improve. Every time Jeptha picked Jared up, he screamed and cried. It took Jeptha until noon to remember that he wore diapers and probably needed a change. His diaper was well past the saturation point, and Jared's bottom was the ferocious red of cheap hot dogs. Lucy checked in at eleven and again at three, and Jeptha had stepped outside the trailer, far enough away that he hoped she couldn't hear Jared screaming. He lied to her, telling her they were fine and Jared was napping both times. Truth was, Jared slept about twenty minutes the whole day long, and ten minutes of it had been at Cody's house on the couch. It had gotten so bad that Jeptha himself had cried twice, pleading with his son to stop. That hadn't worked either.

By five o'clock, Jeptha was done. He'd never wanted a drink more in his life. He didn't know what else to do or where else to go. His whole body was aching for alcohol; his head was pounding from the combined effects of his hangover and Jared's crying; and he wanted—no, needed—someone else to try to entertain Jared for even a few minutes. At ten minutes after five, they pulled into the parking lot at Judy's. Jeptha toted the seat into the bar, aware as he did so that there was something wrong about taking a baby into the place.

"Jared, this is where Daddy works," he said.

"You bringing that baby in here?" Judy asked from behind the bar.

"That okay?"

"I mean, it's a bar. Not a babysitting service. But come on in."

Jeptha settled at the bar and put the car seat on the counter.

Judy poked her head into the car seat. "Hey, Jared. How are you?"

Jared stared back at her, his lips turning down into a pout. Jeptha laughed.

"What?' Judy said, pulling her head back and looking affronted. "It's not like you're so good with him."

Jared smiled at Judy then. "See? He's a smart kid," she said. "You want some water or something?"

"Yeah," Jeptha said, remembering Lucy's warning from the morning. His hands shook as he set down Jared's car seat on the floor beside him. He knew if he had a couple sips of beer, he'd be back to feeling normal again. He'd promised Lucy, but surely half a beer didn't count. "Don't suppose you would bring me half a beer too?"

Judy stared at him, her eyes steely. Jeptha shook, and not just from lack of alcohol. The truth was, Judy scared the shit out of him. He wasn't alone in that feeling—everyone, Jeptha included, liked to blame it on her being a Yankee, but he knew that wasn't it. She was so hard, so flinty, like that buck out at Delnor's place that people had been hunting for years. No one had ever come close to getting it, but sightings came in a few times a season. Fourteen points, a monster of a white tail, with an antler spread that looked more moose than deer. Jeptha had seen him once and been stunned into silence in his tree stand. The buck walked past Jeptha with a fearlessness and pride that no deer ought to have. Jeptha had eased the safety back on his rifle and set it across his lap. The buck watched every move, and not a muscle flinched, as if nothing—not humans, not guns, not death—scared him. Judy was giving Jeptha that same look now: piercing, fearless, and haunting. He looked down at the counter, rubbing the smooth curve of the edge with his thumb. He'd been no braver with that buck. Two minutes after it had stepped off into the underbrush, Jeptha had packed up for the day and gone home to finish a six-pack by noon.

"You are fucking up your life, Jeptha Taylor," she said finally. "It's awful to watch."

"What are you talking about? Because I want a beer?" he asked.

"Not 'cause you want this beer but because you want all the beers. You are circling the drain. You aren't like Delnor—who can maintain this," she said. Delnor shone with a rare, if backhanded, compliment. "You're going down. And I can't stand to see you take Lucy and this baby with you."

"I ain't going nowhere. I'm fine." First Cody, now Judy—what had he done to the world today to deserve this?

"If I had a dollar for every time I've heard a drunk say that . . ."

"Well, you wouldn't have a dollar from me. I ain't a drunk," Jeptha said, feeling the kind of righteous anger that only came when he was lying through his teeth.

Judy nodded at his hands, one frenetically rocking the handle of Jared's car seat, the other shaking as he reached for a sip of water. "So, what's that? Parkinson's?"

"That's none of your business."

Judy was silent for a moment. "Here's the thing, Jeptha. This," she looked around the bar, "is my business. And Lucy works here, so she's my business. That band you're in is my business. And you're making a mess of all of it."

For Jeptha, there'd always been a fine line between anger and sadness. He always had to choose—if he didn't stoke the fire, he'd cross over into the sort of pitiful territory he'd always associated with old women, mourning their life. He tried to summon the same anger that had given him whatever little drive he'd had in life, but at the moment it wouldn't come. He just felt tired, and behind that exhaustion was a sadness so deep and profound he felt that sinkhole sensation again, the earth gaping open beneath him.

"Whatever," he said. It was the only word he had available to him in the moment.

"So that's how it is." She crossed her arms over her chest and shook her head at him. "You told me once that Taylors didn't, quote, 'have no honor.' I guess you were right."

Jared busted out with a squall that turned every head in the bar. Jeptha nearly cried with relief. He hustled him out of the car seat and spent the next ten minutes trying to quiet him down, never once looking at Judy. Eventually, as Jeptha walked up and down the floor bouncing and shushing Jared as he went, she stopped glaring at him and went downstairs.

"We're all right, aren't we, Jared?" Jeptha cooed to him. His son stared up sleepily at him. "Daddy's not as bad as everyone thinks, is he?"

"Hey, Jeptha. Hey," Delnor said as Jeptha passed, his hand wagging awkwardly at Jeptha.

"What's up, Delnor?"

"Here. This is for you." Delnor passed him an unopened beer. "For after. When you get home."

"You sure?"

Delnor looked down at Jeptha's hands, where they patted Jared's bottom. "I know how it is. You need one to steady you out a little."

"Thank you, Delnor."

"It's for after, though, mind you. I'll kick your ass myself if I see you drinking it before you get that baby home."

"I wouldn't . . ."

"Yeah, tell yourself that. I used to," Delnor said. "I'm serious now. Only after Lucy takes that baby."

Jeptha nodded. He looked down and saw that Jared was finally, blissfully, asleep on his shoulder. Jeptha eased him into the seat and carefully fitted the buckles around him. Jared's face creased like an old man and then relaxed back into sleep.

"Lucy's gonna be home soon. I better go," Jeptha whispered to Delnor.

Jeptha stuffed the beer into the bottle pocket of Jared's diaper bag and grabbed the car seat in the crook of his elbow. At the car, he set the diaper bag down on the ground and flipped the car seat to face backward like Cody had done and strapped his son in. He shook the seat back and forth, satisfied that it didn't move and thrilled that somehow Jared was still asleep. He straightened up out of the car, smiling. He felt, if not competent, then at least not totally incompetent.

He picked up the diaper bag, the beer seeming to call his name. He pulled it out, imagining the crisp taste, the exhilarating cold tumbling down his throat. His finger crept under the tab, the cold metal digging into the pad of his fingertip. He wiggled it there, back and forth. His hands shook harder. He closed his eyes, hearing Delnor's words in his head. Home. He'd drink it at home, once Lucy was there.

Resolution made, he opened his eyes to find Lucy staring at him, a fury in her eyes like none he'd ever seen.

— 20 —

LUCY WAS NO STRANGER to anger. Growing up, her house hadn't been the sea of calm that she imagined others were. Her mother burned with a cool flame that grew white-hot when she was really angry, but her father was more like her, fiery and sudden. Their collisions had seemed epic to her as a child. Still, those fights had been nothing to the anger that Lucy felt when they died. It was an anger that seared through her, cauterized her soft edges. It was the kind of anger that made her so mad at God—who she imagined looked down on his creation like some sleazy reality show producer—that she did dumb shit, like get in the back of Jeptha's car. It made her think that nothing mattered, that there was nothing to lose. Because in the end, she was sure, we were all as likely to die too young at the hands of a man so drunk he actually thought it was possible his pig had been driving as we were doing something stupid.

Then, Jared came. Now, everything mattered. She was still angry, but love for him had kicked some of it aside, and for what was left, there was a purpose. So when she saw Jeptha standing by the car with her baby strapped inside and a beer in his hand, his face tipped back like he was about to relish that cool drink before he drove their son home, she found she had scaled a new, dizzying height of anger, one she had never surmounted before. She was so angry that her throat closed up, and the only word she could force out of it was a scaly, hoarse, "No."

Jeptha's eyes dropped to the can of beer in his hand and then back to her face. How dare he look sad that she had interrupted him before he could drink that beer?

"No," she said again, as she stomped closer to the car. She pushed him out of the way and leaned down to unbuckle Jared's car seat. His eyes were half closed, but they sprang open when he saw her face.

"Mama!" he yelled, grabbing her cheeks with his hands and smiling with the glee of a kid who has no idea what's going on. Lucy envied him.

She jerked the seat out of the car and faced Jeptha. She shook her head at him, gritting her teeth as she tried to breathe, tears of rage massing in her eyes and clogging in her throat like a thunderstorm gathering power. She wanted to scream at him, to wound him, to scare him. But none of it would come out.

"No," she said again and walked to her car.

"Lucy, no! I wasn't drinking. I wasn't going to," he yelled behind her. She heard footsteps cracking over the loose chunks of asphalt. "I wasn't—Delnor gave me this, for later. I was about to put it away and drive him home."

Lucy kept walking.

"Please, Lucy. You got to believe me."

She whipped around. "Why? You've been drunk every night for months. Why should I believe you?"

She saw the hurt look in his eyes, and satisfaction surged through her.

"I wouldn't, Lucy. I wouldn't hurt him like that."

"No," she said, leaving him behind her and plopping Jared's seat into the car seat base as gently as she could given that she wanted to throw something.

"Tink!" Jared said. She leaned down and forced her voice into as close an approximation of Mommy-speak as she could.

"Yep, you do stink, buddy. We'll go change it."

"Lucy! Wait," Jeptha said, his hand on her shoulder.

His face was splotchy with worry, and rank sweat dotted his shirt and soaked his armpits. He was sober and terrified. But all she could see was that look, the one he'd been giving the can of beer in his hand, that look of delicious abandon. She shook her head again as she got in the car.

"No," she said and drove off.

Five minutes down the highway, she realized she had no idea where to go. She pulled over and put her head down on the steering wheel.

"Mama?" Jared called from the back seat.

"Yes, sweetheart. Mama is here," she mumbled into her hands.

"Tink?"

"No, Mama doesn't stink. She does need to think, though."

"Dink," Jared said somberly.

Marla was gone, her kids still sick. Lucy had to be at Judy's tonight and couldn't take Jared with her. As a last resort, she could bail on her shift tonight, but Judy's patience wouldn't last forever, especially if both members of her family stopped showing up. She had a vision then of Judy talking about choices the other night. Lucy knew exactly where to go.

She bumped up the drive to LouEllen's ten minutes later, by which time Jared had lost his excitement over his new word and had begun to cry about being in a wet, dirty diaper. She hadn't seen LouEllen in months. Her heart thudded against her chest with fear that LouEllen wouldn't take her in. Lucy didn't care anymore that LouEllen was right. She just wanted to keep Jared safe.

She brought his car seat up on the porch and then got him out of it, balancing him on her hip as she knocked on the door. The look of kindness and love on LouEllen's face when she saw them made Lucy burst into tears.

"Lucy! Goodness, what's wrong?" LouEllen asked, opening the screen door and shepherding them inside.

"I . . . I didn't know where else to go. Can we come in?"

"You know you don't need to ask that," LouEllen said, bringing them into the house and grabbing the car seat and diaper bag off the porch. "You never need to ask."

As LouEllen went into the kitchen, Lucy collapsed into the couch, her entire body melting with relief at being back in LouEllen's house. She held Jared tightly against her and wiped her tears away. When LouEllen came out, she held two glasses of water and a just-made bottle. Lucy almost cried again at the sight of someone making Jared a bottle without having to be asked or directed to do so.

LouEllen set the water in front of Lucy and held her arms out to Jared, shrewdly holding the bottle in one hand. Jared almost never went to strangers. When he looked up at Lucy, she smiled and nodded. Suddenly he thrust his arms out and crawled into LouEllen's. She nestled him into the seat with her, cozied up between her boobs and her arm, and Jared greedily grabbed the bottle and lay back happily.

"He never goes to strangers," Lucy said.

"Well, that's 'cause I'm not a stranger. Am I, little man?" LouEllen cooed at Jared. "No, I'm not. I'm your Auntie LouEllen."

She looked up at Lucy, a worried look on her face. "Is that okay? If I tell him that?"

"Yes," Lucy said. "It sounds good."

"Well, Auntie LouEllen hates to be the bearer of bad news, but you stink, little man."

Jared removed his bottle and looked up at her, his brow creased. "Tink," he said.

LouEllen laughed so hard they both shook. Jared was startled for a moment and then smiled broadly at her. LouEllen grabbed the diaper bag and changed him quickly on the couch. When she was done, Jared lay back on her, stuck his bottle back in, and smiled up at her. Then he looked over at Lucy and said, without removing the bottle, "Mama."

"Yes, honey, that is your mama," LouEllen said, using her broad thumb to wipe the milk that had dribbled out of the side of his mouth. "And she's a good one too."

"I don't know about that," Lucy said.

"I do. I can tell."

They watched Jared as he slowed from vigorous sucks on his bottle to slow, sleepy ones.

"I'm sorry. For everything," LouEllen said. "I shouldn't have made you leave."

"Me too," Lucy said, not daring to speak more yet. Establishing any kind of peace with LouEllen, no matter how fragile, felt good. She had missed her, missed being in this house. Pride bit at her as she thought of what she wanted to say next, but she swallowed it down. She needed help. As Jared's eyes fought against sleep and then finally closed, she said, "Do you still have that baby room set up in the back?"

LouEllen's head flew up, her eyes wide and her face flushed with hope. "Of course! Even got another crib just in case . . ."

"Could he stay here tonight? While I go to Judy's?"

"There is nothing on earth that would make me happier."

"You really don't mind?"

"Never. But . . . do you want to take him home after? Or maybe you can stay for the night, both of you?"

Lucy smiled at the hesitation in LouEllen's voice and looked around her. She was more relaxed after five minutes in this house than she had been in the last ten months. A night feeling like this would be good for her, give her some space to think about what to do next.

"Yes. I'll stay too."

IN BETWEEN GLARING at Delnor so harshly that he finally apologized and left an hour early, Lucy spent her shift at the bar thinking about that word *family*. She had come to LouEllen because she had lost her family and then left her in search of a family for her son. But she wasn't sure how much family was left in that trailer.

When she entered LouEllen's house at 1:00 a.m., she found LouEllen in the kitchen, two cups of tea on the table, both with a smoky whiff of bourbon coming off them.

"For you," LouEllen said, pushing a cup toward Lucy.

"How's Jared?" Lucy asked as she collapsed into the chair with a sigh.

"Fine. Asleep. I'm more worried about you."

"I can tell. Bourbon, huh?"

"Thought you could use a drink."

"Pretty sure that's what got me in this mess," Lucy said.

"Oh, please. The difference between this cup and what Jeptha's doing is light years apart."

Lucy sipped the hot drink as her body relaxed. "I just . . . I thought it would be different. I thought I could . . ."

"Save him?"

Lucy nodded.

"You can't save someone from himself, Lucy. He's an alcoholic."

"But is this him? There were these moments, LouEllen, before Jared was born. He was sober, working, and we were—happy."

"What happened?"

"I mean, what kicked it off was Crystal Gayle getting hit by that car and him having to put her down, but really . . ." Lucy shrugged. "Life happened. It was life."

Lucy stared up at the ceiling, remembering those months before everything fell apart. "I thought . . ." Lucy stopped. "I thought *that* was the real him. But now . . ." Lucy stopped and toyed with the handle of her tea mug. "I'm worried he's going to hurt Jared."

"On purpose?" LouEllen asked, a crease of worry appearing between her eyes.

"No, no. Just accidentally. Tonight, I pulled into Judy's, and he had Jared buckled in—correctly, I will say—and was holding a beer in his hand, looking at it like . . . well, honestly, like he used to look at me. Like salvation."

"Had he been drinking?"

"No. He was sober."

"But you don't know if he'll stay that way."

"I wish he would," Lucy said, taking a sip of her tea. "You know, everyone talks all kinds of shit about the Taylors, especially Jeptha, but when he's sober, he's the nicest guy I know. Even drunk, he's not mean or violent. Just forgetful and drunk."

"I never said he was a bad guy. And I've seen he loves you. There's no question."

"Well, that's something."

"It's something. But is it enough? Especially since . . ." LouEllen's voice trailed off.

"Since what?"

"Since it's never been entirely clear to me that you feel the same way."

Lucy took a sip of tea; she wished LouEllen couldn't see the tears slipping down her cheeks. She knew her love for Jeptha wasn't as strong as his was for her, but she did love him. Not in that soul-crushing way she loved Jared, but it was there. LouEllen waited.

"I want Jared to have a family. I want him to have what I didn't."

LouEllen put her hands over Lucy's hands, still cupped around her tea. "I know, Lucy. I do. I just worry that if you keep going like this, you're going to end up with no family at all."

———

THE NEXT MORNING, after a full night's sleep, Lucy got up and made coffee. She sat at the table in her place from last night and mulled her choices. Rested and relaxed, her pride had stolen back in a little. Plus, she knew she did love Jeptha still.

"You're going?" LouEllen said from the doorway, watching as Lucy put a babbling, happy Jared into his car seat.

"Yeah, we've got to get home."

Lucy could see the emotions warring on LouEllen's face. She didn't say anything as Lucy tightened the straps around Jared and picked up some extra diapers. Finally, everything was ready. Lucy settled the handle of the car seat in the crook of her elbow.

"He's our family," Lucy said. "He deserves one more chance."

LouEllen nodded. "I know. But I want you to know that you are always welcome here. I'm your family too."

—21—

JEPTHA DOUBTED THERE WAS a man alive who had wrestled as hard or as long as he had with that one beer. Here it was, the morning after Lucy had driven off with Jared, and Jeptha still had that same can next to him, hot from holding it close all night long. He hadn't opened it, but neither could he put it down. His hand jittered so much that it was impossible to read anything beyond the large silver Bud Light on the side, and even that moved too much to make it easy reading. After Lucy had driven off, he'd sat on the hood of his car, desperate with longing—for Lucy to believe him, to have her back, to drink the beer in his hand, to be a better man, about whom there would never be a question of whether he was going to drink and drive with his baby in tow. He drove home and sat on the couch as darkness fell, holding the beer until he'd finally fallen into bed and pulled the covers over himself. He woke up early, feeling like the bottom of someone's shoe—he hurt more after twenty-four hours sober than he ever had with a hangover. The pain was immense and all-consuming. He knew he could stop it in five minutes with that piss-warm beer in his hand, but if he did, he'd be living up to Lucy's fears. He'd be the man she saw in the parking lot—and Jeptha still believed there was a chance, even if it was no larger than the ball of lint in his pocket, that he might not be.

He heard the trailer door open, and the sound of Jared's voice came babbling down the hall. Jeptha threw the beer under the bed and ran to the door.

"You came home," he said, helping her with her bag and the car seat.

"For now," Lucy said, looking him up and down. He suddenly wished he had changed clothes. He must look something awful. Her eyes rested on his hands, tremoring as he held her bag.

"You been drinking?"

"Last one I had was the night before last."

"How are you feeling?" Lucy asked. He thought he heard a glimmer of concern in her voice.

"Well, I'm not drunk."

"You're shaking."

"For a couple days, probably. Got the DTs a little."

"You gonna be all right?" she asked.

"I'm trying."

Lucy bit her lip and stared at him. He was flooded with love for her and threw up a prayer to God to help him keep her. "I'm sorry. I wasn't going to drink that beer yesterday. I promise."

She sighed loudly, that one lone piece of hair that never stayed back in her bun puffing out with her breath, then nodded like she'd decided something. "I want us to be a family, Jeptha. To be there for each other and for Jared. But I can't do that if you're drunk. It's got to stop. You've got to choose. Us or the alcohol. Otherwise, I will."

"You. Jared. Us," he rushed to say. "Always."

"I mean it, Jeptha. This is it. Your last chance."

"I know. I'm stopping. I'm sorry."

"Okay," Lucy said. She tucked her hands into her sleeves, fiddling with the edges of the seams. "I thought . . . I thought I might take Jared to the playground, if you want to come."

He smiled then, his relief at her forgiveness overwhelming his headache for a moment.

EVERY TIME JEPTHA gave Jared a push in the baby swing, his son let out a gurgle of laughter that eased the pain Jeptha felt in every inch of his body. So he pushed him for thirty minutes while Lucy sat on the mulch nearby, laughing at Jared's face and taking pictures.

"Does he usually swing this long?" Jeptha asked.

"I don't get to bring him here much. Marla probably knows better," she said. Jeptha saw her jaw tighten. He hated that Marla knew something about their baby that neither he nor Lucy did.

"We did all right yesterday," Jeptha said. "You could leave him with me some." He was forgetting for a moment how the day had ended. "Or not yet."

The look Lucy gave him reminded him of the one from the hospital—weary, full of pity, lacking any hope at all. "Maybe," she said. "Let's see how it goes."

He couldn't blame her. Why would she trust him? He had one chance left to make this right, to get her back. Cody and Judy were right. He had to stop drinking—or else he was going to ruin not only his life, but Lucy's too. He'd never expected much of one for himself, but he couldn't abide being the cause of that for Lucy and Jared. In morning light that seemed harsher for not having seen it in months, he said to her, "I'm going to stop. I got to get through these next couple days, but I'm going to stop. Get myself together. Be there for y'all."

Lucy was quiet for a minute, watching Jared laugh in his swing. Finally, she said, "I hope so, Jeptha."

LUCY TOOK JARED back over to LouEllen's when she left for Judy's at 1:00, and Jeptha was on his own. He grabbed the beer under the bed and poured it out, resolute in his desire to do what he'd promised Lucy. He found a handle of whiskey in the cabinet and poured it down the sink. Then he sat on the couch, not sure what he was supposed to do with himself until it was time to show up at Judy's for his gig at 8:00.

He went to the bathroom then sat back down on the couch. He opened the fridge, shut it, and wished for a drink. He turned on the TV and quickly turned it off. He found himself looking around for Crystal Gayle, even though he knew she was gone. He missed her every day but never more so than today. She had always been good company on detox days, rubbing up against him and barking at him when he started looking through cabinets for stray bottles of alcohol. There wasn't any more in the house, but he knew he'd be scrambling for it in a few hours, unable to accept the truth. Jeptha stood up again and almost fell over with a wave of nausea. The kitchen was closer than the bathroom, and he bolted toward it, heaving over the sink. He hadn't had a drink in thirty-six hours, but he still vomited alcohol somehow, or at least something that tasted like it.

After he was done, he wiped his mouth with the back of his hand and looked out over the farm. It was a raw day, the trees bare and the grass dulled to a wintry green brown from the frost every morning. The fields were bare too. They'd harvested the tobacco months back and, once again, Bobby was assuring him they'd get almost nothing for it. This year, though, even he could acknowledge he hadn't done much to help. He'd shown up late and hungover to the point of almost drunk on workdays and needed a six-pack of beer to steady his hands enough to hold the knife. Bobby had outstripped him by a mile.

Jeptha looked out across the road, to the farm that Cody had mentioned yesterday. His friend was right; the pot idea was stupid. Jeptha knew it, but he didn't know what else to do. The farm across the road was perfect, beautiful, river-bottom land—land where a man could plant a crop big enough and healthy enough to make a name for himself. Land so good he could rewrite his story, his reputation. Jeptha sighed. The chances of him being able to own it were nothing. He rubbed at his head, thinking if he could get rid of this headache, he might have a chance of making it through today. He didn't have any business looking any further ahead than that.

When Jeptha looked up, he saw Bobby struggling over the fence across the road.

"What the hell?" Jeptha said out loud.

Then Deanna came up after him, her face creased with displeasure and her pinkies up in the air as she pushed down the barbwire, like she was the queen out inspecting Tennessee tobacco land. Jeptha had always heard DTs could cause hallucinations, but this was something else. He rubbed his eyes. No, there they were, both of them checking for cars before heading across the road.

He eased himself down the stairs, his stomach tumbling with the movement, and walked down the driveway to them.

"What are y'all doing over at the Gibsons' place?" he asked. He was fighting against a rising tide of anger on top of the urge to throw up again. He'd been suspecting it for years, but now he knew. These two, who were supposed to be his family, were screwing him.

They looked up nervously. Deanna was the first to recover. She'd always been the better liar. "Just checking it out—hear it's gonna sell soon."

"Oh yeah, who'd you hear that from?" Jeptha asked.

"Just people talking," she said, taking him in from head to toe. "Damn, Jeptha, what happened to you? You look like hell, purely wrung out."

"It's none of your concern. Bobby, what's going on?"

His brother had never mastered Deanna's ease with lying, and he was staring at the ground, his hands rooting around in his pockets. Bobby glanced up at Jeptha briefly and then back down. "Just looking," he said.

"Looking my ass," Jeptha said. The anger flooding through his body was like a miracle cure—his headache disappeared, and his stomach tightened up into a ball of hate that he was sure would never go away. "What. Are. You. Doing. Over. There?"

He saw Bobby's eyes widen briefly, and even Deanna's posture faltered for a moment. She started to talk, but Jeptha was focused on Bobby, whose lips were moving with sound so quiet Jeptha had to walk right up to him before he heard it. "It ain't the Gibsons'. We bought it."

"You what!" Jeptha yelled. He pushed Bobby before he even thought about it. Bobby shuffled back two feet and held his hands up.

"Hey now. Don't do that," he said.

"Don't do what? Don't be pissed y'all went behind my back again, bought land I ought to be a part of again? Don't be pissed y'all are trying to take away this farm from me? Take away everything I've ever had?" Jeptha yelled.

"Please, Jeptha," Deanna sneered. "It ain't like you ever had this. Like you could of done anything even if we'd told you."

Jeptha's fist tightened—he hadn't hit his sister since he was ten, but God, he'd never wanted to more. He spoke through lips so tight his voice hissed.

"Deanna, you better stop talking right now. Nothing would give me more pleasure than knocking your teeth in, so I'd shut up if I was you."

She took a step back.

"I can't believe you did this, Bobby. Her, I'd believe it of, but you— again?" Jeptha shook his head and spit on the ground. "You're no brother of mine."

He strode back to his trailer. There was nothing left to say. He slammed up the steps, grabbed his hunting gear out of the Tupperware bin where he stored it, and rooted in the closet through a mass of coats until his hands closed on the vinyl of his rifle case. He threw it all in the car and slammed on the gas, leaving Bobby and Deanna in a cloud of gravel dust.

HE WAS AT the store in ten minutes flat. He sat in the car, breathing like a bull in a fight, thinking of his brother and sister. He couldn't believe they'd done this, not even talked to him about it beforehand or even seen if he might be able to go in with them. He thought of the bank balance he'd seen earlier in the week: $113. He could barely buy food with that. How could they afford to buy that land? They worked the same job he did, split the same money.

"Split the same money," he whispered to himself. Unless they weren't splitting it at all—unless those no-good, lowlife siblings of his were keeping his hard-earned money for themselves. *That* would explain how little he'd been getting these years and how Bobby could afford to buy more land. *That* would explain Deanna's new car. *That* would explain why his life was so goddamn shitty. In that moment, Jeptha knew it to be true. They'd been stealing from him all this time, and he'd been too dumb, or drunk, or both, to notice. But not anymore. He'd show them. They had it coming, and Jeptha aimed to give it to them.

Jeptha tightened his grip—one hand on his gun, the other turning the steering wheel back toward his farm. He pressed down on the gas, reveling in the throaty, murderous sound of the engine, and drove back out to the entrance of the parking lot of the store. Whatever happened to Deanna and Bobby, they deserved every bit of it. You don't steal money from a man, and you certainly don't steal land from a man. They had messed with the wrong Taylor this time.

Jeptha waited for a break in the cars to come, his anger growing with each passing vehicle. Finally, too impatient to wait, he edged out, but a harried-looking mom driving a minivan stood on her brakes, french fries flying through the air from the back seat, before coming to a stop two inches from his car. He saw the faces of two of her kids—quiet and terrified at the near-miss accident.

Lucy, Jeptha thought. *Jared.*

He edged his car backward and closed his eyes. He pictured Jared on the swings and Lucy smiling up at him. He took his hands off his gun and placed them in his lap. He couldn't go home now—mad as he was, he knew he wouldn't be able to control himself if he was within a half mile of his brother and sister. It was too dangerous a risk.

Anger coursed through him, so vivid his hands shook, although Jeptha couldn't tell if his shakes were due to that or not having anything to drink. What he wanted, next to making his brother and sister hurt like they'd been hurting him all his life, was a drink. He pictured Lucy's face again, telling him that he had to choose between her and Jared or alcohol. But he'd already made his tough choice for the day—and it wasn't between her and alcohol, but between her and going to jail for trying to kill his siblings. This kind of anger—the murdering kind—could only be quieted by alcohol. One last drink to get him through today, and then he'd quit for good. Lucy would understand, he told himself as he walked into the store, when she knew what Bobby and Deanna had done—how they'd taken all his and Lucy's money and their land, depriving them of the opportunity to raise their son in the way they wanted. Lucy would get it. She wouldn't kick him out for that. She'd be mad, sure, but she'd give him another chance.

Three minutes later, he was back, a case of cold beer beside him, the end of the box open before he left the parking lot. He drank two on his way to Delnor's, almost causing a wreck in the middle of the first one when he looked up at the sky in praise of how delicious alcoholic salvation tasted.

He hadn't asked Delnor for permission to hunt today, but he really didn't give a shit. Besides, Delnor didn't care none. He called Cody and said, "I'm hunting. Come over." He pulled on his bibs and orange vest, snugged a hat around his head, and tucked the case of beer under one arm and the gun under the other.

It was good to be walking, out in the sunshine, the air cool on his face. The two beers had set him back to rights, and all he had to focus on was his anger. Every once in a while Lucy's face would swim up, and he'd think of the promise he'd made to her earlier, but then he'd push it away and walk faster into the woods. The tree where he and Cody had built their stand stood on the edge of an oak grove in the middle of a hill. It gave them a clear view up or down a line of wild grass that mounded up high against the tree line, giving the deer some ground cover as they poked around for acorns. It had been a prime spot for years. He hauled his beer up the 2x4s nailed into the tree trunk like a ladder and then came back down for his gun and gloves. He settled himself on a milk crate, quickly knocked back two more beers, and took up his rifle.

An hour later, he heard a sound and brought his gun to his shoulder, his scope sighted on the bottom of the hill before realizing it was Cody, huffing a gun and a cooler up with him.

"Thought you was gonna shoot me," Cody said, his breath straining as he pulled himself up the ladder.

"Sorry."

"You look pissed. Could see it all the way down the hill," Cody said, looking down at the beer cans at Jeptha's feet. "Good day, huh?"

"Don't you start."

He held his hands up in front of him. "Hey man, I was just asking. I got beer too. I ain't judging."

"Different song than you was singing yesterday then," Jeptha said, finishing off the sixth beer and feeling, finally, a calm begin to creep over him.

"I wasn't judging then either. I'm your friend."

Jeptha was silent. He kept seeing Bobby and Deanna walk over that fence and try to pretend like they hadn't gone behind his back. The beer was helping, but it wasn't ever going to get rid of it. He was screwed. He'd never be able to make a good life for Lucy.

"Bobby and Deanna went on, bought that land across the road. Didn't even bother to tell me. So now, our farm is huge, but I only got a third of a third of it."

"Oh, hell. That sucks. Is that why . . ." Cody said, looking down at the beer.

"Seemed like the only thing I could do."

Cody shrugged. "Guess so."

HUNTING WAS SLOW business, and today was no exception. Four hours after Cody climbed up into the stand, they'd seen one doe, who'd scampered as soon as the wind shifted in her direction. The only thing they'd bagged was enough beer to leave Jeptha comfortably drunk and Cody buzzed. As dusk came on, Cody packed up.

"You going?" Jeptha asked.

"Ain't nothing coming out tonight," Cody said. "Besides we gotta go play."

"What?"

"It's Friday. We got the gig at Judy's tonight?"

"Oh, shit. Right."

"You'll be there? Judy's getting pissed you keep missing. Frankly, man, it's startin' to annoy me too."

"That's about all I hear these days . . . I'll be there," Jeptha said, popping open the second-to-last beer in his case. He shook his head. Judy was one more person on the long list of people making him angry.

"Sure you don't want to come with me? I'll give you a ride."

"Get on out of here, Cody. I'm fine."

"I'll see you there. Right?"

"I'll be there. You don't need to babysit me."

"All right, man. Mind you don't shoot me on the way down the hill."

Thirty minutes later, the sun was nearly gone, the case was empty, and Jeptha was getting cold. He moved to grab up some of the cans around his feet when he heard something move in the brush, something big. He paused for a minute, thinking it was Cody come back for something, but then that buck, the huge fourteen-pointer, stepped proudly out of the woods, his antlers flashing white against the darkened ground. Jeptha watched him—all his anger with his family and his life raging in his chest as he saw an animal walk with more pride than Jeptha had ever had. He lifted his rifle and sighted through the scope, the deer's shoulder moving up and down in the crosshairs as Jeptha's hands swayed with beer. He took a deep breath and squeezed the trigger.

The shot wasn't even close. The deer didn't dart away like every other deer in the world would have. Instead, the buck eyed Jeptha with a still, haughty look in which Jeptha could only read disdain before slowly and majestically picking his way into the brush and disappearing from view.

— 22 —

LUCY CHECKED THE DOOR every five minutes starting at seven o'clock. She'd been nervous leaving Jeptha after the morning at the playground. She knew he was in a dangerous place, all shaky and needing—not wanting—a drink. But she'd said her piece, told him this was his last chance. She didn't know if he could see it through, but she hoped so. For now, though, she'd settle for him showing up for tonight's gig, and they'd go from there.

At 7:30, the door opened, and Cody banged into the doorjamb as he walked through it. She waited for Jeptha to follow after, but the door stayed closed. She watched as he set his banjo down and started setting up—he dropped the mic three times before he finally got it in the stand and then accidentally kicked his banjo off the chair where he'd laid it down. When he laughed, she knew he was drunk.

"Jeptha coming?" she asked him. Cody looked down at her from the stage and instantly sobered up.

"He said he was, Lucy. I swear."

She nodded and bit down on her bottom lip so hard it bled. There weren't words for how pissed she was.

"He like you? Drunk?"

Cody wouldn't meet her eyes.

"Y'all can get your own damn drinks tonight. Don't seem like you're going to need one, but if you do, don't you dare ask me for it," she hissed.

JEPTHA NEVER SHOWED. She stopped looking after the first set. If any part of her had any doubts about this being his last chance, it was gone. This was it. She was terrifyingly angry at Jeptha, but also at herself. She hated herself for all of it. For getting in the car to have drunken sex with him two years ago, for telling him about the baby afterward, for letting herself fall in love with him, but most of all, for the naïve belief that she couldn't let go of—the notion that having a family might mean something, that having a kid together could correct someone's basic personality, could change his DNA.

"You can go on, Lucy," Judy said at 11:30. The bar had quieted down, and Lucy was trying to keep her tears at bay by cleaning. All she wanted to do was hold Jared, hear his little breaths against her neck, and pack up everything.

"You sure?"

"I got this. Go on. I'm sorry, about Jep—well, I'm sorry."

"Me too," Lucy choked out. She grabbed her bag, tapping the spot on the bar in front of Delnor on her way out to let him know that he, at least, was forgiven.

LouEllen was still up, watching TV when Lucy came through the door.

"How is he?" Lucy asked.

"He's fine. He was tired tonight."

Lucy nodded and put her hand on LouEllen's shoulder on her way to Jared's room. She eased the door open and stood over him in the crib. He slept like a bomb had gone off: on his back, his arms over his head and his legs splayed. But his chest rose with a regularity that Lucy always found comforting to watch. She could hear his little nose bring air in and then whistle it forcefully back out. Finally, when she couldn't stand not holding him another second, she eased her hands under him and picked him up. He stirred and mewed for a second, like a kitten might. She settled him on her chest in the chair and rocked back and forth, singing "Twinkle, Twinkle Little Star" until he settled back into a deep sleep.

"It's you and me," she whispered to him. "Just you and Mama. And that's enough." For the first time, she heard the truth of those words. Her family was this baby. He was all she needed. She'd been a fool to look for more.

Lucy looked up and saw LouEllen silhouetted against the crack of the door. "And LouEllen too," Lucy whispered.

She heard LouEllen laugh softly behind her.

"You gonna take him tonight, or do y'all want to stay here?" LouEllen whispered.

"I'm going take him home tonight. But we'll be back tomorrow, if that's okay. Then I'll figure out what to do next."

"You sure?"

"Yes," Lucy said. "It's time."

— 23 —

JEPTHA VAGUELY REMEMBERED GETTING out of the tree stand, although it seemed to have been a much more rapid descent than it should have been. He remembered getting to his car and realizing he'd forgotten the box of bullets for his gun but deciding to leave it. And he sort of remembered driving thirty minutes out of his way, all the way to the county line, to buy a handle of whiskey, but he didn't remember drinking some of it while he drove down the highway, or pulling into his driveway past 1:00 in the morning, or hitting his dad's car again. And he certainly didn't remember passing out, the bottle in one hand and his rifle in the other. All he knew for sure when he woke up with the sun beating down on him was that he was drunk, still pissed, and felt for the first time like he knew what people meant when they talked about hitting rock bottom.

The sun hurt his brain where it came through the one eye that had actually opened when he commanded it to. He closed them both again to make the world stop spinning. Then he pawed at them, trying to get the sleep out, but found his eyelashes on one side were matted together. Once he'd cleared the debris, he rolled his head over to one side and saw his dad's car off the blocks again. He was home. That much, at least, was good. He thought of Lucy, of the damage he'd done. The memory of the buck from last night pierced his drunken haze. That look. It was the same one he was sure Lucy would give him when he saw her. Neither one had any use for the man Jeptha was. Nor should they.

He eased himself out of the car, offering God a silent thank you for allowing him to do so without falling in a heap on the ground. He was still wearing his camo long john shirt and a pair of jeans. He stood and stretched, then ducked back in to grab his gun. His bibs were in the trunk. He got them out, raised them to his nose, and quickly threw them up near the stairs to his trailer. They stunk to high heaven. No deer would come within five hundred yards of him wearing those. He'd have to go to the Laundromat later.

Walking back to his car, he heard voices down by Deanna's house. He squinted in that direction and saw Deanna and Bobby talking with a man in a suit. It took him a minute to realize it was Lawyer Tom, who'd represented him on a drunk driving charge four years ago. Jeptha still owed him money. Jeptha was sober enough to realize the lawyer hadn't come out on a Saturday for an old closed case like his. He was out for the land deal—they were probably closing today, those cheating sons of bitches.

Jeptha stalked down the hill, wishing as he did that Crystal Gayle was there to lean against. She always helped him stay in a straight line. He knew he was weaving from side to side but couldn't help himself. All that mattered was getting there, telling this lawyer what was going on.

"What are y'all doing?" Jeptha asked when he was close enough.

The three turned toward him suddenly, so occupied in their talk they hadn't even seen he was coming. He noticed Lawyer Tom stepped quickly out of the way.

"What are you doing with that?" Bobby asked, nodding at Jeptha's hand.

Jeptha looked down, surprised to see he still had his gun in his hand. It was unloaded, he was sure of it, even if he didn't distinctly remember doing it, but still, he put the butt down in the grass and held the barrel up to the sky.

"Went hunting yesterday. Just cleaning up," he said. "What are you doing here, Mr. Jenkins?"

"Seeing if we can close this deal today."

"You mean the land across the street? The land what they bought without letting me know?"

"I . . . I don't know about that. I'm just here to figure out the paperwork."

"You're doing it, huh?" Jeptha asked Bobby.

Bobby was silent.

"We don't owe you nothing, Jeptha," Deanna spat. "I don't know why you think we were supposed to cut you in on this. Everybody in town knows you don't have money to pay for it. We're supposed to give it to you free? The world don't work like that."

"Interesting you mention free. The thing I can't figure is where you're getting the cash from," Jeptha said. "I mean, you said the tobacco barely cleared nothing this year. And I can't figure that neither." Jeptha turned to the lawyer. "You know anything about that, Lawyer Tom?"

He held up his hands in front of him. "Now, Jeptha, I don't know anything about y'all's family dealings. I just know Bobby's waiting on his check from RJR for eighteen . . ."

Jeptha was listening to him and watching Bobby shake his head back and forth more and more violently. Finally, the lawyer saw it. His voice trailed off.

"Eighteen, huh?" Jeptha said, rounding on Bobby until he was up in his face. "Your share is eighteen thousand dollars? And what'd you say mine was gonna be again—about three thousand dollars?"

Jeptha's anger was all-consuming. He knew in his bones they'd been cheating him, knew he deserved more for all that work, knew it couldn't be right to be so broke after breaking his back working on that damn field all spring and summer. And here, finally, was the proof. He waved his hands around, the rifle coming with him.

"Whoa, Jeptha!" the lawyer said, his hands up again as he ducked his head.

"Don't talk to me like some damn animal needing to be broke. I don't need to be reined in," Jeptha yelled.

"Why don't you put the gun down?" the lawyer said.

"It ain't loaded. You think I'm an idiot? That I'd be out here waving around a loaded gun?"

He raised his eyebrows and held Jeptha's gaze, the look on his face making it clear he had no doubt Jeptha was capable of waving around a loaded weapon. Finally, he looked to Bobby and said, "Seems like y'all got some stuff to figure out here. I'm gonna head on."

"Yeah, Lawyer Tom, why don't you? We got more than a few things to talk about," Jeptha said.

"Bobby, I'll see you later. Jeptha, be careful."

As soon as Lawyer Tom had driven down the driveway, Jeptha rounded on his siblings. "Eighteen thousand dollars, Bobby? How'd you manage that? And, Deanna, how much did you get? You came out in the field, what, once?"

"You got your fair share, Jeptha," Deanna said.

"Deanna, you wouldn't know a fair share if it bit you in the ass. You've never even touched a tobacco leaf, and you still get twenty-five percent."

"I put up this land—it's part mine," she said, her red-taloned hand jutting out from her hip.

"What else would you do with it?"

"Sell it, if I had my way. I only keep it so y'all can farm on it."

"Yeah, I can see how it must be real tough to stay out here collecting rent for doing nothing."

"Jeptha, the only one out here doing nothing is you. And you know what? For your information, I get forty percent. I put up the down payment on the land next door, and I make the payments to the bank so this place doesn't get sold out from under us. How's that for a fair share?"

"Deanna, hush," Bobby said quietly.

"Forty? Forty?" Jeptha was dumbfounded. He had never in a million years imagined that Deanna got any more than twenty-five percent of what they made each year.

"So, what . . . Bobby and I split the other sixty?" Bobby still hadn't looked up from the ground, still hadn't made eye contact with Jeptha. For a guy who used to talk a lot of game, he'd been silent as a mouse these last few minutes.

"Bobby . . ." Jeptha said, a note of pleading creeping into his voice. He expected this of Deanna, but of Bobby? He knew they weren't close, but he felt betrayed by his brother. "I got a wife, a kid."

"Jeptha, you are dumb as a rock. Y'all don't split that. Bobby takes the other fifty. You get ten. And that's only 'cause Bobby argued we should. I voted for nothing," Deanna said.

Ten percent. That's all his brain could see. 1-0. He got next to nothing out of a farm that he broke his back for. Ten percent was why his wife had to kill herself working all damn day, why his son lived in hand-me-downs, why they stretched out his diaper changes for as long as they could. Far as Jeptha could tell, ten percent was why his life was total shit. His eyes were full of tears, his throat too choked to speak.

He picked up his gun, careless with it now, too angry to even care. "Y'all is as bad a people as I've ever met. You're lucky this gun ain't loaded, or I'd shoot you myself."

Jeptha turned away from them and walked right into one of the kids'
bikes, abandoned hastily on the grass. Sober, he'd have been able to save
himself, but drunk and angry as he was, he couldn't stop the fall. He went
flying, the gun too, and as he face-planted into the grass, he heard a crack
near his head, a shot from his apparently still-loaded rifle flying out wild
over the farm.

L UCY HAD WOKEN UP with a smile on her face. Her decision was made. It was time to say goodbye to the vision of family she'd been toting around for too many years to count. She stretched in bed and turned over to look at her phone, only to see it was 7:30 and Jared was still asleep, or at least quiet. She felt better then about coming home last night. He got to sleep in his own bed one last time, and she could pack up her stuff and, most importantly, say goodbye to Jeptha. She didn't have to do that, but she wanted to. She was oddly unfazed by the confrontation that was coming, as unpleasant as she knew it would be. She was ready. It was time for her to be her own family—her and Jared. She thought of Knoxville then, a dream that had seemed impossible a year ago, but for some reason now felt back in her reach. If she wanted to go to college, she'd have to go. She and Jared would make it work, somehow.

She had expected to see Jeptha passed out on the couch when she came into the kitchen, but he wasn't there. Instead, Jared was paging through a book she'd left in his crib, talking to himself.

"Mama!" Jared yelled, tossing his book aside and quickly pulling himself up. He held his arms out to her. "Mama, Mama, Mama!"

She picked him up and held him against her. He tucked his curly little head into her neck and rested it there, his breath soft against her shoulder.

"Hey, buddy," she murmured. "You ready for our big day?"

"Mama," Jared answered.

"I'm gonna take that as an okay," she said and took him into the bathroom with her, where she turned on the water. It was her last shower in this house, the last time she'd be in this bathroom, where her son was born. She swallowed back tears, tracing the dog-shaped image on the fake marble that had gotten her through labor. It had never occurred to her that it'd be hard to say good-bye to this space, with its broken accordion door, tilted toilet, and tiny shower, but there it was. You can miss anything, even a shitty little trailer bathroom, if given enough time and memories.

Before she stepped behind the curtain, she said, "Mama's gonna get a shower. I'll be right out. Then we'll pack our stuff, say goodbye to Daddy, and go."

"Oh!" he said.

"That's right! Go."

The day called for celebrating. She poured a larger-than-usual dot of her orange shampoo into her palm and breathed in the scent before rubbing it into her hair. She peeked out at Jared, her hair piled on top of her head, and said, "Boo!" He laughed. She hid again and poked her head back out.

"Boo!"

His whole body jiggled with laughter, his curls bopping around and his eyes squeezed shut with glee.

"Boo!" Lucy said, joining his deep belly laugh with her own, his love for her and this moment contagious.

She rinsed out her hair and finished her shower, listening to him trying to say "boo," which came out as "ooo." She wrapped her towel around her chest after drying off and picked Jared up to get him out of the way, but he clung to her like a spider monkey.

"Do you need a snuggle?" she asked, sitting down on the closed toilet seat. She held him to her until he squirmed away from her wet hair dripping on his face. She lay him on her lap, so she could look at him. He put his feet on her chest and grabbed at her nose.

Lucy bent down to kiss Jared on the forehead, smiling as she saw his eyes cross with the effort of tracking her face coming toward him. When her lips touched the tiny cleft between his eyebrows, he squeaked. Lucy loved that sound—the kind only babies make. She stayed there for a few minutes, peppering that spot with kiss after kiss, listening to him squeak after each one, laughter beginning to gurgle up softly from his belly. The sound and smell of her child made her feel even more calm. It reminded her all over again why she was leaving. She kissed him on the forehead once more.

"Guess we better get going, huh?" she said.

She walked into the bedroom and finished drying off while Jared crawled behind her into the room. He played peek-a-boo with the sheets hanging off the bed as Lucy pulled on her favorite pair of jeans and her dad's old UT sweatshirt and wrapped her towel-dried hair up in a messy bun. She pulled a duffel out of the closet and emptied the contents of her dresser into it. When all her stuff was packed, she folded Jared's clothes from the bottom drawer she'd emptied out for him and placed them carefully on top of her stuff. Looking at all their possessions collected there, Lucy suspected someone else might have found it sad. She just felt ready.

Jared's boos were fading into whines—he needed a bottle. She was done in here anyway. In the kitchen, she dropped the duffel by the door and settled Jared into his bouncy seat. His feet stuck out five inches over the edge—she couldn't count on it as a containment device for much longer, had probably pushed it too far already. One less thing to bring with her.

"Let's get you a bottle, buddy," she said.

"Mama." His fist was opening and closing frantically in the sign for milk.

"That's right. Mama's going to get you some milk. Don't you worry. It's coming."

She shook the bottle until all the powder dissolved. Jared shoved it in his mouth and closed his eyes with pleasure for the first few sucks, like his dad with a beer.

"But we aren't going to have to worry about beer any more, are we?" she said, rubbing his cheek with the back of her hand. "Are we, buddy?"

Jared smiled at her around his bottle. "Mama," he agreed, his mouth full of milk that dribbled out and down his chin, where it puddled under his neck.

"Messy baby," she said and turned to the kitchen to get a wet washcloth. She would wipe him up and move him over to his high chair for the rest of his bottle. May as well get used to it now. By the sink, though, she saw his baby dishes and silverware on the drying rack. She stacked them, searched the rest of the kitchen for his stuff, and put it all in the duffel. Satisfied she'd gotten it all, she grabbed a washcloth. Jared hated having his face wiped, so she smiled at him from the sink and opened her mouth to sing the "clean up" song.

Before she could sing a note, she heard a sharp crack resound through the air. A fraction of a second later, she heard something smack through the sagging aluminum siding of the trailer. Jared's bottle fell to the floor.

She was still looking for where the bullet went, and it took her more than a few seconds to realize the two events—the sharp crack and the bottle thunking to the floor—were connected. She stared at Jared, at his blue eyes, Jeptha's eyes. His whole body let go. Everything relaxed. She ripped him out of his chair and felt his body, heavy against her chest, like when he was really, truly asleep. When he fell asleep at night, or during his naps, he fought against the physical act. On the verge of surrendering to sleep, his upper lashes tangling with his lower ones, he would suddenly rebel, his eyes opening to look at her once more. She looked at his face, waited for him to push his eyes open, to fight sleep, to surprise her again with one more laugh. She kissed his forehead again.

"Boo," she whispered. But nothing happened. His eyes stayed closed.

"Jared," she said against his ear as she kissed his face again. "Wake up, buddy. Open your eyes."

She shook him slightly, his body jostling loosely in her hands. Then something wet dripped down her wrist. A stream of blood pooled under her bare feet, shiny and thick.

"Wake up! Jared, wake up!" she screamed, holding him against her chest and frantically brushing the blood off. Then she saw the dark mass of blood on his side.

"NO! NO!" she yelled. She shook him. "Wake up, Jared, wake up. Wake up. Please wake up," she said, over and over again, rocking him back and forth, sobbing.

She grabbed her phone, smearing the numbers with the blood from her hands as she dialed.

"My son," she screamed into the phone. "He's bleeding. He won't wake up."

"Is this Lucy?" the voice said.

"You have to help him, Ethel. He won't wake up. I think he might be . . . Just get them here. NOW." She threw the phone down and held Jared tight against her body, applying pressure as best she knew how.

"You're okay, you're okay," she sang in a ragged half-whisper. It was the little made-up song she always sang to him if he was sick or hurt. That, and a kiss, had always made everything better. As she sang, the blood dripped down his leg, wound around her wrist, curled down the side of her hand, and fell, drop by drop, off her pinky into the puddle below her feet. The puddle grew to twice the size of her foot as she sang.

"You're okay, You're okay. You have to be okay," she sang, rocking him back and forth and back and forth. His eyes were still closed. She stopped singing and stopped breathing, listening for his soft breath, willing his chest to move against hers like it had the night he was born. She waited and waited and waited. Finally, she gasped for air.

"No!" she screamed, her voice frantic and ragged. He was so still, so unbelievably still. Lucy held Jared to her, breathing him in like she had when he was born, screaming with abandon as his life left him, one steady drop at a time.

– 25 –

THE CRACK HAD TERRIFIED Jeptha, and the direction of the barrel scared him even more. He scrambled to his feet and ran for his house, Bobby and Deanna right behind him. As they came up the stairs, they heard screaming. Jeptha skidded to a halt—overwhelmed by terror.

"Go, Jeptha," Bobby said, gulping breaths in as he ran up the stairs behind him.

Jeptha pulled the door open, dread and fear drying out his mouth. His body was shaking as he opened the screen door and slammed through the front door. His mind froze at the scene there.

Lucy clutched Jared to her chest—wild screams tearing her apart as blood dripped off of her arm and onto the floor. Jeptha had never seen Jared so still. Some part of Jeptha, some awful caveman instinct, knew he was dead. It was impossible, he thought, for it to have happened so quickly, and yet, Jared's skin, usually suffused with a pink that glowed with life, had already taken on a grayish tint. He had only ever seen deer, killed with the perfect shot, so still. So gone. It was not a question of being at peace or not; it was a matter of presence. Jeptha could not stop looking at him, taking in the blood and the ragged hole in the new green frog pajamas Lucy had shown Jeptha a few weeks before. He measured the stillness of Jared's body, holding his breath without meaning to, but there was no approximating that lack of sensation by not breathing. In Jeptha's body, there was blood flowing, little cells doing whatever they do, a hum of work he couldn't hear. With Jared, all was quiet.

Lucy stared at him, a plea in her eyes for what she plainly knew would be a miracle. A plea for a miracle from the man who had done it. Standing there looking down on the scene, he knew he would never *not* see this vision, knew he had known his last moment of peace on earth. He deserved every moment of horror this memory would forever hold.

"Call an ambulance," he croaked, as he heard Bobby come up behind him, retching as he saw Lucy and the baby.

"Jeptha . . ." Lucy said. "I can't wake him up. Help me." Her eyes were hollow and her face ashen. When he did not move, she screamed, "Help me!"

"Lucy . . ." he said. How could he confirm what they both knew but neither wanted to accept? "Lucy . . . I think he's . . ."

Jeptha couldn't bring himself to say the word out loud. He reached out for Jared, but she snatched him to her.

"No."

"Okay, you hold him. But sit down. I'm here," Jeptha said, guiding her down to the couch.

He knelt beside her, his knees splashing in the puddle of blood on the floor, and put his hand over hers, feeling Jared's soft skin underneath. It already seemed cooler than Lucy's. He wanted to scream, to shout, to do anything to make this not be so.

"I'm sorry," he said to her. "I'm sorry."

There was a moment then when he thought of running. Not away, not to disappear, but straight down the hill to where his gun still lay in the grass. What he wanted more than anything was to swallow that barrel whole in the hopes that he could exchange his life for his son's, even though he knew it was an exchange that had passed its expiration date. Then he thought of that deer—and all Jeptha could do was stay there with his frantic wife and dead son to face the bullet of pain and regret that would forever be coming for him. He ground his knees into the bloody floor until they hurt.

"He's not dead. He's not, he's not," Lucy kept repeating, rocking back and forth with Jared like she was trying to put him back to sleep on a particularly cranky night.

They both knew Jared was gone, but Jeptha understood that Lucy needed to hold the full truth of that awful knowledge at bay as long as she could. He wished he could do the same. Instead, Jeptha rocked with them, hugging his family in his arms for what he knew would be the very last time.

— PART THREE —

— 26 —

THAT A TAYLOR HAD finally killed someone surprised few in town, but that it had been Jeptha killing his son, or more accurately, Lucy's son, as everyone thought of Jared, struck everyone as grievously wrong. That Lucy had lost her Jared that way, after losing her parents years before, shook the faith of even the most devout church ladies. The town had gossiped on it for months—on the tragedy of that kind of accident, on how they were sure that it wouldn't have happened if Jeptha hadn't been drinking, on how Jeptha deserved every minute of his three-to-five term for involuntary manslaughter, and how glad they were that Jeptha, at the very least, had recognized that fact when he'd walked up to Officer Mullins, his arms outstretched, and pled guilty to every charge they threw at him despite Lawyer Tom's advice to the contrary. The church ladies, even those who'd never met Lucy, went full crepe—they brought every casserole and every Bundt cake they knew to make to LouEllen's house and chatted about Lucy behind her back after they left. But a few months before school let out, Travis Cartwright ran off with his teacher, and a few months after that, tobacco prices bottomed out. No one forgot what happened over on the Taylors' place, but they picked up on new gossip and new stories until finally, three years later, the story of how Jeptha Taylor accidentally killed Lucy's son was old news, which meant Lucy got some pitying looks when people chanced on her unawares, manning the line at Walmart or serving up drinks at Judy's, but she was no longer the chum of daily gossip.

Lucy still found the pity on people's faces nearly impossible to bear. It reminded her all over again of what she had lost. She barely remembered anything from that first year beyond a deep and abiding sense that she never wanted to see another casserole in her life. She'd spent the first three months on LouEllen's couch, huddled under an afghan that Miss Irene had knitted especially for the occasion. A mourning quilt, she had called it, when she dropped it off. Lucy didn't remember LouEllen laying it over her, but she remembered spending every day cuddled up with it whether on the couch or in her bed, trying in vain to sleep at night without seeing the images of her son dying in her arms. Hundreds of times a day, she thought of LouEllen asking if she wanted to stay that night and never once understood why she hadn't said yes. Jared would be alive if she'd left him with LouEllen that night, gone on her own to tell Jeptha. Her hands shook when she thought of it, of how she'd failed her son, so many times and in so many ways. Her obsession with family, with doing what she thought was the right thing, had gotten her son killed. One tiny decision gone another way and she could have kept him alive and safe. He'd be in her arms or unsteadily trying to walk around the coffee table.

Trying to keep those visions at bay, she curled up on the couch, immersed in the soap operas that had become her passion. Lucy quickly lost herself in the manufactured drama of the soaps, obsessed with the affairs, illegitimate children, and the many marriages and re-marriages. Somebody was always trying to kill somebody else, and that person would end up living due to the caring ministrations of some insanely attractive doctor to whom the patient would reveal a terrible family secret that inevitably unraveled in spectacular fashion in the patient's recovery room. In the soaps, a character's accidental killing of his baby son would be the beginning of the story, the beginning of whatever crazy new plot twist was about to happen. In the soaps, everyone's husband or wife had been to jail at least once, and most of them had at least one murder to their name. Having a father who had spent a good chunk of his life in jail was the necessary prelude to becoming one of the city's leading lights. And Lucy had quickly homed in on the first rule of soap operas: no one ever actually dies. No matter how gruesome the death, the supposedly dead character was always alive somewhere just off camera, ready to be called back to the story line at the right moment. For those first three months, Lucy needed to believe that such a thing was possible.

Even after she'd begun to leave the couch, down twenty-five pounds, her hair a matted, stringy mess, she hadn't done much. LouEllen fed her every comforting food she'd ever known, took her on long drives, staying far away from the Taylors' farm, and helped her shower. Showers, for some reason, were the hardest things. She still remembered her first one after that day. While LouEllen sat on the toilet beside her, Lucy had soaped up her hair into a beehive that rivaled those sported by the Mennonite women at Shoney's on Sundays. She let her arms fall down to her chest and faced the flow of water, knowing that the next step was putting her head under it. She hated being in here, naked and exposed against the white plastic walls, with nothing but a shower curtain to protect her. She took a deep breath, though, and forced herself to walk into the stream of hot water, trying to remember the days when it felt good to stand there as the water blocked out the world and pelted her worries away. With her eyes closed, she saw spots on the backside of her eyelids that were the exact color and size of Jared's wound. As the soap flowed down her shoulders, the spots expanded, growing larger and thicker, looking like nothing so much as the puddle of Jared's blood that she had watched form on the floor beneath her when she held him. Her eyes flew open, and the soap stung as it mixed with her tears. She breathed harder and louder, irregularly, until finally she was screaming with rage and fear. She took baths for the next year and a half.

But these days, three years on, Lucy congratulated herself for being able to shower, for going to work, for getting through what seemed like a normal day. She tried never to think of Jeptha, but thought of Jared every day, all the time. Every three-year-old caught her attention at Walmart, all their whines and tantrums over not getting the toys they wanted, all their smiles and laughs. She longed for him then, stalking young children through the store on her break. Each one destroyed Lucy to watch—but she couldn't stop. Now, Lucy could watch them and still manage to get through her shifts without having to run in a panic to the break room. She was starting to slowly—very slowly—think she might survive the havoc Jeptha Taylor had wreaked in her life.

"ANOTHER ONE CAME today," LouEllen said when Lucy walked through the door. "I put it away, but I can get it if you want."

Lucy shook her head. She didn't want to read Jeptha's letter. He had sent one every week that Jared was gone—162 in total. Or 163 with this most recent one. They always came on Fridays, which was, not by accident, Lucy's busiest workday. The less time she had to think of the letter arriving, the less stressed she was. She'd never opened a single envelope, each one emblazoned with the Tennessee State Prison system logo and prisoner #1070589 stamped on top. She had considered them long enough to have memorized Jeptha's prisoner number but had never made the leap from holding one in her hand to actually opening it. Even unanswered, the letters kept arriving, regular enough that Lucy had finally noticed a creeping sense of dread steal over her on Wednesdays, getting steadily worse and making her snappish and angry over the tiniest things until the day she found the letter in the mailbox and could get rid of it. In the beginning, she had taken care to place the letters deep into the trash can—burying them under a debris flow of coffee grounds and leftovers showing the first faint fuzz of mold. But one night, six or so months after Jared died, she came into the kitchen and found LouEllen digging a letter out of the trash, carefully wiping coffee grounds off with a just-wet paper towel.

"What are you doing?" Lucy had screamed at her.

"One day, you may want these. Not now. But one day, it might help."

Lucy had been so infuriated that she stomped out of the room, but not before she noticed LouEllen tucking the letters into a Tupperware that she slid up onto the cabinet above the refrigerator. There had been nights, particularly in the beginning, when Lucy had stolen into the kitchen at three in the morning and sat at the table staring at that cabinet. Sitting there, unable to sleep, she considered digging them out, her loneliness at such a pitch that even Jeptha's mutterings sounded like something akin to comfort. She had never actually succumbed, though—the closest she had come was pulling out the Tupperware and resting her head on it until the feeling passed. She'd fallen asleep there more than once, Jared's lovey in her hand.

Lucy saw LouEllen's face then, her lips pursed, her cheeks drawn. "You think I should read them?" Lucy said, angrily. "Three years later? Do you really think there is something in them that might help?"

"I think you are still so angry you can barely breathe. Maybe the letters would help."

"I can't see how."

LouEllen shrugged her shoulders. "There's something else there for you."

Lucy pawed through the pile of mail on the table. A large white envelope with a bright orange UT symbol had her name on it. She brought it with her into the living room where LouEllen had gone to sit on the couch. "What is this?"

"Why don't you open it?"

Inside was a folder of brochures, pamphlets, class descriptions, and a letter describing the Older Adults Bachelor program. "What is this?" Lucy asked again.

LouEllen sat up, as excited as Lucy had seen her in years. "I saw it on-line. It's this program at UT where they do a special thing for older adults applying to school. I know you've been wanting to go, have forever. But it's not like you could go as a freshman, living in a dorm. Not after everything . . ."

Lucy busied herself looking at the happy people in the pictures. Getting drunk in a dorm was definitely not something Lucy was interested in. But going to college? It had been so long since she was excited about anything that it took her a minute to recognize the sensation. But then Jared's face swam up in front of her.

"No," she said. "I can't."

"You can't stay here forever, Lucy. Not because of him."

"It's where he is."

"It's where he was. You can't stay for him. He's gone, honey."

Tears streamed down Lucy's face. She couldn't leave. She couldn't leave the only place where Jared had ever lived. It was disloyal, wrong. She had finally relinquished her soap opera fantasies of him coming back, knowing her baby was gone forever. But leaving this place when he never could? Growing up, moving on while he was stuck here forever at ten months old? She shook her head at LouEllen and stood up.

"I can't. I have to get ready for Judy's. Can you throw this away for me?" she asked, dropping the envelope on the couch beside LouEllen.

"LUCY!" DELNOR SAID as soon as she walked through the door at Judy's. His was the first condolence note that Lucy had received and the only she still had, scratched out on a faded piece of nicotine-stained stationery. He'd also been the first person to drop the pity smile and treat her like she was normal. Every time she saw him, she felt more so.

"Hey, Delnor. How're you?" she asked, throwing her bag behind the bar.

"You're here. I'm good."

"You're an old charmer," Lucy said.

"Definitely old. I'll have to take your word on the charming," he said, a shy blush creeping up on his face. "How are you?"

"I'm all right, Delnor. Thank you," she said, more serious now. It was funny how easy it was to tell when people were asking for real or just to be polite. Good ol' Delnor. He always asked for real.

"How's everything here?" Lucy asked. Since Delnor spent most of his waking hours at the bar, he usually knew more about the place than Lucy did.

"Judy's in a bad mood. Says the new mandolin player is awful. Says he's so bad even she can tell."

The sound of the mandolin, which used to be her favorite, clawed at her brain now—she even hated the word. She swallowed past the lump in her throat and nodded. "I'm sure they'll find someone."

Delnor looked worried and hurriedly said, "Um, could I get another beer?"

Lucy looked at him with her eyebrow raised. "How many have you had already?"

"This'll be number two. Promise."

Lucy stared at him, but he didn't drop his eyes. "Promise," he said again.

Lucy grabbed another can for him. After everything with Jeptha, Delnor had asked Judy to keep him to four drinks a day. He couldn't quit, he said, not now. He was too old, too dependent. But he didn't want to do anyone the way Jeptha had done, he'd told Judy, and meant it.

"Thank you," Delnor said as she slid the can over to him. "You figured out what you're going to do yet?"

"Do?" Lucy looked around the bar. "You're looking at it."

"Not here. After this, I mean."

"There is no after this, Delnor. This is it."

"It doesn't have to be," he said. "You're young. Smart. You could go to school, be a teacher or something. Hell, even a lawyer. Don't never seem to be too many of those. Move out of this town."

"No, I cannot, Delnor," Lucy said, with finality. He stared sadly at her, his eyes full of pity, and then dropped his gaze. She picked up a rag and wiped off the bar.

THE IDEA OF going to school, though, wasn't as easy to dismiss in her head as Delnor had been. It stayed with her all through the early part of the evening, niggling at her, always competing with Jared's face. She was so consumed by the thought that she barely registered the bar filling up and didn't notice the band had begun to play until they were four songs in and she finally heard the new mandolin player. He was, as Delnor had said, truly awful. For the first time in three years, the mandolin had no impact on her. She heard it and not even a single tear threatened. There was something freeing about the realization, even if it wouldn't be the case if she were to go to the Fold and hear someone truly gifted play.

Still, when Cody came up to say "hi" to her, as he did every week, she wasn't her usual pissed self. She smiled at him as he walked toward her.

"Hey, Lucy."

"Hey, Cody."

"Did you hear?" he said, jerking his head back to the stage.

She grimaced. "It wasn't good."

"Nope. Hopefully Judy will let us keep playing."

"Well, she let y'all stay when you didn't have a player at all, so I guess she'll let you stay with a bad one."

"Speaking of . . ." Cody said, casting his eyes down.

"Cody, don't."

"He had his hearing. He's probably getting out. A couple months."

Lucy dropped the glass she was drying, which struck the bar with a bounce. Judy grabbed it before it fell to the floor. Lucy's hands shook. She couldn't breathe.

"I'm sorry. Marla said someone should tell you. Maybe this wasn't the best time."

Lucy bit her lip and stared into the crowd, not seeing anything but Jeptha holding her and Jared, rocking with them at the end. She ground her jaw tight, her teeth creaking, trying to tamp down the scream that wanted to escape her lungs.

"Go, Lucy," Judy said, her chin pointing in the direction of the back door. "Go on home. I got this."

LUCY DIDN'T REMEMBER getting in her car, driving home, walking up the stairs to the house, or clambering up on the kitchen counter to pull down the Tupperware from above the refrigerator. But suddenly, there she was, a pile of letters in front of her, tears flowing down her face as she read the first one, written two days after Jared died.

> *Oh, God, Lucy. I wish I had the words in my head to tell you how sorry I am, to change what happened, to have had it be me. Me gone would've been no great loss to the world. But Jared . . . I am so sorry.*
> *There is no hell hot enough for what I done.*

She slowly read through the pile, her sobs filling the kitchen. She recognized her own hurt in the words, as if in grief she and Jeptha had finally become the partners they had never been in marriage. He mirrored her fury, her sadness, and her despair that there would ever be a life after that day.

By the time she got to the last letter, her sobs had subsided.

> *Had my parole hearing today. Told them I shouldn't get out, that I never deserve to. There is no atonement for what I done, no way to make amends. Three life sentences wouldn't do it. I took everything from Jared, from you. There are not enough sorrys in the world. I'd kill myself if I didn't know it was the easy way out. Only thing I can do is live with this, all my life.*

"Live with this, all *our* lives," Lucy said out loud. She'd felt so alone the last three years, like she was the only one whose job it was to remember Jared. As much as she hated Jeptha, she was less alone in her grief—she wasn't the only one shouldering the burden of remembering him.

Lucy walked over to grab a paper towel for her eyes. There on the counter above the trash cans was the envelope from UT, like LouEllen had started to throw it away and then stopped. Lucy pulled out the folder inside and scanned the application. The essay question on the back of the application was, "Why are you applying to college later in life? Why are you ready now?"

Lucy opened up LouEllen's computer and started typing.

— 27 —

FOR WEEKS, JEPTHA HAD been staring at the letter from the parole board, eyes on only one word: approved. He shook every time he saw it. He'd meant what he'd said to Lucy in his letter—he had told the parole board in no uncertain terms that they should never let him out. He would never deserve it. Apparently, they disagreed. Quaking, he wondered if he could refuse to leave. When his hands shook too much for him to stop, he picked up his mandolin and began to pick out a new song he'd been writing.

The mandolin had saved his life in here; it was the only thing that got him through the long days and even longer, nightmare-filled nights. Remembering that one throwaway comment from Lucy one night at the Fold when she told him he had a nice voice, he'd started singing. It was whispered mumbles at first, but when the guys on either side of him, hardened men both, had asked him why he stopped singing one morning, he'd kept going with it.

Then, one day when he sat with a pen and paper to write his weekly letter to Lucy—knowing she'd never respond, but he didn't care, he'd set himself a penance and he'd be damned if he wasn't going to stick with it—he wrote down words. He'd never been much for writing, and it took him a few days to realize it was a song he was putting together. When he reread the lyrics, the music came to him all in a burst. He tinkered with it all that morning, and when he finally put it all together that afternoon and sang it in his cell, long slow claps came out of the cells around him. He remembered then where he was—in his head, he'd been holding Lucy and Jared in his shitty trailer. He figured he'd spend most of his life in that room, never able to let go of that moment. As he listened to the slow claps around him, he'd have been glad to remain there in jail for the rest of his life. But the parole board had other plans.

The day he got released, three months after his hearing, the guard handed him a pair of stiff-legged jeans and a white t-shirt to change into, his first clothes in three years. Scratchy and cheap as they were, there was something nice about being in clothes again. Jeptha immediately began itching to take them off. It was one more thing he didn't deserve. He sat on his bed with his head in his hands and stared at the concrete floor, tears slipping down his face.

Then he took a breath and tried to, as they said in his AA group, "change the narrative" in his head. He'd been sober since the day Jared died, the need to drink scared right out of him by what he'd done, but going to AA had helped him come to terms with the many mistakes in his life. Counting the ones he'd sent to Lucy, he must have sent hundreds of letters to the people he needed to make amends to: Ethel and her husband for giving him chances and him missing the job; Brandy Anne, for treating her like shit; Cody, for messing up more times and in more ways than a friend should; his boss, Tom, at that last job, for not being someone he could count on; and Deanna and Bobby, for not working harder and for blaming them for his own mistakes. The list went on and on. Every letter helped, made him feel like maybe he'd be able to find a place in the world that wasn't completely worthless. He wrote Lucy most, of course, even though he knew she'd never be able to forgive him. He didn't want her to. He could forgive himself for some of the shit behavior he'd been capable of all those years, but he knew he would never forgive himself for killing his son, even if it had been an accident. His whole shitty life had been an infinite number of stupid, drunken mistakes leading up to that one horrible moment. No father would be able to forgive himself for that—maybe the goal was just accepting all the reasons why he'd done what he'd done and trying to never find himself in that place again.

He wiped the tears off his face when he saw the guard standing by his door. It opened with a slow groan and metallic clang.

"It's time to go, Jeptha," he said. When Jeptha stood, empty-handed, the guard nodded at his mandolin. "Don't forget that."

Jeptha's steps were slow down the hall and even slower walking through the fence. He wasn't sure how he was going to get home, or even whether he should go home, but then he saw Cody's familiar truck parked outside and the man himself leaning against the fence. Jeptha never thought his heart would swell from seeing that old too-small Harley shirt, but his steps quickened toward Cody. They hugged each other, hard, and Cody pounded him on the back.

"It's good to see you, man. You look good."

"You too."

"Ah, hell, I look the same. It's good to lay eyes on you, though."

Jeptha nodded. It was wonderful to see Cody. For a minute, he thought it was the kind of good that meant he shouldn't be enjoying it, but he shook the thought from his head. Acceptance, he reminded himself.

"You should of let me come see you in there," Cody said.

"You don't want to see that place. 'Sides, I didn't deserve any visits in there."

"It was an accident, man."

"Don't matter much. He's still gone."

Cody was silent as they got in the car. After a few minutes of driving, he nodded at the mandolin case in the seat between them. "You been playing?"

"A lot. Been writing some stuff. Singing."

"You? Writing?"

"I know."

"I'd like to hear it. Our new mandolin guy is something awful. We'd love to have you back."

Jeptha didn't know what to say. He wasn't sure he could ever play in front of people again. It felt wrong.

"I got to study on it," Jeptha said.

"Well, let me know—we still got the gig at Judy's." Jeptha's heart went cold, and he shook harder than he ever had since he got the notice he was getting out. What if Lucy was still there? How could he sing those songs in front of her? He'd written them for her, but he had never supposed she might hear them.

"Would Lucy be there?" Jeptha finally asked.

"Would you want her to be?"

"I don't know," he said. He had never wanted anything more in his life than to see her, apologize to her in person, but he'd never been more terrified. "Depends on what she wanted, I think."

***

JEPTHA THOUGHT HIS heart and his body would seize up with every step he made toward Judy's two weeks later. He could handle the looks, none of which were exactly friendly; it was his own fear that was killing him. Cody had said Lucy wasn't going to be there—on purpose. But he was still terrified. After a walk that seemed to take years, he pulled open the door. The smell of leather, beer, and sweat was the same, as if it was just yesterday, and not years ago, when he'd started down this road.

Judy came out from behind the bar to give him a hug. "It's good to see you," she said, and—Jeptha had to check twice—smiled at him. In the moment, he couldn't speak, but he made a note to thank her later for stocking his fridge at the trailer with tiny bottles of real Coke, the kind from Mexico, full of real sugar that was so much better at soothing the cravings he still had sometimes, three years after his last drink. He started to the stage. A few feet in, though, a calloused hand grabbed his arm and pulled him to a stop.

"Hey there, Jeptha," Delnor said.

"Hey, Delnor," Jeptha said, nodding at him.

"You playing with them boys tonight?"

"I am."

"I'm glad of it—been too long since we had some decent music."

"I'll do my best," Jeptha said.

Delnor squeezed Jeptha's arm and held his gaze with his piercing blue eyes. "I know you will."

THE AUDIENCE GREETED his appearance with silence, but Jeptha didn't care. He slid his strap over his head and began to play, following Cody's lead on the first several songs. It felt good to be playing with a band again. His fingers flexed and yearned for the strings for the pleasure of it, as opposed to the desperate heartache that had driven his playing for the last three years. A few songs in, Cody stepped away from the mic and nodded at Jeptha. He shook walking over to it.

He wanted to sing the simple truth, whether Lucy was there to hear it or not. For that, it had to be one of the old songs, a touchstone for Jeptha since it'd always felt true. It felt even more true now. He looked at his bandmates and said, "Follow me, real slow."

> *I am a man of constant sorrow,*
> *I've seen trouble all my days.*

I bid farewell to old Kentucky
The place where I was born and raised.

For six long years I've been in trouble
No pleasure here on earth I found
For in this world I'm bound to ramble
I have no friends to help me now.

It's fare thee well my one true lover
I never expect to see you again
For I'm bound to ride that northern railroad,
Perhaps I'll die upon this train.

The sorrow and the joy flowed out of him. He sang, loud and true, his every thought of Jared and Lucy, of their lives, and of the devastation he was responsible for. He whispered the last few verses.

You can bury me in some deep valley
For many years where I may lay
Then you may learn to love another
While I am sleeping in my grave.

It's fare you well to a native country
The places I have loved so well
For I have seen all kinds of trouble
In this cruel world, no tongue can tell.

Maybe your friends think I'm a stranger
My face you'll never see no more
But there is one promise that is given
I'll meet you on God's golden shore.

The song ended on a long, drawn-out note from his mandolin. Silence followed. Jeptha wiped a tear off his cheek and looked out at the silent crowd. He peered past them, to where a light was shining down on a woman in the back—her long blond hair hanging wavy down her back and her nose upturned in a way that was more cute than beautiful. Lucy's face was lined with the same tears and etched with the same never-ending sorrow as Jeptha's. The saddest smile in the world flickered on her face as she nodded at him. Then the audience burst into applause, and she walked out the door.

———————

THE NEXT DAY Jeptha sat on his porch, mandolin in his hands. He looked out over the land. The hills, the grass, and the tobacco were as green as spring caterpillars. He closed his eyes for a moment and enjoyed the sun beating down on his face. He was so glad to be home, and yet so guilty at the blessing of it all. "I'm sorry," he said to his son, as he did whenever he got to enjoy a moment that Jared should have.

His new puppy licked his ankle, and Jeptha looked down at her with a smile. Bobby had shyly brought her over a week back. She was a little nip of a thing, blonde and fluffy and cuter than Crystal Gayle had been, but with those same awful teeth. Jeptha took it as a peace offering and snuggled her up on his chest where she promptly fell asleep. She'd followed Jeptha everywhere the last week and, like Crystal Gayle before her, most enjoyed sitting in front of his feet while he played, wagging her tail as he tapped his foot against her back in time to the music. Jeptha played a few bars but, hearing a note out of tune, bent his ear to his mandolin. He fiddled with it for a moment but stopped when he heard a car crunching up the gravel. It was Lucy's beat-up Honda. His hands froze.

She left her door open when she got out, clearly not meaning to stay long. He watched her walk up the hill, her blond hair as tangled and gorgeous as it had been the night that had started their whole story together. Jeptha was oddly relieved to realize he felt neither desire nor love for her. Their shared history had left him scrubbed raw, cauterized of all the emotions that had gotten them both in so much trouble. He saw her now and felt nothing but sorrow.

She stood, one leg on the bottom step, her hands in the back pockets of her shorts. Her face was hard and planed. Unlike years before, when he'd seen this same look on her face when she was angry, he knew this wasn't temporary; everything he'd done had permanently shaved the young, cute girl she used to be from her features. He saw her looking around at the place, knowing she hadn't been there since Jared died. He choked up thinking about it and saw the same look on her face.

"You got a dog," she finally said.

"Patsy Cline."

"She's got teeth like Crystal Gayle."

"I know. Poor thing."

Patsy Cline's tail thumped, and she looked up at Lucy with an interested woof.

"Bobby brought her over last week. Think he was trying to apologize."

"Heard they put you on the deeds to the land."

"That's what they say," he said, shrugging. What had seemed like the worst insult in the world and the only thing that mattered three years ago now seemed so small, not remotely worth the worry and the people he'd thrown away over it. His plan these days was to work the land he got told to, get paid what he got paid, and focus on playing his mandolin and staying away from alcohol. He'd given up on the larger picture—he was just trying to get through each day.

"Last night . . ." She stopped and swallowed. "You were good."

"I was just trying to apologize."

"You did. You have."

He stood up. "I'm so sorry, Lucy. Every day, every minute—I am sorry."

She looked away, over at the tobacco field, nearly ready to cut, and Jeptha saw her eyes fill with tears. "Me too."

They both stared at the land. The cicadas switched on, filling the low, oppressive air with their steady, pulsing drone, punctuated by the maraca shakes of katydids.

She cleared her throat. "Just wanted to see the place. One more time."

He nodded. She walked back to her car. Leaning on the door, she stared up at the trailer behind Jeptha. He saw a tiny shiver shake her frame. Suddenly, the insects quieted, the world gone silent between them.

"Take care of yourself," she said and pulled the door closed behind her.

Through the dust her car kicked up, Jeptha could see the cardboard boxes in her back seat. He guessed they were the ones labeled Knoxville, the same ones she'd been saving since he first came over to her house to assemble that crib so many years ago. He waved and saw her hand rise in reply. Then her car rolled toward the road. He watched long past the time when it disappeared from view. Around the time Lucy would have been turning onto 11W, her headlights pointing west to Knoxville, the cicadas came back on, the sound flooding Jeptha's thoughts. Patsy Cline nudged her body into the space between Jeptha's foot and the edge of the porch and whimpered low in her throat until he began stroking her fur with the toe of his boot.

Jeptha picked up his mandolin and began to play.

ACKNOWLEDGMENTS

It's been a very happy year for me, in large part because I have spent my days talking with an amazing team of women—the most talented, smart, and fun bunch a writer could hope to fall in with. Huge thanks to Ann Collette, my agent and guru for big necklaces and red lipstick, whose love for this book made me love it even more too, and whose perseverance found it a very happy home. For everyone at Blair, thank you for being the best publisher I could have hoped for. Robin Miura, editor extraordinaire, who "got" this book in a way that writers can only dream of. She's an amazing editor, a joy to work with, and has a laugh that just makes you smile when you hear it. Lynn York, the best publisher one could hope to have, who brought all her know-how and genius to Blair and makes it a thriving house for books about the South and beyond; Carla Aviles, in-house publicity goddess for keeping it all straight; Arielle Hebert, the ops genius who keeps everything working smoothly; and Callie Riek, for beautiful banners. Laura Williams, for a cover that knocks me out with its beauty and depth every time I see it. Beth Parker, for laughter, good cheer, and having patience with me for every shitty idea I tossed her way but really celebrating the good ideas and making them better!

This book wouldn't be what it is without Grub Street. Thank you to Eve Bridburg, Chris Castellani, Sonya Larson, Kathy Sherbrooke, and everyone at Grub for the amazing work they do making Boston home to the very best writing community in the world. For my first teacher there, Yael Goldstein, whose support for the first twenty pages helped me keep writing the rest.

I count myself so lucky to have gotten into Grub Street's Novel Incubator many years ago—a million thank yous to Michelle Hoover and Lisa Borders for their wisdom, insight, and support for me and this book, and for all the authors you've nourished through that program! And for my

Season Two friends and readers: Ashley Stone, Jerry Whelan, Mike Nolan, Mandy Syers, Stephanie Gayle, Patricia Park, Hesse Phillips, Lisa Birk, and Carol Gray. For everyone in the other Incubator classes (we are a crew, y'all!) but especially Kelly Ford, beta reader and project manager launch extraordinaire; Jennie Wood, who has known and loved this book and me (and the feeling is mutual!) for too long; Susan Bernhard, who inspired me to keep writing and keep submitting; Michelle Ferrari, for being a burst of life and support when I needed it; and Rachel Barenbaum, an incredible writer and friend whose hard work is an inspiration. And to Sarah Pruski, whose web design genius brought y'all an actual website instead of the sad shell I would have put together. Thank you to Jamie Vacca Chambliss, Yun Soo Vermeule, and John Boveri who read parts of this book eighteen or more iterations ago. To William Dameron, Katrin Schumann, and Louise Miller for answering frantic debut-year questions. For the Facebook Debut Authors 19 group, y'all are like an encyclopedia and therapist all rolled into one. (With special thanks to the very generous James Charlesworth!) For my post-Incubator classmates Bob Fernandes, Janet Edwards, Bonnie Waltch, Andrea Meyer, Julia Rold, Desmond Hall, Sharissa Jones, Rebecca Rolland, Leslie Teel, Helen Bronk, Julie Carrick Dalton, and Louise Berliner: your wisdom and laughter kept me going! To E. B. Bartels and Natalie at Shay's!

Thank you to the team at MFN Partners, who let me turn your conference room into a WeWork and talked to me over cups of coffee in the kitchen, when I emerged from the dark lair of writing, starved for human contact. Special thanks to Nicole Whitney for making our trains run on time and cheerfully printing things out for me; to Rosemary Concepcion for catching all my editing mistakes; and for Avery Strassenberg, for making sure I got something to eat!

I want to thank Rinn Mandeville, Indra Ali, and Lisa Lincoln who helped me with my human babies in too many ways to count, all of which helped me be able to think about these characters and write this book. Indra, you are missed. And to our beloved Val Brocco. We miss you, too.

For blurbs and support and general lifetime awesomeness: Lisa Borders, Patricia Park, Jennie Wood, Kelly J. Ford, Susan Bernhard, Whitney Scharer, Michelle Hoover, Amy Greene, Bret Anthony Johnston, Lauren

Groff, Ron Rash, and Lee Smith. Your amazingly kind words about this book left me speechless.

I've got some amazing friends, y'all, and I can't believe I'm so lucky as to know them: Lauren Margulies, Abby Freirech, Karlis Kirsis, Jill Brennan, Joanna Lydgate, Katie Pickett, Marion Min-Barron, Kate Flaim, Caroline Adler, Jennie Weiner, Debbie Goldstein, Elli Bonnett, Cristina Ferrer, Missy Schneller, Lisa Alpern, Karen Nanji, and Ellie Chu. With a special shout-out to Ivana Ma, my friend and unpaid West Coast publicist!

For Raven Ladon, the best nanny any family could ever have, whose hard work and love for our kids has allowed me the space to write this book.

For Mike's family, into which I have happily been adopted: Diana and Pat Ryan, Paula Studzinski, Viola Vanderzwalm, Stefanie, Manny and Tino Velez, Katina and Brett Henderson, and Kara Studzinski.

For my grandparents, my first models for readers and thinkers and talkers: Lesley and Betty Shelburne and John Russell and Sarah Parham Chiles.

For Amherst College, which taught me so much about books and about the world. I am so grateful you gave this Tennessee girl a shot. To *The Atlantic*, when it was here in Boston, who gave me my first real gig and taught me to keep asking questions.

For my mom, Sally Chiles Shelburne, who wrote fearlessly and beautifully in the face of people who wished she wouldn't, and continues to parent fiercely every day of her life—thank you for being the model. For my dad, Thomas David Shelburne, who taught me the value of telling stories and listening to the people whose stories don't get told. Plus, the value of a great punch line. For my sister Sarah, and brothers Tommy and Will, who are the best siblings one could ever hope for. I loved growing up dirty and half-wild with y'all as my pack. And to Lesli and Sara, the best sisters-in-law!

Eliza Jane, David, Theo, and Charlie, y'all are the most awesome, hilarious, adventurous, and personable lot I've ever seen. See, Mama told you she was working! Keep reading and writing and laughing. I love you.

For my husband, Mike: I'm not sure how twenty years has gone by, but you've made me laugh every day and given me the space and ability to write. I thank God that I drank all that gin and kissed you that night. I am beyond lucky to have you.